RALPH

Diary of a Gay Teen

ANTHONY MCDONALD

Anchor Mill Publishing

Anthony McDonald

www.anthonymcdonald.co.uk

Anchor Mill Publishing

4/04 Anchor Mill

Paisley PA1 1JR

SCOTLAND

anchormillpublishing@gmail.com

For Steve Gee

And remembering JBA, JLA, PJB, RJB, AAC, CG, DG, GAJH, PPH, NJ, SRJ, FK, PMK, AGL, DML, PJM, RP, DR, AJS, DMS, HAS, PJS, CBW, MW, JWY and other friends

Anthony McDonald

ACKNOWLEDGEMENTS

The author would like to thank Roger Mills for musketeering on this one – and Steve too, of course.

AUTHOR'S NOTE

Ralph might have literary ambitions, but his syntax, punctuation and spelling sometimes leave a bit to be desired. He persistently misspells poltergeist, and the plural of handkerchief and the past tense of pay, among other things, and is convinced that literally is spelt with two Ts. He is also still in the dark about when to use *my friend and I* and *my friend and me*. (For anyone in doubt, it's *my friend and I* when *I* would be correct in the same place, and *my friend and me* when you'd write or say *me*.) Ralph makes some valiant efforts, but – a warning to other aspiring authors – his writing is not always a model of stylistic or formal excellence.

Anthony McDonald

These are not children. This is not a rough draft for adult life. Later life is a copy. These are not childish things and they are not put away.

Michael Campbell: Lord Dismiss Us

ONE

Queer, Foggy Place

Monday Jan 13th 1969

So, what did you do today?

Back at school for six days now. The books have come for the play: Max Frisch's Andorra. As usual, so much to do. A room that is no home. Perpetual aimless wanderings from room to room, unwelcome and welcome. Wind blowing a gale down the sealed-up chimney. Andorra, Hadrian VII, Chaucer and Book on French Vineyards to read, as well as a heap of French and History, and vain efforts to ease the comfortable, lead-plated, lonely, laughter-filled, precarious existence in this queer, foggy place.

Maybe it's no worse a beginning than that of other sixteen-year-olds' diaries. I don't know. I've never read anyone else's. I rather like the alliteration in the last bit. At least I think I do. As for the opening... Nobody will ever get that reference to David and me. Two years ago. That was special. Private. I'm Ralph, by the way. Ralph

McKean. Though everyone who knows me calls me Rafe. To those who don't know me I'm Mac.

The impression one gets of the school today is one of darkness, high-roofed and primitive, and harbouring all sorts of beasties, timorous and otherwise. Blond-hair, limping along a corridor, smiling when necessary. Good at Biology, like me.

Jan 14th

Stayed up till two o'clock last night reading Andorra. This morning the wind has changed. The sky is blue. Almost a foretaste of spring.

The O-level results came this morning. Everyone seemed pleased to be alive this morning. Even those who'd failed.

Then I found myself appointed Chairman of General Studies. It's certainly a feather in my cap, but just what the hell I'm supposed to do, I haven't a clue.

No scrambled eggs for breakfast – just toast to last us till lunch. Then a Magazine Committee meeting. Chris Kirkman is now chairman and we waffle and wrangle as before.

Jan 15th

I was a bit nervous this morning. Chairing Sixth Form General Studies in the grave and teak-shelved surroundings of the Rathbone Library at twelve o'clock. I took my grandfather's shillelagh with me in case of heckling or worse. To be honest, I didn't know what to expect. I'd never chaired anything in my life.

With some embarrassment I introduced Father Cosmos as speaker. With even more I found my request for questions afterwards greeted with bewildered silence. In desperation I asked: 'Does everyone, then, agree with every word he's said?' Two points were raised. Well, it could have been worse.

First reading of Andorra went well, though Rory, for all his enthusiasm did not turn up.

Blond-hair has his bandages off now but still walks with a limp.

Bandages or no bandages, limp or no limp, he still looks nice. When I wink at him he smiles a bit uncomfortably, but he doesn't wink back.

Jan 16th

Zebedee spouted some of my own more outrageous opinions at General Studies. I wound up the proceedings with: 'Has anybody got anything important to say? Then let's pack up!'

Jan 17th

Politics! Rivalry with Rory. Who will be tops next year? Who nose? We get tea at tea-time now. It involves shouldering through a seething mass, sliding over the tea-lubricated floor, seizing a cup of lukewarm pre-milked, pre-sugared tea, stir it with a fifteen-times-used plastic spoon. The damp cake still accompanies it. Steve is incredibly talkative. It is now quarter to nine. He has been talking since seven and still is.

Steve is my room-mate this term. He arrived halfway through last term. He's my age less five weeks (we're both sixteen), and is a bit smaller and skinnier even than I am. Black hair, dark eyes and skin. Endless energy and very forthright. When he sees a spade, that's what he calls it. Last weekend he told me, a bit circuitously, how and why he got chucked out of his public school. But he told me it in confidence. I'm not planning to share it. It involved a girl. I'll leave it at that.

Saturday Jan 18th

Barney lectured at General Studies. Very humbly. Sitting next to him at the top of the table I was able to see at one moment that he was shaking. I realised how nervous he was.

I haven't got used to dealing with the idea of fragility in adults. Barney – real name Father Barnabas – is our headmaster and, for all his Benedictine modesty and self-effacement, a very tough guy indeed. He needs to be, dealing with us two hundred delinquents. Since my own father died when I was eleven Barney is the nearest thing to a father that I've got.

In the afternoon I read the whole of Ecclesiastes. I shall have to read it again in order to understand it properly.

Zebedee is out. Gone to a wedding.

Somebody suggested a Current Affairs section in the School Magazine.

Guess who would be expected to write it…

Jan 19th

Sunday, and such a sermon from Father Cosmos at Mass in school chapel. It lasted twenty minutes, ending finally amid sighs of relief.

Zebedee had evidently drunk deep at the wedding, for he returned on the wrong side of the motorway, sloughed across the central reservation and badly scratched his car. But he is his usual self today.

In the afternoon I walked down to the Hoverport. It is still under construction and everything is very informal.

You balance on parapets, cross planks to avoid squelching mud – very amusing to watch a lady in high heels – scrunch over concrete blocks, gravel and sandstone waste, over clinkers and cinders, steel girders and pipes to the sounds of drilling and hammering and are eventually confronted by a bleak emptiness of concrete slinking out onto the mudflats. A row of concrete blocks marks the nearest you can get to the apron, and then the hovercraft, like a turtle studded with windmills, sweeps in between the marker buoys shrouded in mist, climbs the ramp, blows clouds of spray and grit from under its palpitating skirt, and settles on the tarmac. Then it rises and bobs out to sea again.

Supper was revolutionary. Kidneys on toast. I suppose it's too much to hope that it will last.

I do try hard with descriptive prose. It feels big and powerful when it's still in my head. But it looks somehow puny and pathetic when I write it down.

Jan 20th

I went to see Alex in the evening but he was most uncommunicative. It was quite embarrassing and the meeting was an obvious failure – though it may have broken a little ice.

Alex... Three months ago? Four months ago? Feels like a lifetime. I was just 16, he was 17. I shared a room with Will on the ground floor of Number One, Grange Road, (it's the same room I now share with Steve) while Alex shared with another guy on the top floor. Alex was about 5 ft 11, though not of a very athletic build, while I was about 5ft 5, skinny and wiry. He was from the US of A, by the way, his father the cultural attaché to a US embassy somewhere in the world.

Alex had formed the idea, from lack of evidence either way, that I was a rather prim and proper boy, sexually un-developed and unlikely to have had sexual relations with anybody in the past. There was no reason for him to know that Will and I had been wanking each other off for nearly a year, and had toyed with the idea of anal and oral sex, though at the time I had shied away from both. Alex had formed the habit of asking me teasingly, as we crossed on our pyjama-clad ways to the bathroom, 'What would you do if I tried to rape you?' and similar questions, to which I replied things like, 'Well, you'd just have to try it and see.' In an inscrutable tone of voice. This non-committal fencing with words went on for some weeks. We had a senior common room over in the main school, among the outlying buildings, in which we could smoke, and listen to discs on an ancient record-player. One evening, and it's funny how these things happen, we found ourselves the last two people to leave. We sat on adjacent arm-chairs. How did we end up there? Because life's like that.

Alex leaned towards me and said, 'What would you do if I put my hand on your leg? Would you scream and run away?' I said, 'You'll have to try it and see.' He did, and saw that I was quite cool, calm and collected in the circs. He said, 'And if I moved my hand up here?' Which he then did. I said, 'Try it and see.' But by then, he already had. 'If I felt your cock....?'

I don't need to write my response to that. Though, actually, it felt wonderful, and I was totally erect in my trousers of course. 'And if I unzipped you? And if I took it out?'

Of course, when he took it out it was enormous, and he said, 'Not bad,' but realising that the windows were un-curtained, and we were on the ground floor in a very frequented part of the school grounds, after giving it an exploratory feel along its length and a fondle to its now wet head, said, 'However, this is neither the time nor the place,' and attempted to stuff it away again. Which he couldn't have done without impaling it on the teeth of my zip. 'You'll have to do that,' he said gently, and reluctantly I did, although it wasn't easy, even for me. Having done that I reached across and my hand dived into his own crotch, where it encountered... 'Of course I'm bloody stiff,' he said. 'What d'you expect?!' And then, 'It's time we went.'

A few days later Alex had to come to my room. His French teacher – Teacher Trev, who was also my French teacher, in a different group – had suggested that if he needed help with something he should ask me. So we had an arrangement for one particular afternoon, a time chosen when my room-mate and ex-wank-mate Will was at a class. Alex knocked and came in. He sat in the arm-chair next to mine, and we placed the French text-book between our two nearest thighs. We didn't concentrate for very long. As we pointed to phrases in the text our hands strayed along each other's thighs more and more until the pretence could no longer be maintained and we dropped the book on the floor. We unzipped each other and hauled our stiffening cocks out.

At this point I made a discovery. Being very small for my age, I'd assumed that my cock was tiny in relation to everyone else's. And perhaps a few years ago it had been. But the only person I'd ever wanked with, Will, who was six-foot two, had a much bigger cock than mine – although mine was gaining on it week by week. Now, seeing Alex's for the first time, and pulling out his balls, I discovered that his prick, which was a perfectly decent size, was slightly smaller than my own, and that his balls were much smaller than mine. You didn't have to be the bigger or older one to have the bigger sodomy set. That discovery did wonders for my ego.

Alex was circumcised, like me. His glans a flattish mushroom-cap. We pulled on each other quickly for a minute or two at most, then felt and saw the eruption of our spunk, which in both cases simply overflowed into our hands. Alex used a hanky. I just stuffed my soggy prick back in my trousers and zipped up. We grinned and got up 'Come again,' I quipped as he left the room. We exchanged conspirators' smiles. We never did finish sorting out that French.

After that I would make regular visits to his room when his room-mate was out. 'Just a social call,' I'd say, and he'd know exactly what was meant. We wouldn't say anything else. We'd sit side by side on his bed, or lie back across it, pull each other's trousers down and wank each other off. He had big hairy thighs and a hairy tummy, which I liked, because I had nothing like that myself, and neither did Will, for all his greater penis size. Neither of us would moan or say anything as we came. An arm around the shoulder was as close as we came to anything intimate. Then we'd get up, zip up, say, 'See you again,' and I'd leave the room.

On one occasion we started to grope each other's legs before we unzipped. Then suddenly I felt Alex tense up, and he let out a little gasp. 'Fuck it,' he whispered, as I went to unzip him, 'I've already shot.' I went on unzipping him, though, and saw his deflating penis, bashfully lying among thick matted pubes, with streamers of spunk all over it, and among his hairs and in his underpants. I plunged my hand in and washed it in the warm wetness. 'Waste of a go,' Alex said, removing my hand and zipping up. But he was gentleman enough to unzip me and give me the relief that I was waiting for. I think it only took seconds on that occasion, though...

Oct 6th 2014

Well, there's Ralph for you. He wasn't sure, when he embarked on the adventure of diary writing, what would turn up in its pages. He did know, though, that there would be no plotline, no beginning, middle or end. A diary is just a diary. A day-by-day account of things. To look for a pattern in it, to find a shape to it... Well, you'd have to be very prescient ... or else wait until the end. Because, inevitably, there is an end Not that Ralph thought about that at the time....

Anthony McDonald

TWO

The Meaning of Deep

Jan 21st 1969

Zebedee talked to us on the stairs till 11.30, touching on entropy, Mr Gough, nature, sin, development, personal relationships and homosexuality. He was most interesting.

It appears that Blond-hair is taking up fencing. Paolo is to teach him!

Otherwise ... nothing.

Paolo, a year older than me, six feet tall, handsome and muscular, with frizzy dark hair, is a sort of Italian stallion. I've known him five years now.

Jan 22nd

Mr Gough gave us a General Studies lecture on 'isms' in art. I had to use the shillelagh twice.

I set out glumly to play football on a sea of mud in the afternoon, but to my great surprise I found I enjoyed myself. People actually said I played well.

After that there was a play rehearsal on the stage in the Assembly Hall. Blond-hair was practising fencing moves by himself in the empty hall below us, he the performer, we actors his audience.

Now I suppose I ought to get down to reading La Symphonie Pastorale. Then I shall have to write up this History essay. But, as usual, I don't feel much like working. I feel I could only survive if my work became my life, living not as a man who works to earn money to live by but as a man who lives by his work. Zebedee, for example. Then work would cease to be a bore. That is why I should like to live off a vineyard. But that is unlikely. What will be will be.

Mr Gough is the art master, obviously, and has the beard to prove it.

Jan 24th

Bad cold. Zebedee put me 'off Games' and off I went. I bought a box of handkerchieves as a birthday present for my mother.

In the evening I had some bread and jam and cocoa in my old friend Smith's room in Number Three, then up to Jagger's room where I had some more. We read extracts from The Hothouse Society, the book about boarding-school life that we've all been reading, accompanied by the inevitable conversation about homosexuality.

Jagger drops in on Steve and me every day now on his way to Maths, but never stays long.

Rimbaud's Bateau Ivre ... a view of sparkling clear sharp clouds with a light openness above it – like the smell of a scarf when you breathe the frosty air through it, and I thought how hazy and dusty everything looks down here.

Rimbaud's idea was that knowledge you gained through joy, and not through pain, is of no value. Profoundly disturbing.

Because he might be right?

Jagger said, in contrast to his last term's outburst on the subject of Blond-hair, 'He's got taste.'

Blond-hair has taste – meaning that he's a little bit drawn to me, and Jagger doesn't disapprove of that? Well, that's very big of Jagger. Given that Blond-hair has been Jagger's property since the year dot.

I've known Jagger since I was nine, and he was ten, down at Stella Maris. He's a big and stocky handsome boy with wavy blond hair, amazing blue eyes, very fair skin, and very sexy big lips, hence his nickname. He also has a short, slightly turned up nose that is cute. He's easy-going and comfortable to be with, though sadly I've never had sex with him. He has very good farmer's boy legs. Overall he gives the impression of a nice cuddly polar bear, especially when in cricket whites and jumper.

***

Perhaps I ought at this point to give a brief account of the Geography and Hierarchy of this place.

The school's main building was designed by one of the less imaginative sons of Augustus Welby Pugin, the Victorian architectural giant. It consists of high-roofed, Gothic-arched halls and dormitories, like churches, that are impossible to heat. It is not only tall but very long and narrow, running west to east. It lies edge-on to the road, Grange Road, which runs downhill, south, to the sea. Its big windows are south facing. They look out over the school lawn and beyond, to the buildings of the monastery precinct, which are half hidden behind trees. In contrast, the back of the school building is mostly blank wall, with rows of bathroom and toilet windows in it.

Next door to this back wall, and close to the road are the two attached Edwardian houses in which we sixth-formers live. You can get from the main school to Number One via the alley that runs alongside the kitchen door, or else via a cast-iron, roofed and glazed-in bridge that leads between the dormitory floor of the main school and Number One's attic, the 'bridge room' under the roof slope.

Zebedee is the sixth form master, and house master of Number One, Grange Road (where I live), on whose staircase he holds forth most entertainingly night after night. He's also head of science. He has very deep dark eyes and is prematurely bald, so that he looks more than his thirty-eight years. The house master of Number Three, next door, is Johnnie, He is a very decent man in his early thirties, and head of English, for which he has a talent as a teacher. But he is not a man to hold forth on the staircase on any night of the week. You can get from Number One to Number Three by any of three ways: walk up the road like any neighbour, go through the two back gardens full of apple trees, whose dividing wall has been breached, or via a door between two bedrooms, one in each house, on the second floor. The whole system is quite a Labyrinth.

We have prefects. Alex is one. The rest of us are not. Not Chris Kirkman, not Steve, not Rory, not Jagger. Not I. Next year perhaps. On the other hand, we are, most of us, heads of mealtime tables, keeping order in the refectory ... up to a point. We all live in Number One. Except Jagger, who's next door in Number Three.

Saturday Jan 25th

Father Cosmos bored us with a talk on The Morality of War at General Studies. Nobody understood.

Nobody really understands Fr Cosmos. He is the most intellectual of all the priest-monks of our monastic community. Grey haired and nearly bald he has a head the size of the planet Saturn. When he preaches or lectures there are two veins in his temples, known as the Tigris and the Euphrates, which stand out and throb. He pronounces words differently from everyone else, putting the accents in unexpected places. *Con*troversy instead of con*trov*ersy. In*di*gestion instead of indi*ges*tion. We like to imagine him saying mas*tur*b'sh'n instead of masturbation.

He can do The Times crossword in three minutes, and understandably gets bored quite easily. He has recently been given the empty title of deputy headmaster. Just for being there. And saying school

Mass on alternate Sundays. He's a nice bloke, though.

...Then, feeling very fed up during English class, and interrupting Will's incredibly boring criticism of poetry by a long and noisy blowing of my nose, I was told to (by Will) shut up. I replied that if I'd thought the class would be taken by him I'd never have bloody well come. 'Fuck off,' he replied. I did.

I apologised to Johnnie in the afternoon in the staff room. 'Sometimes I wonder,' he said, raising his head from The Times newspaper, 'if it's a menagerie I'm teaching.' He buried his face in the paper again. I closed the door as I left.

Monday Jan 27th

Lovely mild morning. I revised History sitting, legs dangling outside the window, lampshade on head. Lovely feeling of carelessness.

Breakfast was frugal, lunch was light, tea diminutive and supper nearly non-existant.

Zebedee spoke tonight about next year's prefects. How Rory has not improved yet and how Paolo is also an unlikely candidate. None of 'us' got a mention, though.

He also spoke about Blond-hair, How Todger was found with him, and also Rajahan, on different occasions, on the Regency football field. Zebedee said that his background is unfortunate and he's looking for affection. How many others of us does that apply to?

This mention of 'us'. Who are 'us' exactly? We are the Bloomsbury Group, the artistically pretentious gang at the top of the sixth form hierarchy. We comprise myself and Steve, Jagger, Chris Kirkman and Chris's best friend Rich. That's about it really.

Obviously, if there's an 'us' there must also be a 'them'. Sharks and Jets. Montagues and Capulets. 'They' are the Haemorrhoids. Hope I've spelt that correctly. The trouble is that their membership is a bit vague. Changes from day to day. For example, Rory is a Haemorrhoid some days and a Bloomsbury-Set other days. Perhaps that says something about Rory. Perhaps, though, it's a warning sign that the Haemorrhoids are simply a shorthand-think grouping for 'Everybody else'.

Jan 28th

I spent the afternoon in Jagger's room. He was sketching Blond-hair's football jersey. I thought I might write a poem about Blond-hair. Steve was there too, which annoyed me. But nobody spoke much. Except Steve, of course.

Someone gave a talk about Nietsche at General Studies. But nobody had heard of him, and the discussion afterwards was a bit feeble.

With a heavy cold, a scarf, a shower of rain, a Macintosh and a library book I trudged miserably down town to the public library and looked at old photographs of the town. How A. W. Pugin's Abbey church looked, gaunt and eerie with its entourage of tombs, perched high on the chalk cliffs – alone. Now it is just another part of the huddled suburbia around Grange Road. There used to be fields and windmills where I am writing now.

Well, I did the poem about Blond-hair. It's not brilliant. A bit embarrassed about it actually.

Two ships at anchor, all sails lightly furled,
While still in port, yet seeing all the world:
That pair of eyes that know and understand,
Are aching for a glimpse of friendly land.
Astride a cheeky nose, beneath a brow
That wrinkles in enjoyment, sometimes, now.
Lips soft, expressive; hair blond, silky, new:
Of mirror waves that to themselves stay true.

Bit of a bastard offspring of Browning and McGonagall. I won't show it to anyone.

Jan 29th

Dreamt that Winston Churchill had died again, and that Fr Cosmos didn't like me.

Jan 31st

The first crocus is out.

Sunday Feb 2nd

Rehearsal of Andorra after Mass. I wore a watch and chain, the former being my father's old American pocket watch and the latter being borrowed from the wash-basin.

I thought once again about one of my reasons for

opening this diary: to convey the atmosphere of Here, Now, February 1969, and it isn't easy. It will just have to be left to creep into these pages by itself...

Now that wasn't original. John Steinbeck wrote it. About his novella, Cannery Row. But even the greatest authors steal from each other. Or so I've heard.

Feb 3rd

The last thing I expected on waking was to find an inch or two of smooth clean snow outside. Revelling in it I walked the half mile down to Stella Maris early with Steve in a cold world suddenly surprised by its beauty. We were due for a History lesson at Stella Maris, our school's preparatory school, with Teddy, who is now headmaster there, as well as continuing to teach History to us sixth-formers. We found Teddy a sort of father figure with children at his feet in the cloisters.

A new side to the severe and remote Teddy we've known for five years: most professional teacher in the school, head of cricket and former Rugby coach, now a prep-school headmaster, his wife the new matron, and still a golden-haired thirty.

In the afternoon I walked out of Johnnie's class again in a fit of temper. It sounds awful but there is no other way of releasing one's tensions. There is no booze, no girls, no really deep friendships, no country walks, no peace, no dark, no comfort...

Deep friendships. When do friendships become deep? When did anything become deep? When Father Luke taught us the word in the fourth form, when I was thirteen, I began to think about my friendships of the past in the light of that new word, or new meaning of it. Deep... The friendship I'd had with Micky at the age of four. With Tim, and Roger, age seven. My thing with Roger going until I was eleven or twelve, by which time I'd met Phil, who I see at school daily still, but who I'm no longer so close to... Because, in that last case something has passed, gone out of it. It can't be the deepness that's gone. It must be something else. Something that applied to all those just named. Something more of the emotions. I hesitate to call it love. Perhaps infatuation and or romance... (And I realise they're all boys' names, of course.)

'My friendship with you is one of the greatest I've ever had. And one of the deepest.'

My Canadian friend David that was. I used his words to open this diary. *So what did you do today?* That's what he said to me every evening that summer term as we started our evening walk around the deserted Regency Field. We were both fourteen, but in different classes, so our paths didn't cross until this point at the end of the day, when the evening star grew big and lustrous out of nowhere, in the west.

We would tell each other all the little triumphs and minor humiliations of the day just ending. We felt something for each other, of course we did. The difference now – in contrast to what had gone before – was that we were just beginning to be old enough to know and articulate it.

One thing we hadn't done in the course of the day would have been to masturbate. We were almost the only two fourteen-year-olds at the school who hadn't started yet. We knew this about each other and sometimes dispassionately discussed this shared unusual circumstance. We once kissed each other, arms around each other, for a joke in front of another friend, the friend I've had since the age of nine: Smith. And once David said, also joking, 'We could go down behind the bushes. I've never had a wank, and you could wank me.' I didn't take him up on it. It was only a joke. Though now, nearly two years on, and armed with experience as well as hindsight I wish I had done the deed with him. He returned to Canada at the end of that term, and that was that. I missed him and I still do. There's been no-one to step into his shoes since. And I wonder about him, of course. He had a sort of girlfriend in the holidays, which I did not. But I wonder if, like me, he started playing with himself in earnest when he turned fifteen. I wonder if he started playing with other boys' private parts around the same time – as I did. In short … I wonder who's kissing him now.

Feb 5th

Aroused by Alex this morning.

That's actually a cryptic joke. Alex is duty prefect this week. He comes into every room and puts the light on. He, like all the other prefects, will shake the shoulder of anyone who hasn't surfaced in response to the light. With me he does things differently. He comes over to my bed, reaches into it from beneath the covers from the bottom, and runs his hand up my leg. Sometimes his hand makes contact with my penis. Then he withdraws and turns the light on to wake Steve up. Steve probably sees this happen from time to time but pretends to be still asleep. At any rate he hasn't commented.

Feb 6th

General Studies was a lecture by Father Nicholas. He was headmaster of Stella Maris when I was there all those years ago. Teddy's predecessor. Today he was supposed to be talking about the state of the Church before the War, but it turned into a string of hazy reminiscences about seminary life in France. It was quite pathetic seeing this tough disciplinarian reduced to faltering senility. His memory has almost gone and he is in and out of hospital all the time. He is due for another operation shortly. His old white scar on the forehead now takes in one of his eyes. All in all he's a poor wreck of a man. He is only sixty-seven and is obviously dying.

Feb 7th

In the afternoon we had Games. It was freezing and after half-time snow began to fall on the muddy pitch. It became almost a blizzard and so we packed up early. Immediately I had a rehearsal to attend... Supper was something awful – I don't know what. In the end they gave up trying to get people to eat it and served out potatoes and bread and cheese instead. By the time our turn came the bread had, of course, run out.

Saturday Feb 8th

Last night the blizzard sent the snow flying like solid mist, swirling back and forth. Within minutes the ground was inches deep. Around 10.30 half a dozen of us ploughed out in dressing-gowns and Macs to push a floundering car through it.

In the morning, after a night of thunder and lightning as well as gale and snow, there was an inch of snow on the inside window-sill, which the wind had forced through the crack.

As we'd eaten all the bread last night there was only Mrs Aldiss, one boiled egg and five crackers each for breakfast. Though lunch was quite good.

Spent the morning pushing cars and vans out of drifts on the road to the harbour. In the afternoon, whichever room I went into – there Steve was! I eventually walked out. It struck me that, though I appreciate his wit, his intelligence and his warmth, I don't feel much affection for him. I see his strengths and weaknesses, but it's a purely intellectual realization. I don't feel for him as a human being at all.

Feb 9th

Sunday. Johnnie sent me onto the roof of Numbers One and Three to bale snow over the parapet before it melted and seeped indoors. Up into the bridge room under the roof-slope, and up through the hatch onto the slates. Never before had I realized how terrified I am of heights. Even with a two-foot parapet wall on one side I hardly dared look over. Once, absent-mindedly, I sat on it, with my back to the thirty-foot drop down into the road. I still reel at the memory of that discovery...

A good film in the evening. The Loneliness of the Long-Distance Runner.

And now, tired and empty, I turn in to my cast-iron, lumpy-mattressed bunk for eight hours of unrefreshing sleep before another week of work – and explanations about why I haven't yet done last week's.

Feb 12th

Bought a couple of rolls in a blizzard to eat in the evening. After which I fell out with Steve. I was trying to mend the chest of drawers in our room but completely broke one of the drawers by mistake. 'Your character in a nutshell,' he said. I like him less and less.

Apparently, though for this I do not blame him, it was he who left a bowl of water on the doorstep, so that, in the dark, I put my foot right in it.

An absentee today: Perez left for good at 3 this morning at Barney's suggestion. He'd pulled a knife on Barney, refusing to take strokes for calling Johnnie a bastard. You'd never have thought it of the apparently harmless little boy.

Feb 13th

Snowball fight indoors in the evening. Rory with Steve and me in our room throwing snowballs out of the window at all the others in the garden throwing them in. Johnnie comes to complain. Tries handle of our locked door. Then, bam, bam, bam. 'Stephen Hooe, what are you doing…?'

'Sorry sir,' flannels Steve. 'I didn't… Yes. Oh, I see. The *door!*' Slow unbolting while Rory escapes through the window. Johnnie enters at full speed. While Zebedee issues solemnly, all innocence from his room above. 'What's been happening?'

All the others were made to mop up the mess we'd made earlier in Number Three. Not me, though. I was made to clear up the mess in our own room in Number One…

Feb 19th

Tale of woe over late supper. Mrs Aldiss had made one of the kitchen staff cry and had then gone off in a huff. We ate our fried fish and pudding in a sombre mood and then I went and listened to Mozart and

Beethoven. Then it was Compline in the chapel in the main school building, up to which very few people turned, then said goodnight to Blond-hair as we passed, then a snowball fight and a small cigar. And now to bed.

(Compline is a service consisting of chanted prayers and psalms. For the monks it forms the last office of the day - their night prayers. We sing it just once a week.)

Feb 20th

Steve and I nailed up blankets over our big windows to keep warm. They seem quite effective.

Saturday Feb 22nd

We watched the end of Doctor Who on television, and then I looked at the sun through the hall front window in the main school. It was setting and orange, and shone either side of the central rib between the two glass plates. It brought with it that atmosphere that comes only in the evening of the beginning of Spring days when one is exhausted after a long day.

Feb 24th

Revising for History, the usual Monday Marathon in the afternoon, a rehearsal in the evening, conversation with Jagger before supper while the power-station blew streams of black smoke across the face of the setting sun. We talked about Zebedee and about seeing the world.

Then prep. More work and an ingrowing toe-nail being troublesome… And after – a talk with Zebedee about room arrangements for next term. Nobody, it seems, wants to share with Chris Kirkman. The talk dragged on, and no decision was reached.

(Nobody wants to share with Chris Kirkman. Was Zebedee laying a bait for me? Was he looking into my eyes and expecting to read I'd love that more than anything in the world there? Well, I was too sharp for that. I gave nothing away. At least I hope that was the case.)

Feb 25th

Walking into Zebedee's room to ask permission to work late, I found Alex and Johnnie there, and Alex and I were asked to do the House notes for the magazine, working jointly. We tried not to catch each other's eye as we said, yes, we'd be happy to collaborate on that.

Soon a crowd collected and Zebedee and Johnnie went on at Will about his not doing enough work. Poor Will was almost in tears; I don't blame him. Then we talked about little boys for nearly an hour, inviting Johnnie (for a joke) to take his pick from the school photograph on the wall. He didn't, of course. 'In comparison to us, The Hothouse Society is a refrigerator,' I said. Ha-ha.

Feb 26th

I gave a paper at General Studies, feeling not too well. The subject was the Papal Encyclical, Humanae Vitae, the controversial one that dealt with artificial means of contraception, and in particular, The Pill. After I'd finished I was harangued by Fr Cosmos. Will occupied the chair but was not too effective. On the whole, though, the talk was a success.

In the afternoon Alex and I enjoyed ourselves writing the House notes. Every other word had queer connotations and we ended up describing the end-of-term booze-up as, 'a credit to King James I.'

We went to History class at Stella Maris in Daniel's Mini-Moke, arriving safely after just missing Mr Fuddington's Jaguar, which was parked on a bend.

Stella Maris. Memories... How I remembered the sound of Grace being murmured in the dining-hall at quarter to five, and the arrival of Mrs Grazer to teach dancing...

In the evening Steve and I tried to make Will's ceiling light fall down (he lives in the basement now) by jumping on the floor, but only succeeded in bringing Zebedee down from his room above.

March 4th

So, what did I do today? ... The unanswered question tails off into the dusk, and we walk in silence to the end of the Regency Field, about turn, and in silence we are swallowed up.

THREE

Kiss Me

March 5th

No lift down to Stella Maris from Daniel in the Moke.
Being late, we ran the whole mile and a half, arriving
panting. 'You needn't run next time,' says Teddy. We
won't.

I did well at rehearsal this evening; it was the Inn
Scene. After that I went along to the Common Room.
The Billiards table has been removed, and there were
only about four of us down there, sitting in the dark
corners. We told a few jokes periodically, but socially
the evening was a failure and we retired to bed.

 (Daniel is one of the two most handsome boys in the
school. The other is Chris Kirkman. Between them they
have the pick of all the girls for miles around. Daniel's
family own the best restaurant in the region. Just three
miles away, in Broadstairs. He's a day-boy. He's also
the only one of us who owns a car. The Mini-Moke.
He's definitely Bloomsbury. Some people have all the
luck.)

March 6th

Stella Maris again. The Moke had its roof and sides
off and, being early, we took a spin round Pegwell Bay.
Sad to relate, Steve beat me at history.

Father Sebastian on Sex at General Studies. Ears prick
up at the word perversion...

March 7th

In the evening a fascinating TV programme 'Civilisation', dealing with the 12th Century, its leap in architecture and thought. Superb pictures of Cluny Abbey, Chartres Cathedral and of course, quotes from St Bernard. The story of the development of flying buttresses, of Peter Abelard and his Heloise, of pilgrimages and crusades, of sculpture and metalwork...

(St Bernard was an extraordinary, wonderful man. So preoccupied with the things of the next world rather than this that he never noticed if his bed-chamber was wood-roofed or stone-vaulted. So determined to suppress his earthly appetites that he considered the eating of an egg to be luxurious to the point of sinfulness. 'An egg,' he wrote. 'Consider how many ways in which it may be prepared...' I never think of him without thinking of Barney, our own Father Barnabas, headmaster here, and the nearest things I have to a father of my own.)

March 9th

Sunday. A shortened Mass. If it gets much more mundane they might as well do away with it altogether.

March 10th

I borrowed some money and bought a loaf, which was gobbled by hordes of people and made a cup of coffee that I spilt while climbing in through the window.

March 12th

It is marvellous how a few unlikely looking and ill-fitting bits of hardboard on stage have become a seedy inn overnight, and although the stage is still a forest of stepladders, paint-pots and paper – the set seems mainly to consist of the latter commodity – it is, none the less, really Andorra. No longer ill-starred the play is proceeding full tilt. One week and one day to the last performance and only three days to the dress rehearsal. But now, 'Time for bed,' said Zebedee.

March 14th

No General Studies exam, so I read a book about Bumblebees.

In the afternoon I went on stage and found the hall full of planks being sawn, boards being nailed, supports being hammered, scenery under construction, costumes being sorted. In came Mr Gough like a medieval master mason and to him flocked a buzzing mass of the juniors engaged on the job. The whole thing was proceeding so smoothly; the whole mass behaving as one body… Like the building of Chartres Cathedral when lords, ladies, peasants and yeomen harnessed themselves to carts to draw the great weights of stone…

Now it appears to have been decided to do the General Studies exam tomorrow – which is bloody infuriating … at 11 o'clock the night before.

Saturday March 15th

Feeling thoroughly sulky we went to General Studies exam, some – day-boys – at only 20 minutes' notice. We answered the questions as facetiously as possible, then doodled on the answer papers.

Lunch early, then cast meeting, then make-up and costume for the dress-rehearsal. I wore a bow-tie and white trousers with brown slip-on shoes. Also a beard and moustache… I was great in scene eight but poor in scene four, on account of an attack of cramp. I took

Andri's (Rory's) pulse using a magnifying glass instead of my pocket watch, as the watch-chain had got caught up...

Afterwards Blond-hair condescended to speak to me, and one of the juniors who seems to like me, Patterson, put his hand in my pocket and had a feel around, which was nice. The soldiers' costumes have come, along with magnificent rifles and sub-machine-guns.

Monday March 17th

Mrs Gladwish brought me a Gladstone bag for me, as the doctor, to use in the play. Thanking her I said by accident, 'Thank you for the Gladstone, Mrs Bag.'

March 18th

First performance day. The hall is packed. Press in the front row, juniors, waiting to wreck it, in the background.

My first entrance... I mounted the steps, cigar in hand ... and my bow-tie came off. I ripped open my shirt collar and started. Mediocre. Very mediocre. I felt the indifference of the press...

But scene twelve has never gone so well, and everyone got emotionally involved.

Chris Kirkman is fantastic as the Señora. Quite fantastic.

We had sandwiches and coffee after, me chatting the while with Blond-hair. Told him I'd come top in History. So the day ended on a triumphant, reconciled note. He returned my 'Goodnight.'

March 19th

The House Notes for the magazine had to be re-written, by Alex and myself. Our first effort had been turned down by Johnnie as unprintable and not to be taken seriously. We started off down in my room but then adjourned upstairs to his. We found very little to write about, so we sat and looked at each other. I liked his smile – first time I'd ever seen it properly. So, as the cars and buses passed in the street we briefly found our everlasting home... Together, lying on his bed. For the first time in a long time. Our everlasting home. Is this it?

At General Studies we had a man who'd been on TV about Padre Pio. He got great attendance including two monks, half the fifth form, Barney, Johnnie. As well as the whole sixth form, of course. The speaker very interesting, reconciling the natural and supernatural. But one of the teachers from Stella Maris, who'd also come along, couldn't accept that. After five minutes I had to shut him politely up.

After lunch a cast meeting. Blond-hair sitting in an armchair, eating an orange. Smiling. Funny how people seem to be smiling today. Even me...

Scene one went without a hitch. Scene eight... Fair, I thought. Scene twelve was good. Even me. After, Father Malachy, our director, came into the refectory, where we were eating sandwiches, and said, 'I'd just like to say a word.' We listened anxiously. He jumped in the air and shouted, 'Yipee.'

Back at Number One I sat on the stairs next to Alex, while Zebedee held forth, and we argued, on the subject of the value of such accomplishments as acting and music.

***

Father Malachy is one of the youngest priests of the monastery community. He has sandy, swept-back hair, kind and thoughtful blue eyes and glasses. He teaches on our A-level English course when it comes to anything to do with modern plays. He especially likes plays that are political and left-wing. While other schools do uncontroversial things like Charlie's Aunt and The Importance of Being Earnest, he has us doing thoughtful plays by Shakespeare, John Arden and Max Frisch. When he preaches occasionally at a Parish Mass in the Abbey church, people complain (he has told me) about his socialist opinions. Perhaps they should read the Gospels...

He is a deep thinker, but great fun to be with, always interesting and enthusiastic. And a good teacher.

He doesn't live in the school but – like most of our teaching priests except for Fr Barnabas and Father Cosmos – comes over every day from the monastery, just the other side of the tennis courts.

March 20th

I got to sleep at 2 o'clock. At half past one there was a poultergeist – though this seems silly now – which tapped at the window and then banged the chest of drawers about – sounded as though it was breaking it up with an axe – which had me quite terrified. But when I put on the light the noise stopped and the chest of drawers was intact.

I was up at seven sharp though, and tidied the room, packed busily, and washed socks, and hauled tables and ladders in the hall to black out the windows for the afternoon, final performance.

House meeting, room inspection, then cast meeting, then make-up call...

...The witness-box scene and scene twelve were perfect. Michael P fell through the stage at one point, though nobody in the audience noticed. And this was the day of Rory's never to be forgotten spoonerism. 'In front of your kind eyes. In front of your kind, kind eyes…' became 'In c**t of your frined eyes. In c**t of your frined, frined eyes.'

My mother was there. Afterwards, though we talked about many things in the play, she never mentioned that.

There was a buffet tea. I was congratulated on my performance by Rich's mother. She's a professional actress. So that meant a lot. Then Blond-hair told me he would be leaving at the end of the summer.

Had to think about the implications of that – of Blond-hair's leaving.

My mother drove me the fifty miles home. I had a homely supper of bacon and eggs, washed my hair thoroughly, and went to bed. Easter holidays began. Spent much of the time in France, touring Brittany and Normandy. But nothing happened in the course of those weeks that has any bearing on this story. The next term began on April 22nd.

…Nothing happened that had any bearing on this story…? Well, all right. There was the boy waiter in the bar outside Rouen cathedral who looked like Blond-hair, and whose glance at me told me he was having the same thoughts about me as I was having about him. And the two nearly naked men working on the deck of an anchored yacht in the bay of Bénodet, on the sun-shivered water… Which made sharing a hotel bedroom with my mother that night a bit difficult.

April 22nd

The first person I saw when I got back to school was Alex, who gave me a knowing smile. He it was who told me a few minutes later that Blond-hair had been expelled for skipping off early at the end of last term.

April 23rd

Conservative party campaigners came to the door. We gave them a copy of the Peking Review while Johnnie was talking to them. In the explosion that followed he threatened to resign.

April 24th

Made it up to Johnnie by being brilliant interpreting Dylan Thomas's obscure poetry.
Will is still afraid of the fire he has lit, and in the evening I talked to Steve about Alex for two hours and resolved to do something about it.

That last sentence was a masterpiece of compression. I'd better complete this chapter by expanding on the first half of it, ...Will is afraid of the fire he has lit... with a look back at the past...

(...And leaving: Alex, and resolving to do something about it... *till the chapter which follows this.)*

Will, though... I sort of knew Will from home. Or at least, from out of school. He lived on the outskirts of London, about sixty miles from both my home address and from the school. But his parents were neighbours of, and friendly with, a grown-up cousin of mine. Will was nine months older than me and, at six foot two, ten inches taller than I was. He was well-muscled, blond and blue-eyed, half Swedish, but without the sunny self-confidence that increases Jagger's charm. We would meet up when my mother and I went to visit my mother's sisters – my aunts – and my cousins during the holidays. At school we were friendly without being close friends. I hung around with younger, smaller people (I'm talking about a year and a half back, when I'd just turned fifteen). As for Will, he didn't hang around with anyone very much. He'd joined the school at fifteen himself. He didn't have those bonds, for better or worse, that went back to the age of eleven or even before, that I did.

A year and a half ago… It was probably November or early December. While I was sharing a room with another boy in Number Three, Will shared an alcove in a dormitory in the main school building. It was a pretty public space. This particular afternoon we went to Lavin's shop in Grange Road and bought two bottles of bitter lemon drink, then we went up to Will's lair to drink it and chat. He sat on his bed, I sat opposite him on the bed of his alcove mate Jimmie, who wasn't there, of course. There was nobody about, although at any second there could have been. Will relaxed backward on the bed, spreading his legs (we were both wearing our charcoal-grey school uniform two-piece suits) and lightly rubbed his crotch. 'I feel all sexed up,' he said. 'Will you give me relief, Mac?'

'I'm not sure what you mean,' I said, although of course I understood his words exactly. But this was nearly a year before anything started with Alex, and I had no experience to look back on, nothing to guide me as I wondered how to – excuse me – handle this. I wasn't even sure that I wasn't being tested, being set up. That if I touched him he wouldn't spread it all over the school that I was queer.

He said, 'Feel me, mate.'

Taking my reputation in my hands I stood up, leaned over him and did just that. He felt big, bigger than me, but reassuringly not as much bigger as all that. I could make out the V-shaped underside rim of his cock's tip. He was more than halfway to being hard, but there was still some way to go, I thought.

'Go on,' he said.

I had never touched a grown-up dick before. I hadn't touched any boy in that way since Roger and I were both eleven. I was a late developer. I'd only been able to come for about two months, and still hadn't learnt to wank properly. Now I gave Will's dick a couple of rubs with the flat of my fingers through his trousers. Then I took fright and stood back up. 'Someone'll come in,' I said.

He reached forward quickly and tried to grab my own dick, which was pointing forward like a bowsprit. My trousers looked as though someone had just put up a horizontal tent.

'Don't,' I said. I couldn't let him touch me. First I thought he'd find me wanting in terms of size. Second I knew that the instant his hand made contact with me through my trousers I would erupt and that his fingers would know all about that at once.

That was the end of that encounter. But shortly after the beginning of the next term I went back. Sat opposite him on his alcove mate Jimmie's bed. Felt him through his trousers as he stood up. This time I let him feel me too. He just squeezed the tip of it and I shot hotly into my pants, making them and his fingers wet. I pulled away from him and gave him and his dick no further help.

I would remember that moment when, a few months later, I first read Lord Dismiss Us, the boarding-school novel by Michael Campbell that all of us read that year, shocked by its intensity … and by the scenes of sex. Michael Campbell had captured that moment of mine, of mine and Will's, beautifully…

And the most appalling, unbelievable, terrible thing began to happen, and he could not stop it. He tried but he could not stop it. And the worst part was that it was wonderful too…

Exactly how it was for me. Except that in the book Terence Carleton and his adored Nicky were lying in a lovers' embrace at the time. Incredibly, they called each other Darling… There was nothing like that between Will and me.

Yet despite the shock, and the guilt, of that occasion, I sat on Will's knee in the Rathbone Library a few days later. Incredibly risky, as anyone could have walked in; the door even had glass panels in it. But we were not interrupted. This time I held out for maybe half a minute, he for half a minute beyond that. Then I was gratified to feel his sudden hot spurt of wet, and, after I took my hand away from his trousers, to see the evidence in the form of a half-crown-sized blot.

I was also gratified that Will made no complaint about, nor even expressed surprise about, the relatively small size of my cock.

It went on in this way for weeks. The two of us sharing a chair together, either in my room or at his, rubbing each other off through the fabric of our trousers, admiring each other's spots of wet. Not until the summer term did we get sight of each other's cocks…

…We took a walk together along the cliff path. With no-one to see us we each had a hand in the other's pocket – we both had holes in them – and were gently touching the other's dick. Both were very wet. 'Come this way,' Will suddenly said. He was only nine inches taller than me by now, not ten, but he was still my senior by nine months. He was still the leader in everything we did.

He led me through a gap in the thorn hedge, and onto a clearing of rough grass, ringed by tall-standing fennel plants, just yards from the cliff edge. The blue sea lay below and stretched mind-bogglingly towards France. 'Lie down, Mac,' he said.

I obeyed, he followed me down, and we lay side by side on our backs. I started to feel him through his trousers, but he said, 'Let's do the job properly this time,' and undid his waistband button, then his zip, and wriggled his trousers down to his knees along with his underpants. His thighs looked massive and handsome. His cock, fully erect, was thick, long and uncut. His balls were heavyweight.

I was small and scrawny, my thighs skinny, and my circumcised cock a mere four inches. My pubic growth, which was still very recent, was a tiny circlet of thistledown, where Will had a virile curly patch. Nevertheless I followed his example. If he wanted to laugh or comment, that was up to him. I was younger, after all, and he'd suggested it in the first place. But actually I was pretty certain that he wouldn't comment. And he did not.

That was the day I saw another boy's spunk for the first time. Floods of it. And now I look back on it I wonder if that was perhaps a first for Will too.

*

The summer is kind to people who for whatever reason have difficulty in finding opportunities for sex, and the great outdoors is a wonderful venue for it. Well, that's how it was for me at any rate. We even managed to celebrate my birthday, midsummer's day, with a session in a small copse behind the town's seafront promenade. Unfortunately a small girl, aged about three found her way in among the trees and saw us just as we were both coming, watching for a second, wide-eyed and with thumb in mouth, before turning and running away. We both felt bad about that.

But it was indoors, a few days later, that something else of significance occurred. We were in my room, Will was sitting at my desk and I was sitting astride his left leg, facing him, and we were groping each other through our trousers. It would have been dangerous to take our cocks out, as my room-mate could have walked in at any second, and so could anyone else: I've already mentioned the pass-door between Number One and Number Three at top floor level, and my that-year's room was part of this corridor between the two houses. Passers-through were usually good enough to knock before opening the door, but not all did.

Will removed his hands from me and, with his Schaeffer fountain pen, which he was very proud of, and kept in his jacket's inside pocket at all times, wrote something on the corner of the pink sheet of blotting paper that lay on my desk. He tore off the small corner he'd written on and handed it to me. The words were fuzzy, as they always are if you try to write with a fountain pen on blotting paper, but I could still make them out. KISS ME.

I leant in to him and we kissed. We didn't open our mouths, we just pressed our lips together warmly for about a second and a half, the way mating birds do with their anuses. It was a major moment. Yet nothing much seemed to happen. No surge of emotion accompanied it. No erotic feeling. There were kisses between teenage boys in Lord Dismiss Us, which by now both of us had read. Those were highly charged events, that excitingly changed the course of their participants' relationships. But now in real life it didn't seem to be the case. And Will and I never called each other Darling. It was inconceivable that we would want to do that. They said, on one occasion, *I love you, I love you, I love you.* Those words never even tried to tumble out of us. We didn't *feel* like the boys in the book.

*

In the autumn I was given a new room – the one I've occupied ever since. I was given a new room-mate. Will. Zebedee knew that Will and I got on well. How well, though, did he know that? Could he see what was going on, and did he want us, consciously or unconsciously, to enjoy the experience more fully? Or did he, more coolly, want to give our affair the opportunity to burn itself out?

It did burn itself out. Sex with Will in a bed, his sperm and mine all over the sheets and our pyjamas, began to feel a bit squalid after a few weeks. The rapture of summer trysts in the open air, atop the cliff, a thirty-mile view of blue to look at and the mewing of the seagulls sailing overhead, was difficult to conjure in the bottom half of a narrow two-tier bunk. Will asked me once if I'd like to suck him off. He'd wrap his cock in a polythene bag if I didn't want his sperm in my mouth. I said no to that. He also asked me to turn over for him, saying he'd do the same for me in return. No, I said again. I shied away from both those opportunities. I wasn't ready for them yet. A bit too queer, I thought. And if I ever did want to do that – whichever way round – I had the feeling that Will wouldn't be the person I'd want to do it with.

Then Will got less interested in me as a sex partner. A year had passed since that first encounter over the bitter lemon drinks. Will was growing out of me. I was growing out of Will too, as far as friendship went. Though – in contrast to him perhaps – I wasn't losing my interest in boys as the objects of my sexual impulse.

At the beginning of the following term I was given a new room-mate. So was Will. He ended up sharing a basement room with Chris Kirkman, directly beneath the room we'd shared, and which I was now to share with Stephen Hooe, who had arrived in the middle of the last term after leaving his previous school 'by mutual agreement'. That was the end of my affair with Will. Though even before the start of term I knew that.

Over Christmas my mother had taken me to see the Royal Shakespeare Company in Julius Caesar at The Aldwych. Brewster Mason in the title role. Ian Richardson as Cassius, with the 'lean and hungry look' which he did to perfection. Ian Holm as Casca. Arriving at the theatre in a taxi my mother found she didn't have a small enough note for the driver. I reached into my wallet and handed her a one-pound note. 'Oh,' she said, 'there's something with it.' She tried to see it in the dim light of the cab's interior. 'A little pinky piece.'

It was the scrap of blotting paper on which, six months before, Will had written *kiss me*. I'd kept it carefully ever since. Now I took it from her, scrunched it up and let it fall to the floor of the taxi in the darkness. 'It's nothing,' I said.

Oct 6th 2014

Home was home and school was school. It was always a major shock to Ralph's system when the twain met. But why had he been sent to boarding school in the first place? As the only son of a widowed mother, who would very much have appreciated his company in her lonely home.

Because he was Roman Catholic. Simple as that. Catholic children had to be sent to a Catholic school. And if the nearest one – a Benedictine monastery school – was fifty miles from home, then boarding school it had to be...

FOUR

Proximity Is Comforting

Day-boys were different. They had other norms. But we boarders could be pigeon-holed roughly as follows.

Type A: Had girlfriends in the holidays, term-time a desert. Examples: Steve Hooe and Chris Kirkman.

Type B: Had girlfriends in the holidays but enjoyed sex with schoolmates during term. Examples: Will. And Jagger,..? and Rory…? I was never a hundred percent sure about that.

Type C: Had no girlfriends but enjoyed sex with schoolmates during term. Holidays a desert. I can't give percentages here. All I can say is that I belonged to type C. And so did Alex.

Type D: Had nobody at all. That probably went for quite a lot of us.

April 25th 1969

(Alex, and resolving to do something about it.)

Our room was full of people all day. Because it's on the ground floor opposite the front door it usually is. At one point Barry M. came in with an alarm clock which he was lending to Alex. To await collection. I thanked him and took matters, and the alarm clock, into my own hands. Leaving the others talking and reading I took the alarm clock up the four flights of stairs to Alex's room.

It was hard to know what to say, and he was no help. I gave him the clock and made some silly remark about its being useful. We stood close to each other in silence for some time. 'Better not,' he said.

He sat on the bed. I asked him when his room-mate would be back. I put my hand on his big leg. 'OK,' he said. 'But this time it's just me to you.'

'Why?'

'It's … a bit too much.'

I didn't pursue this. I presumed that he had masturbated very recently and had run out of juice.

It was a funny, restrained sort of business, half-lying, half-sitting on the bed, and afterwards I said, 'Will I be seeing you?' We laughed awkwardly and I left him still sitting on the bed.

Later, plans were laid for the cast of Andorra to visit the Royal Court Theatre in London on Thursday next.

Saturday April 26th

I found my photo on the notice-board. The photos of Andorra are printed and mine are very good. It was quite matey in the smoking-room. Everyone sat on me at once.

Then I started to write up the inspiration I'd had for a story while looking at the gorse blossom a week or two back. It's a conversation between a man and a honey-bee, in which the bee talks about its way of life and its view of other people's.

Sunday April 27th

I finished the bee story. It is not very good. Some day I'll make it better. Then everyone went to the cinema except for me and Jagger. Just the two of us out of all the sixth form at supper.

Later Will was sulking – everyone had avoided him on the walk back from the cinema. Then Zebedee arrived back to liven up the scene. He'd been out to dinner. 'A whole bottle of burgundy … mmmm!' He couldn't stand at first, and when he could he spent the evening hacking at people with his sword, biting Rory, and throwing

Alex's transistor radio out of the window. At ten-thirty we were all in the garden picking up the bits and saw Johnnie at his window. We sang Happy Birthday to him in honour of the following day, its date having been ascertained when some curious people found his Birth Certificate in one of the drawers in his bedroom.

Then we went to bed.

April 28th

The usual Monday Marathon. Including an essay on the Battle of Bosworth. Someone bought a pair of stockings for Johnnie, who spent the day with a puzzled frown repeatedly assuring well-wishers it was not his birthday.

Supper was good. Minute pieces of fried pork and tomatoes and potatoes. One could have wished for more however.

After supper Steve tried mixing milk and electricity using the light-socket in the table-lamp on my desk as a mortar. Results: steam, smoke, bangs, blue sparks and a blown fuse, a ruined light-socket and a nasty smell. Then Steve tried breaking the window. In this he was more successful. It broke.

April 29th

Said Goodnight, almost silently to Alex in the bathroom. Almost silently he said it back. Best thing about the day, perhaps.

April 30th

Did no work. Walked to the harbour. Robin Knox-Johnson was there, signing autographs, before setting off on his trip round the world. At General Studies Zebedee discussed the film 'If...' I met Alex's eyes for no more than a few moments. Rory has German measles, a great pity, because he can not go to London tomorrow.

Curry and rice for supper, at which I presided, everyone else, including all the prefects, having gone to The Killing of Sister George at the Marlowe Theatre. Including Alex.

I pondered lightly on security and my wonted side of these relationships.

May 1st

Woken early by Will. Breakfast of poached eggs for the two of us at seven o'clock, then up to the station to catch train to Canterbury. We got to the college too early for our French Oral exam, so bussed a mile back into town for a coffee. Then had to run all the way back...

Afterwards we had to run the whole mile back to the station and caught the London train with seconds to spare. The sun was hot. We had a shandy in the buffet.

Arrived at the Royal Court Hotel in Sloane Square we had a Martini cocktail which wiped my wallet out, then the others joined us and we had lunch. Tomato soup, rump steak, fruit salad and Beaujolais. We just did the 100 yards to the Royal Court Theatre in time to sit down and see David Storey's 'In Celebration', with Constance Chapman and Fulton Mackay. A powerful piece about a reunion on a wedding anniversary, in a miner's house.

The discussion afterwards was a bit feeble. Too many dumb schoolgirls, too few questions. It was soon over.

We went by tube, bus and feet to Marble Arch, to see the film 'If...' Before it started we went to Speakers' Corner...

I had an altercation with 'Aggie' a little old lady who loved Jesus but not Catholics. She called us a brood of vipers. I told her the devil could cite scripture to his purpose.

I was called a second-hand little monkey by a black chap called Mafu, listened to a Pakistani boasting of his abilities as a lover, there was a furious dispute after somebody insulted the Queen and a few blows exchanged when a man objected to being photographed. It was all rather fun.

Then into a pub where I had a lager, then to 'If…', an excellent film about a public school – symbolising a society authoritarian under a veneer of broadmindedness, whose instruction is: Fight for what you want. Fact becomes fantasy as three rebels decide to end the regime, the story culminating in a massacre with machine guns on parents' day.

We missed the last train back because we got on a bus going the wrong way. But Father Barnabas, when Father Malachy phoned him to explain, said, not to worry. So we descended on Michael P's family in Kensington. The twelve of us dossed down in blankets in a basement bedroom. I went to sleep next to Jagger at two o'clock.

May 2nd

We woke up gradually as it began to get light. I remember remarking the dawn light catching the contours of Jagger's face, and his eyelashes too, a few inches from mine. We were all freezing, but proximity is comforting.

We put on ties and stood to breakfast in the kitchen, toast, cereal, coffee.

On the train from Victoria we sang and talked. We convinced ourselves we all had German measles and all ended up lying down across one another. And I laid my head in Chris's lap and went to sleep for a bit…

Walked back to school from the station. As we entered the refectory just in time for lunch it felt as though people should have been applauding us. But nobody did.

In the evening I sat next to Alex in the smoking room. Later, passed him on the stairs after looking for a pen in Rich's room. I brushed my hand along his shirt. He smiled and I whispered Goodnight.

May 5th

Rory is raucously back from his sickbed. English class was out of doors where amazingly I found a four-leaved clover in the grass. I smeared it with Vaseline to preserve it. I should like to put it in a locket or something. It is not a particularly beautiful object but it's rare and supposed to be lucky. And anyway, I like it.

Steve has decided to adopt my doodles as wallpaper.

May 6th

Four sheets of my doodles, cartoons or sketches hang on the wall now, beside our bunk. They are popular with visitors.

Latest piece of news... Someone has written on Rory's door: *Arselickers Anonymous. Crawl right in.* We found out who wrote it later. It provoked a bit of criticism from Rich, who believed we were all ganging up on Rory.

I was a bit gruff with Rory later, but he was very nice to me.

In the smoking room Jimmie – Will's last-year alcove-mate – sat on my lap. Nearly squeezed the life out of me as he's a year older than me and nearly twice as big.

May 7th

Alex said Good Morning to me very nicely when he woke me up, but in the smoking room, didn't talk to me, sitting the other side of the room. What thoughts are going through his head?

I was table prefect at supper. The rest of the world had gone sailing.

May 8th

Heard the horrifying version, according to Chris Kirkman, of the prefect list next term. Neither of us is on it. Neither is Steve.

I tried to turn handstands on the garden wall. In the evening we Bloomsbury lot watched Alec Guinness and John Gielgud in a 30-minute Theatre on TV. Very good. It was after that that Steve, Chris and I had our depressing talk, convincing me that I was in the wrong camp altogether.

May 9th

Alex, duty prefect this week, returned to his old way of waking me this morning. Hands in under the covers from the bottom of the bed, working their way up...

Skipped cricket in the afternoon, and went up to Alex's room. But he was out, so no luck.

Then there was a rehearsal for Joseph and the Amazing Technicolor Dreamcoat. I am doing the song about Potiphar's wife. Then we played in the garden and on the wall. After some horsing around with Jimmie in the garden, he led me into the refectory for supper pulling me by my tie, announcing to the whole school that I was the reincarnation of King James I.

Piggyback races down the hall to the chapel for night-prayers. I was on Rory's back. He carried me all the way into chapel…

The Jimmie thing is interesting, and surprising, as he's definitely Type A (has girlfriends in the holidays, never touches boys). Maybe it's just the effect I have on him.

***

My diary doesn't record this. Too hot a topic, too difficult, I suppose. But it was tonight that this happened…

In bed, as we were – perhaps – drifting towards sleep, Steve and I talked about wanking. For the first time. We never masturbate at night in our shared bunk. Shared vibrations… I've been there before, with other room-mates, but with Steve… Well, we don't.

Usually I do myself after sport, a run, a Rugby game, or PE or soccer. Throw myself down on my bed on my bottom bunk, legs planted on the floor at the bottom, pull my shorts down to my knees and go for it…

I asked Steve this night how often he did it. When he'd done it last…

'Um… The night you were all away in London,' he said.

A week ago. I felt myself stiffening. There was a long silence. I broke it. 'Steve, would you ever let me toss you off?'

A bit of a pause. Then, 'I might,' he said.

Another silence while I considered this. 'Would you let me do it now?' I asked.

Steve's silence was eloquent. I took it as a yes. I climbed down from my top bunk (confusing, isn't it? But we did change and change about) and got into his. He already had his pyjama bottoms down and his top pulled up He was as stiff as I was. We felt each other with eagerness, as well as a kind of dispassionate interest. He wasn't circumcised. His cock was marginally smaller than mine and very hot to the touch. I'd never thought Steve beautiful, but I now thought that his cock was. His balls were small and tight-hauled up. His pubes were scanty but like tough wires. He was scrawny and skinny, but his muscles were harder than mine. In the darkness between the sheets I was strangely, acutely, conscious of the chocolate colour of his gleaming skin, and could imagine the black-cherry colour of his dick-head. The feel of him, the smell of him, the imagined colour of him were wonderful. He was a black forest gateau of delight.

'I'm going to come,' I said suddenly. We'd been masturbating each other for a mere minute and a half. And I did. Wetting myself and him, and his sheets.

'Sorry,' I said. I leapt out of his bed in a panic. I ran to the toilet and pissed. I was shaking like an aspen leaf. So much so that I could barely get my stream into the bowl. When I got back into our room my teeth were chattering. I leapt up into my top bunk. Glumly silent. I don't know if Steve had finished himself off in my absence. I suspect not. After a minute Steve broke the silence. 'We shouldn't have done that,' he said.

'No,' I said. We didn't speak after that. We lay awake in our separate agonies, unsure about what had happened to us, and what it meant. Then at last, inevitably and mercifully, we went to sleep.

Sunday May 11th

In the morning Chris Kirkman and I discussed the cartoons I'm doing for the school mag. Then Jimmie came in and asked if he could feel me. There were about three other people in the room. Chris laughed and called Jimmie a queer – which he is certainly not – but Jimmie and I took no notice. I said yes, and Jimmie squeezed onto the bed beside me and grabbed my cock through my trousers, giving it a quick but thorough grope, along with my balls. I did the same to him. He's reputed to have the biggest prick in the school, and is known as Hammerhead. I've never seen it, but now have a clear idea of its dimensions. Amazingly, I'm now nearly as big myself. Despite being a year younger than Jimmie and five inches less in height. I'd give the world, though, for his muscular arms and legs.

Later, in Chris's basement room, he and I sat together on his bed listening to an LP and reading the Sunday Times Supplement. Proximity is always comforting. Lunch was quite good – me table prefect – but Chris is out of favour with Zebedee. However, I like him.

FIVE

I'm Right and You're Wrong

May 12th

Chris and I spent the first part of the morning getting opinions on the Mag section illustrations. My cartoons. Father Barnabas liked them, all liked them, even Mr Gough, but Johnnie thought they shouldn't occupy a full page each. Father Cosmos thought they were worth a try…

English class was on the lawn. Chris and I wore daisies behind our ears. Spent the evening sitting in his room.

May 13th

After lunch sat on the garden wall with Chris while a blazing afternoon began. Later I perspired my way down to Winter's for some new shoes. Passing the antique shop on the way back and noticing the antique proprietor sunning himself in the doorway, I enquired about the price of gold and silver watches and chains. About £20 or £30 for the former, £3 for the latter. I had never before appreciated the difference in value of gold and silver. Three quid didn't seem too steep. But I only had sixpence on me.

Supper was quite good, me table prefect, and after supper Steve and Chris staged a duel. I was doctor. For twenty minutes they cavorted in the garden. By the end both showed with pride a tiny scratch inflicted by the other's foil. They were both voted dead by the bystanders, but neither would admit to having lost.

May 14th

Woken first by Alex and then by Chris, about whom I had just dreamed in connection with T.E. Lawrence… or D.H. I'm not sure which.

After breakfast Chris and I lay on my bed together, scandalising Mrs Pring (our youngish, pretty cleaning lady). 'Are you very tired?' she asked us. 'Not tired,' I said. 'Just queer.' Which is one thing that Chris is certainly not.

Rich brought John Lennon's In His Own Write, thinking that he and I could do some of the poems for the Speech Contest. We started to rehearse.

Lunch was good. Veal, ham and egg pie with picaninny. I had diarrhoea afterwards.

After Compline in the school chapel Chris and I made Steve an apple-pie bed, then span him a yarn (which he never quite believed) about how we were going to be expelled for writing a critical article in the magazine.

May 15th

Down to Stella Maris in Daniel's Moke. Chris and Jimmie piled in with us, so it was more than crammed. We met Tricia, Daniel's girlfriend on the way. Chris and Jimmie both very keen on her also.

I had butterflies about the afternoon's Speech Contest. On the way back from history class we seemed more than ever piled on top of one another in the Moke – rather like the pilchards that followed with lunch.

The Speech Contest was adjudicated by Mrs Lodge, a senior voice coach at one of the top London drama schools. We are only lucky enough to have her because she's also Barney's aunt. She certainly knows how to make an entrance onto the stage, with broad-brimmed summer hat, flowing cape and leg-of-mutton sleeves.

The juniors went first, and were giggled over by some of the bawdy boarders on the back benches. Though I'd like to see some of them try.

Then Phil did quite a good speech from Julius Caesar. Rory did his speech from Andorra. Smith did an impersonation of the Queen opening the school swimming pool – which was rather good. Jagger bravely sang a song – the one he'd done in Andorra. Then Rich and I went on, me with tie undone and splay-feet, Rich with bare feet and pigeon-toed. So we got a laugh before we even began. I forgot my words and had to take my piece of paper from my pocket. And improvise. Rich laughed at me and I stuck my tongue out at him. And the audience loved it – thought it was all part of the act. We did Liverpool accents too. 'Good Dog Nigel' went down especially well.

Compliments flowed, and medals too. Rory got the silver, and every other sixth-former taking part got a bronze, including Rich and me. 'Accent not quite right, but well done,' said Mrs Lodge.

Chris had done W.H. Auden's Miss Gee very nicely. About him, Chris, does it matter that next term I may think him a bigoted fool, a pseudo, a ridiculous pathetic little shadow of a dashing young man? Does it matter what he'll think of me next term? Because he doesn't think so yet; neither do I. For the moment... And isn't it just the moment that matters? These moments of illusion, these tastes of perfection, in the grip of alcohol or emotion, tobacco and affection, religion or sex? Perhaps or perhaps not, but there's no point putting away bliss for a rainy day. It's better than money. Because it's real.

Anyway, I also have Jimmie breathing down my neck and wonder: what does matter?

May 16th

A day in a glass dome. Hardly saw Chris. Went down town to the public library. Umpired cricket badly but amusingly. Went with Smith to buy bread, brie and expensive marmalade, which we ate with Jagger. Cod-pieces for supper.

The evening was better. Went down with Chris to the music room where some of the others were listening to the LP of Hair. Silly, or funny, or previously unprintable, the songs conveyed an atmosphere that was terrific.

One day our existence in this queer foggy place will end. Horrible! To be replaced by another, Cruel. Unbelievable, but fortunately true. Poor David, poor Phil, poor Chris... Poor everyone, and poor lucky Rafe.

Saturday May 17th

I started reading King Lear. Alex passed the window, looking in. I went upstairs one at a time, nervously. He was in his doorway. I said I had come up to see him. He signalled with his eyes. I sat down on the bed. Afterwards he put on the radio. Then we left together. We hardly spoke more than a dozen words.

May 18th

Sunday. Nothing doing in the morning. After good beef and Yorkshire for lunch Chris, Steve and I talked about our childhood experiences and memories. Then went into Number Three, where they were furnishing an outhouse to turn it into a sixth form common room / smoking room, like ours in Number One, which is called

The Pit. We drew pictures on the walls, carpeted the floor and put chairs in the place.

'We want Mac', chanted the juniors at supper, as Will became table prefect. I dissuaded him from joining our party to the cinema after. I'd borrowed a quid for this. We went, Michael P and Jimmie, Steve, Chris and me, to see Lady in Cement, not bad, with Frank Sinatra, and Secret Life of an American Woman, not good but funny. Will did not join us. Afterwards we went into 'Pit the Younger' as we've christened the new Number Three smoking room and watched Rich and Rory have a ball competition. They were fairly evenly matched, I thought. Chris and I said Goodnight, and I said it to Alex too. The house is beginning to subside into Monday.

May 19th

Talked all morning with Steve and Chris. We said nothing at all during English class, and Johnnie actually walked out. After all these years of threatening!

May 20th

Tons of work to do. None done. Went to Broadstairs in the Moke for a cup of tea and petrol. Johnnie was conciliatory. Back to Broadstairs with Chris and Steve to find history books. No books. We had a glass of Kirsch instead.

Went downtown with Chris and Steve in the afternoon. Got library book about Battle of Bosworth. No work done.

Steve and Chris went to the mayor's induction in the evening. I stayed in, and failed to control the table at supper. Too depressed after that to do any work in the evening. I'd have liked to have got drunk, but as usual I had no money... Shit!

May 22nd

Spent French class discussing our forthcoming trip to France. The trip is really for the juniors but Will and I are going as supervisors along with Teacher Trev.

At Stella Maris we found Teddy had made history by forgetting about our History class. We had to run him to earth on the cricket field where he was coaching the kids in the nets.

Toneless afternoon. I borrowed a library book on Richard III, intending to write a tragedy about him, though come to think of it, someone may already have done that. In the Pit I very publicly climbed onto Chris's knee and sat there for a bit. Chris seemed OK with that. More than OK, I think. Perhaps a little bit proud of this new friendship – as I am, of course. He even laughed and ruffled my hair at one point when someone made a pointed comment.

After supper I finished some bread and salami, and had to explain to Steve why I felt my relationship with him was devoid of emotion. A bit sad, that.

May 23rd

Did precious little work, and after lunch fell into a depressed slumber in my chair, waking in the middle of French class – but too late to go to it – finding my neck all but broken by the uncomfortable position. I intended to stay on my bed all during Games, but the cricket team was short, so I reluctantly turned out. I didn't bowl, I didn't bat, but Will split his trousers from ear to ear while at the crease, so entertainment was provided at least.

After that I had a cup of coffee with Jagger and we had a most interesting talk. I like talking to him. He doesn't force the conversation and never gets het up. I reluctantly bade him farewell and walked out into the warm sun to await the coach for the House outing. (Jagger is in a different House. That's why he lives in Number Three.)

First we drove across town to Zebedee's bungalow – it's actually his mother's – and had a buffet tea. Our host's 'tea' consisted of two sherries, two vodkas and a port, and then we set off for Herne Bay, singing a selection of songs on the coach.

At the cinema in Herne Bay the manager showed Zebedee a note in the local press about our visit. I installed myself between Rich and Steve. The main film was 'If...' Again. I enjoyed it just as much as the first time.

We returned singing, and retired to our (respective) beds.

Saturday May 24th

It got hotter and hotter.

The storm broke while I was having a bath, after reading Alexander Pope, in the afternoon. I washed my hair. After that I went up to the off-licence with Smith, claimed without a blush that I was eighteen, and then went back with beer, which we ate with bread, cheese and marmalade, with Jagger.

Table prefect at supper; horrid to the juniors.

After night prayers I had a fencing match with Steve and Chris and then we challenged Johnnie to an indoor duel in his house-master's room in Number Three. Johnnie was in a good mood and we all read the magazine proofs. Then Jimmie joined us. Johnnie told me my long hair looked effeminate. We turned Johnnie's radio on. Steve climbed out of the second-floor window. I hauled him back in again. In the mayhem that followed, the contents of Johnnie's fruit bowl went missing and his medicine cabinet got knocked over. Johnnie was screaming for lost apples, almost for blood, and chucked us all out.

We consulted in the garden and found we all felt penitent and at last borrowed some money from someone, not for the 'pound of apples' but Chris and I combed the local off-licences for a bottle of Carlsberg for Johnnie by way or reparation.

Flushed and apologetic we returned to his room after a successful expedition. Johnnie was really touched to receive the unexpected gift. We were all friends again. For now.

May 25th

Sunday.

On our morning expedition to the corner shop Steve and I staged a duel with imaginary foils in the street. At the end of it an old lady came along to find me prostrate on the pavement. 'You on a sit-down strike?' she asked.

'Actually he is dead,' replied Steve with dignity.

After that we walked to the cliff edge on the upper promenade and pretended to push each other off the railings. Jagger met us as we walked back and said he'd been invited to lunch in the monastery and could bring one other person. Would I like to join him? It was already five to one, and it was Whit-Sunday, so a feast, so there would be wine, so I said yes. It was a bit hard on Steve and the others, but there it was.

Inside the monastery we were introduced to the abbot who called me Paul (which is Jagger's real name) and called Jagger Rafe, and had to be put right.

Grace was said and soup, tomato, came round, followed by chicken, sausages, carrots and roast and boiled potatoes. I drank two glasses of Ste-Croix-du-

Mont '62 while Jagger had Beaujolais. It's only on feast days that you eat like this in the monastery, or have wine. It's only on feast fays that the rule of silence at table is relaxed. I talked to Father Malachy about the House outing, and to Father Sebastian about monasticism, then a trifle came along, followed by biscuits and stilton.

We adjourned to the senior common room for 'something to drink' which was, in my case, two glasses of port and a cup of coffee. I declined a cigar, re-introduced myself to Father Nicholas, my old headmaster at Stella Maris – he might have forgotten me since he spoke at General Studies. He told me that on the whole he'd enjoyed his headmastership at Stella Maris, said that some people had criticised him at the time for being too heavy with the cane, but that discipline never hurt anyone. Then we went on to talk about French authors.

Barney was there – he'd had school lunch, presumably, and then come along for the drinks – and I asked him if Jagger and I could have a chat with the abbot, so we were re-introduced. He's actually quite human. We talked about the possibility of his coming to talk at General Studies, about overpopulation, the broadening effect of travel, about the last school play, Andorra, and about Ireland. He thought the current situation there was very sad, but was only prepared to see one side – the Catholic side – of the question.

Then we left, and meandered back to the school. I went to tell Chris about it all. He said he was thinking of doing voluntary teaching overseas in 1971, and would I join him? I'd like to, I said.

Back to Jagger's room, (he now shares with Smith and Todger) talked quietly. Smith was obviously quite jealous about our lunch. Then it was time for vespers in the Abbey Church, which were sung rather beautifully in Latin.

Supper was revolting.

Steve, Chris, Rich and I went to the cinema, a poor Western, then a good Norman Wisdom, then fooled about all the way back, fencing, and chasing each other about the back streets.

Before bed Steve and I had an argument about something. 'Well, that's where you and I disagree,' I concluded.

'No,' he retorted smugly, 'that's where I'm right and you're wrong.'

So typical of Steve.

***

School, abbey, monastery… A little more history and a few compass points.

Augustus Welby Pugin built his home, The Grange, here on the cliff-top, in 1843, and next door to it one of his most beautiful churches, with its exterior of knapped flint. A road separates these two buildings from the domestic buildings of the abbey (or monastery – they're two words for the same thing), which are arranged around four cloisters that take the form of the cross. To get to the Abbey church – the Pugin church – the monks have to come out of their front door and cross the road or – their cosy secret in wet weather – take the private underground tunnel beneath the traffic.

The Grange is now the home of the school's junior boarding house. No tunnel links The Grange to the main school buildings (the ones built by Pugin's less talented son), which lie to the northern, landward side of the sprawling abbey buildings. Juniors come to the main school for meals, crossing the road (under strict supervision) and via a twisting back route which doglegs past the abbey itself, past the Regency Field, the Monks' Park, the tennis courts, the Coppice (territory of the

Scout Troop officially, but sometimes annexed unofficially for other purposes after dark) and the School Lawn, where Prize Day happens when the weather is good. This northerly migration occurs three times a day. Its northerly limit is the refectory or dining hall. Number One, then Number Three lie even further north than this, but the juniors come nowhere near these hallowed precincts.

And our migrations southwards take us seniors to the Abbey church sometimes, or beyond it to the cliff-top promenade and the sea below, but rarely to The Grange.

Most of us lived in The Grange when we were juniors ourselves. From the hallway a tunnel behind a locked door dives down through the chalk cliffs to the beach two hundred feet below. Sadly the final yards were bricked off during the War...

SIX

An Infinity of Stars

May 26th

Getting my stuff together for French class. Chris comes into the room. 'Come to Mass,' he says. I dropped my pen and followed him. We walked through the abbey grounds, across the road and into the Abbey church. 'It's the only time in the week when I can – you know – contemplate – and there's the added attraction of the juniors.' He has added that last bit for my benefit, as he isn't remotely interested in the juniors, immune from their (very occasional) charms. But the thought is appreciated just the same.

After Mass we went down town together, Chris wanted a haircut, but it was a bank holiday, so the barber's was closed. We looked at the watches and chains together and returned.

After supper Chris and I discussed my caricatures with Johnnie for an hour in Johnnie's room in Number Three. Also my English essay. I'm just not a scholar. I can't confine myself to the job in hand – I must explore all the exiting generalized things that lead from my work – I think.

Then Jimmie and I had a climbing competition in one of the apple trees in the back garden of Number One. He got higher, I got nearly as high; all were amused.

To night prayers with Chris, fooling around all the way, later piggybacked on Chris with Rich underneath him, and after running races to the pillar box, scrounged a coffee off someone, pretended to be drunk and went to bed.

I said Goodnight to Alex, after he had demanded to see my caricature of him, for Zebedee had told him about it. (It shows Alex bent over, with Rory standing on his back, holding a set of reins.) I put it about though that I had destroyed it, so everyone is happy – at least I hope so...

...The answer is very faint now, but it will live for ever. 'G'night,' in a beautiful Canadian accent and blue pyjamas.

And today the lunar astronauts splashed down. Big deal. Mind you, my Canadian friend wanted to be an astronaut.

May 27th

Good grades in history, so coffee in Broadstairs.

Afternoon and evening consisted of listening to Steve and Rich criticising my relationship with Chris. I'm a 'sycophant', the relationship is 'political'. Untrue.

I told Steve not to analyze, defile, destroy the dignity of the individual, to rob. But the truth? Perhaps because it is part of my character to behave this way. Because I need Chris? In fact, because I am Ralph McKean Esq., and why should any other reason be necessary?

However, we sorted things out, but I am dubious about the future.

I did some work on English and French poetry – Verlaine is exquisite – and intend to work late tonight.

***

This was the evening I overheard Rich and Chris talking in the bathroom while I was climbing the stairs. I stopped in my tracks, of course. Rich was warning Chris to be careful with me, not to get in too deep.

'Why do you say that?' Chris asked him in an injured tone.

'Because I know what you're likely to do, Chris,' Rich said. I took him to mean that Chris would at some point go off me and I'd get hurt. Ah well, we'll see.

Chris and Rich have been friends for years. They're both about eighteen months older than Steve and me. Bigger too. Chris is five feet nine or ten, while Rich has just topped six feet. I'm five foot six now, same as Steve.

May 28th

Amazingly, the abbot has taken me up on my invitation and has come to General Studies. This after a visit I paid to him in his Spartan office in the monastery. His talk was about modern unrest, and was a great success.

Chris and I went along the prom together, read Journey's End aloud together, went to Compline together, observed France together and talked about the 'opposition' to our friendship. We agreed on one point: that it 'just happened'. Neither of us forsaw it, as these pages bear witness.

We listened to 'Emily Butter' on the Radio, a spoof programme about an opera written by a very masculine – and we imagined lesbian – woman composer called Dame Hilda Tablet. It was very funny.

May 29th

History at Stella Maris – the Moke fully opened up. Extreme onions at lunch.

English class was quiet. After it a whole crowd of us went down to the prom and the beach below. We took the lift back up the cliff. Steve got up and offered his seat to a very large woman. I stood up also. 'Take two,' I said.

We all had ice-creams when we got to the top, talked about homosexuality and sexual equality, then made our hot way back.

I read French poetry during prep, enraptured as usual with Verlaine, and then, after night prayers, Chris suggested we went out to a pub – just the two of us. A wind got up as we set off and billowed our jackets as we walked, talking about Chris's new poem he's written…

…Chris chose a small backstreet pub that other people don't go to. There was a woman behind the bar, and just the two of us. My first time in a real pub. There was a fitted carpet, which was red. The cosiness of it was lovely. I didn't know what to have. Chris suggested a lager and lime. We both had one. It came in tall glasses with stems and looked beautiful. I'd never had a more important drink.

We didn't talk much. We were just being together. I looked into the elegant glass in front of me. A multitude of bubbles was rising from somewhere near the bottom. In that glass I seemed to see a whole world, and among the bubbles something like infinity. I was seeing inside myself and seeing something I hadn't known was there. That was strange, because it was so big, this thing. Bigger than I was.

We'd been read a story by GK Chesterton in which a character, walking home one night along his familiar route, finds the road climbing steeply, unexpectedly. He asks someone why it's so changed suddenly. He is told that the road is not heading for its usual destination this evening. It is going, instead, to Heaven. He glances down through the hatch of a pavement-side coal cellar that has been left open. Instead of the dark, closed space he expects to see, he finds he is looking down at the night sky and an infinity of stars.

This is what I remembered as I looked down inside myself. I'd looked down into this space before. The hatch that led to it had been opened a few times in my life. Most recently with Canadian David, two years before. Before that, with Phil, with Roger, Tim... And Micky. When I knew Micky I had only been four...

The magical big space I found myself confronting had not been so big back then, wonderful though it was. It seemed to have grown each time I found myself experiencing it. It had grown just as I was growing. Now, like the night sky, it seemed infinite. And I was in it now. I was falling in it, and not caring where I would land, or even if...

I came back from the stars by way of the rising stream of golden bubbles. I was in a small bar, in a tiny pub. With Chris. He was telling me about other evenings, creeping out of the school, breaking bounds, to visit pubs.

Over the last few days I had come gradually to realise what was happening to me, and how big it was. But tonight I understood clearly and for certain that it was happening also to Chris...

...Soothed by the bubbles we made our way back, up the alleys, up the road and into the school, into Number One. Inside the front door we parted, said 'Goodnight.'

Now the rain begins, foreshadowed in the gusts that blew in the faces of Chris and I. So the reckoning always comes.

Every farthing of the cost,
All the dreaded cards foretell,
Shall be paid, but from this night
Not a whisper, not a thought,
Not a kiss nor look be lost. (WH Auden)
Though there was no kiss, of course. Just all the rest.

May 30th

I woke up this morning and... Michael Campbell had

written this in Lord Dismiss Us…

Suddenly he remembered. Another being existed in the world. That was it. The world was made more gracious by the mere existence of Carleton. How strange that someone's mere existence – without even meeting – should work this magic.

I remembered that moment in the book now. For that is exactly how it was for me.

We did the Amazing Technicolor Dreamcoat to a try-out audience of sixth-formers. At lunch Chris and I acted out the joke about the man who couldn't hear because he had a banana in his ear. Much laughter from ther juniors.

Umpired cricket. There was a bit of a silence between Steve and me in our room, so I escaped to go over to the playing fields with Chris, who was practising for the high-jump. Then we played French cricket with Jagger and returned to fish-pie supper. The Old Boys began to arrive, in readiness for the annual cricket match, and Chris and I shared a bag of chips – provided by Zebedee – and separated, bound for bed.

France was faintly visible on the horizon, and the abbot's laundry turned up in Number One, amidst merriment.

June 2nd

Woke up at 5.15. Went back to sleep. Woken by Will at 6.30, got up, walked down to the sea – it was calmish – and on the way back found our coach driver already parking outside the school. An hour early. He'd got the time wrong.

Breakfast on the prefects' table of egg on toast, then into the coach with the juniors and Teacher Trev, and we were off into the early morning mist…

Dover. Walking through passport control, reversing down the slope into the hold of Free Enterprise I. Soon sitting on deck at a table with Teacher Trev and Will. One of the juniors was sick over the side, and Cap Blanc Nez appeared out of the haze...

We drove round the Capes, the White, the Grey, and stopped at a café near Wissant where I had a glass of wine. One of the juniors, who had bought a litre bottle, was by now quite drunk. Will bought a bottle of *vin très ordinaire* which we swigged at intervals as we continued along the bumpy sea road to Boulogne.

Strong smell of fish where we parked on the quay-side at Boulogne. But our packed lunch was good. Egg roll, sausage roll, chicken, apple, biscuit and cake – and Will's wine. We ate it near the beach, watching the ferries coming and going on their regular journeys to Folkestone.

Later we met a cripple hanging round the coach. The poor man had no teeth, told us the story of his two prisoner-of-war experiences. We didn't dare leave him near the unlocked coach, but eventually we offered him a couple of cigarettes and he went away chortling happily.

The cathedral looked near, so we went to have a look at it... After climbing a half-mile hill we found it, airy and classical but full of scaffolding. We saw the ancient crypt with ancient coffins, ancient pillars, ancient wall paintings and ancient darkness.

Back at the port, found all the juniors had bought flick-knives. Back on the coach. Back to Calais. Will and I found a moderate place to eat. Beer, mushroom omelette, camembert and bread.

At the docks, Free Enterprise II welcomed us in with gently smiling jaws. On the way in the coach scraped against a bulkhead and everybody cheered.

We pulled out astern, turned, and crept along the coast, past the wreck of a paddle-steamer towards Blanc Nez, while a wind arose and the sea rose with it, and we lurched between white horses and heroic seagulls.

Three juniors were sick and on the lonely deck the lights went on, white, red and green. Down below, holding onto the moving furniture, I had two whiskies, and went up on deck again. Now Cap Blanc Nez and the South Foreland rivalled each other in bulk, one white with sun behind us, the other black and beckoning ahead. Then a mist wheedled its way up the French cliffs till they appeared to be floating on cloud. Dover Castle, like a barnacle on the cliff-top, came into view while the dark shadows crept like an octopus and ate France.

The people in the flats on Dover seafront began to put up their lights, and the train ferry appeared, heading across our path for the harbour entrance. The cry, 'Harbour Stations' went up...

We awaited customs with trepidation. Some had bought nearly 1,000 fags each. But we got a nice officer, obediently showed our two packs each and charged through.

Barney met us off the coach in his bedroom slippers. It was ten thirty. I went down to see Chris, and told him about the trip. Then went to bed...

***

In a way, telling the story to Chris was the best bit of the day. It had seemed funny, spending the day with Will. Although it was quite amicable, it seemed hard to believe that – even as recently as seven months ago – we'd done the things we had. Unthinkable that we shall ever repeat them.

Back in those days of having sex, and one kiss, with Will, I'd worried that I should have felt more for him, or that we should have felt more for each other. Was this it?

I'd wondered. In Lord Dismiss Us, there had been quite a lot about schoolboy sex leading on to infatuation, at the very least. I had worried because nothing of the sort had happened, in the end, between Will and myself. I'd worried that perhaps there was no more to it than that.

I wasn't worried now, though. I hadn't known back then what I did know these days. I'd learnt this wonderful thing, and had learnt about myself in the process, through what was happening between me and Chris.

Oct 8th 2014

Michael Campbell said it in just six words: Another being existed in the world.

SEVEN

It <u>IS</u> a Beautiful World

June 3rd 1969

Chris cut my hair in the afternoon and far from working in the evening, Rich, Will and I trooped down town to see Belle de Jour and M. Hulot's Holiday, one marvellous, the other very funny. After watching two French films, smoked two French cigarettes and returned late. We found front doors to both Number One and Number Three locked, so we had to climb over a neighbour's wall. Heard that two fifth-formers had been expelled, had got violent, had to be drugged and were now awaiting collection.

June 5th

Revised History ready for tomorrow.

Zebedee, holding court on the stairs in the evening, says the arts are inferior to the sciences, when it comes to university study. Asks me which Oxford college I'm going to apply to. Six more expulsions.

June 6th

Woke up at 8.50. Soon Greg and KP were in the room and it came up in the course of conversation that the History A-level exam was not in the afternoon as I'd thought but in 20 minutes' time. –What! I gulped down coffee and bread and dashed up to the exam, which was in the Physics lab. 1st question… I'm dying for a shit.

I put this to Zebedee who was invigilating.

'Most unusual, but I don't see why you shouldn't.' Dashing along the corridor, then back again. 2nd question was on James I. 3rd and 4th questions, and now … look back.

So I've taken a real live A-level. In the afternoon a trip to Broadstairs, then a trot along the beach with KP and Smith, standing about on rocks till almost cut off by the tide then leaping onto a new rock fortress. When you've taken an A-level you can afford to be childish.

Borrowed some money and went to see The Great Escape, a magnificent film. We got back very late. And in bed I had terrible indigestion and wrote a poem.

Saturday June 7th

Had to supervise litter-picking detention in the morning.

In the afternoon I went down town with Jagger, trying to find Lord Dismiss Us in the library, to re-read. In the end we went to Uncle Ron's flat – Uncle Ron's the school's bursar – where we talked about the expulsions, drank coffee, ate cake, and watched Doctor Who on TV.

Later I read a bit of Oscar Wilde's biography and played the piano badly. Heard the story of how Joe Davies had stayed out very late the other night and when he got back, found Barney asleep in his bed. He'd gone to sleep while waiting to catch him…

About the Grateful Dead (formerly known as the Haemorrhoids), it's not that I don't like them, or their attitudes, or what they symbolise. It's just that they're the present excuse for a bit of anger, as the WC gang were, five years ago. So much has changed since those bitter-sweet summer days and these, through pearls of wisdom in a tent – 'I don't want to grow up' (Phil to me) – through 'If ever you feel you have no friends you will always have me,' (me to Canadian David), and the words *kiss me* on a scrap of pink blotting paper – to now, and 'It just happened.' But it's always the same me. 'You will always have me.' Or someone will.

Sunday June 8th

A poor lunch but a good pudding, then I nicked some cheese and biscuits from the staff dining-room and talked to Jagger before he and Steve left for the House cricket match.

While I was reading Oscar Wilde Alex appeared at the window. (The steps down to the Pit are just outside our window, that's why it's such a social place.) He asked if I had any matches. 'No,' I said.

Ten minutes later he was back again, uneasy. I said, 'Come in if you like.'

He said, 'Come up if you like.'

We climbed the stairs to his room together. Inside, he drew the curtains. Then I sat on his knee and put my free arm around his shoulder while we did it.

Afterwards I simply left. I feel much more kindly towards him than I've done for some time past.

Back in my room I went to sleep and was woken by Steve. He'd retired hurt from the match. Had taken a cricket ball in the eye and was badly bruised.

Smith was in France, I hardly spoke to Chris, Steve was in bed, Jagger out, the music room occupied… I was depressed and weary of weariness. I walked along the sunset-lit promenade and was pursued by two revolting little tarts. ''Ere – got the time?'

I returned to school and joined the nine o'clock set (alias the Grateful Dead) who were quibbling on the stairs with Zebedee about House cups. If only one could talk to Zebedee without his circle of morons!

***

How weird to be having sex with Alex while right in the middle of falling in love with Chris. Yet Michael Campbell observed this phenomenon in Lord Dismiss Us. Carleton goes off into the wood with Naylor (I saw our Coppice, on the edge of the school lawn, here, including the detail of the masters' lit windows) and Naylor masturbates Carleton (although Carleton doesn't come on this occasion) despite Carleton's having fallen in love with Nicky Allen that very afternoon, when Allen is sitting on Carleton's lap in the back of an overcrowded car, coming back from a cricket match.

June 9th

Woke up late. Breakfast and then Shakespeare A-level English paper. Not bad questions but lousy answers!

After it I walked with Smith to the Hoverport and back. On the way back we sat on the grass on the cliff-top, at the spot where Will and I had first pulled down our trousers together. Now Smith and I looked at each other's crotches and we almost... But we didn't. Though we looked into each other's eyes and knew we were both thinking the same thing.

After supper I read a bit, worked a bit, talked to Chris a bit and, after prayers, talked to Jagger, eating bread and marmalade, and then, in the bathroom, to Zebedee, for once not surrounded by his grateful-to-be-dead zombies. We talked about religion and logic. Interesting.

June 10th

Down to the public library in the morning. Read a poem by Patric Dickinson about a redwing and liked it. In the afternoon returned there with Jagger to look at the exhibition of paintings there. We looked at Stephen Spender's autobiography, World Within World, and had a coffee at the Wimpy Bar. Later, watched Chris balancing on a beam in the garden from inside my room. He seemed miles away. Listened to Hair with Smith, returning to my own room in a thoroughly good mood which was promptly smashed to bits by Steve, still slit-eyed after his cricket-ball accident, who was in a bad mood.

Bad.

June 11th

Had the House photo on the school lawn in blazing heat. I sat next to Chris. That was followed by a species of lunch and after that we watched and cheered the House tug-of-war. We won. And still the sun was hot…

French A-level paper, jackets off. Not bad, wrote a Verlainesque essay about autumn. I liked it and afterwards, while eating bread and stilton, translated it into English, and made it a poem. It goes like this: –

Autumn,
What is it?
The necessary counterpart of spring,
Succeeding to summer tastefully,
Not brutally, but with grace.
Colours subtle, pale, mysterious,
That characterise the spring,
Borrow for autumn wear a cloak
Of gold and copper
And sensual flame
From the shimmering summer sun.
And the autumn carries it off
Without vulgarity.
A season with good taste,
Autumn.
The cartwheel mists of autumn,

As veils to women's features,
Return to the dry,
Taken-for-granted stubble-land
Its pristine mystery, reserve, completeness.
Mists, too, have taste.
One morning, sun-threatened like the rest,
On the telegraph wires no longer
Sit the swallows, their places taken
By great fieldfares, golden, purple,
With wild eyes like black diamonds,
Night-blown.
Autumn,
What is it?
The fruit of the plant of which
Spring is the flower;
The season of liquid gold,
Frozen.

I've written worse. Johnnie liked it. I talked to Jagger, had coffee with him, then returned to 'a fiercely mourning house' as Dylan Thomas puts it. For Zebedee was out and those dynamic bundles of character, the Grateful Dead, were unplugged, lost and silent.

June 13th

Free day. Filled in Oxford forms, got a form for a driving licence, filled that in, went with Barry M and KP to buy a car from a prostitute but founds she was already sold.

Then down to the beach with Daniel, Rory, Chris and Steve. Daniel's girlfriend's sister Lucy joined us.

After supper I read World Within World and let Steve read these pages – on condition he made no comment on the more personal passages.

Saturday June 14th

Ate three hefty pieces of veal and ham pie at supper; this succeeded in keeping me awake until 12.30.

Sunday June 15th

After supper Chris and I sat on the lawn of Number One. We watched punishees moving the stones of the wall that was collapsed, and Chris said he thought he was going mad. Actually, I think he is homesick. He said – as Canadian David said long ago – 'The best people have skinny fingers.' They both included my fingers as well as their own.

Chris, *je t'aime beaucoup*. But that doesn't alter the fact that you've gone to Tricia's house (that's Daniel's girlfriend's house) with Steve and left me feeling thoroughly depressed.

June 17th

Went out with KP in the morning. We found a dog and walked four miles with him, taking him up and along the cliff with us. He only agreed to leave us when we got back to school. On the journey we watched the hovercraft manoeuvring (or failing to do so) in a high wind and choppy sea, then back to the sea-front for a cup of tea. I decided to become a Russian monk, or build a tall tower where I would intern myself. Chris (who sits on our table at meals now) decided he would join me.

Now I'm tired and with aching legs, and anticipating a gloomy future. But captivated by mysticism and Siberia, by a world that IS beautiful and trying to make sense of the unwieldy tangle that has somehow got to be shaped into Rafe McKean.

…Nearly forgot to mention the fire in the main school cellar. Smell of burning, Father Barnabas seen directing a hose-pipe through a hole in the floor of the staff lavatory where someone appears to have dropped a cigarette end.

***

It wasn't a famous person who said this, but a famous person who recorded it. A curmudgeonly person who had never had a good word to say about anyone or anything lay dying. He opened his mouth one last time. The words that popped out were – 'It IS a beautiful world.' I don't know who the curmudgeon was, nor remember who the famous writer was that told the story. But I don't think that matters.

June 18th

Day of hysteria. Chris was late back from Lucy's last night. Zebedee wants him thrown out. I had French Literature exam.

After lunch I had French Dictation and a bath. Later a talk with Chris and Steve. Supper was a piece of pork fat, and after Compline came the disaster of Jimmie being expelled by mistake, for throwing a pebble through Barney's window.

Later the edict was withdrawn.

…I understand. I always do. I play along. I do nothing original. I give an impression of independence, but depend for everything on whoever is my current father-figure. I lack strength of character. But perhaps they lack it too? (Divided we are weak, united strong?) Perhaps.

June 20th

£2 from my two Aunts, who anticipated tomorrow.

A three-hour S-level English exam, in the Reception room and so constantly interrupted, but I was quite happy about my efforts.

Zebedee can not see me doing Oxford scholarship exam in History. Johnnie can not see me doing Oxford scholarship exam in English. Hmm.

Saturday June 21st

Sweet 17. Two minutes before midnight my pyjamas split; I didn't get to sleep for ages. Missed morning prayers and got a card, procured by Chris and Steve, that everybody had signed – even Alex.

In the late morning, Barry M, KP and I made our way to a pub the other side of Stella Maris, stopping off at a kids' playground on the way, to play on the swings. We bought a round each – I had lager – and returned home.

Chris and I waited for Steve to finish his class and when he turned up we drank the first half of my Apricot Burgundy bottle. We were all happy when we went in to lunch.

I read Thomas More's Utopia in the afternoon. Later Jagger and I bought bread and cheese and ate it, then walked down to Uncle Ron's and had coffee. Doctor Who was a rounding-up episode. It's going off the air for six months and a new actor – John Pertwee – is taking over the title role.

At supper I took charge of Jagger's table but found it difficult to manage his rather peculiar form of discipline. I sat next to Joe Davies who told me he had overheard a couple of girls in the street saying I was sweet. (Nice!)

Read More Utopia (excuse the pun) and after prayers down to the pub with Barry M and KP. A spectacular view of Blanc Nez across the water. Though it's 30 miles away, the fields shone bright green in the low sun, the cliffs were dazzling and the monument on the cliff top was visible with the naked eye as were the buildings of Calais. Never saw it looking so clear and bright before. Had three more lagers in the pub – met and chatted to some boys from St John's. After returning we were joined by Jagger and had some Scotch, and some Cognac.

Steve came back from another pub and I wrote a note to Chris. Soon heard him clambering in through his basement window, immediately under ours. I climbed down the wall and said, 'Come up for a drink.' A few minutes later he did. We drank the rest of the Apricot Burgundy, just Chris, Steve and me, and chatted happily in whispers.

***

I wrote 'returned home'. Instead of 'returned to school'. Without thinking. First time that's happened.

In Lord Dismiss Us the narrator Terence Carleton muses: *'It's funny, once upon a time – and not so long ago – home used to be the real place and this was just somewhere I had to be. Now it's exactly the other way round.'* That was just after he fell in love with Nicky Allen. Now it seems to be the same with me.

Sunday June 22nd.

Rory's birthday. Now he's 17 too. Rich and Chris quarrelled at breakfast and Rich asked Chris to return to his old table.

After breakfast Rory was tossed in a blanket in the garden of Number One. I went next. But being lighter, and because the 'tossers' were now more confident I flew much higher, and was in danger of missing the blanket on my return. After about seven take-offs and landings I clutched at the blanket, and the others did their best to dislodge me from it. Till Chris yelled furiously at them, 'Stop. Can't you see he's frightened?'

Then they stopped, and I tumbled onto the ground. As I stood up Chris ruffled my hair. He's only done that once before.

Anyway, it's over now. I told Steve that if he wanted a key to my character that was it. That I can do anything, provided I'm hanging onto something. If f I hang onto nothing I can do nothing. That's why I need things – like booze, friends.

After Mass, down to the seafront with Chris, where we ate ice-lollies and met the others, Steve, Jagger and Rich. Chris took a photo of us all, sitting on some steps that had been sprayed with acid weedkiller, though we didn't know about that till alerted by a lifeguard. I wasn't sure if I was going to walk back to the school after that. Rich said, 'He'll go if Chris goes.' It was probably true, but I wasn't too happy about him saying it.

At lunch I was on Chris and Steve's table. Afterwards I sorted out history essays and then, hearing Alex go up the stairs, I followed him to his room. He was starting to undress for a bath. I sat on his knee. 'Last time,' he said. And, 'Strictly for school.'

We were going to go hetero from now on, we said. Alex is leaving for good in a few days anyway. I walked out, saying goodbye. His face surrendered to a transformation that could possibly have been called a smile.

I walked along the prom feeling a sense of release. Alex will be a happy memory. I hope I shall be one of his, but that's it. I walked to the harbour. Saw the Agenor had smashed her bows in, and that her sister ship, the Aphaia, was back from Bremen. Then looked through the telescope and could see the North Goodwin lightship clearly. Later the Aphaia glided out of the harbour and I wandered what sort of a place was Bremen.

June 23rd

Revised History. Wrote thank-you letters. The rain came, and so did the school magazines. My sketches are printed, and so are Alex's and my House notes.

Chris declared that I was the person closest to him in the whole school; that cheered up a rather miserable day. Steve is annoyed with me, Smith disgusted with me, Johnnie says I lack perseverance.

June 24th

Woke up at nine and was told that History exam would be in the morning. Bustled frantically, only to be told it was only a joke.

Washed my hair, ate bread and butter and coffee, and set off for Stella Maris with a pile of books that Teddy had asked for. I met Miss Moyne (she had taught me piano there all those years ago) and we talked a bit, then Teddy hove into view. I gave him the books and asked him about Oxford, so he knelt down at a table in the cloister and wrote a list of colleges. 'Christ Church is easy to get into if you've been to the right sort of school.' He didn't need to say that wouldn't include a school like ours. 'Worcester is good, it has a pond with ducks on. Jesus College is full of Welshmen. Avoid Exeter – Victorian buildings, very nasty – and St Edmund's Hall does nothing but rugger.'

On the way back I was offered a lift by Mr Fuddington, form master of form one since the year dot and, this year, the town's mayor. I dodged the traffic and ran to his battered Jaguar. Jumped in, thanking him. 'Better a bad ride than a good walk, what?' he said. It was all of a hundred yards to the school, but he then had to drive two hundred yards past it to find a parking space. We had to walk back.

In the afternoon we took History. Not bad questions. After that I felt empty, tired.

After supper a gruelling two and a half hours rehearsing Joseph. Nothing was quite right for the man who had come to tape it and in the end he arranged the mikes so we could not hear a word we sang. We didn't even get to hear the recording.

When I went to see Zebedee about Oxford he was sitting in near darkness. He said – get my hair cut. You'd think my hair was painful to him. What does he take me for? Samson?

June 25th

Walked in the afternoon to the harbour where a replica of the Nonsuch was moored before crossing the Atlantic.

Wondering what to do with the evening, got a surprise from Jagger, who invited me down to Uncle Ron's. We talked about Oxford, then Uncle had to go out, leaving us to watch The Avengers and The Laugh-In and eat biscuits and drink coffee and address school magazine envelopes. It made a change.

June 26th

Rushing round with Chris from form to form, dealing with magazines. In Uncle Ron's office, sealing the envelopes, stamping them. Talking to Teddy who said he used to quarrel with his own housemaster over the length of his hair, talking to Father Barnabas about the length of mine, working in the library, walking on the prom, filling two pillar-boxes brim-full of magazines, sorting out my room after supper, wearing a hat – for my hair was by now all cut away – Jagger tapping on the window, cup of coffee together (everyone else gone down the pub) walking along the prom with him, breaking and entering Doctor Boulting's spooky house, finding a recently opened bottle of homemade wine on the table, but not daring to taste it, back out of the window across the overgrown lawn, and back to school for a further chat in Jagger's room, followed by the discovery of Chris's return. Goodnight. Then bed.

June 27th

More magazine rounds, listening to a recording of Joseph's Coat, rehearsing in the open air, drinking orange juice, more magazine work. Fish curry for supper, down to the Wimpy with Jagger after. Back for Bournvita, polishing shoes, and depression, resulting in listening to Beethoven's Number Five in the music room with Smith. Everyone else was at the pub. Even those who, like Steve, have no money.

Never mind. I am to be presented with a cheque for a guinea for my sketches in the magazine... Tomorrow, when it will as much use to me as it would be on my death day.

France is visible, rain imminent – and would you believe from these pages that this is the last night of term and tomorrow night I shall be in Sussex. 'Adieu humiliations, degrading tasks, hatreds, sarcasms, Adieu.' To quote Vigny.

And, to misquote the Earl of Bute, 'God knows what consequences the room next term with Chris may have.' ...I only hope we'll manage.

Saturday June 28th

Beautiful morning, bustle and scurry, packing and tidying. Over to the sports field. Mother arrives. Is introduced to Steve, talks about my haircut to Barney, we watch a few races, exchange news, then it's over to The Regency for lunch this year. An interesting cold soup called Vichyssoise, tons of chicken, salad and chips, a glass of white wine, a cup of coffee... And *I drive* back to school, parking outside Number One!

My mother and I are also introduced to Steve's father. He has the most extraordinary eyes I have ever seen. The colour of amber. He's a doctor. Luckily for him he's a consultant surgeon, so his title is Mr Hooe. Had he been a physician...

I help move a piano, and arrange chairs, for the performance of Joseph in front of the parents. I wore a huge borrowed boater for my number, which I sang amid laughter and applause. But it was very soon over.

Then came the speeches. I thought about all those I was saying goodbye to. To Alex. To Will. To Rich, who is going to drama school. To Jimmie. Then the prizes were given. For the first and only time I went up a ridiculous number of times. I received a Music Dictionary, The Faber Book of Aphorisms, my cheque for twenty-one shillings, and my bronze speech contest medal.

Tea and goodbyes all round. Goodbye Alex. Were you my 'boyfriend'? Goodbye Will. Were you a boyfriend too? Anyway, out you both go, into the flow and eddy of a wider and – a straighter? – life.

EIGHT

Bull's Blood, Beefballs and the Beatles

June 29th

Sunday. A watch and chain, a present from Mother, appeared at breakfast. I call it Peter'n'Paul. As it's the Feast of Sts Peter and Paul today.

June 30th

Mounted my four-leaved clover, to be worn on my watch-chain.

July 1st – 4th

A week of sunshine. Working on a market garden – Stocks Farm at Wittersham. Cutting and packing lettuces, rotary hoeing, eating strawberries, driving a tractor – a Ferguson. On Saturday my first (car) driving lesson. Did quite well. In the afternoon went to the fête at St Mary's School, hoping to pick up a second-hand waistcoat on which I could wear my watch and chain, but there were none for sale.

July 23rd

Learning to reverse with tractor and trailer. Mother's old friend Miss Bennett has had three toes chopped off in an accident with a motor-mower.

Watched a pig having eleven piglets.

Sunday July 27th

Drove to church, and hit a fence for the first time on the way back.

August 28th

Driving test day in Hastings. Very nervous. Many mishaps. But I passed…..!!!!

Sept 3rd

Drove back to school and installed myself in my old room – with new roommate Chris. Steve is now on the top floor, vertically above us, though with one room in between.

Other changes. New prefects, including Daniel. Paolo the Italian stallion is the new head boy, already re-styled *the 'ed boy* and among the other new prefects is … of all people … Rory.

Johnnie is no longer housemaster of Number Three, he has moved to The Grange. Probably to get away from us lot. His place and his room have been taken by Fr Cyprian. Cyprian was my form master in the fifth form two years ago. He's the same age as Fr Malachy – about thirty – and they studied together in Rome and are good friends. Otherwise, they are very different. Malachy is introspective and thoughtful, Cyprian, though just as clever, is very ebullient and extrovert, votes Conservative while Malachy votes Labour. He has an unruly thatch of black hair, is tall and thin, with prominent cheek bones and coal-black eyes that always have the spark of a laugh in them, and a love of life. He looks on the bright side of things – an unusual disposition to find in a celibate monk.

After revolting supper – me table prefect – we trotted down to Tricia's for the evening, and Daniel gave us a lift back in the Moke. We were then talked to by Zebedee and, in spite of indigestion (mine) Chris and I consumed between us a bottle of bloody good Bull's Blood of Eiger. So the indigestion went away, and we talked ourselves to a sound sleep.

Sept 5th

The summer holds…

The morning passed. Beefballs, new sports coach, divided us into PE-ists and musicians, and I decided there and then to have nothing more to do with him. Lunch was OK and in the afternoon I got as far away from Beefballs as possible by going down town and looking at the shops.

The afternoon passed. Teddy is prepared to write my Oxford recommendation, and everybody is happy. The summer holds…

Saturday Sept 6th

Chris and I are so carefully not taking each other for granted that our relationship is ridiculously polite. We talk to each other like two lunatics who both believe they are Christ but don't want to quarrel over it. The future remains to be seen.

There is a new boy on my table. Mark Javen, aged thirteen. He is easily the prettiest of the new term's intake. Small and lively, he has straight blond hair with a fringe at the front, neat dark eyebrows and eyelashes that frame a pair of laughing china-blue eyes. Oval face, nice mouth and cheeky nose. He is well-spoken, friendly, and full of a confidence I would envy if I was still his age.

Sunday Sept 7th

After a reasonable lunch, now at the head of the table, I read Jane Austen all afternoon and evening until Steve returned from an expedition to Tricia's house, where he hadn't been too welcome.

Anyway, having had nothing to eat, he took me down town for a Wimpy, through the street-lamp-lit streets, and we returned, singing, *Potiphar had very few cares...* And I had a bath.

Sept 9th

Father Malachy was at General Studies, recruiting for the next school play, which is a typical Malachy choice: Brecht's Mother Courage.

After lunch I read half of a book about Oxford, washed my hair, ricked my back and, seeing Chris sound asleep on his bed, followed his example, and awoke to find myself – and him – school captain(s) for the rest of the evening.

I banged my fist beautifully on the refectory top table, said Grace, and after supper, and reading more Jane Austen, took night prayers.

After that I smoked a cigar, washed it down with a piece of chocolate presented by Chris's younger brother, and then prepared for a long evening reading Jane Austen's Emma.

Sept 10th

Took morning prayers, then went down town. Skipped off Games, to read more of Emma in the public library, but returned to find that Beefballs wanted to see me. So I didn't enjoy my evening, although it terminated with a trip to the pub and two whiskys. I enjoyed that, my companions being Chris and Steve.

Life is a shell of crystal, with swirling waters all round. How long before it breaks? How long before the idyll disintegrates in a cataclysm of breaking glass? For how long in other words will things go on?

Sept 11th

Horrible day. Intense depression. I felt quite ready to burst into tears. I don't know what I want to do, what I will do, where or what I am. I saw Beefballs in the morning, and my hopes of making a dramatic speech decayed into acquiescence. 'Yessir. Nosir.' I despise myself.

Sept 12th

...Dutifully I changed for running. At the roll-call for the 'extra' Games session Beefballs called my name three times. I yelled it back and Beefballs looked daggers at me but did nothing. Then Gollum pressed me into his rugger game. 'Hurry up.' I had to change yet again. I went into my room and – to my utter astonishment – wept. However, I changed into Rugby kit, and played dutifully for ten minutes, after which time, on being counted, we totalled 16. So I was released. Got back into running kit and charged down to the Viking Ship, on my own. There I spotted another lonely white figure on a distant road and made towards it, across a field following a path labelled, 'Trespassers will be persecuted'. I was not. The figure turned out to belong to a chap called Monty, in the lower sixth, and we ran back to the school together. There I changed yet again, and tried to do some Latin...

An hour and a half, but only three sentences, later I gave up and lay on my bed till supper time.

After supper I talked across the wall – the one between the gardens of Number One and Number Three – to Phil, for the first time, in any depth, in years. Then to Rory. He hasn't grown as much during the summer as I have.

Sunday Sept 14th

Translated Latin in the morning after Zebedee had compared Chris and I to a couple of babies – quite groundlessly – and then I had lunch in the monastery with Smith. I did a bit of work in the afternoon and then there was a play meeting. Who will be Mother Courage?

Sept 15th

Monday. Things cheered up a bit in the evening, when Chris and I worked late, and Zebedee dropped in for an hour to talk and joke about Beefballs.

Sept 16th

Anti-Beefballs morning. General Studies – which Beefballs walked out of after 30 seconds, and a good lunch. After that, Chris, KP and I went down to see Carry on Camping and Counterfeit Killer – both quite good and, though I got a headache on the way back, we bought some bread and peanut butter, sat on a table talking to Fr Malachy and, after singing along to Leonard Cohen – went to supper.

After, I visited Johnnie in his Spartan new room in the junior house, The Grange, while Fr Richard, who is still housemaster there, shouted through the door, 'Have you just been to the toilet, Mr Johnson?' Fr Richard hasn't changed a bit.

After night prayers Chris and I and others were auditioned by Fr Malachy. I am to be Mother Courage, and Chris to be the Cook. Everybody happy. We went to bed.

Sept 17th

Chris and I both overslept, waking simultaneously at 8.35. (Tut-tut.) I did some work in the morning and after lunch there was a run. God was it tough! Only to the Viking Ship, the Hugin, and back, but fast and without a stop when we got there. Such a stitch. I nearly died, but didn't.

Sept 18th

'Rafe, we've done it again!' Chris's words woke me up. We had indeed done it again. It was nearly nine o'clock and when we opened the curtains the whole sixth form, who were standing outside, smoking, clapped.

I revised History in the morning and Paolo rebuked me for non-punctuality and not turning up for breakfast. At lunch Smith upset a bowl of fruit salad all over me. Then I borrowed an Earl Grey tea-bag from Smith, scrounged some sugar and partook of my first drink of the day.

Finally I read Twelfth Night, and at supper collected the first penance I'd ever dished out. Supper was curry but after it, and in spite of two helpings, I was still hungry. After supper Rory came in, and together we wrote up the sailing club notes for the magazine, adjourning to the prefects' room. We filled the text with all the innuendos we could muster, while a violent squall raged beyond the window pane.

After night prayers, first reading of the new play…

Saturday Sept 20th

I spent almost the whole day making a waistcoat out of Jimmie's old suit, as he'd left the school back in the summer, and wouldn't need it. Then someone told me he was coming down at the weekend specially to collect the suit. I was horror-struck and, while Chris went to the pub with Rich – now at drama school but back on a visit – I went miserably to bed.

Sept 26th

Last night Chris and I read each other (heavily censored) extracts from our diaries and resolved to work all night the next day. After Mass – complete with singing – Chris and I sat on the bed, he playing the guitar, me listening, and at midday the [new, untitled, white-covered] Beatles LP was played during music class. It is a melancholy piece of work, the brilliance in it is ghostly, a mere echo of past glory, and the whole is a blatant proof of the beginning of the end of the Beatles' era. Maxwell's Silver Hammer is the only really good one although it too has a sad 'past-it' quality.

After lunch I wrote a History essay, attempted a run, gave up and walked back, rehearsed for hours in the Monks' Park after Zebedee had called me affected for reading Punch in a P.E. vest, and was volunteered for practises of a four-part choir for Christmas carols. Supper was lousy, and Johnnie talked in our room during prep, after which I roughed out some sketches for the school magazine.

———

I write this at ten past two tomorrow morning, having struggled through Mansfield Park since ten o'clock. Chris went to sleep soon after midnight, and I was left alone, listening to those strange clock noises that come from everywhere at once. Something Steve said at Night Prayers depressed me, and now I sit here while a wind blows outside and Chris snores. Yes, I stayed up later than him, I am still independent, but still, for all Steve's cynicism, I like Chris, as I did last summer, no more, no less. And now it's Saturday and I am sad.

Saturday Sept 27th

Play rehearsal. Some of the lines between Chris and I are rather ironical, at least Steve would find them so: 'I had no idea you were such a close friend of this gentleman and had to account to him for everything.' And – 'Because the Cook says so,' sneers the chaplain, reminding me a little of Rich on the beach in June.

So the day ends, but without the special something of last spring and summer. Witness May 27th...

Chris and I went along the prom together, read Journey's End together, talked together, went to Compline together, observed France together and talked about the opposition to our friendship. We agreed on one point: that it 'just happened'. Neither of us forsaw it, as these pages bear witness.

The wording of Chris's diary is similar, but of course he didn't read out anything about the last bit – if indeed he put it in.

He keeps his diary in the same drawer as that in which I kept these pages last year... But I'm turning into another Alex, living off his reminiscences. That must not be. There IS a future. Leaving school is not the end of the world. But my prophecy about the future not mattering with respect to Chris last term has not yet come true. And I do not like to see anything beyond our present situation, which could only lead to loss. Perhaps there is no future?

Now I polish my pocket watch and look at the world reflected in its silver back, look at the peculiar phenomenon we call silver. Silver is not a reality, it is a vehicle of reality and as such is understandably precious and valued. It is a proof of our world existing in our attitudes towards it, the explanation of Heaven and Hell and such ... Oh chuck it, Mac, enough of this rubbish!

Sunday Sept 28th

I showed my cartoons to Johnnie and Fr Barnabas, both liked the unprintable one, then Chris and I went up to Fr Cyprian's room – that used to be Johnnie's room, in Number Three, where Fr Cyprian has replaced him as housemaster – and we talked about the cartoons and about Father Nicholas and smoked a Gauloise each. So passed the evening until Paolo came in to tell Fr Cyprian there was to be a fire alarm in ten minutes. There was. We rabbled together, and then were dismissed. Chris and I went to talk to the kitchen staff, then I took a bath. After that I said to Chris, 'Would you think me a fool if I stayed on till next Christmas when I fail my Oxbridge entrance exam?'

'I might,' he said.

'So might I.'

Then we sang old Beatles' songs together and now, after a cup of coffee, we must do some work for a change.

———

We did. Unable to sleep for the coffee, Chris wrote a History essay and I did two Latin proses, all the work I had to do – and all the work I ought to have done into the bargain. Even when in bed, we didn't sleep till long past three, and then only in a half-awake sort of way, so we were a wee bit tired the next morning...

Oct 2nd

A cold day. Chris and I are late for breakfast. I finish my caricatures and sleep as much as possible. I read Gulliver's Travels. For fun, Chris asks Mrs Pring if she will make him and me a coffee while we lie on our bunks in the morning. To our surprise she does...

After supper (ugh!) Chris and I go up to our familiar Off-Licence and acquire a bottle of cheap, sweet, white plonk, and owe the man a shilling. So we return in trepidation to school and after producing some glasses from the staff dining-room, taste the first sip. 'There's only one thing good about this wine,' says Chris. 'Alcohol.' At least there is that.

Oct 3rd

Got up early. In an Octopus's Garden was played at sixth form Mass. School was amused. Abbey was not. I payed the Off-Licence man a shilling.

Saturday Oct 4th

I went to Stella Maris to collect the Stella Maris Chronicle for the school magazine. Looked out of the cloister window as I'd done do long ago when I'd resolved to look upon myself as a prisoner of a system I could not fathom. Then Chris walks round the corner with the news that KP is waiting outside in the car.

So we drove to Broadstairs, where Daniel is in bed. We visit him. But we're then in a hurry to get back for sixth-form meeting. However, someone has padlocked shut the car park we've put the car in. I run to get the key, but after frantically trying it in the lock we find it is the wrong one. KP runs back this time, gets the right one, and the gate swings open. Panting, we get to school just in time for form meeting. Paolo threatens to read out names of those late for morning prayers at next Assembly. Fair enough: it won't happen again.

Then Assembly comes. I am obliged to remove a stray basketball which is wedged in one of the nets. Climbing the wall-bars I just manage to do this, amid cat-calls. The place is in an uproar. Technically I am in charge for the moment. To be treated with perhaps a bit more respect? Anyway, my name, and Chris's and Steve's are read out by Paolo. We are to see Rory. *To see Rory!*

We wait outside the door of the prefects' room and a messenger at length arrives, saying: 'Rory is ready to see you.' Rory will condescend to vail his regard upon his miserable subjects…

In the ensuing heated discussion I lost my temper, insulted Paolo, and Rory walked out. The discussion continued in the garden but when Rory's henchman Dick-the-Dick called me a sneaky little bastard I had to walk away. I tried to eat lunch but couldn't. I took a walk to Pegwell Bay to calm myself down. The walk seemed the longest I'd ever taken. The countryside showed a preview of winter. Sloes quivered in the wind. I returned, hating myself and everyone. I went to watch the rugger match, in a daze. Near the end, someone was on the ground. I realized it was Chris. Unconscious. Matron was fetched. We were sent away. My feelings were beyond my feeling them.

I made some tea. Michael P came in, and Daniel took a party to Margate hospital to see Chris. There was no room in the Moke for me.

I played the piano, badly, then finished some sandwiches left over from the rugger tea, then went for a walk. Fr Cyprian inadvertently called matron 'a monstrosity rearing its ugly head.' Matron was amused, and assured me that Chris was only in hospital for a check-up. I continued my walk and watched the sun set over the bay and the Agenor enter the harbour. The sea was calm.

Supper was Scotch eggs: I had little appetite and debated about my course of action. At the end of the meal I decided. I told Rory I apologized for all the things I'd said due to bad temper, and stood by those that were rational opinions. He was condescendingly understanding. Good. Now let him work out what caused the bad temper. He is the prefect, I am not. That is where the insult, and I believe it to be fairly deliberate, lies. I don't blame Chris for getting shirty with Dick-the-Dick when he said the same thing to him. Now I'm beginning to come round to a more balanced view of the situation and can afford to philosophize a little. But I will never forget today.

(Though of course I did…)

And now I am to spend a night alone. No Chris in the top bunk… So I shall read Gullible's Travels and then go to bed, and tomorrow will bring – tomorrow.

Sunday Oct 5th

Spent a miserable night, with an itchy arse and a twisted shoulder. Somebody read a Bidding Prayer for Chris at Mass. Jeff takes the prefects' side over yesterday. The itch has cleared up but Chris remains in hospital. Steve, Jagger and I went down to the Foy Boat.

Steve gets the drink I owe him – and most of the rest of my money as well. After lunch I do very little. Pick a purple dahlia and put it in a glass, make tea. Steve comes in and notices I am depressed, so he makes me more so. The afternoon is beautiful, and I sit indoors, playing the piano until Benediction. Short and snappy. After supper I play the piano until I'm exhausted, sight-reading impossible chunks of Wagner, and Bach's Fugues. I scrounge a cup of cocoa from Smith and take a bath. Then a Latin unseen. Now bed.

Oct 6th

I got up depressed. Mrs Pring admired my purple dahlia. Everyone is still adamant Chris will not be back from hospital till Wednesday… But KP and I went up to the shop – and when we got back we found Chris returned, none the worse for his stay in Margate.

I sit and stare,
The record plays,
The creatures on the pavement move,
Sadly, unwittingly,
Dying by walking,
Lying by speaking,
Damned by being saved.
I sit and stare,
I feel for them,
But nothing more.
For I am on the outside looking in,
And the glass-pane thwarts the touch,
Lace curtains fence their view,
They don't see me.

NINE

Convent Girls and a Big Journey

Oct 7th

Breakfast was disgusting: we were naughty in Johnnie's English class, and later in the morning I went to the library with Jagger. I borrowed some books on wine and reawakened my interest in growing vines in England.

After a lunchtime rehearsal I had no money to go to the flicks with so I sat and read, and consumed Todger's honey and bread with him, in the room he still shares with Jagger and Smith in Number Three. (I had a very sore throat). Then another rehearsal, curry for supper, and choir practice. The staff had their supper by candle-light – Father Barnabas seen at the top of a step-ladder mending an electrical appliance.

Chris and I went to see Johnnie, but the front doors of The Grange being locked, were obliged to reach him via the garden wall, the fire escape and his window. Which gave him a bit of a surprise. We read magazine articles, and adverts in the paper for teaching posts. *To teach girls PHYSICAL EDUCATION* read one of them. Goodnight, we said, and left.

Oct 8th

Kipper for breakfast. Naughty again in Johnnie's class. I promise to be a good boy in future.

Rehearsals as usual, and I slept all afternoon, dreaming of being pursued by a fox, only it turned into a cow. Later, I awoke.

After supper I played the organ in the chapel – and rehearsed. Joe Davies talked for hours in the evening and I read Pope and discussed with Chris the interesting question of Being Somebody Else. I am determined to write in Heroic Couplets one day.

Oct 9th

I was a good boy this morning – did some work and washed my hair. Then in glorious sunshine, went with Jagger to draw Pugin's Abbey Church, from the vantage-point of the cemetery.

Lunch was mediocre, and during the ensuing rehearsal Chris and I found a picture of a plate with a tiny rasher of bacon on it. I stuck it up on the kitchen hatch in the refectory.

Oct 10th

A misty autumn morning, a summer's day, and a Christmas evening with fog. One went to Mass, the sunlight flowing down the cloister behind one, and I read a Bidding Prayer. One then spent a boring morning till Jagger took me down to the Wimpy, where we analysed his magazine article on Pugin. We returned for lunch, Danish blue on toast, and then came rehearsal. I sat on the stone steps outside the school, dreamily happy…. The summer holds – even though it is October. (How I used to hate October!)

I wrote an essay on James I, attended a History class, and determined to have a cold and do no Games. Did my Latin instead. Chris has a septic foot. More rehearsal and then, at a loose end, I went to Vespers which was sung in Latin, but not all that uplifting.

Supper. Someone had filled the salt-cellars with sugar… Ever had sweet fish-fingers? I was told to take junior prep over in The Grange and since supper ended late because of the sugar debacle we started prep in fits and starts. But once Fr Richard had had his nightly explosion we got through it fairly well, while I wrote an essay about Gulliver's Travels.

Returning through the fog I found Chris with his feet immersed in a pail of water. Bad, very bad. After night prayers I played the piano and the organ and talked to Fr Cyprian about Vespers (the monks' evening psalms and prayers) and the Cistercians. Then – Time for bed, said Zebedee.

(The Cistercians are an order of monks who follow the Rule of St Benedict, just as our monks do. They broke away from the Benedictines in the eleventh century, as they wanted to follow a stricter interpretation of the Rule. St Bernard was their most charismatic abbot back then. These day they tend not to run schools, but to farm in silence or – particularly in Belgium – earn their living by brewing beer that they are rarely allowed to drink. Their strictest congregation are known by a more familiar name: Trappists.)

Sunday Oct 12th

Fr Richard's sermon at Mass. Amusing. Afterwards, Chris, Jagger and I sat Steve in a bucket of water which the last-named threw back at me. We both changed our suits but Steve sulked so we went down to the pub without him. We had two pints and, between us, consumed the whole of the bowl of cheese and biscuits that was laid out on the counter for customers. We enjoyed our profitable morning thus, and returned to a chicken lunch.

After that I wrote a letter to my mother, and went for a walk up Nethercourt Hill to absorb the suburban autumn atmosphere that I now rather like – misty evening beginning at two o'clock.

Then I spent a most enjoyable afternoon sitting on my bed, Bob Dylan playing in the background, feeling very much at home. Out of four room-partnerships this is undoubtedly the most homely. By way of contrast to Jan 13th, I can say that I can now walk into my room and need not leave it; there I am, settled.

Oct 13th

Dreamed I'd died of hanging on the stage. It is a Monday and after failing to sleep in the morning I did no work – save French class, had pork for supper, had music, and rehearsed as usual. Despite my desire for an early bed I talked to Zebedee about arts and sciences till midnight and then scarcely slept, dreaming of an undertaker falling from a theatre gallery, of school, and finally, of Chris serving Mass for the Bishop. Then I awoke and just stayed awake for breakfast, after which both Chris and I went to sleep for the whole morning...

Oct 15th

Learned at English class that Johnnie had been at school with Paul McCartney. We asked him if he'd fancied him. He said he hadn't. Had a walk to the sea with Jagger and Chris.

In the afternoon I accompanied Steve to Winter's and turned out the entire shop looking for a shirt. Then we went to the Wimpy. Steve payed.

Played the piano and had a revolting supper, followed by a general discussion about what drinks to take to the Westgate convent party on Friday. Now I resolve to stay up all night – and work.

Oct 16th

I went to bed at 6.30 a.m., after reading most of the Canterbury Tales. I got up at 7.15 and was quite alive at breakfast, but had to go to sleep after going down to the library – fruitlessly.

Lunch came – then rehearsal, supper, prep, and more rehearsal. Then Barney – Fr Barnabas – wishes to see me. My hair unkempt, tomato sauce on my shirt. Inevitably I'm anxious. What does he want?

I knock on his door. The *Enter* sign flashes up. 'I've boobed,' he says.

He had, too. I was supposed to have taken an academic aptitude test today, but now must do it tomorrow. A three-hour paper of Eleven-Plus drivel, and a mock exam, and rehearsals, and the party in the evening... So here I sit, racking my brains over Pythagoras's Theorem.

Oct 17th

Chris read the Epistle at Mass. Then I did my mock test paper for the Eleven-Plus then I lay on my bed and listened to Beethoven. Lunch was disgusting as usual and afterwards, rehearsal, plus three hours Eleven-Plus with a happy five minute break, during which I was told I'd got a Grade A for my essay on James I. After the tiresome exam I had another play rehearsal. When it came to an end I dressed for the evening, including the tail-coat I'd borrowed, and went in to early supper, escaping as soon as possible from the cat-calls of the sex-starved juniors. Supper was Hungarian goulash, but neither Hungarian, nor goulash – as Chris said, and his parents are posted out in Hungary so he should know. Neither was it even edible. But, 'All bad things come to an end' – Chris Kirkman.

After a singsong we piled into Mr Vaughan's car (he's the new head of music: there has never before been a head of music) and he took us to a pub in Westgate. We chatted to the public in the public bar and then walked to The Red House, home to the sixth-form girls of the Westgate convent, while the traffic lights ahead of us turned to red, to green, and back to red again.

We knocked on the door nervously. Was this the right place? Yes it was. Sargent's sister is cute – she has a look of Blond-hair about her – but in the end I found myself with a girl called Charlotte, (sister of one of our juniors, called Williams) who admired my tail-coat, but on whom I seemed to manage to spill beer every time I sat down. She's also cute – her birthday one day before mine, and I managed to get my hand inside her shirt and feel her right breast. First time I've ever done that.

But then nuns interposed and we had to go. We danced down the street, found the station and found the train. A fight at the station. Todger got knocked down, civilians intervened and we returned happily, talked a little to Zebedee and went to bed, with a vomit-streaked KP sleeping on the floor of our room.

Saturday Oct 18th

Awoke with hangover at 5 a.m., slept till 7 and woke fresh as a daisy. Had breakfast with KP, went for a walk on the mist-curtained prom and as the day wore on felt more and more depressed, unhappy (there were ants in the salad at lunch) sick, and tired. At 2.30 both Chris and I went to sleep. 'Wake me at four if you're awake…'

Next thing, it was dark and Steve was hauling us off our beds to go to supper. Jagger had slept too, and I spent a gloomy meal under the impression that it was breakfast, hating everyone.

Had a sulk with Jagger, who feels as sick, depressed and exactly as I do and now, after a pair of Codein, I'm going to bed.

Sunday Oct 19th

Zebedee nasty about girls at House meeting. Then a monumental sermon from Fr Cosmos. Down to Foy Boat. Jagger, Steve and me. No Chris. Two pints. Very pleased. Good lunch. Read The Knight's Tale, encouraged by the beer, in double-quick time and turned out to watch the House match. The convent girls were on the other side of the pitch. Didn't dare talk to them with Barney, Zebedee and whole school watching. After the match the girls became a Prefects' Perk, so the rest of us all sulked till Benediction, Jagger and I arriving late and sitting in the front row.

Oct 20th

Steve made me sit on a drawing-pin at night prayers. I got up and walked out.

Oct 21st

Didn't do a stroke of work. Spent the morning lying on bed and making a Z, then went down to the Wimpy with Jagger.

Went for a cross-country run, with Fr Cyprian among others. Ended up in second place. Cyprian got back first.

In the evening, after a cast meeting, Chris and I set off in the dark, through the Coppice and across the lawn to Gilbey's. Pitch dark down there and we fumbled with the lock without getting it open. After ten trembling minutes we gave up and returned across the patchwork lawn to sulk in our humble abode. Eventually Zebedee entered the evening, pissed, and diverted us somewhat.

***

Gilbey's is a code word for the monastery's wine cellar. The Z is an elementary pick-lock, made by bending a piece of stiff wire into a right angle at each end. When I was in the lower sixth my room-mate's brother used to have one and the three of us would occasionally make expeditions down to the cellar. It lies under the monastery library, which is an isolated building, separated from the main building of the monastery by a lawn. In addition to stocks of (unconsecrated) Communion wine – a sweet white wine from Australia that didn't interest us – there were racks of the wine that the monastic community drank on occasional feast days during the year. The red was a heady Gigondas from the Rhone valley, the white was a sweet Bordeaux from Ste-Croix-du-Mont, in the Sauternes region. Very occasionally we used to help ourselves to a bottle of one or the other and share it in our room at the top of Number Three. The Zs made by my then room-mate's brother worked perfectly, and so quickly that we barely had time to get frightened. The one that Chris and I made on this occasion, though it looked the part to perfection, did not work at all.

Oct 22nd

Jagger announced that he dreamed he had married me, and I watched Scene 11 being rehearsed. Atrocious.

Oct 23rd

'There cam a privee thief, men clepeth Deeth,
That in this contree al the peple sleeth.'

– As you can see, I've been reading Chaucer. Magnificent lines. I also filled in Form P, wrote the first paragraph of yet another novel… (It's not that I've written any novels yet, just a lot of first paragraphs…) Then rehearsed; slept an hour in morning and a further hour in the afternoon after going down to the Wimpy with Barry M, Steve and Jagger. Steve passed judgement on my relationship with Chris yet again, and it was ages before we were served.

More rehearsal, then nothing to do till supper. A dismal meal. I even become depressed at mealtimes if I can't talk to Chris: or possibly I just get depressed because there's Nobody to talk to – I don't count the two juniors I was next to today.

Still, the supper was quite reasonable and I did a bit of French, then listened to Hylda Baker on the radio in the 'new' building with Fr Malachy. I'm supposed to be studying her accent for my performance as Mother Courage. For the same reason I also get to watch Coronation Street. Then there was a talk on the stairs with Zebedee that began as an interesting conversation but degenerated into the usual tripe. I began to read more Chaucer. The Miller's Tale. I quote: 'He gan pullen up hire smok and in he throng.'

Saturday Oct 25th

Teacher Trev suggested I might do a term in a French school. I was aghast. No, I said. But I liked his next idea. A job with a friend of his in St Emilion. Fantastic. I hope I get it.

Oct 25th – Nov 2nd

Half term. Drove all the way, both going and coming back.

Returned to find Number One patrolled by a cat –
belonging to Zebedee. She's called Florence. There is
mail. Lots of it. After corned beef supper, Jagger, Steve
and I traipse to the Foy Boat. Pint of bitter, and a
Harvey's Bristol Cream.

Back to school. Open my post. A letter from Durham.
They want me to travel up tomorrow for interview the
next day! I showed it to Chris, who was already in
pyjamas. He has accidentally bitten through a cigarette.
Showed letter to Zebedee, had a bath and, with mind in
turmoil, try to think about tomorrow. Perhaps after a
bottle of elderberry wine with Chris, I may be more
prepared...

We drank and enjoyed the elderberry wine and felt
'nice' and sentimental. I told Chris how I wished he
could be coming up north with me, and he said (with
sobs in his voice) how he wasn't academic enough for
Durham and I said (with sobs in my voice) that of course
he was...

Fortunately we were obliged to fall asleep at that
moment.

Monday Nov 3rd

Hecticly did laundry, told everyone about my
forthcoming event, drank buckets of milk at breakfast,
rang home, went to Pain's Travel Agency after a chat
with Barney and at long last found Uncle Ron to get
some money from and phoned Durham against a
background of chatter. Difficult. From the way people
spoke at the other end you could tell what it was like at
Durham, nearly four hundred miles away to the north:
dark and oppressive, with rain torrenting down.

Got my money, said goodbye to Chris – without sobs
– and walked to the station. Passed a couple of the
convent girls on the way.

Conversation in the train to London was about midwifery in hushed whispers. I did not participate. Arrived at Charing Cross with just half an hour to get across London to King's Cross.

I got there. Found the train conveniently situated and situated myself within it. It moved, and I moved into the dining car for lunch. Soup, fish and Danish blue and the train went through Barnet and Potter's Bar, where the first fields appeared, and then we were in flat open country – Huntingdon, eventually Peterborough with its stubby cathedral.

Crows became numerous, pheasants abounded, so did one kingfisher. Darkness came upon us by three o'clock and we entered Yorkshire in rain. How appropriate. Selby Abbey, York Minster, Thirsk... Scraps of old moorland mingled with ploughland, and all coated with the same perpetual Yorkshire rain. Not a hill. Everything was flat.

It got lighter and a sign said, County Durham. Actually, it looked rather like Yorkshire.

Darlington. Stop. Start, and half an hour to go, through coalfields now. Then the train slows down, circles bends, undergoes cuttings and at last emerges onto a ridge with Durham underneath. Dusk was just beginning.

The lights were on in the shops, and I got off the train, finding that the only other interviewee in my carriage was going to another college – still she wasn't all that pretty.

Durham, as I found it, was dark and oppressive with rain drizzling down. I walked round the tortuous streets and eventually up and up and up and up to Cathedral level, where Durham castle found itself, lit by an old carriage lamp. With help I found the porter's lodge and found the porter to be a She. She showed me my room in the castle and showed me the dining hall. She introduced me to a fellow interviewee from Bristol. So here I sit, with a view over the city far below, to the railway viaduct above the house-tops, half a mile away. Here I sit, 'without you,' Chris. Sad, but there it is. Still, Durham's not a bad place. There's only the interview to worry about now. Still, I've got my four-leaved clover with me.

*

Now I've climbed the stone steps that once echoed to the footsteps of the Bishops of Durham, and now echo to mine, to my room under the battlements, where I retire for the night. We had a good supper in the 40 ft high Hall, with panelled walls and mushroom soup, roast beef and long waits between courses, talk about other students who came up from my school, and gooseberry tart. The place has terrific atmosphere. I like it.

After that I set off to look for a pub, but finding one not, watched Panorama, Counter-Strike, and an amusing lecture about explosives in colour, in the TV room at the bottom of my staircase. Zebedee would have despised it but we viewers in the half darkness (I think we must have been mere artists for the most part) enjoyed it.

Now, remembering that breakfast is at 8.15 a.m. I'd better get to bed. Well, there's not much else to do.

Nov 4th

Woken up (thank God) by my neighbour, my fellow interviewee from Bristol. Time was just past 8.15. I dressed in 2 minutes and raced to breakfast – but it is an informal meal and less than half the college had turned up. We had a diminutive pack of Ricicles, some bacon, kidneys and fried bread. Not bad.

After that I went to see the cathedral, which, unbuttressed, stands, a rock of Norman masonry, opposite the door of the college, across Palace Green. It is a magnificent building, gigantic drum-like pillars, rose windows, and Norman slits.

Eventually I left it and, after a wait, made my way up a beautiful oak staircase to the enquiries office. Then to the waiting room. 'The senior tutor will see you now, Mr McKean.' That was the secretary. I'm not used to being Mr McKean.

The senior tutor wore a waistcoat with a collar, and a Scots accent. He said he detected one in my voice too. Anyway, we talked a lot of nonsense and I returned to the waiting room.

'The Master will see you now, Mr McKean,' and he did. A burly Mr S., who asked the same questions as Dr R. had just done, and seemed quite pleased with my answers.

Then I walked round the town, a little city in the country, reasonably unspoilt, with colleges nestling in cobbled streets, old Georgian houses adapted. I found the times of trains to the Kent coast at the station, bought a little bottle to keep out the cold (although the sun shone it was bitterly cold) and wrote a post-card to Mother.

So now I sit up in my eyrie and await lunch, looking out at the trains on the ridge, and beyond them, the country, fields of brown, woods still green, even as far North as this.

Lunch in fifteen minutes. Back at school in ten hours. It seems impossible; I must have been in Durham all my life. Will I ever come here again?...

Lunch was chicken soup, egg, chips, beans, tomato, and rhubarb tart. I sat with a certain James, John and Jeff and after lunch had coffee with them in James and John's room in another Georgian-fronted house that hid old cruck-beams behind modern furniture. After that and a tidy-up I traipsed to the History Department and was welcomed by the secretary. I waited in her office.

'Durham is a friendly city,' she said. We talked. Professor O was going overtime overhead. At last I was called.

Professor O is a rotund little man with spectacles, pipe, and with huge red beetlecrushers on his feet. After rotating around the room a little he came to rest at his own desk and talked in an inaudible voice for the next half hour – nothing about History.

When he was through I dashed helter-skelter to the station and just caught the train to Darlington. The first spits of rain fell...

In Darlington station I admired Stephenson's Locomotion for twenty minutes before the arrival of the fast train from Edinburgh. On board I read Scottish newspapers and it began to get dark. Rain settled on the windows. I bought some sandwiches, Guinness, lager, and ate my mother's shortbread. A sad lady got in at Grantham.

We passed Hitchin, Welwyn Garden City and Finsbury Park and as we drew into King's Cross the sad lady, glowing suddenly with an Evangelical light, pressed a pamphlet into my hands, 'On Becoming a Christian, about our Lord and Saviour Jesus Christ.'

I dashed along the platform and tubed successfully to Charing Cross in time for the 9.00 p.m. I shared the compartment with an elderly professorial fellow who got out at Ashford.

The train divides. Ashford becomes Canterbury. Canterbury becomes Thanet. I hastened down the road from the station. 'Three Children Found Murdered,' the news headlines leap up at me from the billboards, to cheer me on my icy way back to school. I get in. Chris is still awake. I tell Zebedee I'm back, and return to my palace. I offer Chris some whisky and have some myself. We get into our (respective) beds and then Chris professes his conversion to homosexuality. But on the mental plane only, he says.

So near and yet so far. Will it always be like this?
And so we went to sleep.

Oct 10th 2014

Hmmm.

TEN

Where Do We Go From Here?

Nov 5th 1969

Hardly a firework! The school seems quite homely. Not bad to be back. I walk to the Hoverport and have passport photos taken, I get thrown out of Johnnie's class, read Punch and talk to Jagger, then eat lunch and go to House meeting, then sleep till four o'clock.

Supper could have been worse. No going to the pub, though. Malachy wants rehearsal. Scene eight. He describes it as a love scene. Between Mother Courage and the Cook. Alias me and Chris. It's a little embarrassing…

Nov 6th

Frankie G comes up from his basement room to work in ours. Steve farts a lot – it's understandable, it's the onions – rehearsals go badly but it's not that bad a day. Not really.

Nov 7th

I read a Bidding Prayer at Mass in the manner of a toast-master. 'Lord bless the Bishop.' The congregation all turned and looked at me. Johnnie was quite upset about it and said so afterwards.

Steve reads my diary these days and, although he often can not decipher the handwriting, is amused, but liable to quote it at embarrassing moments.

Supper not bad. Plaice.

More work after. Jagger is being interviewed in Oxford.

More rehearsal, and bed.

Saturday Nov 8th

I spent a horrible night, hardly sleeping, but feeling sick, and only got up for the post. But there was nothing from Durham.

Spent the morning on my bed, feeling ill, and the afternoon sitting reading Pride and Prejudice feeling ill

Supper, squashed eggs, nearly turned my hair grey. An enforced silence became a riot, and it was a relief when it was over. I did a Latin unseen and then there was a rehearsal of Scenes 1 to 4 which – except for Scene 1, up to which we had not quite warmed – did not go badly.

Now I feel sufficiently nostalgic to write an increasingly rare Opinion Section. I don't want to go to Oxford. Durham would suit me better: teach me a lesson. I like the idea of the journey through Hertfordshire – St Neots and Hitchin, which sound so ugly, bleak and inconvenient … and Yorkshire, appealing to my particular brand of masochistic sentimentality…

As far as Chris is concerned the beginning of the end began years ago. We are now in the middle. The end is not far. Nothing can last for ever. The world is a *tricheuse,* sad to say.

I remember the first day of this term, the shy exchanges of remarks on the stairs, the warmth imparted by the Bull's Blood drunk from one shared cup, sitting on the same bed, the subsequent reserve, the descent to triviality.

Half-term, more wine, the expedition to the North, Chris being the one reason for wanting to get back here that night... And last term, the photographs, the ivory tower we were to build, the tower that collapses on completion. The long unsuspecting years before, the surprise eventually, and now, perhaps the most intensely emotional relationship ever.

Anyway, all must be swept away, so how could I go to Oxford? It must be the black hole of Durham, or else Russia, or become a Trappist monk.

I wrote a (non-heroic) couplet today -)
The world's not divided by rich and poor
But by those who've enough and those who want more.

But as the thought can't be all that original, I guess someone else has written it before me.

Now one record player blares next door, while overhead another is playing Sgt Pepper. A school evening in winter. Chris is asleep.

Sunday Nov 9th

Up quite early. Miserable breakfast. The table mutinied and stole my bread. Zebedee takes a sudden dislike to me. Mass is a bore. Down to the Foy Boat with Jagger, Steve, Chris, and now also Frankie G and Simon H. They share the basement room, just below ours. It was a nice relaxed drink all together. Dealt better with the table at lunch.

Read Pride and Prejudice in the afternoon. I like Sunday afternoon this term. My room-mate is usually with me. Over to Benediction in the pouring rain. At supper I bring the table to heel finally. After that, more Pride and Prejudice, a P.O.W. film and a bath.

Dick-the-Dick demands I have a haircut. A suitable excuse for Chris and I to consume a bottle of hawthorn berry rosé. Delicious. Now we are happier.

Nov 10th

Last night Chris and I talked about previous room-mates and our quarrels with them. Woke up depressed, spent the morning with Jagger, down town and in his room. I have my hair removed and wear a hat till the afternoon.

Saw Smith and got my old book about Oxford back from him. Though I still prefer Durham. Supper abominable.

My hair, or lack of it, is atrocious. Last time I have that cut for a long, long time.

Nov 11th

An abysymally depressing day. No work done, no good books except The Psychology of Sex, which we are all reading at the moment. A cheering chat with Steve and Jagger, a choir practice, a good supper. But no work done, and not even happy because of that.

Fuck my haircut, fuck Zebedee, fuck the school. Still, Scene 9 went well...

Nov 12th

A better day. Mother Courage's wagon has been built, though it looks awful.

Wrote two letters in fifteen minutes, then spent an hour finding a stamp...

Workmen try to push a two-ton second-hand safe up the front stairs of the main school.

Nov 13th

Rejection slip from Bristle University. Never mind. Didn't want to go there anyway.

Simon H tells me his family history. His father running the family like a business, his mother running her life like a brothel, Simon running as far as he can… Makes my mother seem quite normal.

Chris expounds on the concept of Fuck All, and Homo-sympathy.

Punch is good this week. Supper likewise. Chips, REAL tomatoes, bacon, sausages, beans. Then I read Hamlet and Chris reads letters to The Times.

Saturday Nov 15th

Another dull day.

Worked, read Scottish History, grabbed Kay Jay (who's Zebedee's pet, and in the fourth form) by the throat, but couldn't go through with punching his face. I banged his head against a wall instead and left him, went down town, read about sherry production in the bookshops, had salad supper, and it winded and stormed and hailed…

We rehearsed the second half of the play. Scene 11 a catastrophe, but Scene 9 was highly praised.

Sunday Nov 16th

Nothing was said by Zebedee about the Kay Jay incident. Nothing said by me either.

Cosmic sermon. 15 minutes.

Then Jagger and I went over the Soldier Lad song, and went down to the Foy Boat, finding Chris there with Simon H and Frankie G. I had two pints. Then, to steady my nerves for the afternoon music rehearsal, I had a sherry. Tio Pepe, of course.

Then we returned to school, had pork for lunch. Then our three-hour marathon. My performance was nothing if not mediocre. I sang the songs flat, although I was accompanied my Mr Vaughan on the piano, but there is already a unity of action that the last play lacked at this stage – or perhaps that's just my view.

Anyway I nearly died of heatstroke in my costume, including overcoat, in Scene 9, but it was very moving as usual. Our rival House – that's Jagger's, Todger's, Smith's and Fr Cyprian's House – had a House outing, while the rest of us had Welsh Rarebit for supper. I did half a Latin prose, then went to the pictures with Chris, the two of us sheltering under his black umbrella. Film was The Virgin Soldiers. Good film.

Nov 18th

Walked down town with Steve during Games. We looked at the displays in Court's furniture shop, disgusted that a table was laid with Champagne bottles but Hock glasses. We turned out Winter's clothes store again. Went to Geering's Books, where there was a new girl at the till. Steve explained the meaning of the word heterosexuality to her. Then we marched on the Albion Bookshop, Pain's travel agency, the Wimpy Bar, Austin Russell…

Steve was in a helluva good mood. He has an interview at U.C.L…

Nov 20th

Battered potatoes for breakfast. Read Pope and other things. Read about grape-growing in the Public Library. Dull rehearsal. Good supper. Chicken fricassée with sherry in it.

No word from Durham. I do want to go there.

Nothing else to say, really. Sorry, Posterity.

Nov 21st

Incredible that two people as unable to get on with anyone else as Chris and myself should have spent eleven weeks in one room without one strain or difference; that a familiarity I dreaded, and that he probably did as well, should be so illogically successful. Despite all prophecies (other people's) and (my own) fears. It's a thing that's never happened to me before, like having yr cake and eating it.

Sunday Nov 23rd

Fr Richard's delightful sermon. Me nervous about tomorrow's exam. Pub with Chris, Jagger, Frankie and Simon. Smith and Phil were there too. I had a pint and a Tio Pepe. We talked about Alex. I became more depressed, thinking of William of Orange, but I cheered up when I was nearly run over by a car but escaped unscathed. Lunch was not too bad.

Supper was abominable. My hands shook. Chris had no money. I saw Steve. He in good mood. We watched an amusing TV programme, then down to the Foy Boat, then we got bored. Walked around town and saw a pub bearing this illuminated sign above the door. *Tart n Bitter.*

Then walked back. Both in a good mood. Where would I be without Steve on one side, and Chris on the other?

Had a bath, ate some chicken sandwiches and am going to bed with a Codein.

Nov 24th

Went to bed, records playing overhead, and at last fell asleep to dream of missing trains, of interviews, of spaghetti, and awoke to find the fuse blown And the room pitch dark and icy. Chris and I got up, dressed with difficulty in the darkness and went to breakfast. I left the meal early: I had to see Fr Barnabas, make my bed in the dark, do my laundry, get some foolscap paper. Captain Gladwish, my invigilator, arrived. It was still almost dark when I started my Oxbridge entrance exam at nine o'clock.

There was beautiful poetry to analyse, the sun began to shine, I turned out the gas fire and my fingers lost their pallor. Johnnie dropped in for a chat at mid-morning and in the fullness of time it was mid-day and I left the room. Told the world about the exam. Only Chris was interested. Steve is having his interview in London.

I was bored, and glad to get my teeth into the second paper. Not too bad. I shared the room with Mrs O the secretary who kindly abstained from typing, and wrote my essays.

I felt parched. Mrs O appeared like a ministering angel with a cup and a jam tart. Never was tepid tea more welcome. Johnnie thought it was a good paper.

When it was finished I read Scene 3, felt bored, and was delighted to meet Chris in the main school. We talked to Uncle Ron till supper, draped over the chairs in his office, an enjoyable interlude. We talked about the play, and disputed the meaning of *academic*.

Supper was quite good, but conversation nil. Music. My last piano lesson with Miss Baker. She is leaving. Then I went over to The Grange to return the books Johnnie had lent me and we discussed the papers. Quite a nice chat about university.

By the time I got back to our room – now re-christened the refrigerator – the lights had gone again, so in candle-light and frosty breath we decided … Chris's exact words: 'What we need is whisky.' Said with a mischievous smile. We couldn't find anyone who could afford to accompany us so after night prayers we went down to the pub alone. We had one whisky and left. Returning, we found Barney and an electrician buried in the fuse cupboard in Number One so went down to the basement and had a long talk with Frankie and Simon about witchcraft. Now, time for bed.

Nov 25th

Up, sprightly. More exams. Abominable Latin, easy French, dull lunch. Steve and Chris have a quarrel. Over which of them is the more inferior...

Afternoon paper. Off-guard. Longer than I'd expected. Semi-balls-up. Mrs O brought me tea and promised to come and see me play Mother Courage. Outside, snow fell. Time up. Straight over to choir practice in the Abbey. In the choir stalls. Elegant setting. Talked to Uncle Ron until supper, after which I finished my book on Scottish History. After night prayers I talked in the kitchen of Number Three for ages with Fr Cyprian and others, then changed for bed and had coffee and chicken sandwiches with Chris. Now I don't feel like sleep, and have nothing to do... I know. I shall learn Scene 3.

Nov 26th

Spent the morning doing lettering for Mr Gough. Gothic script for the notice on the side of Mother Courage's wagon. Found a model for most of the letters in the masthead of the Daily Telegraph. Slept in the afternoon. Groggy at long rehearsal. Better after supper. Now unable to work because of room temperature. Bed the only solution.

Nov 27th

Steve got a 2E offer from UCL...

I got another book on Oxford from the library. Found Johnnie being teased by the juniors and felt really sorry for him. And awful. How much of that is my own fault?

At 8.30 I went on stage to find the orchestra already there, with Smith all smarmy and official, and my mood darkened. Reluctant, nervous and angry – angry because I had been looking forward to an enjoyable evening – I sang the first two songs badly but scored a hit with 'The Great Capitulation' and 'If war don't suit your disposition'. The Cook's song was fine and 'Lullay' went well. The piano has been doctored, the hammers have been impregnated with drawing-pins.

Then Chris and I talked as usual to Fr Malachy.

I brightened up a little then, but it became bedtime and, Chris having tried on my waistcoats, I prepare for sleep.

Nov 28th

At breakfast some bastard unscrewed the cap of the salt-cellar which promptly emptied itself over my egg and bacon.

Watched the snow fall. Flake after flake it came at first. Then with clockwork regularity. God's dandruff.

In spite of the wet ground it found places to settle and after an amusing History class the ground took the momentous decision. At five o'clock it froze. The snow had stopped.

Supper was quite good. Fish fingers and chips. Inexplicably the kitchen was festooned with balloons and Xmas decorations.

On TV The First Churchills. William III dies. Chris and I watched it in the dark, with the electric fire on. We stepped back into last summer.

Then we rehearsed Scene 9. It went well.

Saturday Nov 29th

Flakes fell onto the skid-pan of Kent and by mid-morning a blizzard was under way. I washed my hair and spoke to Fr Malachy about props. I went down town to 'prop-shop', searching for an 'unusual' purse. ('Nothing unusual in THIS shop, sir. All our stock is perfectly usual, thank you.') But I found some pipes and cross-gartering.

Lunch being abominable Smith and I trudged to the Foy Boat for a couple of pints and a sandwich which we enjoyed, and then trudged back again. We made some toast but burnt it, though still ate it, and all in time for a play run-through.

It snowed violently, the wet ground was quickly covered. Helping to push a car through it I was joined by Jagger and Chris and we then ran, or slid, down to the prom and had a snowball fight against the juniors.

Supper was a leek, shrouded in ham and with a cheese sauce. It would have been delicious had not the leeks been full of gritty mud. But it was still nice.

Then the prefects disappeared for the annual prefects' dinner and – temporarily head-boy, and in between the duties required by that high office – I trudged with Jagger, nay, we trotted, down to the Foy Boat for a Harvey's Bristol Cream and a Scotch. We trudged back and I took night prayers. Then a pep-talk from Fr Malachy and a rehearsal of Scene 1.

Young Williams has been telling me I ought to write a letter to his older sister Charlotte, so I do this on an impulse this evening. Then undressed and washed – and was summoned by Steve to go across to the main school to watch The First Churchills, so I went across in my dressing-gown, while my shoes and rugger socks dried themselves over the fire.

Sunday Nov 30th

Woke up early. Woke up Chris. He didn't like being woken up. Neither did I.

The salt fell on my egg again. I was annoyed.

Another cosmic sermon from Fr Cosmos. Awful.

Watched the Old Boys' Rugby match, then practised smoking my pipe. Had supper, then a chat in Steve's room. By 8 o'clock I was in the Foy Boat, where a lot of us already were. Chris turned up. He and I parted from the others. We walked to the Wimpy, but Jagger and Steve weren't there, so we walked back to school deep in friendship, the frost appearing beneath our feet like stars as walked.

We talked for ages in bed(s) about how we were the only decent blokes in Number One. I told him the term would have been murder but for sharing a room with him. And that was the truth.

Of course I ought to have written this up at length, including all the amusing – and nostalgic – incidents of the day. But one point stands out. Though that will not be written here, if it be allowed even to cross my mind.

But it has crossed my mind of course. That Chris and I seem to have fallen in love again. But where can it conceivably go from here?

ELEVEN

Oxford, and Another Kiss – Sort of…

Dec 1st

Chris slept all morning. I practised smoking a pipe. In the afternoon I read about Oxford and then it was the House outing. Wine cup and good sandwiches at Zebedee's mother's house. Kay Jay very much the little son of the house. Then to Folkestone for the Virgin Soldiers. Depressed on the way back. Sang songs on the coach. Not too bad a day but a little flavourless.

Dec 2nd

Protracted goodbye to Chris as he leaves for his interview at U.C.L. I try to sleep. No luck. Walk to Stella Maris with KP. Then we drink coffee and disinfect the carpet where someone has trodden dog shit into it. Coffee good.

After lunch journeyed to Boot's and bought bags full of make-up on Mrs Gladwish's instructions, then we went to the antique shop and bought a brass jug from Mr Charrington.

Choir practice. Curry for supper. Worked on stage, rehearsals. Rigging up a line of metal tea-pots on a string inside the wagon to jangle when it moves off or stops. All great fun. Talking to Fr Malachy afterwards.

Fr Cyprian drops in later, as I'm making coffee, with the exam papers for tomorrow. This time I'm not taking the exam, but invigilating someone else's. Fr Cyprian takes Jagger and me across to the monastery for Horlicks and bread and Marmite in the kitchen. We remember the fifth form days of making ginger beer here...

Then I stay up, reading, learning Mother Courage. Now I'm going to stay up and do caricatures for the magazine. It is lonely...

Dec 3rd

Late breakfast. Invigilated juniors' exam. Example of Mrs Gladwish's tact. 'Have you got scrawny arms?' All day on stage. My wig has come. I look like William of Orange in it. A run through in the busy Assembly hall. Sorting out ticket sales. Talking to the kitchen staff. There is a new arrival today: a coffee vending machine. I get a cup of chocolate... And at last Chris is back.

Dec 4th

A glass of Graves and two pints of beer. Must have been quite strong beer because I found myself stroking Chris's hair and face, and babbling about Blond-hair. Then at last fell happily asleep.

Dec 7th

Sunday. I packed my trunk, had lunch and got changed. We went over to the Abbey church for the carol service and after a long intense wait in the cloister there, marched into the choir. Not bad on the whole. The readings sounded good and I quite enjoyed the carols. We marched out...

...Little expecting to find beer and cider awaiting us in the music room. We dutifully consumed this with pleasure and were entertained by some of the more adult members of the choir on various musical instruments. Charlotte came in and I spoke to her briefly.

Then I had supper in a thoroughly good humour, and the dress rehearsal began. Make-up by Mrs Gladwish. The first half was a fiasco for me; one big mental block, wrong lines, no lines, bad singing. In the middle of the 'Great Capitulation' I gave way to bad temper, yelling out, 'Damn,' and asking for a prompt. Things were not made better by everyone's insisting I was ill... They never are. I was told to sit still and suffer the indignity of drinking a cup of tea, but fortunately I was able to drink it in an upright position with the orchestra.

The second act ran better, but Chris became depressed about Scene 9, and then everyone insisted that he was ill...

Some bastard bit the end off my pipe and didn't tell me.

Now I'm tired, but there's a lie-in for Me & Chris tomorrow, and we hope for lunch in the monastery. Then there will be the Number One house outing – generously paid for by Zebedee each year – and after that I sincerely hope this book will be filled in for a night or two in Oxford.

The great worry is Money. Barney is tightening up on outgo. There doesn't appear to be enough income. How can I have enough for the end of term???

Anyway, now to bed. Tomorrow may see Chris'n'Me in a better temper.

Sabres and swords are hard to swallow,
First you must give 'em beer to drink.
Then they can face what is to follow,
But let them swim before they sink. (Mother Courage.)

Dec 8th

In costume early for press photos after lie-in. Lunch came, then I went to Pain's for ticket to Oxford. Then back to the school and down to the cinema. 'Here we go round the Mulberry Bush', and 'The Graduate'. Then we all went to Henneky's, where there were some suspicions of under-18-itis, but Zebedee assured them we were all older than we looked. Then to Marchesi's in Broadstairs in taxis after two schooners of fino sherry. I paid the taxi driver and we entered, found a table – Chris and I sitting next to each other of course – and after a plate of whitebait I had a rump steak, and shared a bottle of Ch. Grand-Puy Lacoste with Chris. People sang and I winked across the tables at Simon H. There was stilton, camembert and biscuits. Bristol Cream, Drambuie and brandy – the last in a hurry, causing temporary hiccups, for the taxi was coming. Then pretending to be more sober than I was, talking to the taxi driver till we reached the school.

Just the right dose, said Zebedee. I had sat with him in the bar, talking about tomorrow. Now, after a cop scare, we prepare for bed...

Dec 9th

I seem to have missed quite a lot out when I wrote last night. The taxi driver wishing me good luck for Oxford, the unexpected kindness shown me by Zebedee, my burning my fingers in a candle, then singing songs from Mother Courage while dancing with Boing in Grange Road, letting off a fire extinguisher, water pouring through the ceiling, talking in bed to Chris, about the Viking Ship, about interviews.

Then throughout the night we seemed to sleep and wake simultaneously. 'Time?'

'I'm dead nervous about Oxford.'

'That's tomorrow.'

'True.'

But now I must get ready and get going. More later.

*

I set off up Grange Road, after screwing £5 out of Barney, and read Mother Courage before Ashford. It was misty. Charing Cross arrived at last. I walked to French's bookshop and looked at the pictures of Helene Weigel, Brecht's wife, playing Mother Courage. She looks more cynical than me. But most of all, she is what I am not: a woman and a mother.

I had a cheap lunch in a café, walked briskly through Westminster and St James's Park and tubed to Paddington.

In the train I sat with a group of people who made a living travelling up and down the country collecting old cars. Conversation had turned to homemade wine by the time I caught sight of the steely spires through the mist.

Feeling anything but nonchalant I walked around the town for an hour. Feelings mixed. There were beautiful old colleges, but seeming hard and unfriendly. There were traffic lights, traffic noise, shoppers. Oxford is foggy. Oxford is too good for me. There are no hills in Oxford. The colleges would look better in the country.

With beating heart I entered the classical arch of Worcester College. Was I perhaps not required for interview? I had heard nothing, after all. What a feeling of relief when I saw my name on a list. I asked the porter – he gave me an envelope: notices to read. I was shown the Nuffield Building, where I am now: modern but in an ancient style. Stone. And I have a panelled sitting room, with desk, dining and coffee table, armchairs, sofa, electric fire, ground-length velvet curtains... Though the bedroom is a bit dingy.

I strolled around. The college is a delightful mixture of the medieval Benedictine cottages of Gloucester Hall, and the 18th century classical.

I saw the lake, and the ducks. Mist was rising off the surface of the blue water, and through the window of the

Provost's Lodging a rich chandelier glittered. Oxford is too good for me. I am uncomfortable here.

Perturbed to see a request to stay till after lunch on Thursday. First performance of Mother Courage is in the evening. I shall have to sort this out. Also, how do I find out if Hertford or Corpus Christi want to interview me or not? Find out tomorrow.

Oxford is secretive.

I hung around for dinner, talked to a Liverpudlian – the only genuine bloke on my table, cauliflower, grapefruit, roast lamb, potato, apricot and rice, mint sauce, cheese and biscuits. The Hall is very modest and classical. Absolute contrast to Durham.

I walked about the town, had a pint in a pub, had a Wimpy, returned to my glorious abode, wrote a long letter home…

I wish Chris were here to cheer me up. I wish Steve were here. But especially Chris. Just how much does the bugger mean to me? Now at quarter to ten, I'm going to bed.

Dec 10th

Awoken at 7.55. Good. Breakfast kipper. Not bad. Posted letter home and wrote to Chris. Explored Oxford. Not much more impressed. Lunch was abominable. Interview – a cosy chat in one of the medieval cottages. 'You don't write enough,' they said. I didn't say enough either. Negative.

Bought port and Madeira. Saw ducks. Worcester begins to appeal. Met a fellow interviewee called Richard. We both saw the ducks, then went for tea, as invited, at 4.30. Where we heard about life at Oxford. Then we hung around till supper, which was also abominable, and went to the Lamb and Flag together (quite nice) for a couple of pints. Now here I am in my sitting-room. My feelings for Oxford are quite negative. If I get an offer I'll take it. If not; well, I'll prefer Durham anyway.

Dec 11th

Up early and bright. Caught up with Richard walking about near the lake after bacon and tomato breakfast. Time passed till nine o'clock.

Had my interview in the History department, with Mr Sandwell, who was quite nice. We talked about Kingsley Amis and D. H. Lawrence and Chaucer. Only a little bit about History. Then the play problem had to be raised...

...I caught the 10.20. I may have to go back on Sunday. I didn't look back at Oxford from the jam-packed train. Soon in London. Crush at the barrier. Mad dash to Charing Cross, but actually caught the train easily. But the buffet car was closed for lunch. Had to wait for a meat pie and a Guinness at the station when I got off.

Everybody seemed relieved to see me back. They had done the dress rehearsal without me of course. I talked to Chris, waded through chaos on the stage, talking with Fr Malachy, had a hurried supper, got changed, made up...

Nervous, very. Shaking hands with cast behind the curtain... Up it goes.

I missed out great chunks of dialogue. Scene shifting was bloody. I had to hold the death-mask expression for ages before the curtain closed.

Over at last. I hardly believed there'd been a play. I felt slightly drunk. I'm told it was a success.

Talking, here, there and everywhere to people, then finally Chris and I sat on his bed and drank Madeira and port, talking loudly and happily till 1 o'clock. Zebedee came in. 'For Gawd's sake shut up.'

We repaired to our own beds and carried on talking. We slept badly…

Dec 12th

…And were up for the morning performance. Not too bad for a hangover. Audience terrifyingly unresponsive. Mad chaos as usual…

Bad lunch. Chris and I go up the road to the Scotch pub. Beer and AT LONG LAST I tasted malt whisky. I wonder why they ever bother to blend it. It is just what I imagined. Creamy, and heavily smoked. Chris and I began to compliment each other on our good looks. With a start I realized we were enacting a dream I'd had in Oxford. Chris and me sitting on bar stools, legs open, and telling each other how good looking we were. We were quite happy, chatted to the barmaid, mistook the Ladies for the Gents and were amused. (So were the other people in the place.)

We bought a bottle of cheap sherry, and Chris went to bed.

I packed, bustled around, and all too soon I had to dress, make up, have supper, drink a large dose of sherry and go on stage. Lots of blunders but a good show. I was shagged out.

Chris and I got pissed on the wine left over. I found myself lying on the bed beside him, my arm round his shoulder, telling him he was the best friend I'd ever had. That was true.

We became less and less sober, talked about everything under the sun in hushed whispers. The booze ran out… We said Goodnight. I kissed him on the back of his neck, and went back to bed.

I soon got up again, to be violently sick out of the window. It was raining. Then Chris got up to be sick in the bog. An enjoyable evening; life's like that.

Dec 13th

Woke up in awful hangover. A bit ashamed of last night. But on second thoughts; no, I enjoyed it. Late breakfast of fruit juice. Fruitless search down town for a pipe. Bought a sausage instead. Back to school. Queasy. Chris had returned to bed.

Up for a malt whisky and a half pint with Smith. I feel worse than ever. Lunch was poor. I ate a little, bought a bacon and egg pie. I ate it with some brandy liqueur chocolate. I had to change in Big Ed's room. He plays the Chaplain. Chris was entertaining his grandparents in our room. Make up... Done.

The play opened. After an uncertain start it became, incredibly, our best performance. Incredibly, because my mind was a whirl of thoughts about leaving school, of waiting for a phone-call from Oxford, talking to Charlotte in the interval, wondering where a certain bleeping noise was coming from (it turned out to be from Surgeon-Commander St-John-Thewliss's hearing aid) and thinking about Chris. When I came to pluck the capon on stage, blood dripped from its beak. At Scene 8 I looked at Chris. And for a horrible few minutes thought that my kissing him last night had finished everything. Remembering last night I wanted to vomit all over again. But in Scene 9 I changed my mind. At the end of the scene we patted each other on the back.

Bustle, changing, drinking soup, tea, eating, talking to Charlotte, to Mother and my two aunts, to Father Malachy... Saying Goodbye to Chris. We shook hands warmly. See each other soon. I packed his laundry for him. We left.

...One extraordinary thing. Zebedee told me, in a 'just by the way' sort of way, that the cute new boy Mark

Javen is Barney's nephew. Who would have believed it?! To be called The Boy From Uncle now, I suppose...

Very tired, driving back home. Heavy cold. Supper. Bed.

I lay awake, while faces from school came looming towards me as I drifted into sleep. They swelled like balloons, bobbing on strings. I burst them with the pins of compasses.

I dreamed of Oxford, of Charlotte, of quarrelling with Chris – From that dream I awoke with relief. Great relief. After that I slept soundly.

Oct 11th 2014

Sometimes the whole of Ralph's diary reads like a dream. It is a fading tapestry, after so many years. Or a series of locked boxes, the keys to some of which are lost to memory.

TWELVE

Who Will Stroke Mine?

Dec 14th 1969

Watched a Noël Coward play on TV in the evening. Very amusing.

I thought about the crossroads I had reached. To become a man or stay a boy. Perhaps I ought to become a bit schizophrenic. Stay a boy in personal relationships – can't stop thinking about Chris, you see – and be a man in all else.

Dec 16th

Dear Reader, you may be beginning to wonder if there is perhaps something odd about my relationship with Christopher D. Kirkman Esq. But I think I can explain this by saying that this diary is an unusually frank and honest one, and that, whatever might seem to be implied in these pages, there is nothing more going on than is written in them. Chris himself might be a little embarrassed, though perhaps also a little pleased, to read this diary, but no more so than would anyone who peered into the depths of another's mind.... End of explanation.

To grow up or not to grow up: that is the question. Maybe I should be an actor. Maybe we both should?

Dentist in the morning. I walked around St Leonards, saw teal hanging in the shop window and watched the Primary School children playing. One minute they were arm in arm, the next, arm against arm. And aren't adults merely grown-up children? But there is some beauty in that brief intensity of firework emotion. May I never lose it.

And in the evening, watching Lawrence Olivier on TV, making a speech to Noël Coward on his 70th birthday, and ending with the words, 'Noël, I give you my love,' I realized that these people, actors, had retained the simplicity of childhood. Actors.

Dec 18th

At long last I got round to dismantling my old train set! That took most of the morning.

Now I wait for the post with trepidation – ever heard of anyone who hoped against hope that he wouldn't get into Oxford? At least I haven't got a scholarship: those were announced in the paper today, and my name wasn't there. But I may still be offered a place…

Dec 19th

We saw a redwing on the lawn. In Rye, in the afternoon, curlew were on sale in the poulterer's. Watched the last bit of The First Churchills on TV. Mother retires to bed wth a cold and I stayed up alone, playing through old music I used to play on the piano when I was a little boy. The past is better than the future. Much better. I am like a man on a ship: everyone tells me to look ahead at the open sea but I dare not turn round for fear of losing sight of the handkerchieves waving on the quay. How long can they stay in sight? Can't they come on the same boat with me? I always promise myself that when they are out of sight I will look straight ahead. But always there comes a new port, with new handkerchieves. Fate has decreed that I shall walk backwards through life. *Ergo,* I walk backwards.

Saturday Dec 20th

Chopped up the old garage doors for firewood in the morning. In the afternoon a letter comes from Oxford. I'm not in. Mother very disappointed; I was delighted. A bit of a blow to my pride, perhaps, but I look upon it as a lucky escape.

Sunday Dec 21st

When we got back from church a letter was waiting. Durham postmark. They are waiting before making a decision till Oxbridge are more definite. I wrote letters, to Fr Malachy, Zebedee, Durham, Smith, and Chris. It's my halfth birthday.

Dec 24th

After lunch, the second post. There is a letter addressed to me, postmarked Tonbridge, where Chris is staying with his grandmother. Quick work Chris. I've never had a letter from him before. It is reassuringly different from letters written by anybody else. He is with me over Oxford, of course, but his own university position is dodgy. Rejected by Sussex. Oh dear. He is thinking of becoming an actor. He's not the only one. Poor, dear old Chris.

Last night I dreamed I got a letter from Tonbridge, and today I got one. Now I can not get Chris off my mind. A stupid, sad situation, because sooner or later it must stop. At the moment we're only prolonging the agony...

Dec 26th

A phone-call from Jagger. He's dropping in around the 4th or 5th.

Dec 27th

A letter came from Fr Malachy, all humility, enclosing a gushing review from the East Kent Times. The lady says she hopes I'll make a career in the theatre, just as Rich is aiming to do. There's a good photo of me, though Chris looks decidedly odd in it, and so does Big Ed, who's also in it. We are 'the high spot of the amateur year in Thanet'.

Dec 28th

In bed I didn't sleep for hours. My thoughts ran in a kind of soliloquy that went something like this…

Sometimes I see myself as John Gielgud, Bernard Shaw and Peter Sellars all rolled into one, and sometimes I imagine myself as John Kennedy and William III rolled into one. But then appears a picture of James I, who knew how well he could manage affairs of life and state in theory, but never quite managed it in practice. Then there is the warning presented by Zebedee. A perpetual bachelor school teacher: a big fish in a very small pond. But even worse is the picture of me coming home at night, opening the door, 'Evening darling had a good day what's for dinner kids home from school yet?'

Brings me to the question: what is my future? Where does my happiness lie? Perhaps in the theatre… But to act and find it all an empty shell – what disillusionment. Perhaps happiness lies in mediocrity. I hope not. Perhaps it's falling in love with a woman, saying, 'Clear off,' to all my friends because, 'I've got what I want.' ...Only to find then that she too was nothing? Perhaps happiness is embracing God – becoming a monk – but then I would know when my finger-tips met that I had embraced nothing. Perhaps happiness is sitting on a bed, getting drunk with Chris. But this is sad happiness, bitter happiness.

Digression: My one moment of pure happiness – sitting on a bench at Stella Maris. On a morning in May. Time stopped. Just that one time in my life. And eternity was. That was happiness. Then the bell went and time started again. Since then all happiness has been mixed with bitterness. I am happy when I'm with Chris. But sad too because it's not a very realistic friendship – is it? I am haunted by the idea of the play Staircase – about the two old queer hairdressers who live together.

It's all very well now to sit here like this. We are young and both fairly popular and with reasonable looks (me) and splendid ones (Chris). But suppose forty years to pass and see us still sitting here, too fat for our school suits, the world laughing like the waves on the shore...

Easy to live for the present, for idleness, for luxury, for pleasure, like Oscar Wilde did – and what happened to him... Then suppose that I become an embarrassment to Chris, or he to me – or worse: that our friendship becomes "adult" – that we see each other four times a year, admire each other's children, fancy each other's wives, remember old times, having forgotten everything. End of Digression.

Oh, to commit myself to something. To say, 'God is all that matters,' and die for a shadow. To say, 'Chris is all that matters,' or 'Pleasure is all that matters,' and find nothing. Vanity of vanities, says the Preacher, all is vanity...

'Why, you're nothing but a pack of cards!' said Alice. 'At that the whole pack rose into the air...' The

diamonds, my friends; the hearts, the theatre; the clubs –
that's politics; and spades: the drugs, the alcohol, the
searches for security in this world, the vices, the hopes
against hope that the umbrella is the firmament; the
spades that dig the graves... The joker: that is God.

But Alice woke up to find her sister stroking her hair.
Who will I find to stroke mine?

Dec 29th

Decided to make a start on reading The Bible. All of
it. Read Genesis this afternoon.

Dec 30th

Read Exodus in the afternoon.

Dec 31st

Read Leviticus. Very boring. Quick lunch, then drove
to Robertsbridge station where the train was on time for
once. Took the tube to Hill's in Bond Street where
Mother bought some stuff for her violin.

Back to the Strand for a meal and then on to the
Haymarket. Paul Daneman is extremely good as Hadrian
VII; the theatre too is magnificent as one would expect,
and if the Underground trains rumbling beneath, and the
ushers with their hobnail boots were a trifle disturbing,
well that was no fault of the production. The entry of the
cardinals was less dramatic than at the Mermaid, the
shape of the theatre precluding such a long procession
down the aisle. But it was a thoroughly pleasant evening.

Crowds were gathering in Trafalgar Square as we
made our way back. As our train drew into Etchingham
station it became...

...1970

…and back home I had some hot soup and went to bed.

And so ended the sixties. The decade that changed the world. But I changed anyway. Inevitably. I was seven at the beginning of the decade, seventeen at the end of it.

Attitudes to sexual activity had changed dramatically. But we were still expected to have heterosexual feelings – all of us – and to behave accordingly. The pop songs of the time made this clear. Baby, you can drive my car. How do you do what you do to me? I wanna hold your hand. *There was no mistaking the fact that a boy was addressing a girl in each case. You fell in love with someone of the opposite sex at fifteen, broke up after six months, then started again, one rung further up the ladder. Only it didn't seem to be working out quite like that for me.*

Jan 4th 1970

Expecting Jagger to turn up. He didn't.

Saturday Jan 5th

Made a wallet etc. At 4.30 Jagger arrived … with Steve! They had hitch-hiked from London and had to walk the last three miles in below-freezing temperature. I couldn't drive out to meet them because Mother had the car. We had some homemade beer in front of the fire, and then talked, between tea, tee-vee etc. until bedtime. And even that didn't stop Steve and me. We were still talking at one o'clock. Steve had the second bed in my room, Jagger had the spare bedroom to himself.

Sunday Jan 6th

Did almost nothing in the morning except church, taught Jagger some chords on the piano, had homemade champagne for lunch, drove to Rye, Wittersham and Rye Harbour in the afternoon, and made orange burgundy. Cosy evening with primrose wine and chestnuts. Bed and another long talk with Steve.

Jan 7th

Took Jagger to the train, and drove Steve to his new girlfriend's house in mid-Kent, on the way to see Mother's cousin at Elham.

Jan 12th

Mother out all day. Awaited Jan 13th. Received a letter from Fr Malachy enclosing another good review of Mother Courage. The Rayburn had to be let out, following the collapse of the fire bricks. Rotten evening for TV.

Jan 13th

Nothing from Durham. Back to school (by train, because of the bad weather and roads) after a lunch cooked on oil stoves. Arrived at 3.45, carrying my case down the road to the school. Had tea with Uncle Ron, and the first face to pass the door was ... Chris's. Quite a jolly reunion. We brought my trunk in. Yes, we still share a room.

Today is my diary's first birthday. A lot of water has passed under the bridge... But the feeling is much the same. If less despairing than last year's entry...

Jan 14th

Chris's birthday. Got up. Bloody school, bloody breakfast, bloody House meeting…

Yes, I was thrown out of Johnnie's class, but didn't go, of course. Shit lunch, went down town, read about sherry, met Jagger, returned to school, talked to Chris, had supper, called Fr Cyprian a shit and then went down to the Foy Boat for one pint and three schooners of sherry. The occasion was slightly marred by the presence of prefects. I told someone I'd come back to school for the purpose of seeing Chris. I was joking, of course…

I think I was.

We enjoyed ourselves anyway, Chris and I, and are now preparing for bed with the help of some homemade hock. Goodnight.

Calling Fr Cyprian a shit… That came about because we were larking around in Pit the Younger, Fr Cyprian included. We were talking about sit-ins, and I said, joking, 'Let's have a shit-in. Come in, Fr Cyprian.' I thought he'd take it as a joke, but he looked dreadfully hurt. This was the day I discovered I had the power to hurt people who were twice as old as I was. But it was too late to do anything about it. Perhaps I could have apologized. But I'm not very good at doing that.

Jan 15th

Ran the gamut of emotions from A to B. (As Dorothy Parker said, reviewing Katharine Hepburn.) Ran all the way to Dumpton Park Road to meet and check out Miss Jane L. Essex, Chris's latest one-woman fan club, but only succeeded in meeting her mother and seeing her Victorian house. Returned.

Listened to King Crimson with Chris. Decided that all was false, illusion: alcohol, friendship... That the only reality is pain. Not even Chris can save me from that.

Read Somerset Maugham and cheered up. Talked to Steve. Read a book about lesbianism, according to which I'm obviously female – or else a hypochondriac. Steve and I scandalised Big Ed by cuddling and romping on my bunk while he watched from the armchair. (There was no-one else in the room.) We were pretending to be queer. Actually I've never felt more hetero in my life.

During prep Chris and I read Howard's End, drank wine, and talked happily.

Night prayers a riot! A day of ups and downs. Long live self deception.

Long live self-deception indeed. While pretending to be queer in order to wind up Ted I lay on top of Steve, opened his fly and put my hand inside, pulling down his underpants so that I could grasp his warm cock, which was stiff. He did exactly the same to me. And me, I was hard too, hetero though I was, notwithstanding.

Jan 16th

Thrown out of English. Went.

Washed my hair. Read Howards End. Had a rotten lunch, but an amusing History class. Teddy drove us down there in his van, showing off his driving skills. Began to read Parson Woodforde's Diary on his recommendation. Very good.

Went for a cross-country run with Jagger. We had coffee at John-for-Teas, on the corner by the nursing home between Stella Maris and the Viking Ship. Brought back memories of years ago...

Afterwards, fell asleep in Jagger's room in an armchair and we both slept soundly till supper…

…Which was followed by my taking junior prep and reading Parson Woodforde.

After that I continued, reading out amusing passages to Chris, who was looking at the books of old photos lent by Teddy.

Night prayers had to be abandoned due to laughter. Not entirely my fault, surely?

Saturday Jan 17th

Missed breakfast on account of oversleeping. Ate it afterwards. Had a form meeting, still tired after falling asleep after talking and drinking with Chris half last night, finished Howards End and continued Parson Woodforde. After lunch I slept for two hours before supper while Chris went joyriding.

Joyriding, or treasure-hunting, means nothing more dangerous than smoking pot. I just have to be a bit careful what I write in these unlocked pages. Anyway, not really my cup of tea. I'd rather have a cup of tea, actually. Or a whisky.

After supper I read Somerset Maugham and played the organ. But nothing much worth mentioning happened. I didn't even read the newspapers; I never do. And I used my voice less today than I have done for ages. I suppose I must just have vegetated.

But Zebedee gave me my Oxford interview report. It said, in more than enough words: 'Good, but not good enough.' My brevity they discuss at length.

Sunday Jan 18th

Craved for food. Had breakfast. Zebedee vetoes further pub visits. Approx 12 of us set out for the Foy Boat. Two pints. The landlord dislikes winkles and unburdened a bag on us. We ate them with paper-clips. They gave Frankie diarrhoea but made me hungry. I ate two lunches – rosbif. Read Parson Woodforde's Diary, but had to raid masters' dining-room, run half a mile in the rain, nick Todger's salami supply, all in aid of my raging hunger. Had some coffee in Jagger's room, talked and went to sleep in my own, walked along the prom with Chris and Simon. Went to Benediction and sang rather over-lustily with Jagger. Me very merry at supper. Lousy supper.

Read Parson Woodforde, had a bath, went for a walk with Chris, Steve and Simon, who were having a cool-off after another treasure hunt. Nothing else to record. Oh, except Chris thinks Steve is rushing to lose his virginity on his, Chris's, advice.

I could have told Chris enough on that subject to startle him greatly, but have made a promise of secrecy I don't intend to break.

'Vanity of vanities, Quoheleth says.'

Jan 19th

Sat through an entire English class.

Steve breaks the ends off my front teeth while play-fighting with me on my bed, Chris gets 'Learning to Drive in Pictures'. All partake of lunch. Steve calls me a queer after lunch. Sleep before supper. Supper not bad. Liver and real-peas. It feels odd eating with the sharp edges of my chipped front teeth.

***

KP has been around for years. We were quite chummy when we were eleven, but then drifted apart. Especially as he was a day-boy. But now he spends a lot of time with us boarders in Number One, and stays the night on our floor if he's had too much to drink, or has missed the last train back to Canterbury. He's tall and rather thin limbed but with unexpectedly broad shoulders. A very square jaw and a long thin neck, and ears that stick out like the handles of a House cup. I'm glad he's around. His ears distract people's attention from mine which, though not really sticking out, are large, like a fruit bat's.

Jan 20th

Did nothing but read Parson Woodforde. Had a long talk in bed with Chris. From this point of view, as good as Steve. Two freighter planes roared over after midnight, taking off from Manston. En route for Biafra with relief supplies, I think. The outside world does permeate the walls of Number One occasionally.

Jan 21st

Everyone watches boxing on TV, so I eat cheese and biscuits alone and drink a pint of beer collected in an icy gale from the off-licence. Then I talked to Zebedee. I asked him if he wanted to be a headmaster. Yes, of course he does. I always knew it.

And finally a talk with Steve. A most enjoyable talk. All over the place. Dear old Steve.

Jan 23rd

Fought with, and talked to, Steve. Chris fell asleep during prep. After, down to the Foy Boat. Chris buys me a pint. Tim the Deal buys me another. We talk about drugs. They seem an expensive substitute for imagination. But who am I, alcoholic that I am, to talk? Seriously though, their descriptions of acid trips are my descriptions of country walks on spring mornings, or half a bottle of wine.

Saturday Jan 24th

Steve came down to our room last night and he, Chris and I talked till past midnight. In the morning we had sixth-form meeting and very little else. I began reading Joyce's 'Portrait of the Artist' and enjoyed it immensely. Bad-tempered at supper (the salt-cellar trick again) and have still not quite woken up. Still nothing from Durham. The world ticks on.

Sunday Jan 25th

Reading Portrait of the Artist, discovered a lack of discipline in my own education. As Steve and I said to each other, 'Why were we not made to read Thomas Aquinas?'

Steve and I talked from 5 till 10. Very nice. Chris came and joined us. Pleasant evening, splitting headache. Good time. Hell, what am I writing! G'night.

***

I got interested in wine and wine-making when I was just fourteen. In the fifth form. It was Will, who told me his parents made apple wine in demijohns. It sounded fun. Another boy lent me a book called Country Wines, and I couldn't wait to get started. After that autumn half-term the floor of Form Five was ranged with fermenting jars of wheat wine, raisin wine and tea wine, which I'd made in the school kitchen. Fr Cyprian, whose family were very keen on wine-making, was a very understanding form-master. He and I went on to make mildly alcoholic ginger beer – in the monastery kitchen, in big stone crocks with taps at the bottom, which we sold in the playground at 2d per glass.

Later, when I'd moved into Number Three, my then room-mate and I fermented out some molasses and spent a whole Sunday distilling it in the chemistry lab over a Bunsen burner, using a Liebig condenser. We flavoured the resulting clear spirit with caramel, which we also made, from a few spoonfuls of sugar, over a Bunsen.

I borrowed a book from the monastery library, called 'Through The Wine-Glass'. A collection of magical accounts of tasting wine in different parts of Europe. One chapter told of eating lampreys in St Emilion – a rare example of a fish cooked in red wine, the writer said – while looking out over the walls of the old town at the river Dordogne in the distance. Made me want to go there.

I didn't know how I was going to taste all the expensive wines described in the book. Wine only ever appeared on the table at home on Christmas Day. But here at school, the staff, or some of them, had taken to buying cases of assorted Lupé-Cholet Burgundies and Thoman Hocks and Moselles, which they would have a glass of each at staff dining-room lunch. The empties were left outside the kitchen door. If I got there quickly I could tip the dregs into the palm of my hand and lick them up. As the weeks passed I began to learn the slight differences in weight, colour and – just maybe, taste – between Chambolle-Musigny, Volnay, Gevry-Chambertin, Nuits-St-Georges, etc., and to recognize the distinctive flavour and texture of German Hocks and Moselles. And then, thanks to my room-mate and his brother's Z, I gained my more extensive experience of Gigondas, Beaujolais and Ste-Croix-du-Mont...

THIRTEEN

Nothing From Durham

Jan 26th

After supper we took Big Ed to pieces. Then I read all about Breugel. Chris and I tried to get something to drink but only succeeded in amassing a vast quantity of food which we are now eating, judiciously quoting from our diaries. Steve came in, said I had B.O. Perhaps I have. Chris was loyally silent on the issue.

Jan 27th

Chris, KP and I wandered down town, this lovely spring afternoon, and did fuck-all. Then we came back to school and did fuck-all. Steve joined in. He has had his hair removed. He looks funny. And sweet.

Supper was a riot. All my fault, for showing Kavanagh his face in a mirror I'd brought in specially. 'Now do you see why I don't like looking at you?' And then picking Todger's pockets and passing the contents down the table.

After supper we had a laugh at Big Ed. I described his penis as a skinhead in a life-jacket, though I hadn't seen it for about five years, then read about Castlereagh and Canning, while Chris went in search of an expensive cube of truth.

After night prayers I decided that if I couldn't afford alcohol I'd just have to get pissed without it. I played the honky-tonk piano for ages and sang around at the top of my voice. Kathy the kitchen maid gave me a pair of oranges. Probably to shut me up.

Then I visited the treasure-seekers in the basement. Steve was unusually introspective and called me Rafe for the first time ever. (Until now, he's insistently stuck with Mac.) Others mucked around with water. It seeming absurd to stand foolishly in the middle of the room I suited my mood to the company, and my feelings lead me to suspect that with the right quantities of relaxation, will power and imagination, the state could be self-induced. I know I can induce the effects of alcohol in myself at times; why not other drugs? Nothing changes, surely, but reality hits one harder. Perhaps hard work can produce this acceptance of reality without drugs?

Anyway, for this evening I took advantage of the state of my companions to be my natural self, unimpeded by the thought that if I wave my arms in time to the music, or stare in wonder at a light-bulb, I will be laughed at, since everyone else is doing exactly the same thing.

***

When you go to boarding school you lose your first name. Only much later is it grudgingly returned to you. But you have to earn it. In the sixth form people begin to call their close friends by their Christian names. People with very few friends tend to be referred to by surname only, right up to the bitter end. Though I was McKean for years, I'm now Rafe to most people in the sixth form. But, like Jagger, I have a nickname that is current throughout the school, which confuses the issue a bit. So that sixth-formers who don't like me or know me well enough to call me Rafe tend to call me Mac, like the juniors do. (Yes, I know some of them also refer to me as Scruff when I'm not listening, but that's not my official nickname.)

Jan 28th

Breakfast. A board appeared in the refectory now informs us of the menu for the day. Unfortunately it is written in chalk and so subject to unauthorised alterations.

Thrown out of English class after taking down in longhand every word Johnnie said, and asking him to stop and wait for me to catch up when he was going too quickly.

Beefballs on the warpath. No sixth formers turned up at Games. I bought mother an apron for her birthday… Beefballs tracks me down. Asks me what my name is. Doesn't he read the papers?

Varegated grill for supper… Good. Bored afterwards. Talked to Zebedee. He's after the headship of B. School at Goudhurst, the other side of Kent.

Jan 29th

The day I told everyone I'd hear from Durham. But I didn't, and I think a few people were rather glad. I talked to Steve and KP in the afternoon, slept in the morning, and talked to Barney and Beefballs all lunchtime.

Which all sounds very reasonable. Actually all the sixth-formers who'd skipped Games were summoned for interviews with Beefballs and Barney in Barney's office. In pairs. I went with Rory. Barney, trying to be serious, asked us where we'd been. 'I was in a cupboard,' Rory said. (That was true. Beefballs had gone to his room, Rory had nipped into the wardrobe when he heard him approach, and Beefballs had opened the wardrobe door…) I said I'd been in a haberdasher's (buying my mother's birthday present.) 'What's a haberdasher's?' Rory asked me, catching my eye with a twinkle in his

own. 'A place where you hab a dash,' I said. Barney
was making such an effort not to laugh that he had to
look at the floor. Even so, the corners of his mouth kept
twitching. As for Beefballs, he looked as though daggers
would melt in his mouth. I told him, in front of Barney
and Rory, that he was too efficient for our school, that
his face didn't fit, and that anyway, I wasn't really that
much of a sportsman. Rory said the same went for him
too, though actually he's better at Rugby and cricket
than I am, and was, I think, just being supportive and
comradely. This was the day that Rory and I began to be
friends again, I think. Barney was very reasonable about
it all. There was a compromise. Those of us who wanted
to drop out of team games could go running. But we
must do it seriously. Fair enough, we said. But Barney
surely had bigger things to deal with.

Later I practised memorising the Brahms A-flat waltz
at the piano. Supper was overdone chicken. After it, in a
fit of manic inspiration I began to rewrite the Bee
Article. We watched Henry VIII, Wife V. Very good. On
the theme, *Stipendium peccati mors est*. However, the
space on the sofa large enough for Simon was apparently
too small for me too, and since Fr Cosmos took my usual
armchair, I saw more of Big Ed's shoulder than anything
else.

Jan 30th

My depression at hearing nothing from Durham
increased hourly. We discussed Beefballs during
English, a ceiling came down in Number Three, Steve
annoyed Jagger by correcting his spelling mistakes,
Chris alienated Jagger by teasing him about it.

But not everything is bad; coffee is easy to come by, I
dislike fewer people than ever before in my life, and
Chris and I decided to go to Edinburgh. However, for

practical reasons we only got as far as the front door before turning back. It's cold outside.

Jan 31st

A firm but polite rejection from Cambridge. Hopes of Durham fade astern. What about acting?

The Bee Article is useless. I could have completed it but...

I worked late last night. So did Chris. The world held no terrors then.

I had a nightmare: I sat at the head of my table, and people began to advance on me. I sensed that they were armed. They were. I awoke.

The ex-Bloomsbury set talked about the death of close relatives. I suspect a hardness near the bottom of my heart, like the 'splinter of ice' that Graham Greene said every writer must have. It angers me.

Chris, KP and I went to the pub in high spirits but for some reason I became depressed. I dared not speak on the way back. I felt like crying but I don't know why.

Only gradually did my depression lessen as the dull afternoon became five o'clock and Jagger and I met Uncle Ron and walked down to the cinema together. Midnight Cowboy. It really IS tremendous – a beautiful film. *(Why? It spoke to me in a very special way. It was about a love between two guys that could not be articulated. By now I was pretty much an expert on that subject...)* On the way back Jagger talked about architecture and I held my tongue. We had dinner, the three of us, at The Savoy. Mushroom omelette, steak fruit salad with Kirsch, and Mateus Rosé. A very enjoyable evening. But now, like Maxwell with his silver hammer, I am back at school again.

Sunday Feb 1st

Chris and I talked about Midnight Cowboy late last night. This morning Zebedee's room inspection. Fr Hellfire preached at Mass.

Down to the Foy Boat. One and a half pints. We ran back in the icy wind. It tried to snow. Lunch not too bad.

In the afternoon I read a little Joyce and slept. Chris wrote an essay. I awoke and we set off on a food hunt. The school kitchen was warm but devoid of any nourishment, and failing to find Fr Cyprian we cautiously invaded the monastery precinct and went into the kitchen there. We got some cold potatoes and I found a hunk of bread with which we had to be content. We returned to our room and ate it. No better than Mother Courage, I observed, huddled together on a storage heater, gnawing at stale bread. So we stayed till Benediction. After that we went to supper, where we split up. The Boy From Uncle took it into his head to slap me on the back every time he passed my chair. That was not surprising but when he graduated from my knees to the inside of my thigh I was rather taken aback. All in a day's work for a head of table, I suppose.

After supper I froze to death at the piano. So I decided to write this instead.

Feb 2nd

Lazy. Got up late and found myself no longer a table prefect. O'Dowd is instead. I suppose it is only to be expected. The Boy From Uncle is Sorry.

Talked all day. The Bloomsbury Group re-emerges. I discussed this with Johnnie. In the evening I wrote him an essay. He always complains that I don't illustrate my essays. This time I did. Litterally!!!

Earlier Chris and I had walked through the dusky rain to Stella Maris. Memories… We saw the poor little bastards doing prep in the inky prep room. We walked back.

I sat on O'Dowd's table at supper…

Feb 3rd

Breakfast was torture. Smith appeared on the table. I moved. Steve made a sarcastic comment about my jagged-toothed smile. Nothing from Durham.

I gave Johnnie my 'illustrated' essay. Luckily he was amused. Lunch was abominable. Talked to Chris a little and bought some bread and cheese.

Bertrand Russell died.

At supper all my frustration rose to the surface and I found myself rapping the table with a knife. I became aware that the refectory had gone silent. I went on banging. I wanted to stand up, scream, and overturn the table on top of Smith, over Dick-the-Dick, over everyone and everything…

It was unfortunate that Paolo called me up. Even more that everyone got excited and clapped, and some got childishly conspiratorial. Paolo was livid during prep, he apologized later. After night prayers I talked with Chris. I enjoyed that.

Peace between men and peoples is impossible. Bertrand Russell must have been mad.

Forgot to mention my long chat with Uncle Ron. Saw the school account books. Red. Pondered future of school, of monastery, of organized religion, of the world. Very interesting.

Feb 4th

Breakfast was a silent hell. I knew it would be. I had dreamed I was smoking pot in Grange Road. After breakfast was English. We excelled ourselves. Poor Johnnie. Then I read Somerset Maugham and it grew lunchtime. House meeting followed, then Steve tried to smarten me up, combing my hair and dealing very intimately with my clothes. After that I donned a track-suit and pottered around. Down by the sea I got involved with a blind lady who'd lost her grand-daughter. I began to suspect that she wanted me to dive fully clothed into a sea so rough that it had caused the hovercraft to limp home, tail between legs, but fortunately the child turned up.

Had an interesting chat with pissed-Zebedee. We talked about The Boy From Uncle and his Uncle Barney and about an old photo of a boys' cricket team. 'Everything in their lives is ordinary now,' he kept saying, 'except this, their big moment when they were pretty.' He kept repeating this and asked me attach great symbolic importance to it. I think there is a little of the artist in Zebedee.

After supper I scrounged some of Fr Cyprian's St Bruno tobacco; unfortunately it is rather strong and made me rather sick.

Then I lay down on my bed. Next thing…

'Don't you think you'd better get changed?' It was Chris. It was also after eleven o'clock, so we got into our pyjamas and ate bread and cheese and Chris recounted his swimming-pool adventures.

Chris is always doing bits of dialogue from Midnight Cowboy. He's especially good at doing Dustin Hoffman playing Ratso. Or sometimes he does Jon Voight playing Joe Buck, and whichever way round it is, I have to try and do the other role. He has a bit of an identification difficulty, I think. He likes the character of Joe Buck but doesn't look remotely like Jon Voight. He does look a bit more like Dustin Hoffman, though, although taller and much better-looking. And he admires his acting techniques hugely. He can recite whole chunks of The Graduate also, getting the accents more or less right in each case. He's remarkable in that way. He goes to every film that's on about twice. And can then remember most of the dialogue and produce it at will. I can't do that.

Saturday Feb 7th

Table prefect again at breakfast. Cheered by the juniors.

Later, met an ex-Vietnam American soldier, Guy Kent, very young, who is staying in the monastery.

After night prayers I looked forward to a quiet conversation with Steve. But the publicity of our coffee hunt (resolved, courtesy of Zebedee) attracted Chris, Frankie and Simon, and we eventually all started talking about homosexuality. I seem to have missed out on a lot.

The Boy From Uncle is in sick-bay.

Sunday Feb 8th

In the afternoon Simon and Frankie, and Steve and Chris'n'me went for a walk on the prom. More than a walk. A spiritual experience.

We went to Stella Maris and explored the dormitories. 'I slept in this bed,' I showed off to the others. I must have been small then; the bed was tiny. Teddy joined us and gave us a somewhat grudging conducted tour. Visits to this place are always nostalgic.

Back at school we ate tons of celery and went to Benediction, which was celebrated by Fr Nicholas, who broke down in the middle of the singing. That was pathetic. I more than feared him once, I respected him, and in respecting him came to love him a little. Poor man.

Feb 9th

Jagger came over to my table at breakfast, pointed to The Boy From Uncle who is out of sick-bay, looked meaningfully into my eyes and said, 'The sun's shining today.'

After lunch there was a bloody row that upset everyone, and nearly developed into the first argument I'd had with Chris. It was about racialism, politics and inferiority complexes. After that I kept Steve company on his way to Stella Maris and talked to him till supper when I lapsed into the usual silence. I wrote Nothing From Durham on the refectory table.

Shrove Tuesday Feb 10th

Chris and I talked for hours last night, I say talked. I didn't realize how jealous he was of Jagger's hold on me. He needn't be really. Then there was a long uncomfortable silence. I think it's just that he's a bit jealous that Jagger has been down to my mother's house with Steve and he hasn't. At the end we said, 'Goodnight.' Has something died in our friendship?

This morning there was a big argument with Daniel about religion. Lunch was foul.

Afterwards we talked all afternoon, very happily, until Chris left to play football and I told him I was very good at it but didn't tell many people, and I found Frankie and together we invaded the refectory where our Under 13s team were entertaining some diminutive opponents, swiped their tea and sandwiches and made off with a couple of pancakes...

For supper we had more pancakes. I felt quite bloated. Then everyone went to auditions for the forthcoming opera (All The King's Men, to be conducted by Mr Vaughan) except me.

I talked to Steve during prep. He was very depressed. I felt very sick during prep and Night Prayers but practised the organ afterwards and after a brief talk to Jagger retired to my room with a headache. Chris returned, equipped with the lead part in the opera. I'm glad. Smith would have got too big for his boots.

Ash Wednesday Feb 11th

Thrown out of English class. Rissoles for lunch. Stroked Chris's hair: a symbolic gesture.

During Games went down town with Jagger, watched a little of the football match and had a nice time scrounging food from the refectory with Steve. He has become very sweet lately. Then some of us went to the Abbey Church, for a variety of motives, to be sprinkled with ashes.

At supper I was entertained by TBFU. (The Boy From Uncle. To be referred to from now on as Tibby.)

After supper I talked with Steve for a bit, then had a cup of tea with the kitchen staff, sight-read a bit of a Beethoven Sonata, and found time beginning to hang heavily. Chris had gone off to the cinema.

Todger, Frankie and I, an ill-assorted company if ever there was one, set out for the Foy Boat, which reached at 10.00. We had a pint of Trophy each, and engaged in childish arguments. When they turned out the lights we took the hint and left, pissing around in the frost: Frankie pretended to throw himself off the cliff and I pretended to save him. We bumped into Fr Cyprian on the way back.

Now I sit here waiting for Chris to return. But as it is nearly half past eleven I think perhaps I ought to turn in.

– Hey, I forgot. Miss Jane L Essex rang up the school. I told Uncle Ron to shove her off. Chris was out at the time.

Feb 12th

Fucking bad mood all day. Breakfast a disgusting meal.

Just getting to sleep afterwards when Chris woke me up for English class. To be taken by the newest monastery guest, Guy Kent, the American ex-soldier, writer, bum, lecturer and knife-man. Interesting but long.

Steve attacks me for no reason at all in the refectory.

The room, mine and Chris's, is a refrigerator. I wrapped myself in a blanket, and Gollum walked in. We had only met once before, when I played in a Rugby game he was refereeing, so the situation was a little embarrassing. Then just as I was getting to sleep Chris woke me up. We put blankets up at the windows, then Chris went to sleep. I went and talked to Mr Roland the new deputy science head, in the staff room. He talked about his experience in 'tough' schools. It sounded rather fun.

Then just as I was getting to sleep again, Chris woke me up.

Super was horrid. Everybody has become most objectionable, though Chris and I got on better after supper. Our room has become so cold that we migrated to Dec's room during prep. (The wind has swung to the east, and there is no high ground between here and the Urals.)

Ibsens's When We Dead Awaken was on TV, with Wendy Hiller.

Fr Cyprian annoyed me. I've written him an angry letter.

Chris is in bed. My eyes are 'like dross of lead', and my fingers white and bloodless. I confuse people's names, and I was forced once again to write on the refectory table – NOTHING FROM DURHAM.

Friday 13th Feb

A unique day.

Went to Mass. English good. Looked at two poems about Narcissus. Walked to Stella Maris through yesterday's snow in my dressing-gown. Mr Vaughan, who was there, was amused.

I stood around in the sun with KP at midday. The postman arrived. He walked into the school. I skipped along behind him exuberantly. I was certain. He laid the letters down on the hall table. I looked.

I couldn't speak for several minutes. There was nothing, nothing, nothing. I have only the haziest recollection of that lunch-hour, wandering around in an absent-minded state, thinking of nothing.

History was OK. I talked to Steve for most of the rest of the evening – and to Father Cyprian, with whom I am now reconciled. Steve and I have never been greater friends. We are in danger of becoming intellectually complacent and apathetic, though, just as on Dec 28th I feared emotional apathy and stagnation with Chris.

No man is an island, but it is fatal to imagine that two people constitute one.

Supper – my throat hurt, the food was tasteless. Have I got flu?

Read Verlaine during prep.

Saw The Forsytes with Steve, then talked, for a change, with Smith, about Phil, and about Number One. Painful.

I returned to my room and the day fades out of existence. How different, and yet how similar, to May 22nd last year.

(May 22nd 1969

In the Pit I very publicly climbed onto Chris's knee and sat there for a bit. Chris seemed OK with that. More than OK, I think. Perhaps a little bit proud of this new friendship – as I am, of course. He even laughed and ruffled my hair at one point when someone made a pointed comment. After supper I finished some bread and salami, and had to explain to Steve why I felt my relationship with him was devoid of emotion. A bit sad, that.)

(Oct 4th 2014

But what was the similar thing, what was the different one? The tapestry is very faded at this point. And yet this still moment in Ralph's diary resembles those moments in Bach or Beethoven when momentum stalls, the harmonies drift, and the listener awaits the return of the theme, or fugue subject, or whatever it may be... Ralph was waiting for it at this time. Though he didn't know it then. A few more weeks had to pass...)

Saturday 14th Feb 1970

Valentine's Day.

Didn't get up but slept very late and I dreamed that Chris and I were running, running along streets, country lanes, cart tracks, and everybody else, Paolo, KP, Steve, dropped behind us as we left the suburbs. We were just in danger of being run over by a bus when I awoke to find Steve lying on top of me on my bed, telling me

Barry M had invited me to lunch at his father's house in Margate.

I got up. After sixth-form meeting I went for a little drink (breakfast) in the Regency with KP and Chris. We returned to school and after Assembly Daniel took me to Broadstairs, lent me some clothes, and took me to the station where I said Good-bye to Chris, and in doing so, missed a train by 15 seconds. It snowed as I waited and got more and more depressed for 29 minutes 45 seconds. Then a train arrived and I went to Margate.

Found Steve, Jagger and Barry M waiting there and we took our way through the back streets to Michael M's house. I had some of a friend's hawthornberry wine and my depression lifted slightly. We had chicken casserole and nuts for lunch, and finally left the house for the bowling alley, me clad in the dressing-gown, which caused us a bit of trouble. We later returned, changed, and soon hit the road again, buzzed to Westgate and had two Jameson's Irish whiskies in the Walmer Castle. Nice, but I felt fluey and really ill.

We walked through the wind to the convent and entered, early. I sat on a heater and surveyed the scene. Charlotte arrived. We each had a Martini. During the evening I could only get through six small glasses of beer. That's how ill I am.

Charlotte and I talked of all sorts of things. She said she loved the record that I liked. Ironical, because it reminds me of Blond-hair, who liked it also. She was feeling more randy than I was. Chris came late and left early. I missed him.

I sang some songs, but the party was less successful than November's, and though I kissed Charlotte goodbye, and played with Simon in the street, losing his cravat in the process, and talked to Barney, who was looking curiously like his nephew, and who smirked on catching sight of Charlotte and me in a corner on the floor, I could only think of Durham on the train, and though I tried to cuddle up to Steve who was sitting next to me I found the back of his neck rather ugly, it is not the same without Chris.

Back from the station I gave Phil a piggy-back ride, then walked quickly home. But Chris wasn't back yet. I tried to get blankets for KP. No good. He is now asleep on the floor in the cold. And I am waiting for Chris – clad in the article of clothing that made the afternoon and nearly ruined my evening.

Not a bad day on the hole... But not good either. B...e...cause... there was – Nothing From Durham. Now it is twenty past twelve tomorrow morning, and Chris is not back, and I am sad.

FOURTEEN

Why Don't You Write All This Down?

Sunday Feb 15th

A wretched day. Morning as usual. No-one spoke to me at the pub so I left. Sat on Jagger's table at lunch. Slept most of the afternoon. Tibby came and sat next to me at supper, and after that Chris and I entertained the kitchen staff. Barney arrived... and shoved us out. Chris and I are now working late. I'm prepared to stay up all night if necessary. Tomorrow I will hear from Durham. I know it.

Feb 16th

Monday. Nothing from Durham. Very depressed. Talked all morning in Steve's room. Onions at lunch made me fart and demand Milk of Magnesia in the evening.

In the afternoon I finished my essay and then did nothing. After supper I took junior prep. No incident, though Tibby was very matey and called me Macky.

Nothing happened. People complain I am eccentric. I resolve to take a firmer grip on myself, tense though the situation may be.

Chris and I are the only two worthwhile people in the world.

Feb 17th

Snow at dawn – quite a blizzard; thaw all day.

Elated in morning. Depressed as thaw sets in. My chair collapsed during English. Tibby insisted on rubbing his buttocks up and down against my genitals in the refectory queue.

I talked to Jagger all morning. He is depressed, believes his relationship with Steve to have folded up. We talked about intellectual and emotional relationships.

Feb 18th

Chris and I lay talking for a long while last night. His way of saying, 'I see what you mean,' is quite different from Steve's or anyone else's. We made tentative plans to spend a few days in the monastery over Easter. Something we've both wanted to do for a long time. Just out of curiosity, though. We're not really the religious type.

Feb 19th

Fuses blown so got up in cold and dark. After breakfast I wrote eight lines of an essay, then changed to drawing plans for a new wing for the school which, though interrupted by English, lunch, and feeding Chris on biscuits and butter, occupied me for most of the rest of the day, practical help being contributed by KP and constructive criticism and cold water being contributed by Jagger. It is to be mock-Georgian.

Chris is depressed. I am suspended in the eye of my own hurricane, for the moment, calm and motionless. The lull before the storm?

Feb 20th

Zebedee has gone out of his mind. He has thrown Frankie and Simon out of their basement room in

Number One and into the Cock-Loft – the fifth-formers' dormitory at the far end of the main building. I helped them carry up their effects during prep.

Someone yelled, 'I hate you,' at Johnnie during English class, which I thought was going a bit far, and the Bidding Prayers were ballsed up at Mass.

I slept during Games, watched The Forsytes, watched Frankie put his fist through a window, heard Paolo denounce Dick-the-Dick (in private), heard Chris rage and rant about his haircut, heard everyone rage and rant...

Saturday 21st

Paid a flying visit home, travelling by train. Mother met me at Hastings. She was horrified to see my jagged front teeth. I told her how it had happened. Well, up to a point. 'Wait till I see Steve,' she said. 'I'll have something to say to him.' She was only half joking.

Friends of hers have seen the advertisement for a science master at my school in the Catholic paper.

Sunday Feb 22nd

Back at school. Found Chris.

Feb 24th

I spent the morning in a homosexual mood, waiting for KP to finish his History essay. We drove down to Stella Maris in the Moke, and Teddy returned Steve's latest essay with the one-word comment: *Adequate*. 'Surely it was better than that, sir?' Steve protested. Teddy looked at the paper again, frowning thoughtfully. He took his pen out and adjusted his comment. It now read: *Admirably Adequate*.

I felt unusually affectionate towards Chris this afternoon. We called on Uncle Ron briefly – Mrs Pring was working there again, then went back to school where we had some coffee and I lay down with my head on Chris's lap.

Then I had a bath and procured cheese from the kitchen. Supper was chicken fricassée. In the queue Tibby tried to lie down with his head on *my* lap. However, I was standing up at the time…

Feb 25th

Rewrote my Bee Article late last night while sharing a bottle of wine with Chris. Then Chris drew a self-portrait of himself and went to sleep.

This morning dawned bright and fair. Spring.

Thrown out of English class. Went.

Chris and I went for a walk. Seeing a funeral in progress at the Abbey Church we joined it for a while, eating peanuts furtively in the back pew, leaving at supper time. Depressing meal.

Feb 26th

Last night late Rory came in and told us the news: Zebedee has been given notice to leave at the end of term, at this evening's Council meeting. We are all rather stunned. Perhaps we should have seen it coming, with Mr Roland (now already nicknamed Roll and Butter) joining the staff as deputy head of science.

I became inexplicably depressed but soon got to sleep. This morning I overslept breakfast, and dreamed of Alex, of all people. We were walking arm in arm in the street and met Chris coming towards us. We went to a pub, while overhead, records played, people danced, and

I realized it was in celebration of Zebedee's leaving. I woke up. We are jackals sometimes.

Had a late breakfast. Told dayboys the news. Wrote to Mother about Chris'n'me's plan to spend Easter in the monastery.

'La journée a été rude,' as Créon says to his Page at the end of Anouilh's Antigone. A great part of me has been turned upside down today. It is the end of an era.

We talked and argued, discussed and disputed, all morning. I felt a longing for something; I'm not quite sure what. Apart from anything else I wanted Jagger back. He is away in Newcastle, being interviewed for the Architecture course.

But still discussion raged. Chris and I got angry with Steve for trying to sum up the situation too soon. A too-early sixth-form meeting dissolved into a slanging match and after lunch Chris and KP went down to the cinema without me. I lay down and dozed, lonely and unhappy, till Chris returned. We collected Steve, and decided to visit Mrs Pring. Then suddenly Jagger was back. All four of us set off together, up the hill, across the footpath through Nethercourt Farm and consumed the worthy lady's coffee and sponge cake, watched TV, and left with a jar of pickled onions.

Supper was vile.

Then – this was Chris's idea but I was happy to go along with it – we decided to go and call on Fr Barnabas. 'He needs to know where we stand,' Chris said. He meant, on the subject of Zebedee's being sacked. 'That not the whole sixth-form is on Zebedee's side.' So we went to his office and asked if we could come in for a chat. The three of us had a long heart-to-heart, sitting round the fire, Barnabas smoking his pipe. All three of us needed reassuring. The gas fire was warm, Barney's conversation sane; we talked about Zebedee, about Daniel's party tomorrow night, about the monastery, about Fr Nicholas's retirement from the Headship of Stella Maris... Barney said, 'He was quite gaga by the time we got him out. It was the women who were covering up for him...' And we talked about Barney's own, though still far-off, retirement from the Headship here, about haircuts, about Kay Jay, homosexuality, and Beefballs... Among other things.

(I didn't write this in the diary: that when we parted at Barney's door he said to us quietly, 'Thank you for your support.' I can't speak for Chris but to me that meant a lot.)

Then we went back to our own room. I ate some garlic, cleaned my teeth immediately afterwards, and then we asked permission from Zebedee to go to Daniel's party tomorrow. It was granted.

'Qu'est-ce que nous avons à quatre heures?'

'Conseil, Monsieur.'

'Eh bien, nous y allons.'

And King and Page go off together, the King's hand on the boys shoulder, to get on with the rest of the day's business at Council meeting – the afternoon has seen the King sorely tested by being obliged to execute his daughter Antigone – and the curtain falls.

Feb 27th

...And today, half the bottom was knocked out of my world in a series of incidents that mounted up to nerve-shattering proportions. First, an envelope at breakfast. Eyes followed me. I opened it and showed it to Chris. Rejection from Sheffield.

I was thrown out of English for no reason. I hardly felt like going to class. I could have thrown the whole table at Johnnie. But I thought of the guinea I was going to be paid for the Bee Article and went out peacefully.

I ate garlic raw and no-one would come near me.

Steve annoyed me by comparing me to Tibby – not boy-from-uncle Tibby, but the ineffectual Oxford student in Howards End.

Jagger and I ate Irish cheddar in my dressing-gown before lunch, and after lunch it snowed. It had snowed last night. The situation – in a Rousseau-esque way – had demanded it.

Teddy's class was a bore. But it finished early. Chris and I decided to go down town. In the midst of waiting for Uncle Ron, in raincoats outside his office, needing to get money, we saw the postman. Odd time of day for a post!

We walked into the post room. 'Nothing from Durham,' said Hilton the post monitor, sorting it. But there was a letter. Faded postmark. Durham. Chris had one from London. Feeling rather unsteady, but glad we both got it together, we sat down on the bench in the hall. People were looking at us. 'Open yours first,' said Chris. It was rather like Christmas. ...A blur of print... *Waiting List.* Chris read his. ...*Rejection.* We climbed unsteadily to our feet. We went up the stairs to Barney's office. He was rather shocked.

Uncle Ron had arrived. When Chris and KP had got money we went down town. Shopped around the Albion Bookshop, sat in the Wimpy, bought sherry and beer. Returned to school. Zebedee was not in. I took two Codein and sat down to write this.

Supper. A pretence of merriment and casualness. Then to Broadstairs for Daniel's party. An ordeal. I had to tell the Durham news to a few people. Had a pint at the Foy Boat on the way, then at Daniel's another half, then two sherries, two red wines, (one was a Côtes de Beaune Villages) then two or three Guinnesses. A chap called Jerry, who left the school over a year ago but has come back for the party, told me that it was the eccentrics that made the world. A lot of girls.

Steve tried to comfort me but failed. The evening has been a strain. Carol was nice about Durham. Listened to 'Alice's Restaurant'. God, I'm confused. I think I know what it's like to be grown-up. No I don't really. I always had Chris to talk to and support me. Jerry and I ended up talking about parental love…

Saturday Feb 28th

Forgot a few things about last night: Rory's hectic driving on the way back, a girl called Jo disentwining my arm from around Chris's neck (what a cheek!) and… well, all the little things that go to make a party 'admirably adequate'.

Today I spent in a trance. Got up for breakfast after just a few hours' sleep. Chris did not. I found I couldn't talk to Zebedee till the evening. I told the dayboys and Jagger my news. Got given a lecture by Johnnie – on the subject of Hard Work.

When Chris was awake the 'gang' went to the Regency for a drink. I had nearly two pints and thoroughly enjoyed myself.

Lunch was vile.

Later Steve and I pissed around on my bed, play-fighting. One tends to attribute one's own feelings to other people, in which case both of us conducted ourselves in a purely intellectual manner. But it was very nice.

Then I got depressed and we talked and read old diaries. Steve said he hated, 'being unable to walk out of a room without someone calling him back.' I replied that my greatest fear was of, 'being able to walk out of a room and no-one calling me back.'

I decided Steve was a little like Pococurante, the character in Voltaire's Candide who has the world's treasures of art and literature at his disposal, yet cares little for any of them. Then we had supper, which was not too bad. I waited and waited for Zebedee, but he was away at a job interview.

In the end I had to tell the news to Fr Cyprian instead, and asked him what was the latest hour at which Barney could be contacted.

Then the weekly Headmaster's Conference. Poor Barney called for loyalty and tact and was at once greeted by the first mass outburst from the Sixth Form at this meeting for over three years (the nine-o'clockers, of course, the Haemorrhoids and the Grateful Dead). It's the kind of 'kick him when he's down' policy you expect more from the Second Form.

I went and talked to Jagger. He talked better sense than I did. I thanked him. It was a long talk. Then Zebedee's return is announced… I ran up the stairs, got a private audience. He talked a lot of rot, seemed to advise me both to leave school and to stay, but agreed my mother ought to come and talk to Barney and he agreed to write to Durham and say, 'What the hell are you playing at?'

I went over to the main school, to Barney's office. Barney said little, but it was good to talk to someone. We played guessing games about my future. Lawyer? Librarian? Novelist? Diplomat? Actor? Journalist?

I went back to Jagger and told him all this, then phoned Mother. She's out. She's probably died. (It never rains but it pours, and it might as well all come together.) Then I talked to Chris. Zebedee came in. Electioneering? Interesting, but stupid.

Sunday March 1st

Woke up, decided I was a shit, a sycophant, one of nature's subordinates. But then I heard Alex had failed his first term exams over in America and had been drafted... Can you see him holding a rifle? Poor old Alex.

But I had to get out of bed, dress, phone Mother. She is coming this afternoon. Then I returned to normality, had breakfast, made my appointment for my mother and me to see Barney. The place is still under siege. Everything is locked in case Zebedee breaks it.

Zebedee said little at House meeting. Except that, as the school held £20 from each of us as caution money against damage, we should all do twenty quid's worth of damage each.

Barney was evidently too busy to say Mass. Fr Cosmos...

After Mass we went to the pub. Chris was reading a magazine when Jagger came in and said, 'Come along,' and walked out of the door. He expected me to follow. Chris expected me to stay. I went with Jagger, and a few others joined us at the Foy Boat. Then Chris turned up, alone. Not nice. I made him sit next to me and gave him a bit of cheese. We're still friends.

After a pint and a half, Jagger and I left poor Chris to the tender mercies of Todger. We had been invited for lunch in the monastery. Back at school we cleaned our teeths and learned from Frs Cyprian and Malachy that as it was the abbot's feast day there would be beer. And there was. With roast pork and the usual trimmings, and Fr Nicholas was the waiter of the day. It was a bit embarrassing being served soup by the man who could make Religious Instruction interesting, and would then beat our bottoms.

After lunch the abbot allowed Jagger and I to finish our beer and then we talked, mostly to the abbot, whose favourites we appear to be. There was coffee and I met Fr Ethelbert, who is the parish priest. We talked about the grand-daughters of Pugin and about the Hastings railway line. He's one of those people one would call a lovable old rogue, meaning nothing of the sort. Then Jagger and I and Fr Cyprian continued our talk in Fr Cyprian's room in Number Three and talked about Zebedee etc. Fr Cyprian said to me, 'You're a writer. Why don't you write all this down?' Why not? The discussion was brought to a halt on the stroke of three by the arrival of my mother.

We saw Fr Barnabas and he quoted some reassuring statistics. His room is getting familiar. The gas fire, the rug, the chairs. My respect for my mother's intelligence was increased this afternoon. We drove to Stella Maris and saw Teddy, who wasn't all that helpful, then to the St Benet's Hotel for a cup of tea and more talking, and then my mother drove off, to home. I talked to Chris for a bit, read The Times, talked a bit to Jagger and then we went to Benediction.

I sat with Mick at supper. Tibby told me that he and I were the only decent people on our table. This situation is nice, but not entirely comfortable.

After supper Chris went to the convent at Westgate. Steve went with him. I spent the evening with Jagger, who thinks Chris is as big a hypocrite as he is.

(As big a hypocrite as who was? Jagger? Steve? And who did Tibby think were the decent people? Ralph and Jagger, or Ralph and Tibby himself? Ralph was not as good a writer as all that.)

I had a bath; my thoughts raced in circles. I and all my friends, I thought, are shits, lacking in guts, intercommunication, stability … and the most marvellous, lousy, comforting, nerve-wracking, inferior-superior coagulation of individuals I have ever come across.

Jagger and I got Fr Malachy to take us over to the monastery for a cup of chocolate. We enjoyed it and returned, glanced momentarily at the TV – a programme about Vaughan Williams, and I came back here. Chris is not back yet. This time I will wait for him.

March 3rd

After History I was so depressed I played the piano, then, after Chris and Steve had had their regular 12.15 argument we went to lunch. Chris persuaded me to see the film Alfie. I preferred the idea of a drink, but looked for money. Steve, in Pit the Younger, said, 'Go back to your lord and master and suck his balls.' He meant Chris.

Chris and I and KP went to the Foy Boat. We had a pint. I told Chris what Steve had said. We discussed the matter. The fact is that Chris is older than I am. (And taller.)

We went to the cinema, to see 'Alfie', but finding we'd mistaken the time, returned to the Foy Boat. We had a further two and a half pints, returned to school and got Steve. We coaxed one another out into the cold and went down together to Daniel's girlfriend's house. Nobody in. So we went to Surgeon-Commander St-John-Thewliss's. Chris did the introductions. Surgeon-Commander St-John-Thewliss remembered me from Mother Courage.

I liked his eccentric naval room, full of brass and ship's lanterns, and a yacht's steering-wheel, and he opened a bottle of Cockburn's Fine Old Tawny. The four of us consumed the bottle easily in three glasses each. I intended to record a lot of what we said, but largely forgot it.

At five we left. Chris managed to do something that I never can: while walking along chatting, he got his cock out and pissed in the road without breaking his stride. His is circumcised like mine, and about the same size and shape, but slightly darker in colour.

Supper was spaghetti. I ate it hungrily, and degenerated into an affectionate hangover for the evening.

Chris went to bed feeling shitty and I went to say goodnight to Jagger. We borrowed money and went to the Savoy. They were unlicensed to sell drinks to non-residents and non-diners, but the barman bought us both a half on the house. We tried, embarrassedly, to make him accept a tip, but he wouldn't have it. So we drank, and fondled the hotel cat, and returned to school.

Bed.

March 4th

History class in the morning. No-one turned up. KP's train had broken down in a shower of sparks. History was postponed till 10.40. Eddie was angry. He called Stella Maris a God-forsaken dump. A rat chewed the floorboards from underneath all during the class, and it sleeted a gale and turned to snow. The Moke was draughty. By now the English class back at our school had had to be abandoned and the ground was getting quite white.

After lunch and House meeting, we talked to Johnnie for ages, and he wants us to have another talk with Barney.

After that there was a power cut and Chris and I had to nick candles. Just then the lights came back on again.

We sat around for ages wondering what to do, and decided to phone Mrs Pring. KP wouldn't come with us, nor would Steve, and even the Polar Bear *(Jagger)* found six inches of snow, a howling blizzard and a half-mile walk too much for him.

So Chris and I nicked potatoes from the kitchen and set off. It was rather beautiful. We practised rugger tackles on each other in the drifts, pushed a reversing car for what seemed miles, uphill, and somehow or other got to Mrs Pring's.

We had coffee, talked to the cat, had egg and chips (made from the potatoes we'd brought with us) and cheese scones, then set off for home. I tucked my trousers into my Rugby socks and we trudged, ran and rolled through – by now – a foot of the cool and deep and even.

One road was blocked at each end by a crashed bus (one had knocked over a lamp-post) and imprisoning a motorist. Many cars lay abandoned, and we reached the school at dusk. It was a damp and depressing return.

Curry for supper; my appetite was unimpaired. After that, Chris went drinking with KP, who couldn't get home because there were no trains to Canterbury because of the snow. I talked to Steve who couldn't cheer me up. Neither could Chris, when I went to bed. Oddly enough this was done by KP, who had filled my bed with toilet paper. That made me laugh.

Unused toilet paper. Had it been otherwise it wouldn't have done.

Oct 5th 2014

And still Ralph couldn't see it coming…

FIFTEEN

Tibby – and the Unforeseeable

March 5th

Freezing cold waking. Said so.

At breakfast there was a change around of tables and people. Tibby came to sit next to me; I had no objection. Steve roared with laughter. Frankie's little brother said Tibby and I looked cute beside each other. It made a change.

Revised History all morning, and not realizing how depressed Chris was, left him, to go down town with Jagger, where we spent a while in the Wimpy, celebrating Jagger's getting a 2 E offer from Newcastle.

Back at school, Chris looked like I felt last night. Poor Chris.

Lunch was fish and chips. After it was History and then Chris and I went to see 'Alfie', but it was not on. We watched two blokes engaged in fierce combat in the street and trudged back to school, drank coffee, tried to sleep but couldn't, became depressed, walked up the road, worked, went to supper.

Very sad. Hughes kicked Tibby off his chair and I didn't think it fair to interfere, so had no little friend to sit next to.

Prep. I worked. After prayers I borrowed money from Fr Cyprian, and Jaggy and I went to the Foy Boat. We had a pint and a half of Tankard bitter, and talked about Tibby and … Alex.

We returned to school. I tried to cheer Chris up. Our failure was mutual.

March 6th

Last night Chris and I had the most despairing talk I've ever had with anyone. We discussed Death, and pinstriped mediocrity; however I slept OK afterwards, he didn't, was ill this morning. After Mass Zebedee ripped the blankets down from our windows. Previously, he'd come in and asked, 'Why's it always dark in your room?' with a laugh in his voice. But today he was in *that* sort of mood.

I went to find Matron – she couldn't come till after her mid-morning coffee-break... But Chris was not ill enough to walk through the snow to sick-bay, so he stayed where he was. I sat and revised History, slept a little, was criticised by Steve at lunch, and after quite a good History class I went to sleep again. To be woken by Steve, climbing onto the bed on top of me and caressing me in his unique homo-intellectual way.

Supper was not too bad. Matron unfortunately read a notice that referred to her as a slug, and I gave Chris his supper. Fr Cyprian entertained Chris and me during prep, and after prayers we watched The Forsytes and had chocolate in the kitchen with Jaggy and Fr Cyprian as usual.

Annoyingly, Matron thinks it was me that wrote the thing about her being a slug. And I can't put this right, because I'd have to say that I knew who did write it. It would be easier if I didn't, but I do. Ah well.

Saturday March 7th

Woken by someone battering on the front door. At 7.30? No, 8.30 – and not one of us was up!

Over breakfast I had a rare talk with Paolo, and read The Times in the morning, and kept Chris company till

12 o'clock when I went for nearly two pints in the Regency with Jaggy. Most enjoyable.

I made Hughes kneel on the floor at lunch and, in a good mood at last – following a half-pint in the Vale Tavern with Chris and Todger, I promptly had it shattered by Steve who can always be relied upon not to support one when you most need it. May God damn him to an Eternity of not hearing the sound of his own voice!

It snowed. I went into Jaggy's room and found Chris there to my surprise. Steve came in and we half made up our quarrel.

Supper was leeks. I had Hughes and Davis both 'kneeling out'. Wonder why.

I tried to read Steve's History essay after supper. Couldn't make head or tail of it.

March 9th

Went to a choir practice. We're going to do an Ascension Day hymn-singing publicity stunt on the roof – like they do at Magdalen College, Oxford.

Supper was very good, and after that we were driven to the Westgate convent for a talk on vocations for the priesthood – sixth-formers from every Catholic school in Thanet had been invited. The cloister there is not bad, and their 'Grande Salle' is decidedly richer than our own shabby gym / Assembly Hall. Everyone was there – as well as a lot of other people.

Steve stood up and spoke quite a lot (afterwards somebody asked, 'Who was the angry young Indian?') Father Cosmos frothed, and I jumped up on the bandwagon and told everybody not to get excited.

It lasted two hours. We went to the Red House for coffee, very dull, and returned home, with Chris driving Daniel's brother's car, playing cops and robbers with the Moke. We lost our way. Got back after midnight.

March 10th

Woke up good. Did History test on the window-sill, physically jittery and incapable of writing properly. Durham have written back to Zebedee. They hold out little hope. They say I 'lack drive and persistence.' I must get at least one A if I hope to go there in 1971. It's too awful to allow it to hit one. I joked about getting a job next year, but I shall have to.

I talked to Steve and KP and Steve and I had one of our 'queer' sessions, publicly as usual, groping each other through our clothes, lying on my bed. Then Steve smothered me in Chris's deodorant, so I had to spend half an hour in the kitchen trying to counteract the smell, talking to Mrs Nelson – and to Tibby, who also happened to be there.

Lamb's hearts for supper. Well, Tibby and I liked them.

March 11th

Got up after breakfast had started. I ate mine quickly in the kitchen afterwards. I tried to walk out of English, but the door wouldn't open, so I had to return sheepishly to my seat. Great friends with Steve today, not Chris till the evening.

Why doesn't Steve always sit in bare feet and a red pullover, reading a book about James I? On the other hand, why should he? I don't know, but I think he ought to.

March 12th

I was reminded today that one can not forsee the unforseeable, however obvious it may appear in retrospect.

Missed morning prayers. Breakfast not bad. English class not bad, History test OK. There was a Form-meeting at which I argued with Dick-the-Dick about having Barney as form master next term. At lunch most of the VIth form sat on the same table. This may or may not have been significant.

The afternoon I spent with Steve – and others – in his room. We put the lights out and everyone said there was an orgy going on. I took on Big Ed, KP and Steve with my feet and beat the lot, of course. Then Big Ed left, Steve and I lay down on Steve's bed, and KP sat in the armchair and read the paper. And the incredible and yet inevitable thing happened, though it shouldn't have happened, and wasn't very pleasant when it did. Ironic, the part that Steve played in my resolve last June never to get myself into the position where it might have happened…

…And KP continued to read the paper, not two feet away from the bed, where I lay on top of Steve, we unzipped each other's trousers, got our hands awkwardly inside and tossed each other off. But it left a feeling of (dare I quote Forster?) 'panic and emptiness'. Steve's present situation may require that sort of boyfriend; mine does not. (I think.) Animal warmth is no substitute for love. Going to bed with a boy is one thing, but I learnt long ago that there is no such thing as an intellectual ejaculation.

…And what the hell did KP think?!!

Before supper I went to play the piano in the Reception room. After a while the door opened. Tibby entered with a guitar. 'Damn, you're in here,' he said. 'I wanted this room.' After finishing the piece I was playing I stood up – I was very embarrassed (suppose Barney walked in?) – and walked towards the door.

'You're not going, are you?' said Tibby. I replied that I had been thinking of doing so – I had no wish to create a world homosexuality record – but the pathetic tone of his voice induced me to stay. I played Brahms to him, then, to my relief and embarrassment, Phil walked in. The expression on his face!

He saved the situation by sitting down and playing the piano himself, and after a few minutes Smith walked in. Seeing three of us he was less shocked. When the bell went for supper Tibby left first and I found myself having to explain to the other two how we'd found ourselves in the room together...

Supper was mediocre, after it I did History and Steve came down with some witty writing. After night prayers Steve went to talk to Barney about his own future, and I read the articles I'd contributed to the last school magazine again. My own genius never grows stale on me.

Friday March 13th

Good day. Saw Johnnie before breakfast about the morning's exam. Read the Epistle at Mass, not quite as well as usual, after listening to Easy Rider with Jagger and Chris, and then Rory and I began our exam in the Reception room. Not bad, but I was thirsty... A cup of coffee arrived, appreciated not only for itself but also for the spirit by whom it was brought, namely – unexpectedly – delightfully – Tibby.

Exam over, I ate lunch, did History, slept during Games, ate Tibby's fish at supper, (Tibby won't eat fish) and talked to Fr Cyprian during prep, about everything under the literary and university suns and had a capful of White Horse, which Fr Cyprian produced to my surprise, from a small bottle that had been given him as a present.

No prefects were in, so I took Night prayers, then watched The Forsytes with Steve, and left the TV room – 'Don't leave me,' called Chris, but we did – to go and find Johnnie. But The Grange was all locked up and we returned to my room, talked about the ideal summer term and Steve singed his hair on a candle. We put out the blaze quickly but the odour of frizzled hair remains. Now my arm aches, my eyes ache, I think I'll go to bed.

***

'Don't leave me,' called Chris, but we did. I can't believe I did that. To Chris, whom I love above everyone and everything. Does it have something to do with the fact that Steve and I have had sex together but Chris and I haven't? Is that how it works?

Sunday March 15th

I spent half the evening with Chris; we talked to Fr Malachy about our planned Easter visit to the monastery, then I talked to Steve, Chris and Jagger in varying combinations. Steve wants to join Chris and me at the monastery for Easter too…

March 16th

Today I said to Steve, 'I feel the same way as you do,' instead of, 'I think the same way as you do,' for the first time. Significant?

March 17th

Talked to Fr Cyprian and Jagger over coffee with an Old Etonian monastery guest, the Hon. Robert J. S. Montague-Wilberforce-Stewart. Then went to Fr Cyprian's room – it was St Patrick's Day after all – and got slightly intoxicated on homemade wine, talked about films, school, and this and that and the other, till we went over to the monastery and the Hon. Robert J. S.

Montague-Wilberforce-Stewart gave, or lent, me a cloak that had belonged to a certain Lord Nevus, then, wearing it, I returned to school. Chris is asleep. It is quarter to two. I have spent a good evening and feel slightly pissed. Never mind.

The cloak is nice. It has a high fur-lined collar and a half-cape. Both the cloak, which is black felt, and the half-cape, made of the same material, are lined in black silk, and it is fastened with a chain mounted on a pair of brass lions. It hangs to halfway down my calves and I look good in it.

March 18th

Not a good day. Awoke early but had rather a hangover. Whatever I did was wrong. The cloak, 'didn't suit me,' someone said. 'Everyone despises you,' said someone else. 'Don't get so het up,' someone else said, and, 'Almost an A in History.' Why is it always 'almost'? Chris went out in the evening.

I went out to the Foy Boat with Joe Davies, had a lager, some chips, and now, back at school, I prepare for bed, alone.

March 19th

Forced myself to get up. Down to Stella Maris with Chris and KP. Back again and Steve bragged about his abilities as a lawyer. I like him less. I walked out, put on my cloak and sulked till Steve came down. 'Would you come for a walk with me and KP?' he asked.

I like him more. 'Yes, of course.' We promenaded down on the lower promenade (I was wearing my cloak) and then, back at cliff-top level Steve and I sat down on a bench. KP left us, saying we looked sweet together. Did he know I had my arm round Stevie's waist?

Anyway, we looked at the sun through our eyelids and talked about the colours we saw and, deciding it was cold, spread the cloak over our two selves like a blanket. Steve laid his legs across mine, and what followed seemed natural, almost beautiful – certainly a happy experience…

While people walked their dogs up and down in front of us, probably sure that they could spot a case of homosexuality if they saw it (poor fools) and eventually we returned to school.

After lunch I went for a drink with Stevie, Chris, KP. Back at school I felt depressed (the others had gone bowling) so I went to sleep, and talked to Frankie till supper (curry) after which, down to the Foy Boat with Steve and Jagger, back for a school rules discussion with Fr Cyprian – who took away my cloak, which had been keeping me warm. (I have a hacking cough.) But apparently it hadn't been the Hon. Robert J. S. Montague-Wilberforce-Stewart's to lend me, let alone give me, in the first place.

Then I talked to Fr Malachy and Smith till I went to the latter's room and consumed an inordinate quantity of rough young wine. He was sick, but I enjoyed talking to hm. Now I'm rather sozzled.

Dear old Steve. Never have I been so fond of him. I simply don't understand the new turn our friendship has taken, perhaps he doesn't either!!

G'night. (P.S. Chris is away tonight.)

***

Later I wrote a more detailed account of the morning's adventure on the promenade bench, outside The Grange. It can easily be skipped by those who do not welcome gratuitous graphic sex scenes.

A visitor to the abbey had lent me – or Steve and me – a monastic cloak. I do mean a cloak. I don't mean the everyday Benedictine habit, consisting of tunic and hooded scapular worn on top. Nor the cowl that was worn in choir, a sort of over-tunic, pleated like an academic gown, with very full sleeves, and ankle-length like the habit it covered. The cowl was worn over the habit in choir, and had been for centuries, because choirs were cold and the Divine offices long. For this very reason the cowl might be replaced by a thick cloak on winter nights. This cloak was made of felt and lined with black silk. It had a half-cape around the shoulders, similarly lined, and a big thick collar. It was fastened with a brass chain attached to two lion-head brass bosses, but was otherwise open at the front. (It's the last fact that is the important one.) On our walk Steve and I were taking it in turns to wear the cloak, showing off to each other in it, swirling it around like a bullfighter's cape from time to time. Eventually we came to rest on a prom-side bench. I sat. Steve, who was wearing the cloak at that moment, sat, then lifted his legs and swung them round till he was lying along the bench, his legs across my lap, enfolded in the cloak. Although it was early morning, many people were passing by, walking their dogs.

I reached my hand into the overlap of the cloak and felt Stevie's stiff cock through his jeans. I opened the stud at the top and, pulling sideways, made the zip go down of its own accord. Going by feel only – my hand was inside the folded-over cloak so I couldn't see – I picked my way among shirt-front and underpants until I had Stevie's rigid cock in my hand. I knew it blindfold anyway by now. It was warm and lovely. About six inches long (so is mine) and quite slender, elegantly foreskin-hooded (unlike mine). It was chocolate in colour (I couldn't see this right then, but it usually was, and I didn't expect it to have changed overnight) with a sloe-dark glans. I reached out his little balls. They were always tightly clenched in their ball-sac, like a dark walnut, which always turned me on; they never hung down low in warm temperatures like my own and those of my English friends. (Something about the climate of his part of the world perhaps?) Stevie always boasted they were like the balls on Michelangelo statues. It was not an idle boast. They really were... I started to wank my friend. I went quite slowly. I had no idea how this was going down. I couldn't see his balls or cock and he was choosing to make his face an inscrutable mask. So I just tugged slowly on, while the ladies and gents of Thanet walked past with their dogs and either said Good morning or did not. I actually didn't realise when he'd shot. I didn't feel the wetness. He pumped out into his shirt and pants, wetting them rather than my friendly fist. Only when he said to me, 'What are you doing, Rafe?' did I realise that he'd emptied himself out and wanted me to stop. He reached inside the cloak himself to zip his jeans up, his juices left to dry in due course. We got up from the bench.

March 20th

In charge of school at breakfast.

March 21st

Late last night I went to see Jaggy, but told him to fuck off, which I didn't intend to. Then went to bed. Now the Easter holidays begin. I drove home, not feeling well. It is my three-quarterth birthday

March 24th

Thought hard about over-consciousness.

SIXTEEN

Have You Ever Been In Love?

Oct 14th 2014

Rather bizarrely, Ralph, Chris and Steve have decided to spend a week of their school holidays together in the monastery that lies just across the lawn from the school they are on holiday from. Over Easter each year the monastery hosts religious retreats for seriously religious people. The unholy trinity however have negotiated a special arrangement whereby they will enjoy something that is halfway between a retreat and a holiday. A reflection, perhaps, of their own uncertainties about their religious sides and about their triangular relationship...

March 25th 1970

Dreamed about Miss Jane L Essex in a turquoise trouser-suit. After lunch drove to Rye and caught the familiar train.

Thanet. Just the same as usual. I knocked on the great front door of the abbey and was shown up to the novices' room, where Father Peter, the novice master, was having tea with Brother Nuts. It was cold. The central heating had broken down.

After that I found Chris in the music room. We stayed there a while, listening to a man from Ceylon called Alfred playing the piano. He's a nice chap, on retreat over Easter. Then we walked over to the school and talked to Uncle Ron before monastery supper. Tinned crab with chips and tomatoes, bread and butter and an orange.

Saw Chris again in the school kitchen and Steve, not quite his usual self following a car crash in a friend's car. Surprisingly, Jagger was there too.

Everyone is going out, so I shall have to spend the night by myself.

I went to Compline in the Abbey church, talked to Fr Peter and a visiting priest and a bloke from South Wales, also both here on retreat, over hot chocolate. Rashly decided to get up at 6.30 tomorrow…

…Time I went to bed.

March 26th

Got up at 6.30. Fr Nicholas wished me the joy of my holiday at b'fast, and I went to Matins and Lauds in the Abbey church, tried to light a fire in the junior common room, after finding Chris, having coffee, and then we went to the mid-day Office, going through the tunnel beneath the road, then soup, pork chops with apple sauce, and jam tart.

After lunch we were driven to Minster and met the nuns of the abbey there. The sisters are addressed not as sister but as Dame. The prioress, whom we didn't meet, is Dame Walburga, and the guest mistress is Dame Concordia, a likeable artistic woman who creates statues in alabaster. Back to our own abbey in time for tea.

Maundy Thursday liturgy in the Abbey church. Chris and I read the Epistles. Teddy was in the congregation and so – astonishingly – was Zebedee. After that there was kippers for very late supper, and a talk about monasticism in the novices' room with other retreatants. That thinned out eventually to 'our lot'; we finally dispersed at 12.15 and Steve, the past master of the parting shot told me I was too arrogant for university.

That is true, I know, but it is not the real reason why I did not get in. It is now March 27th, and like a fool I decided to get up early again tomorrow.

Good Friday March 27th

Awoke. Had hot cross buns. Attended Matins but skipped Lauds. The altar is lit with Tenebrae candles. They have been going down in number all week. Today only one last flame flickers among the shadows. Tomorrow the church will be entirely dark, until the Paschal candle is re-lit at midnight as Easter begins. I wasn't expecting the feelings that this gives me.

I went and found Chris and talked to him, woke Stevie up, and the two of them went off to chop wood for kindling while I spent hours trying to get a fire going in the junior common room. Damp wood, bad coke, and Fr Cyprian.

The abbot gave us a talk about God, a caterpillar named James, and Thomas Aquinas.

Fish for lunch that might have been shark, in a sauce that might have been emulsion paint. However, it's Good Friday and penitential fare is the order of the day. Choir practice with Brother Hilary and then I went to an excruciating parish service in the church. Teddy was there, and Uncle Ron, and Zebedee. I talked to Zebedee. He had found the service excruciating too. He has stopped applying for headmaster jobs, and is hoping to become a railway signalman.

Tea-time, music, and I pottered in the monastery library before the frugalest supper ever. It was Barney's turn to do the washing-up. Fr Peter told Barney that I wanted to watch him do this, but in the end it was Steve who attended this spectacle, while doing the drying.

We read Bible extracts in preparation for a church service, and then went over the road to The Grange, had an interesting discussion which continued in the novices' common room and finally in the kitchen. It was getting late. Steve and I ate bits of bread, said G'night to Chris, talked about how much we were enjoying this new experience, then I said Goodnight to Steve. It's midnight.

Jagger was thinking of joining us here. In the end I'm rather glad he didn't. It's complicated enough already.

***

It's curious, seeing the priests I know in their roles as my school teachers at home in their other roles as Benedictine monks. Father Cyprian, my form master in form five, now housemaster at Number Three. Father Malachy, director of all our school plays, and teacher on our English course wherever plays are involved. John Arden, RC Sheriff... Father Sebastian also teaches on our English course. Virginia Woolf is his speciality. Nobody ever walks out of his, or Fr Malachy's, classes.

And Barney doing the washing up... He's our headmaster, for God's sake! No wonder Fr Peter thought it worth winding him up about my wanting to watch him with his hands among the soap suds. Father Peter, now the novice master... For years he was our Latin teacher, and our Religious Instruction teacher.

During a Latin class on Virgil's Aeneid, three years ago, in which Fr Peter was talking about different Latin words for love, and the subtle differences between them, I took it into my head to interrupt by blurting out to Fr Peter: 'Have you ever been in love?' Fr Peter blushed a dark plum colour and his blue eyes stood out like priceless china about to be broken. A boy called Ben, a foot-balling friend, and someone I'd known since we were six – long before this school, in my home town of Rye – called out, 'Hey no, you don't ask that!' and there were murmurs of support for Fr Peter throughout the room. It was my turn to blush, knowing I'd behaved like a turd. I was silent for the rest of the class, and Fr Peter, who now had no need to answer my question, went on to give one of the best classes I ever saw him give. He didn't look at me for the rest of that lesson. He didn't need to. In a way I'm surprised he's so generous with me now.

But that's the Benedictine way. You turn the other cheek. You share your cloak. You walk the second mile. And when the boss says, 'I know you're a wonderful teacher, but now we need you to take responsibility to train up novice monks in the monastery,' or, 'You've been wonderful at dealing with the monastery's share portfolio, saving us the cost of a stockbroker, but now we need you to run a medical mission in Africa and dig wells,' you have to do it.

Fr Malachy told me that a very old monk had once told him – on the subject of the three vows that all monks take on the day they are professed: Poverty, Chastity, and Obedience – that the pains of Poverty and Chastity were nothing compared to the frustration of Obedience.

Holy Saturday March 28th

Just about got up this morning. Breakfast and Matins as usual. The church movingly dark, as the Tenebrae candles are now all extinguished.

Then I lit the fire, helped move an armoire and washed up. Coffee followed, a talk from the abbot followed that, then it was the Midday Office, and sausages for lunch. At which I arrived late.

After lunch we went to Canterbury. 'Have you been driven by Brother Hilary before?' asked Fr Malachy. 'It's an experience.'

It was: we contemplated death all afternoon. We scratched the paintwork before even leaving the monastery grounds, had difficulty parking in Canterbury, but got to the Cathedral at evensong time. Steve and I did pull-ups on the window bars in the cloisters, lost the others, found them again and drove dangerously back, holding up a wedding procession while Fr Sebastian nipped into a shop to buy bread, and got back in time for a vital cup of tea and an erudite lecture on the history of monasticism in Thanet given by Fr Dunstan. Then I had a bath, and supper (Stevie and I arrived late) at which were boiled eggs. Then I watched the Hon. Robert J. S. Montague-Wilberforce-Stewart playing the organ in the Abbey church, which he does very well, and prepared my reading for the evening.

An interesting discussion about prayer and Other Things, which I need not describe at length, because nothing unusually unusual occurred.

Over to the church. The usual people were there. The service proved interesting. I sat next to Steve. Chris and I read the Lessons. At midnight the Paschal candle was lit and the church blazed again with light. The service finished with the Lauds of Easter morning.

Now Chris has just been in to my room to say Goodnight, so I take the hint and, seeing both hands of my watch neatly composed over the figure one... G'night.

Sunday March 29th. Easter Day

It was nine o'clock when I arrived in the refectory for eggs and bacon breakfast. After that I helped wash up and prepared a reading – Chris had another – for the morning Mass. Chris and I sat together at the back, read 'admirably adequately;, couldn't help laughing as the Hon. Robert J. S. Montague-Wilberforce-Stewart read a

Bidding Prayer for 'all the Royal Family,' took the bread and wine up to the altar with Chris at the Offertory, and then sang 'Battle Is Over, Hell's armies flee', rather too loudly, so that half the congregation turned round and looked at the two of us.

Then we went with Steve to the Regency where I had one and a half pints of beer and an assortment of pickles, and returned to the monastery to more beer and then turkey, Danish blue cheese, etc…

Up to now our meals have been taken in silence, with readings to listen to, but on big feasts like today the rule is relaxed, so I talked during lunch to Father Sebastian and Father Cyprian about the lack of intense personal relationships in monastic life, about intellectual discipline, about Johnnie, Barney, and Fr Nicholas.

After lunch a sherry and a Spanish brandy. I talked a lot to Barney about my stay here, Zebedee, Steve and our pull-ups in Canterbury Cathedral. Barney wasn't entirely happy about that last one.

Then I talked with Fr Nicholas until we were the only people left in the room. We discussed theatre, monastic life, corporal punishment. He remembers me quite well now. Later he referred to our conversation as, 'being told how I should have run the school.'

Then we all went to the Bon Secours convent, had two sherries, I gave Steve a rather public hug, had tea, and a ghastly meringue that sent Brother Hilary into more than usually hilarious hysterics. Then back to the abbey for Vespers. After that the church was empty, and I took the opportunity to try out the organ. I played a Brahms waltz, then, finding a hymnal handy, embarked on Oh Come All Ye Faithful, for a joke, not realizing that the church was now filling up with people coming for the evening Easter Mass. Father Ethelbert put his head round the curtain and politely asked me to stop. Oh dear.

Supper was a good turkey salad, followed by a chat in the community room. A mystery piece of music had been played at supper. It was a sort of violin concerto and rather weird and wonderful. In the community room we were all asked if we could guess the composer. Nobody could. Fr Sebastian smiled and revealed the answer. It was the *Symphonie Espagnole* by Edouard Lalo. A Spanish piece by a Frenchman. I'd heard of neither the piece nor the composer, but will try and hear it again.

Compline was quite good. Then I read a humorous poem I'd written about the Bishop to Brother Hilary and others, and we went to a discussion. Left at ten o'clock, returned, had a glass of beer with Fr Sebastian in the kitchen, then returned to my room at the early hour of 11.30.

Steve and Chris have gone out drinking with a dreadful chap called Cyril, who they don't really like any more than I do.

-) I thought a lot today about personal relationships, some particular ones in particular, and concluded that I could not reach a conclusion. Alleluia. -)

March 30th

Woke up with indigestion and made toast for breakfast. Ate it.

Read about medieval monasteries in the library. Felt ill. The others are in bed. Washed up and went for a walk with Bro Hilary in the rain. Somebody burned the soup and the Hon. Robert J. S. Montague-Wilberforce-Stewart and I got thuribles from the sacristy and, swinging them as we walked, we incensed the kitchen and nearby corridors.

Midday Office in the church. Lunch not bad – cold meat and ice-cream. Recreation afterwards.

After more time in the library went with Chris an Steve to Fr Sebastian's aunt for tea, and then Fr Sebastian took Chris and me to his aunt's friend, Mrs Churl, for a sherry.

Fr Sebastian had told us we would find Mrs Churl an interesting study in refined elderly womanhood, and we did. She told us she found the public library increasingly off-putting. 'The books are so dirty,' she complained. 'I borrowed one the other day and found someone had used a rasher of cooked bacon as a bookmark.'

Chris said afterwards, 'If you *did* leave a bacon rasher in a library book, she's exactly the sort of person you'd hope would find it.'

Back in time for supper, a sad meal with cheese on toast and ham, etc, and an apple.

Went to Compline and sat with Chris.

Went over to the school TV room to watch The Hound of the Baskervilles. Returned with Steve through the labyrinthine corridors of the monastery boiler room. We enjoyed each other's proximity on that journey through the dark. A touching scene ensued…

Had a cup of Horlicks and the old depression returned. Conversation with Fr Sebastian and Steve in the former's room did not improve matters.

(So much for an early night: Chris came in and we talked for an hour and a half. It is now 12.30.)

***

A little about the Hon. Robert J. S. Montague-Wilberforce-Stewart. He's in his late twenties, I suppose. Very tall and slim and, I suppose, reasonably good-looking, with attractive thick brown hair. He claims to be descended from one of the illegitimate children of Charles II. That's why Chris and I laughed in church when he asked us to pray for, 'all the Royal Family.'

There's something slightly odd about him though. He seems to pose a bit, and you think you're getting close to him only to find that you're not. I imagine Oscar Wilde might have been a bit like that.

Monasteries have a duty to take in people who request their hospitality – within reason, of course. But it does mean some quite odd people turning up. Not so long since the American Vietnam veteran, Guy Kent, was here. After his lecture to us – which was very interesting: he told us that when you get shot it feels like being whacked hard with a baseball or cricket bat; I'd always imagined a more piercing sort of pain than that… Anyway, he disappeared pretty smartly after that, and no-one seems to have heard from him since.

March 31st

Today's entry was to have been a dramatic and hammy account of why I decided to close this diary, but as the best way seems to me now (slightly less depressed) to be to continue the diary, I shall do this and *carissimus lector* can see for himself why this diary should have gone *tacet* some time ago.

(For readers who find my Latin irritating, carissimus lector *means dearest reader, and* tacet *translates as: it is silent.)*

Rising early, Steve and I (still recovering from seeing old Bro Harold in his underpants) sang Matins and Lauds in choir, made toast and coffee with Chris – poor Bro Hilary is ill in bed, some sort of chill after our walk in the rain, I suppose – had breakfast, then pottered in the library, felt depressed and lay down on my bed, went to the bank with Chris and £500 (all in coppers, to judge by the weight) and stopped off at the Foy Boat on the way back for a pint or two.

Shepherd's pie for lunch, then we all drove to Minster, met Dame Walburga, and then Steve proposed to a married woman in the street while all the rest of us nearly died of embarrassment. Back at the abbey, Chris and I took a photo of each other on the lawn, then I went to look for Steve, finding him in his room.

'Take a pew,' he said. He was lying on his bed as it happened, wearing underpants and shirt but no trousers or socks and I automatically joined him. We lay in each other's arms for some time, discovered erections tenting each other's pants and then dealt with them in a businesslike way. After we had both come Stevie held me, lying on top of me, and said, 'Poor Ralphie,' as he stroked my head. Why poor Ralphie, for heaven's sake? Why not poor Stevie?

Brother Nuts saw me coming out of Steve's room, closing the door behind me and told me that it was part of the Rule of St Benedict that two people were not allowed in a room alone together with the door shut. (Yes, dear Bro Nuts, but imagine the scandal if we'd left the door open!)

Pilchards for supper. Talked to Chris, Fr Cyprian, Bro Hilary, watched TV spasmodically, and sat on Chris's bed talking till now – 12.00. Only this last began to cheer me up (but I see there is no room for more sentimentality. This particular notebook has come to the end of its last page.)

April 1st

New jotter.

Woken up. Got up. Woke Chris up. Had a bite of breakfast and played April Fools on the monks with Chris. Lunch was cod and then we said Goodbye to everyone and Steve and I caught the train. Chris was going to hitch-hike. I got a little less depressed on the journey. Mother met us at Rye, and I drove us all home. Chris turned up in time for supper and we talked most of the evening, and listened to Mahler. Then carried on talking to Chris in bed. He and I have the two beds in my room, Steve is in the spare.

April 2nd

Up less early. Drove to Northiam and to the village shop, (the 'City Stores'). In the afternoon we went to Battle Abbey. We were given a tour by a student from Worcester College, Oxford. It was interesting, and he had enviable sideboards. Drive to Rye and to Wittersham, and back at home in the evening listened to Mahler again. We were all rather tired and didn't talk much.

April 3rd

Woken by Mother at 1 a.m. She's fallen out of bed and injured herself. I put her back to bed with Aspirin. In the morning I explained to Chris and Steve. We cooked breakfast together and washed up. (Chris misheard my instruction to use a cap-full of washing-up liquid, and used a cup-full. The suds filled the kitchen.) Because of the situation Chris and Steve decided to leave soon, and hitch-hike back into Kent to Steve's girlfriend's place. Soon after they'd gone the doctor came, and diagnosed cracked ribs. I drove off to the surgery to collect some medicine and when I got back Chris and Steve phoned from Northiam, the next village. They hadn't been lucky with lifts. I drove out to them, only too happy to do so, and took them to Tenterden, where I left them thumbing a lift towards Ashford.

Before they left, the post came. There was a long, almost hysterical, letter from Father Malachy. He warned me and Steve against further contact with the Hon. Robert J. S. Montague-Wilberforce-Stewart. That this is not his real name, and he is not a safe person to know... I started reading this letter out in my mother's bedroom when the others went in to say goodbye, but had to skip the awkward bit. Afterwards Chris and Steve and I scratched our heads over it. We'll have to wait now till term starts before we can get to the bottom of it.

Cooked supper for Mother and me and ate it in her bedroom, listening to the radio. Then played the piano till bedtime. No Chris or Steve to sleep with tonight.

Earlier Mother said, 'Your friend Chris is very good-looking.'

'Mmm,' I said non-committally.

'Luscious eyes,' she said.

'Mmm?' I said, as if I hadn't really noticed them.

SEVENTEEN

The Roofs of the World

April 21st

Back to school. Father Malachy is the new housemaster, and resident in Zebedee's old room in Number One. Chris is already back. Tibby has had a haircut. The refectory has been repainted…

Supper wasn't too bad. To the pub afterwards. Principally with Chris, but Jagger and practically everybody else was there as well. Two pints, two sherries and a malt whisky. After all, it is my ten twelfths birthday.

Back to a meeting with Malachy, who hasn't got his carpet down yet, or any chairs. He, and all the rest of us, sat on the floor. Steve turned up finally and squeezed in between Chris and me on the bare boards.

Down to the Regency. One pint. Chris's new girlfriend was there. Then we went back to see Malachy for a private chat. To ask about the Hon. Robert J. S. Montague-Wilberforce-Stewart. By 1.30 we (Steve, Chris and I) had heard the whole sad story of Tom Stubbes, adopted, schizophrenic, homosexual, forger of cheques, Associate of the Royal College of Organists, and book thief. He had been caught, finally, selling books from the monastery library. He lived in a shabby room in a queer house with the bogus Lord Nevus, kept a diary of his love life – which he believed had some literary merit – and impersonated priests at convents. Poor old Robert! He is relieved of the strain of pretending to be someone else and is awaiting trial in Brixton prison.

One community of nuns whose silver and priceless volumes he had stolen were less worried about that than the fact that he – pretending to be a visiting priest – had given them Holy Communion, with wafers that he of course hadn't the power to consecrate. But at least I was right about the quality of his organ playing. There was nothing phony about that.

April 22nd

Up early, but with a headache. Sixth-form meeting with Barney at nine o'clock, who looked me in the eye with an amused twinkle once or twice as he made rather pointed references to the conversation I'd had with him on Easter Day, and then, chatted all morning till pub time, two pints with KP and Chris and then lunch, talking to Daniel, then House meeting with Malachy – who was very Malachian. Then I went up to Steve's room, which was full of people, and fell asleep on his bed. On waking I found the room empty except for Steve, and lying down together we did what Alex used to call *'that'* and afterwards I left.

I did an hour and a half's piano practice including something unexpected: Vaughan has given me the second piano part for the opera he's doing. (All the King's Men, by Richard Rodney Bennett. Chris has a part in it, I didn't really want one.) The idea for me to share the four hands piano part with the new piano teacher, Kevin Collyer. It's easy but a bit dull without the other instruments and … there's fifty pages of it!

April 24th

Working, was kept waiting an hour by Beefballs, was waved at by Tibby from the top of the main school stairs, practised the Ascension Day hymn that we're going to sing on the roof, wondered whether this diary is worth keeping, slept in the afternoon, practised the piano for two and a half hours solid, had a magazine committee meeting, at which Chris's story, 'Hell, It Hurts', was read and discussed, and worked a little late.

Oh yes, and I lost the Bidding Prayer I was supposed to read at Mass, and having already stood up, had to make one up on the spot.

April 27th

Didn't get to sleep till past midnight…

Chris had a driving lesson; I drank his coffee. I read about architecture most of the day, and played my opera duets with new piano teacher Keven Collyer, who didn't think I was too bad.

Steve spent most of the day with Chris.

I took junior prep in The Grange, and helped Tibby with his Latin; he was sitting in the front desk for a change. I confiscated a bottle of shampoo and forgot to give it back afterwards, now I feel a fool carting it around in my pocket.

Paolo held quite a successful form meeting about haircuts. I worked a bit late, talked to Chris, opened a bottle of wine… it is now past midnight. Good night.

Before choir practice I found Tibby also waiting to see Vaughan. After talking to him for a bit I noticed a Stella Maris kid looking at me hard, who then plucked up courage to ask: 'Are you Charlotte Williams's boyfriend?' (He was one of that large family himself.) And what he said next was too flattering to be genuine so I won't record it, though it made Tibby open his blue eyes very wide and suggest that this was quite out of character.

… The waterfight season opened.

April 30th

Today was the first lie-in-the-grass day. I talked to
Jagger and Frankie about university, and we invented a
new kind of degree course – one that led to a B.O.

Curry for supper.

Opera rehearsal. Felt very inferior sitting beside
Kevin Collyer, but didn't have to play much, balancing
the music on my lap, and had a cup of tea afterwards.

S. Maugham's 'Jane' on TV. Priceless.

Glass of wine with Chris before bed.

Saturday May 2nd

I had one of my increasingly rare conversations with
Smith. We walked down to the harbour, looked at the
ships. I still have one sixteenth of a mind to be a sailor –
and it was slightly sunny. Smith told me that Robert J. S.
Montague-Wilberforce-Stewart had fallen in love with
him over Easter and they'd had sex together. Smith is a
darker horse than I'd ever have thought, despite knowing
him closely for nine years

May 3rd

Sunday. Didn't go to the pub but went to sleep on
Steve's bed

Cyprian lent me a copy of The Once and Future King
by T.H. White. He thinks I ought to read it, but quickly,
as he wants it back. It's a new copy that he's got in order
to give to Tom Stubbes, alias the not entirely
Honourable Robert J. S. Montague-Wilberforce-Stewart,
who has requested it. When he goes to visit him in
Brixton prison.

May 4th

I read The Once and Future King till 6 a.m. when, after a picnic of sandwiches at 1, being frightened by a poultergeist at 4, heard the birds singing at 4.30, walked on the prom at 5 and, deciding against Matins in the Abbey church, lay down on my bed ... where I awoke in time for breakfast.

Mrs Pring was very frank this morning. She told Chris and me that her husband only makes love to her twice a year. Poor woman. Considering that she's over thirty she's very attractive, and amazingly well preserved for her age. The sun shone. I watched someone tip a bucket of water over KP, who was sunbathing on the roof of Number One in his gym shorts – he wasn't very pleased – and then lay up there myself, slantwise on the hot slates, my feet resting across the gulley against the inner wall of the parapet.

Cyprian told us that Guy Kent, the American soldier who talked to us at General Studies, was also wanted by the police, on behalf of the Americans. He's a Vietnam deserter, apparently. (Come to the abbey and see the underworld.)

Thursday May 7th

Ascension Day. Whole Holiday.

Rory woke me at quarter to seven and I made my way to the main school where people clustered, looking like people that have got up earlier than usual, which is what they were. We all had a cup of tea, including Chris who had come to take photos, and trooped up onto the roof. Tenors and basses were me, Rory, Fr Cyprian, Smith, and Todger. Charlotte's little brother was one of the dozen altos and sopranos. Mr Vaughan conducted. People stood below, looking up, rather bored and disconsolate, and Fr Cyprian read a Collect. We sang, the speakers distorted it, and only the sopranos were audible. Still, it made a change.

After breakfast we went back up on the roof for a press photo, then it was Mass time. Our gang had the choir loft, Chris and I sharing the organ seat.

Did fuck all for the rest of the morning, but after lunch we went down to Stella Maris in the Moke, to repeat the morning's performance there, on the cloister roof. A toilet flushed while Cyprian was reading his Collect. The whole thing was a slight anticlimax. Cyprian, Rory, Chris and I all got back in Vaughan's open topped, two-seater Triumph Spitfire, wedged behind the seats and hanging on for dear life. Nothing like an open car for sorting out those who can grow proper sideboards from those that can't.

Chris slept all afternoon. I tried to, but every time I dropped off, someone would come in, even people who never come in, like Boing. Even Mrs Pring's pickled onions proved an ineffective deterrent. (Steve now calls Chris and me The Onion Eaters, after the book by J.P. Donleavy.)

Spaghetti for supper. Our table last. I ate mine too quickly, trying not to be late for opera rehearsal. Only afterwards did I realize I had given Tibby a friendly pat on the back while talking to him in the refectory queue. I'd been trying not to do that.

May 8th

Friday. Sixth form Mass in the Abbey. Then work. I lay on the roof under a vaulting blue sky, lost my fear of heights, the sun shone, and we did History. I wrote for a job on the car ferry at Dover, and practised the piano. Mr Roland-Butter took over, and played bits of The Gondoliers off the top of his head, then snatches of the

Emperor Concerto, and Take Five. I can't do that. Play by ear, or from memory. By supper time quite a crowd had collected. About twenty people.

I at last showed Rory the cartoon I'd done of him a year and a half ago, with him standing on Alex's bent back, holding reins. 'Poor old Alex,' was what Rory said, but I wonder what he really made of it. (Alex had once taken a photo of Rory's erect prick, with a notice hanging from it that said Reserved, though I have never seen this photo.)

Saturday May 9th

An unexpected delicacy: real tomatoes instead of tinned at breakfast. Sent off to Channel ferry companies. We went to the pub. Then Steve made passionate love to Chris. Then we all stripped naked and threw a bucket of water over Steve. Then we had a waterfight.

Tibby has re-christened me: Fred.

I slept on the roof in the sunshine, awoke with a headache, tried to do History, and in the end did two hours' King's Men piano practice, while Roland-Butter typed and chatted to me.

Supper was a muddy leek. Most people were out.

Steve has chucked his girlfriend. We had a wearisome post-mortem…

…After the pub closed at eleven we all drove to Joss Bay, by the lighthouse, and pissed around on the beach. Of course Steve had to be immersed in the sea, I shinned up to the top of a flag pole, and somebody else banged a slut we'd picked up, behind some rocks. We talked French and sang. No fuzz joined the party. We returned with a red road-works lantern. Now it is quarter to one. Over and out. – Fred.

May 11th

Steve invented a quiz, or rather an opinion poll, so we all took questionnaires around the seniors and the staff. More atheists among the latter, staff touchy about saying who they vote for, Barnabas approves the liberalisation of the homosexuality laws... What to do with the results caused much argument with Steve, me and Chris.

Jagger hasn't spoken to me since Saturday.

May 12th

Mrs Pring has been expecting her father to die. But he has not died. To her own surprise she now suddenly believes in God.

We had a meeting about the opinion poll and a new idea for a radical magazine – to be called Alpha. This provoked a lot of argument. Chris was eventually persuaded to accept the necessary *via mediocrita*: which is my idea, grudgingly approved by all but liked, inevitably, by none. But at least unity is maintained. The opinion poll and survey reveals a large proportion of Catholic atheists, which is interesting. No work done, as usual. Further meetings. Talk to Uncle Ron. What to put in the new magazine, Alpha? Who to write it?

There was a waterfight after supper, and returning from the main school to Number One at bedtime, I heard a scratching noise and looking down – I was climbing the doorsteps – I saw a figure crouched over a stone, scratching it. A pair of big brown eyes looked up and smiled, and it proved to be Chris, sharpening darts. I sat down beside him and while we were talking a woman looked in along the alleyway from Grange Road. Chris made a noise, she looked again, and one of her older companions said, from the street, 'Don't go near the Abbey; you'll get raped. I'm not joking!'

May 13th

We waterfought after lunch, till Malachy put a stop to it, and in the afternoon I read the History of the Papacy on the sunny slates with KP and Barry M, an ice-lolly and Steve. Braver now, I can sit on the parapet with my legs dangling over the road three floors below, no hands holding.

Later I found Frankie and Bernie digging in a neighbour's garden, joined them, and helped them carry a barrel of earth and purloined tulip bulbs into their basement room. It nearly fills the place, stands like a beer keg on a table, with a tap to release excess moisture. Frankie has to draw a tulip for A-level Art. Hence the preparations...

I dug a huge luxuriant weed out of the front garden and flung it into the road to see what would happen. It landed in the path of a car, which swerved, hooted and looked daggers at me. Most of its successors – who included Zebedee of all people! – skirted it, and after supper about ten of us witnessed the first attempt of a valiant motorist to flatten it. By bedtime it was well and truly laid low.

There is going to be a General Erection on June 18th. Three days before I'm old enough to vote – on the 21st. Four days before Rory turns eighteen, too. I mentioned this to Barney, who was watching the news too. He laughed.

Chris returned from an interview with the Foreign Office. He is not suicidal, though 'he has good cause, I admit'. They have told him to wait another year and apply again.

May 14th

And today I got a rejection letter from British Rail Ferries. *Rejected by British Rail!*

I got the book of Kenneth Clarke's TV series, Civilisation, from the library. Slept for ten minutes in the afternoon, was awoken by Daniel, then Jagger asked me to clip his right thumbnail, so we're friends again.

May 15th

Townsend Ferries have sent me an application form, and advice to join the National Union of Semen! Bravo!

School photo was taken. Traditionally chaotic and absurd. Otherwise a depressing day. It is a fallacy that joyless labour induces happiness by itself.

Between everyone there are stone walls. We hear muffled voices, feel vibrations, but what are other people really like? Even our closest friends are sealed off. What are Chris and Steve? Who are the people in the past? Alex? My Father? And we are all haunted by the idea that perhaps, beyond our own stone cubicle, all the walls are down, and all is one. Communication and celebration are rife, outside. We are… I am… the only isolated one. And we must not cry out from inside our stone-walled space – we are English, after all. So we can never rid of ourselves of that sneaking suspicion that we are unique in our isolation.

Question: what, then, is marriage?

(R. McKean pseuds off left; the lights fade, the curtain closes. The audience applauds, and pretend that they appreciated the drama. Sad.)

EIGHTEEN

Abnormal Desire To Be Constructive...

And Sharing the Roof with Rory

Saturday May 16th

Last night Chris and I had a long talk about depression, Steve, and mediocrity. We both felt rotten in the morning, slept long and got up at 11.15, after a cup of coffee with Frankie and Bernie in the basement, and after I'd dreamed about an archetypal Going Home scene, crossing the new-mown hay at Wittersham with Chris and – I'm not sure who the other person was, and taming a pair of young crows, observing the blossom and the birds and reaching the cottage I was born in, which seemed now a bit glorified. There was clean washing on the line there; there seemed to be a wife...

...Then I was studying for an exam at Stella Maris with Steve, then I dreamt that so much had to be done before spending a day in bed that, for the heavily booked businessman I was dreaming about (the future me?) it was just not worth the bother.

Dull day. Read Civilisation, wrote up my dream about the businessman, washed my hair. Everyone Out. Depression. My abnormal desire to be constructive took over and I started to make metal heel-taps for my worn heels, borrowing tools from Bro George, wrenching bits of brass off a library cupboard.

Talked to Johnnie throughout prep, about this, that and the other and, when Chris and Steve returned from the pub – they were thoroughly depressed – I got worse than ever and, Oh Christ, we're still moping. All three of us. Nearly midnight. I wish I could return to that dream world of last night. I wish Steve was accepted as Stephen, I wish Chris was what he ought to be, I wish I was either a person or a symbol, not the half-and-half botch-up I am at the moment.

(What was that about? One of those locked boxes, of which memory has thrown away the key?)

Curried eggs for supper.

Sunday May 17th

Chris and I had been invited to lunch in the monastery (last year it had been Jagger, who had invited me along) and we wended our way there. Almost like coming home, we said. And the routine was as usual. I had two glasses of Gigondas, Brother Nuts to talk to, and – I suppose at a pinch you could call it a five-course meal – grapefruit, soup, turkey, pudding and cheese.

At recreation afterwards Father Angelo (a visiting priest from Italy) told me that he didn't like my hair, that I hadn't got a proper face, that my waistcoat and watch and chain looked eugh!... Nice chap, Fr Angelo.

We talked to Cyprian quite a lot, then Cyprian took me over to the Abbey church, and gave me an insider's tour of it – every part of it, from Abbot Taylor's chapel to the organ pipes, and up into the tower, approached by spiral staircases. As one goes up one looks down into the church and onto the tie-beams, becomes aware that Pugin made the whole thing out of bricks, and that the stonework and knapped flints are actually facings, both inside the building and out. Finally climbed a tiny iron ladder, poked our heads out onto the rimless roof, scaring the seagulls who were perched there, and admiring the uninterrupted view of town and school, sea and – was that a tiny trace of countryside in the distance? And – where was I? – had a long talk about Tibby when we got back to school, and Jagger joined us (I found we were on comfortably casual speaking terms), and we talked about homosexuality and generally spent a good evening.

Later Rory and I made a raid on the kitchen. Rory was clad in only a towel, which wasn't the most suitable thing to go window-climbing in, but never mind. And although the larder opened very nicely with a plastic card, stocks were low and biscuits, whole biscuits, and nothing but biscuits were forthcoming.

***

I realised later that when Fr Angelo said I didn't have a proper face he was using the word in the Italian sense, meaning, appropriate or suitable. He meant it wasn't the right kind of face for long hair. Which is just a matter of opinion. So that was all right.

May 20th

Chris said, would I go with him to see The Mikado. It took a bit of persuading on his part but in the end I said yes and after an early supper we walked through the wind to the Granville Ballroom. Everyone was there. Vaughan and the music set were in the orchestra. Barney was there with Mr and Mrs Roland-Butter. Cyprian was there with the fourth form. There was Smith...

Ghastly production. Vaughan, Cyprian and us went for a drink in the interval, and another one after. Despite topical references to the coming general election etc: 'It doesn't really matter who you put upon your list, they'd none of them be missed, they'd none of them be missed...' and of course 'the student anarchist, the Sunday columnist', etc, the evening was a bore – except for the twisted cue and elliptical billiard balls and the caricature of a face.

Barney said to me, 'Keep off acting.' I call him Father in conversation. I may as well listen to him as one.

Back at school we listened to King Crimson in Frankie's room, more than ever convinced of its distinction, and now – bed.

(Have just re-read diary entry for March 13th. I can't believe it. A geological erratic, I suppose. To walk out of a room after Chris – of all people – had called me back. Never again will I miss the chance of being called back – by anyone. But have you forgotten, Rafe – you didn't walk out of the door alone.)

May 21st

Drink to celebrate my eleven twelfths birthday. Bible. Civilisation. Daniel. Sunbathing. Chris leaned forward and gave me a penny. Opera. Jagger with damp, mildew, library and church tower. April shower. Some soaked. Chocolate spilt. Cyprian soaked. Rory. Rory on diplomacy and homosexuality. Chris joined in. Given up work. New diary style. Success? No. Chuck it.

May 22nd

Rory and I prevailed on one of the dayboys to drive us to the Westgate convent. We went, had a cup of coffee with Charlotte and others, and we came back with a note to give to Charlotte's brother.

Then we rolled up to Johnnie's room, climbing over the wall, up the fire escape and in through his window, and had an informal meeting. In the middle of it I had to open the window to let Tibby in. He was returning late from an outing with his parents.

Johnnie was a little shocked by my turning cartwheels on the floor and handstands on his bed, and Rory explained, with one of his raised-eyebrow smiles, that he and I tended to get uncontrollable sometimes.

(I liked the way he said that, and wondered where it might be leading.)

Saturday May 23rd

Very ill till three o'clock this morning, but got up for lousy breakfast on a beautiful morning. Discovered half term didn't start till 12 but left at 9 all the same and drove home.

I left home in winter. Now it is high summer: the grape vine is pushing through, the roses want pruning, the grass cutting. I did those things, and worked at History, and learned Ecclesiastes.

In the evening mother and I listened to 'Steve's' Mozart piano concerto.

Steve's piano concerto. It's Mozart's one in D minor. The lovely slow movement. It makes me think of Steve – of his gentler side anyway. I've listened to it with him, while holding him in my arms on the sofa last time he was down here on a visit, and told him I always thought of him when I listened to it. He was very moved by that. Not that he said so. But I felt it in the stirring of his arms and body as I held him.

Sunday May 24th

Home-made quote today. 'No man may hope to become adult: he can at most pray to become adolescent in old age.'

(I think Steve may quite like that. Hope so anyway.)

May 25th

Beautiful day. I had a viola lesson with mother, my first.

In the afternoon I sat in the sun, reading Civilisation, interspersed with chopping down and cutting up a dead lilac tree. After bottling beer in the evening, we walked down the lane toward Miss Bennett's cottage to listen for the nightingales. But there were none, and after a chat with Miss Bennett, we returned under the first star, me throwing stones at a bat, the sun having set in a magnificent shower of sparks behind Northiam church.

May 26th

Septic tank was dredged in the morning. In the afternoon drove back to school. Surprised to see KP with his parents looking at the view over a gate near Wittersham. Looked at a Queen Anne house near Minster, called Sevenscore. It's a perfect building, a 'gentleman's' farmhouse set among cherry orchards. Of ruddy brick and roofed with tile. Five equally spaced, white-framed sash windows are set in the front wall at first-floor level. Below them another four flank the centrally placed front door. Around the door a thick-grown winter jasmine forms a topiary door-frame and pediment. Beneath the eaves the closely spaced rafter ends are visible, painted white, so that they resemble a line of pearls. I could live there happily.

May 27th

Chris is asleep in bed. I've returned from listening to Leonard Cohen with Cyprian, after returning early from a packed pub to which I had wended my way with Chris and partaken of beer and malt whisky. I had some chips and onions on the way back and, finding the school's back door locked, returned to Number One via the bike-sheds roofs.

This morning I took the magazine to the printers, saw Zebedee downtown, and went to the pub with dayboys for sherry and beer, after some French wine with Chris.

Sat behind Tibby at the Speech Contest and talked to him about Mrs Lodge, who is, of course, his great-aunt. Good old Lodge. Good old Tibby too, who recited The Hoorgi House by Ivor Cutler: the best among the juniors' performances. Chris's younger brother did well too, but got no medal.

Smith did a sketch by Fr Sebastian – At Your Convenience – which was very witty. Ed did 'Oh that this too, too solid flesh would melt' from Hamlet, Chris did a modern poem, and O'Dowd got the silver medal for a piece by Dylan Thomas.

I have never played to a boreder audience, but no worse than I expected. Lodge praised my daring to sit in an armchair and say my pieces from Ecclesiates. We all got bronzes – Ed, Smith, Chris and I. Pity about little Tibby though.

Walk on the beach, dull. Made an exhibition of myself at supper again, but Jinkins got a penance for it. I only called him disgusting!

Steve is not yet back. Rory has recently returned. Teddy broken-heartedly gave up History classes. I was run over by a perambulator.

One of those days.

May 28th

Corpus Christi. Whole Holiday.

Got up at mid-day, renewed Civilisation at the public library, lazed away the afternoon on the roof with Rory, had an early supper of curry and went to evening Mass in the Abbey.

Lying on the roof with Rory... We were both wearing nothing but our gym shorts in the sunshine, glancing from time to time at each other's muscles and the bulges in each other's crotches, and occasionally looking into each other's eyes. There was a delicious feeling of will we, won't we? about that sunbathing session, but we didn't, and nothing was said.

I do like the physical presence of Rory, though. He has chunky legs and arms, and he fills his tight white gym shorts even more fully than I do mine. His legs are lightly covered with curly, virile black hair. Whereas you need a magnifying glass to see the hairs on mine. I haven't seen his cock since he was a junior. I remember it as thick and chunky, and roundly circumcised. These days it's probably even bigger than mine. There's no doubt about his bollocks, though, since they're very manifest in his tight shorts. Each one the size of a peach. Either of us could have lazily stretched out a hand, during one of those balmy summer sunbathing roof-days, tested the ground, tested the reaction. But what is done is done - and what is not done in life must ever more remain so.

Sunday May 31st

Surgeon-Commander St-John-Thewliss died in hospital. What will happen to his booze cabinet?

June 1st

A beautiful June day. Today I love everybody. I worked in the morning, while it drizzled.

Lunch was very ordinary. Chris and KP went to the cinema. I went to sleep. Awoke. Bored. Walked, fast, to

Sevenscore, looked at my beautiful house. Queen Anne... Beautiful... I imagine the wonderful house described in Howards End must have looked like this. It gives me a very special feeling that I am unable to describe. When I arrived back at school my feet were blistered. I had walked eight miles in an hour and a half.

Found Chris. We went up the road to Lavin's shop together, I ran through the opera at the piano, and we went to supper. Tibby has got the idea I'm some sort of Don Juanish womanizer... But I'm not really.

After supper I became very happy, talked to Steve and we went to the Regency on an impulse. We drank and talked and whiled away a whole prep time. Returning, I took night prayers, then Chris and I went to see Johnnie. We did it in style, climbed over the locked gate, found Johnnie out, got along the fire escape and through the window into Dorm 5, which caused a bit of excitement among the juniors who were by now in bed. We were accused of the obvious perversion by Tibby – who seems to have changed his opinions since supper.

Leaving a note for Johnnie we left, but on our way out over the wall, just as we got up on top of it, we met Johnnie who was coming in. He smelt our breaths and commented on them. Then we finished our climb by dropping down on the outside of the wall.

A good day; now I must do a bit of work.

June 2nd

Another great day, felt like I was drunk all day. Over breakfast had to explain to Tibby the reason for my invasion of his sleeping quarters last night.

Mrs Pring's father has died, Arkle the racehorse has been put down, but the sun still shines...

I played a trick on the school at large, leaving a two shilling bit on a piece of paper, with Nosey Sod written underneath. I left it on the post table in the main school hall, then retreated up the main stairs to the banisters outside Barney's office, from which vantage point I could lean over and watch what happened. Reactions were interesting. Cyprian looked under the paper and read what I'd written. Bro George did the same, and exclaimed 'Well, well, well,' in one of his mutters. Munting, poor little kid, nicked the coin. I yelled down at him and he jumped out of his skin, then returned it.

On the roof in the afternoon, with sunshine and Steve and KP, and walked on the prom, where someone had chalked on the pavement: Tibby and Fred xxx, I'm Fred Up, Fred is exquisite... etc.

NINETEEN

Worthwhile People

June 3rd

Nervous this morning about tomorrow and exams in general, so nervous that I nearly bought a packet of fags, while rumours ran round of an impending police raid. Lay on the roof working and talking with Rory. He admired the bum-fluff on my upper lip. (It's the only facial adornment I have. I have never shaved yet.) But our heads were in sight of the people on the far side of Grange Road, one of whom was Barney on his way to the playing fields, and he motioned to us to come down. But we didn't.

Later in the morning Chris decided to climb over the roof of Number One. Alex's older brother had done it once, years ago, and Chris thought that if Alex's brother could do it, then so could – or perhaps should – he. It was no mean task. He went up from the garden side, the back of the house, while Steve and I watched from below. There were three storeys of drainpipes and window-ledges to go up, with the well of the basement steps yawning beneath. Windows opened as he climbed and heads poked out offering encouragement, and steadying hands to help him on his way. He was clearly frightened, but carried on up. At last he had to go up the sloping slates – there is no parapet to fall back against at the back of the house. He just scrambled and slid and flailed about and it was terrifying even for us watching him, but he made it to the ridge and disappeared over the top.

We knew he would be OK now because he could slide down and land against the parapet at the front of the house. But we all ran inside and belted up the stairs. When I got up into the bridge room under the roof-slope he was just coming down through the hatch, and a couple of guys who had got there first were helping him down. He was trembling all over and could hardly stand. When I had him to myself a moment later I laid my hand against his back and said, 'You're quite a brave little boy, really, aren't you.' Understatement. But he knew what I really meant.

Lunch was light. After it I lay on the lawn at the back of Number One with Chris, gazing at the scene of his morning's adventure. He is obviously jealous of me and Rory, though he needn't be.

Then we had House meeting, then Rory and I listened to Mahler's first symphony in the music room, and I played some of Grieg's Peer Gynt Suite to him on the piano. After that Rory left and I stayed, having a go at some Bach. Then Jagger walked in and calmly put on a record. I walked out. Bloody hell.

Chris, Frankie and I pissed around on walls and ladders and things and ate broken biscuits in the basement while the sun lit up the dust as it poured through the window.

Over supper we discussed homosexuality with the juniors, and Frankie's little brother told me that though most people looked like fools sometimes, I never did. Quite a day for compliments.

Worked, talked to Cyprian, to Chris, listened to Abbey Road, came to a truce with Jagger and we went over to the monastery together and had Ovaltine in the kitchen. Someone was playing a piano in a distant room. Rather well. I asked Cyprian who it was. It was the Prior, apparently – the abbot's right-hand man. I didn't know he could do that.

Back at Number One I said goodnight to Rory (notice the small 'g') and am now going to bed. So is Chris – 'dear Chris' as Rory rather sarkily referred to him.

June 4th

In my History 'S' paper I said that the medieval thinkers used God as an infinitely elastic winding-sheet with which to wrap up all the things they didn't understand. And I waffled a bit about medieval churches and the Age of Reason. There was coffee in the middle. I was very nervous beforehand, but it was soon over and I told Chris about it over lunch.

He told me that yesterday, climbing over the roof, he hadn't cared whether he lived or died, that was how fed up with life he was. I didn't like the sound of that and told him so. And then I thought – what about me? I didn't tell him that.

Sunbothe on the roof doing a satisfying period of revision, did six chin-ups on the apple tree, and lay on my bed talking to Chris about what we would do if an H-bomb fell.

Talked to Boing, Frankie and Tibby in the Rathbone library, pinned up a touching notice about sunbathing on the roof – Barney made me do this, it was his gentle punishment for disobeying him yesterday – and had supper.

Opera rehearsal. A bit subdued. Mr Vaughan's father has died.

Afterwards Rory and I decided to go down to the Regency for a half-pint. We ran races in the street and joined the usual school crowd, including a beautiful Swiss girl names Gabrine with whom everyone is in love – with good reason.

I am reminded of May 29th last year, but only superficially: I offer no quote from WH Auden. (May

29th was the day on which I wrote: ...*Chris chose a small backstreet pub that other people don't go to. There was a woman behind the bar, and just the two of us. My first time in a real pub. I didn't know what to have. Chris suggested a lager and lime. We both had one. It came in tall glasses with stems and looked beautiful. I'd never had a more important drink.*

We didn't talk much. We were just being together. I looked into the elegant glass in front of me. A multitude of bubbles was rising from somewhere near the bottom. In that glass I seemed to see a whole world, and among the bubbles something like infinity. I was seeing inside myself and seeing something I hadn't known was there. That was strange, because it was so big, this thing. Bigger than I was.

I was falling in love that night. But I'm not falling in love with Rory. I know the difference now.)

June 5th

Talked to Cyprian... He has just started working for his A-levels: the monastery want him better qualified and he's going to an Oxford college in the autumn. But he needs A-levels first. They didn't have them when he was at school.

Saturday June 6th

An on-off day.

Last night Chris and I made a declaration of independence; we hate everyone except ourselves – the only two worthwhile people in the world.

Today I became uncomfortably suspicious that Frankie's younger brother is infatuated with me.

Got up with heroic selflessness, read an escapist book and suggested to Chris that we went for a drink, after lazing around on the beach for part of the morning. Daniel's brother drove us down, and Jagger came too.

After lunch, lay on the roof with my hat on but not much else, and Frankie's little brother appeared through the hatch and came and lay down beside me, to my embarrassment. But then other people popped up too and the space filled up, so that was all right.

Chris has walked along the parapet, he told me. Sheer three-storey drop on the street side. If he can do it…

So now I too have walked boldly the length of the parapet in terror of my life. Still, Chris can do 12 chin-ups, I can only do 8.

Talked to Uncle Ron for ages about school policy and staff politics and he told a delightful anecdote about Barney, walking out of a recent Council meeting on the verge of tears, saying, 'Let me make a mess of it then, it's my responsibility,' and slamming the door behind him.

Phil's feet smelt at supper. I asked Chris if I could move onto his table, but there is no room.

At Sixth-form meeting we were told: avoid the Regency; it's swarming with detectives.

Fooled around in the garden, talked to Malachy, later to Cyprian – and Jagger – about developments of the school and adolescent homosexuality. We went up to the Vale Tavern for a pint and sat in the cool air outside the house, then trooped back and ate liquorice.

It is nearly midnight. Chris appears to be spending an evening on the tiles with his latest girlfriend. Perhaps I shall go to bed.

***

Phil's feet smelt at supper. Almost the last time he gets a mention in this diary, and I should hate him to be remembered like that. Smelly feet can happen to anyone, and it's the only time I've ever noticed Phil's.

Phil is a handsome boy, but a bit quiet these days. We used to be the two smallest boys in the school. I've grown taller than him in the last few months, he's remained shortish and stocky. He has Rory's build but on a smaller scale. (Though I'm actually a bit taller than Rory now.)

Phil and I. We used to be...

Well, we used to be best friends. When I arrived here, age eleven, I was the smallest boy in the place by a long way. Then, a few days into the term, Phil turned up, and we were the same size. It was quite a bond. He was a couple of months older than me but in the form below. Form one. I'd been placed straight into form two, and was a bit out of my depth among older and bigger boys. Phil and I were friendly at first, but no more than friendly. Then something happened, during the summer of our first year. It wasn't quite the same as seeing the night sky through a sudden hole opening up in the bottom of one's world as it was with Chris last summer, but something approaching it.

I had a best friend back at home then, called Roger. But Phil began to replace him. Phil is partly Italian – it shows in his deep brown eyes and raven hair, and also in his mercurial temperament. That made him difficult to deal with in a way that Roger never was. We were in the Scouts together. Sharing tents at camp. Cooking. Climbing trees...

(Years earlier I'd had nocturnal fantasies about Roger and me. I imagined us living together in an underground nest, like mice or bumblebees, children forever, snuggled up in quilts of thistledown. By the time I was eleven my fantasy had evolved. It now looked hesitantly forward into young adult life, and involved Phil. Perhaps we'd share a house together... We even discussed it. We guessed we wouldn't have much money and the house would be very small. Privately I wondered

how we would spend our free time: I thought we might spend our evenings reading cartoon magazines and laughing together at the jokes. One day in the school holidays I asked my mother, staring straight ahead of me through the windscreen as she drove the car down Market Street in Rye, 'Could two men live together, do you think?'

She probably pursed her lips and frowned. I didn't look. There was certainly a pause before she spoke. 'Hmm. They could...'

I broached what I thought would be a very problematic issue. 'What would they do about the housework?'

This time her reply was prompt and confident. 'They'd skimp it,' she said.)

Phil and I became bell-ringers together. When I moved from The Grange to the main school at the age of thirteen and Phil stayed on at The Grange, I was early morning and evening bell-ringer at the main school, while Phil rang the main school bells during school hours. There was a big outdoor bell on the roof of the chapel which one of us set clanging at almost half-hourly intervals throughout the day, plus a set of electric bells which I used in the evening. Thus I rang the electric bell in The Grange by remote control. The last bell of the evening – bedtime for the fourth and fifth form – wasn't supposed to sound in The Grange, where the juniors were tucked up already. But I used to give it three short discreet presses, which were a signal to Phil. It was me saying Goodnight. Or perhaps – there were three pips not just two, after all – I was saying a little bit more.

Our friendship survived Phil's joining me in the main school when he entered the fourth form and I went into the fifth. We were in different cubicles in the same big dormitory – which was known as the Big Dorm. (What else would it be called?)

Then Canadian David joined the school. We were a bit of a trio – all aged fourteen, and there was always Smith, of course. Though Smith was one year younger. But Canadian David and I sort of fell for each other and became very close. That began to sideline Phil a bit. Then David left, and I moved into the sixth form and Number Three, and my closeness to Phil didn't survive all that. We've stayed friendly, but we're no longer close friends. It's as though doors that lay open between our two hearts and minds are now closed. I'm frightened to think that perhaps that always happens between people. That it always will.

TWENTY

Rites of Passage.

Good-bye Father

Sunday June 7th

Chris and I were first into the chapel for school Mass and Barnabas asked one of us to read the Epistle. Chris did. Genesis. The Fall of Adam (or The Man as he is now called) which occasioned a 'frank' sermon from Barnabas about nakedness and sex which had his nephew in hysterics.

June 8th

Delayed reaction to last week's exams: Chris and I didn't get up till 10. Then we lazed on the beach with KP. Jagger and I went to Surgeon-Commander St-John-Thewlisss's funeral in the Abbey church. A short Mass, said by Father Ethelbert, with the doors open and sunshine pouring in. Two swallows flew in and twittered around overhead before flying out again – rather clever – then we trooped out into the hot sun and stood in the graveyard watching him go down. My first serious funeral since my father's six years ago.

Repaired my shoes in the afternoon. The brass heel-taps haven't lasted. I'm replacing them with stainless steel ones made from one of the refectory table-forks. It's much harder to work, and has rather damaged the chisel and drill I borrowed from Bro George. Ah well.

June 12th

Got up before sixth-form Mass in the Abbey and read an Epistle about Elijah (or was it Elisha?) Only four sixth formers were there; I had to cart the wine and stuff up at the Offertory.

Felt much better today, had a cup of coffee, a health inspector health-inspected the school kitchen. Labour, Liberal and Conservative posters abound around the school. Steve and Rory went up to Bexley to canvas for Rick, the young manager of the Regency, who is standing against Edward Heath...

Chris took his driving test. The examiner was Mr Birch, so he failed, of course.

In the afternoon I read a book about the development of the English small house, listening to Simon and Garfunkel with Chris.

Barry M did five and a half hours of exams today. I did none, had a thoroughly lazy day – save for doing 10 chin-ups on the apple tree, and designed my own stone farmhouse. It's just like any other stone farmhouse, but it's *my* design.

Only Cyprian could read just one set book for a German exam and then answer all the questions... and of course he did, and is as pleased as Punch, while poor mutts like me can only get through French and English by reading all six books six times.

Supper was not too bad. Cod balls. Tibby asked, 'Who wants my balls?', and a few faces turned in my direction.

Saturday June 13th

Painfully got up for breakfast. Steve read this diary. Said he found it amusing – whatever that means.

Chris's younger brother came in during the morning with his usual nonchalance, wearing only tennis shorts, trying to borrow trousers. He'd left his somewhere but couldn't remember where. He got a torn pair from Frankie, and left with his usual nonchalance. Funny chap.

Walked up and down the prom after supper, revising history, talked to Cyprian and Jagger – Cyprian told us how a bloke once fell in love with him – then to Jagger and Frankie over sandwiches till Chris returned from his girlfriend's towards midnight.

Sunday June 14th

Lousy day. Everyone was at the Westgate convent, save for Steve, who was watching football on TV. *Watching football! He doesn't even like football!* So I had no-one to talk to, till Jagger and Cyprian returned about 10. I put my suit on over my pyjamas and we went out to the pub – meeting Barney in the street on the way! – only to find the pub was shut.

June 15th

I invigilated a third form Chemistry exam, with the door open, and Tibby drawing question-marks in the air.

After lunch I sat on the roof with Stevie, Barry M and Big Ed, who dismantled Chris. Let them.

Talked to Frankie about Alex at supper. Drew cartoons for Alpha afterwards, couldn't work, got depressed, carved my name on the apple tree, and despite Steve's fortunate persuading me to watch The Troubleshooters on TV, I still am.

(What? Still depressed? Still carving my name in the apple-tree bark? Both? Dear Reader, we shall never know.)

Surely more happened today than this? Evidently not. It just seems like a lot more happens when you're in a good mood....

Sometimes I hate myself.

June 16th

Stephen has been Steve all day, never Stevie, a great pity.

June 17th

Did bits of work and got depressed. Wrote up a magazine diary for Malachy, looked at the town bookshops, moped, sat looking out of the window at the wind gnawing at the trees; it's a windy day, cold and bleak. Frankie and I folded election pamphlets so as to maker nonsense of them:

Young Voters, George Brown wants you to ... let us down.

Is this your first election? Ten reasons... why you shouldn't vote.

June 18th

General Election: those of us who were old enough went to the polls. But what was the use when Heath had no brain, Wilson hadn't a soul and Thorpe hadn't a clue?...

...Those of us who were too young affected airs of cynical detachment and stayed at home.

In charge of table at breakfast. People kept forcing me to reprimand Tibby. Shame!

Spent the morning embarrassing Mrs Pring and walked in blazing heat to the beach with Steve. We sat on a rail and watched the eel-like wavelets sliding on sunlit stones, and talked about sewage.

Beefballs found me climbing the scaffolding that has been erected outside Number Three. What was I doing? 'Campaigning, of course. Vote Labour!' Two passers-by looked up. (I now walk the length of the roof parapet every day as a matter of course. It doesn't bother me at all. I've got used to it.)

Stirred up a little enthusiasm for Alpha, read The Times – Chris went to sleep – revised, had a cup of tea at the kiosk with Leonard, and talked to Steve over coffee, one of those times when we ended up sitting on the bed. Bernie, who was there, did not read the paper, so we hauled a blanket over ourselves. One of those occasions when you kid yourself it's not for real – until you find your hand down the other bloke's trousers and his down yours, and are rather surprised, strangely enough, at what they do when they're down there. Anyway, it didn't seem to worry Bernie, sitting in the armchair...

Opera rehearsal, Not too bad or boring. Went for a drink with Chris to the Vale Tavern. Frankie came too. In the public bar the pubic bar-goers were discussing politics.

Back again, chocolate as usual, found no end of cockroaches in the monastery kitchen, and took back some bread for Chris and me...

...It is 4.30 tomorrow. I watched the election programme. Conservatives unexpectedly turned the tables, rather exciting watching. One by one people dropped out and went off to bed. Steve and I were left. He fell asleep. I've just woken him up – nearly broad daylight – and we're going to bed – in our own rooms.

Sunday June 21st

Eighteen today.

Steve and I read Bidding Prayers at school Mass. Chris stayed in bed. So now I'm an adult? Act like one, then.

Steve and I went for a walk on the prom, and ended up lying on the hot grass. People stared at us and we conducted ourselves in an adult manner – after all, it's only allowed in private.

We had anice lolly and went back to school, had lunch and Chris and I had quite a little homemade Madeira.

Spent the rest of the afternoon drinking coffee.

After supper Chris and Steve and I went for a 'liddel trink' and met a few people including a dear gentleman names John West. Had a pint, then three malts, John West bought me a lager, so did a friend of his, I bought another pint, and a married woman who Steve knows bought me a lager, took a fancy to me and started kissing me by the bar, while her young husband stood watching. She soon had her tongue down my throat, and I put mine down hers. Steve said, 'Where did you learn to do that, Rafe?' and I said I hadn't. I'd never done it before. But it seemed sort of instinctive and self-explanatory.

Then Phallus-head bought me a malt. Great fun. Steve and I staggered back arm in arm, that was pleasant. We got in through the back gate to the Monks' Park and there was no-one there and it was getting dusk. We were falling about rather, and finally pulled each other to the ground, collapsing in a heap in the flower bed around the elm trees in the middle. We became children again and undid each other's trousers and pulled them down. I took Steve's cock in my mouth and sucked him. It was the first time I'd ever done this too. But neither of us came, as I suddenly had to throw up. After a few minutes' rest on the grass, during which Steve held me, we continued our walk back through the school grounds and buildings to Number Three, and from there into Number One.

Chris was already back in our room and the three of us took all our clothes off and ran down the stairs to the basement, running round Frankie and Bernie's room starkers – they were both in bed – emitting loud Indian war-whoops and yells. Chris and Steve didn't have hardons, but I did. I was a bit embarrassed about being the only one, but there was nothing I could do about it.

Then I was sick again, and Chris and Steve finished my wine.

June 22nd

Rory's birthday. I got up late, hung-over, had Codein and bath and slept all morning. Did Alpha all afternoon.

Curry for supper. Wrote a letter to Barnabas about haircut muddle, and after helping Chris to move bricks, Paolo invited me for a drink at the Foy Boat. Went. Chris came too. Glad about that. Steve didn't join us. That was a pity. John West bought me another pint.

Back to school. Exam tomorrow, shit. Goodnight!

June 23rd

Took my mind off the imminent exam by busying myself with Alpha. Even so, I was shitting bricks by lunchtime – and when I saw the paper I burst out sweating. Dreadful; hope I didn't do too badly.

Watched a ridiculous film with Terry-Thomas in it during prep, and talked to Steve afterwards, about History and Alpha.

My school life is over. Isn't that funny?

June 24th

Worked on Alpha and on the stage set all morning and afternoon. Got ready for the opera and had supper. Good mood after the dress rehearsal since I didn't feel too lousy beside Kevin Collyer at the piano – just mediocre – and went for a drink, but as Steve wasn't there I returned to school – only to find he'd gone out anyway.

Still I found a female hawk moth and couldn't identify her, used her as bait and set a trap for others. Talked to Jagger in his room. Now Steve is crawling over Chris in a drunken stupor. They look rather cute.

Forgot: Chris cut my hair yesterday, Barnabas smiled cautiously at me, I smiled doubtfully at him. Two days ago I wrote him a reproachful note: tomorrow I ask him for a reference. Goodnight.

…Steve and Chris and I persuaded Cyprian to take us down to the monastery. He did; we had cocoa and bread and Marmite, and crushed cockroaches. Quite a satisfactory expedition…

June 25th

We had a penis competition in Paolo's room, which is next door to Chris's and mine, last night. Me, Paolo, Steve and Daniel. Big Ted was there too, though unlike the rest of us he didn't take his clothes off. The rest of us stripped, while we enjoyed a glass of Paolo's wine. And were all stiff. Paolo's is big and slightly tapering. Very elegant, uncircumcised, like Steve's but on a bigger scale, just as Paolo himself is. He also has beautiful balls. He was very taken with mine, actually, remarking that the head was even bigger than Jimmie's. (Hammerhead, he was known as.) Not sure if I've got the biggest one in the school these days, I haven't seen them all by any means, but mine was certainly the biggest one on show last night.

Paolo asked me, 'Can I touch it?' and I said yes, though I was terribly nervous I'd embarrass us all by spontaneously shooting. As it was, it was streaming with clear juice, which the others pretended not to notice, and trembling on the brink of letting fly. Anyway, I said yes partly because I wanted to touch Paolo's too. Which I did, giving it as much of a little stroke as I dared to without it seeming too queer. And luckily I managed not to ejaculate.

Daniel's isn't particularly big, though it's very beautiful, and gets a lot of respectable heterosexual use. His balls are very big and fat.

Eventually Paolo lay back naked on his bed and Steve lay on top of him, tummy to tummy, chest to chest, and cock to cock. They lay very still and silent, and at last the rest of us left the room and left them to it. Whatever it was.

I asked Steve in the morning. He said they hadn't touched each other's cocks with their hands, had just gone to sleep together for an hour and then woken up and disengaged. Steve had left Paolo's room and gone back upstairs to his own. I knew that. I heard him go; I was lying awake.

Had no breakfast, released my still unidentified moth, worked with KP and Steve on Alpha, had lunch, practised the piano, ran down to the Foy Boat for a quick half – got given two – and had to run rapidly back to help KP and Stevie in their typing, got very hot, and dictated stuff to Rory, who's the best typist among us, it turns out. Including Daniel's vitriolic attack on the school.

Supper, typed a couple of words, hung around, not nervous, just tense, played at the first performance of The King's Men with no inspiration or drive at all – a pity after last night – and went for a drink: one pint, one port, one cognac, came back with Jagger, had coffee, showed Alpha to Malachy, and am about to give this to Stevie to read…

…Forgot – after the opera I went to see Barney. 'Thank you for your note,' he said when we parted. 'I found the last bit very encouraging.' We shook hands and said good-bye…

A couple of weeks ago, during one of the many crises he faces daily he turned to me, as we happened to be walking out of the front door together, and talking about the crisis of that day, and he said, 'You have to be a Solomon.' He smiled ruefully and shook his head. A moment later, as we continued to talk, he turned to me and asked gently, 'What would *you* do?' I can't describe how that made me feel.

Good-bye, Father.

TWENTY-ONE

Waiting

June 26th

My last full day at school…

Got up at 8 o'clock, typed a few words of Alpha till Fr Malachy rescued me and helped for a bit. I got Phil to help with some of the typing too, gave out pages for Jagger and Lemarc to draw pictures on – and in the last minute panic lost four whole pages… I had to re-do the title page… Steve had to go over it all with Mrs O – he's been working very hard on this. Daniel drove into Canterbury to get KP's article, but he wasn't in so we had to make it up. Mrs O typed it out, and I worked out the stencilling, a bit of a headache – still wearing my pyjamas.

Then I changed my shirt, and got Fr Malachy to get the whole thing to Brother George's for running off copies.

Supper was not bad. Middle-aged potatoes.

Played well at the afternoon performance of All The King's Men – after a bottle of lager. Even Kevin Collyer said Well Done, and Frankie's younger brother blew kisses at me from the back of the stage.

Down to the Foy Boat after exchanging congrats with everyone, with Jagger, met up with Steve, had two whiskies, a half-pint, left and went to the Tart n Bitter pub with the Lavins, the couple who run the shop in Grange Road. They bought Stevie and I a half of Tart'n each.

Back to the school. Still no Alpha. Talked for ages to Fr Malachy and Johnnie and to Stevie. I quoted a couple of passages from this diary. Johnnie said he wanted to read it – ha-ha!

Things that ruined the day: Stevie called me a bore. Fr Sebastian said I'd never make an actor.

Things that made it: Kevin Collyer said, 'Well done.' Stevie said my pillow smelt nice. Fr Malachy thought it remarkable that Beefballs still didn't know my name.

June 27th

Got to bed at three o'clock, got up at seven. Still no copies of Alpha…

Bro George wouldn't print it till Barnabas had seen it. Malachy and I went to see Barnabas. 'We need your go-ahead for Alpha to be printed,' I said.

'It isn't going to be printed,' Barney said. I tried to cajole him, while Malachy, who has been known to threaten to resign over such issues, kept a necessary diplomatic silence. Barney was adamant. No Alpha.

…I've got over being bitter about things, so I'm not bitter about Alpha. I hope Stephen isn't. Everyone is very sympathetic.

Mother came for the sports. I told her the sad news about Alpha. The subject came up when we were both talking to Barney. He was very friendly, and had a twinkling smile for me. I find I've forgiven him.

It thundered, lightning struck the loudspeaker, and the sports were brought to an abrupt halt.

We had lunch in the Regency, oyster soup, scampi, gouda and a bit of red wine, watching the weather.

Back to school. Mother, Steve and I talked in what used to be my room, until the prize-giving – which was now, because of the rain, scheduled to be held in the refectory. We, those who could sing, lined up and sang Gaudeamus – appallingly. Then we had to queue at the back for prizes. I got R.W. Chambers' Thomas More, and my Lodge bronze medal for the Speech Contest. In his speech Barnabas launched a broadside against the 9 o'clockers that really hit Bloomsbury as well, and the abbot announced we were moving to Westgate in a year's time and going co-ed with the convent there! Barney may have confided in me a little bit at times but he's kept that one under his hat.

Having talked to Johnnie – I should say, Mr Johnson – on the lawn, we had a crowded teatime. We talked to Mr and Mrs Javen (who weren't to know their son Mark was known variously as The Boy From Uncle and Tibby) and bade a fond well to Tibby himself. Said goodbye to Joe Lavin in his shop, then found Charlotte and a whole crowd of girls from the convent in my room, and Steve there, making jokes about me and Chris.

I escorted Charlotte to the 'op-e-ra' in the best Edwardian manner I could manage, not very good even then, and said Goodbye to Frankie's younger brother, got ready, played very well at the final performance and, after loading my trunk into the car, had a quick can of beer on the stage, said Goodbye to everyone – where was Steve? Never mind, I'll see him soon – and then to Chris on the steps. Of course I'll write, I told him, and walked away giving a thumbs-up sign.

I shall miss him, but again, I hope not for long.

Weather was wonderful as I drove home, I daren't describe the sun and shadow on the fields, the fresh young corn…

Supper back home. Bed before midnight.

*

So I've left school with no offers from any university: rejections from Oxford, Cambridge, Bristol, Sheffield and York, and still on the Waiting List for Durham. I've now been put on the 'clearing' list: offers that have not been taken up by the end of September are reallocated to some of the people who, like me, didn't get anywhere first time round. It means that like Ben in The Graduate, 'I'm a little worried about my future.'

June 28th

Received an old print of Rye from mother as well as a rather nice dressing-gown, to mark my having been eighteen for a week.

Found a killed, to my satisfaction, a flea, also a number of death-watch beetles I didn't know we had the priviledge to possess.

June 29th

Watched the mice and rats while studying the timber construction of the old barn across the road.

John Betjeman discussed Pugin on TV – very well and instructively, with shots of The Grange and the Abbey church.

June 30th

Cycled to Windings nursery. Mr Tate prepared to give me a job but very gruff – says it's not all chatting up girls. I didn't really think it would be. Still, mustn't grumble. I start on Friday.

July 2nd

I wish I had Chris to 'talk to and support me.' (Now I'm no longer sorry he read that drunken entry in this diary.) Not that he ever has been around when I had to do something on my own, but somehow one imagines he has – at least, other people do. Anyway, I hope I'll see him very soon, but in the end of course, we are all on our own.

Friday July 3rd

First day in new job. A day of brick shifting, peat scattering, and selling geraniums to customers, knowing no prices and trying to look as though I knew where the till was... And I did some nurserywork, standardising and staking ornamental cherry trees. Tate was pleased with the result.

In the evening I went with Mother to Jane Manders' annual birthday sherry at Watcombe Farm, where she lives with her old aunt. I liked the house – but so much more could be made of it. I met a fellow there called Jeremy, who has been suspended from his public school for drinking. We got on well and by the time we'd rambled round the garden for an hour we'd psycho-analysed all our respective experiences of being brought up by a mother... We also talked about being skinnier than the average, which we both are. He told me that someone had once said, 'You can never be too rich or too thin.' He's a nice chap.

July 6th

Listened to Segovia (on a record) and killed off a wasp colony. I felt such a brute as the unsuspecting industrious animals hummed down their entrance hall, covered in the white dust that will have left their city silent and petrified before morning... How human they are. We too see the poison dust on our doorsteps, we too ignore it and carry on our pathetic little duties till they are mocked by our being no longer able to carry them out; we too are doomed before we are born, and we too pretend that we are not.

July 7th

86 in the shade. After a long hot day, pruning shrubs and hacking weeds I spent a long hot evening digging up the wasps, but finding the fresh air revived them, poisoned them all over again.

Then I wrote a very long letter to Chris, signed, *Your little brother, Ralph.*

Saturday July 11th

Had an amusing dream last night that unpityingly portrayed my threesome. Steve was walking out of a door with someone else, apologizing to me, and probably meaning it. I was cutting strips of concrete with an axe on the sea-front, when I came across Chris, who had been playing with a toy car on a bit of string and fallen asleep, and was now refusing to be moved and insisting I stayed in the cold with him till morning.

The rest of the day was spent gathering a bumble-bees' nest. I walked across the field to find one, and had soon located a fiercely buzzing colony of *Bombus hortorum* or *Bombus lucorum* – I'm not sure which – and bravely dug it up, and by evening had it in a specially knocked-up bee-box in the shed. I hope they'll be alright. One escaped during the move, and the comb is a little bit on its side. Sort it out tomorrow.

Sunday July 12th

The bees have settled down.

July 13th

Heard about the man in the next village (80 years old) who chased his dog up the hill, saying, 'This dog'll be the death of me,' and promptly dropped dead.

Mother bought a hat for the wedding on Saturday. Unsure whether people would wear hats or not she compromised and bought one that you can only see when you're close to it. I'd call it a rigid hair-net, but then, as mother would say – I would.

July 15th

Worked on the roses and helped Mrs Tate start her car, pretending to know exactly what was wrong, and in the end, swinging the good old starting-handle in desperation. It worked.

Saw old Tom who helps with my mother's garden. He hadn't seen me about much, he said, and asked if I ever got out of bed these days. I self-righteously explained that for once I was doing an honest month's work. Tom, who could do a week's worth of my digging, weeding and pruning in half an hour, smiled.

July 16th

A self-important man turned up at the nursery. He told me, 'I've come about that peach tree your employer put in for me three years ago… I built a wall for it, and this year it's producing fruit. Cherries…'

I'm not born to be a salesman. I laughed in his face, nearly split my sides. The gentleman was astonished and left in a hurry.

July 17th

My bee colony is in decline. From thirty-odd at the weekend the numbers have dropped to three. Inevitable, I suppose, but sad.

Saturday July 18th

I received a letter with my breakfast, from Chris. Signed *Middle-sized brother, Chris,* which I thought summed up the situation better than any pair of monkey's paws. His interview with the TV producer was a fiasco. I am very sorry to hear that, but enjoyed his letter as he obviously did mine.

July 21st

I've only just remembered it's my one twelfth birthday! But it's been a rotten day, felt ill, and did two and a half hours bent double weeding dahlias.

July 27th

Had quite a witty letter from Brother Hilary, who is now Father Hilary, and ham for breakfast.

Hacked down lilac, searched for bees' nests – I want one to replace the colony that died out – and found several, but quite impractical, one being under concrete, another being in nettles and full of large fierce *Bombus lucorum*.

July 29th

Discovered, after searching, a ground nest of *Bombus agrorum*, the common Carder Bumble-bee. They're very pretty with soft ginger and brown fur. The nest was in an old meadow-vole's nest, which is like a circular eiderdown of felted grass and moss laid on the ground, about five inches across, with the comb beneath. I had no difficulty in transferring it – carder bees are docile creatures – into my box, which I left in the field all day, in the place they're used to.

Then collected them after dark, when, hopefully most of them are inside, and put the box in the shed.

July 30th

Spent the whole day transporting lost bees, who had homed on their old nest site in the field, back to their new address in the shed, using a jam-jar. The colony is about sixty strong.

But – you can't write much about catching bees in jam-jars; the public don't buy it.

Sunday August 2nd

The first fog – but it lifted to provide a scorching Sunday of the type on which you do nothing. Even the bees sat around listlessly on the comb, so you can imagine how much I did.

August 3rd

The bumblebees are now feeding a new larval clump which is expanding rapidly, and some of the pupae seem to have hatched.

August 5th

Drove to Margate – dropping off an accidentally stolen blanket at my old school, to the surprise of Matron and Mrs Pring – and found in Margate that my mother's old friend 'Auntie' Doris's house hasn't changed since Victorian days. (Neither has Auntie Doris.) Upstairs are seven boarding house bedrooms with dark-painted doors, faded frills on the dressing tables, clocks going as high as the second floor where lives the bathroom with geyser. In the kitchen is an ancient boiler, and in the scullery an ancient sink. John Betjeman would have an ecstasy.

When we got home the field gate had been left open and the geese were in the garden. The mess!

Old Miss Manders' illness provided an excuse to go over to Watcombe Farm in the evening, and to be shown the Charles II fireback, the hooks where the farmer had kept his loaded gun, the brick floors, the best room, 'the parlour', that nobody ever used because of the damp… I had thought such things went out last century, and was reassured they hadn't.

Miss Manders has had three heart attacks since Easter. And there's something brooding in the calm of that old house…

August 6th

Went back to Watcombe in the morning; it poured with rain but we talked about the war and drank cider.

A bevy of queers on the TV in the evening. In 'The Expert', and then in Marlowe's gruesome play, Edward II.

August 7th

Nothing happened.

Saturday August 8th

I drove early to Wittersham, taking a bottle of elderberry and wild plum wine to exhibit at the flower show, and we had lamb and beer for lunch.

Afternoon and we traipsed over to Wittersham. With great self-restraint I came round to my section last, and found I had won a first. And four shillings and sixpence...

The school magazine arrived, plus my school report, in which I was described as an institution.

Thinking about who else could be described as an institution, Steve would of course be a prime example. And Chris too, because ... because ... because he never knows when he's lost an argument.

Sunday August 9th

The bumblebees sulked because of the mist. A good 45 were crowded buzzingly on the comb this morning.

In the afternoon I offered to cut the hedges at Watcombe Farm, and was commanded to run old Miss Manders to hospital tomorrow.

August 10th

To Watcombe, and drove Miss Manders to the hospital in Hastings and back in the rain.

August 11th

Spent the morning at Watcombe, cutting the hedges.

August 15th

Drove Miss Manders to Hastings and back. The kitchen at Watcombe Farm is good. Cats and onions litter the table, fuse boxes and damp-peeling distemper cover the beamed walls, a wide doorway is explained as being made to carry faggots through, to fire the Dutch oven, and a hand-pump brings water from well to sink. Nice.

August 17th

Found I could still do cartwheels. Otherwise nothing. It is Sunday. Tomorrow a certain letter may arrive…

August 18th

No A-level results. Delayed by strikes of course. I have done nothing but wait for things for nearly 10 months…

August 19th

Off to Suffolk for a few days, with Mother. Worst weather of the summer. Fog and deluging rain. I drove through the Dartford Tunnel. We looked at Gainsborough's house at Sudbury – Georgian fronted but Tudor interior, with Regency additions, and very beautiful, and drove right up to Ely and looked at the cathedral which was well worth it, and I wished I had Paul's address – that's Jagger, of course – because we weren't far from Cambridge where he lives.

We had dinner in The Angel in Bury St Edmunds, opposite the abbey – in a cellar type room with Norman arches – the old monastery guest house foundations, I supposed.

Charles Dickens stayed at The Angel but we could not; it was full. We were directed instead to a secluded and grotesquely Victorian country club in the middle of nowhere. Here the staircase is so huge that it seems a waste not to be fat, and the landlord is so jolly you feel it can't be England.

And at last the rain has stopped.

August 20th

A bit sunnier. We drove to Long Melford and Lavenham – the latter is beautiful and appears to have only just realized its potential, being full of renovating work. Many beautiful black and white houses are for sale, some of them painted pink – which looks wrong to me, but apparently is traditionally correct in these parts.

Lunch in Sudbury, then a tour of Essex villages – Finchingfield, Thaxted and Steeple Bumstead... the last worthy of mention for the name alone.

In the evening we wandered around the abbey ruins at Bury – a poetic heap of rubble, powerful reminder of the transience of splendour, wealth, and theology. Dinner at the One Bull Inn (of the Papal sort, apparently) better and cheaper than last night, even if the chips seemed to have been made from instant mash. Gammon.

Back at the spooky country club we watched a TV programme about gulls. Excellent. And had a last drink. Excellent.

Interesting to note that the area abounds in great noctule bats, that flitter like shadows over the dark lawns and roost in the eaves. Excellent?

August 21st

It poured. We drove around Essex villages and towns, and in the end found a lovely farmhouse near Thaxted for the night. A plain square Georgian exterior conceals six 15th century rooms on both floors. There are brick floors, old rifles, polished horse-brasses, a spacious dog called Magic and a characterful woman called Miss Trembath. She's Cornish.

Dinner in Thaxted at The Star, all else being fully booked. Very large mixed grill. Decided to have Hungarian Bull's Blood with it and naturally my mind went back to last September, and I wished I had Chris with me or could see him again soon. But... *Que sera, sera*.

August 22nd

Drove home. Back through the Dartford Tunnel.

And when I got home and opened the post – I found I had my A-level results, including a merit in the Special paper...

And I have got into Durham. Well, well, well...

TWENTY-TWO

The End of the Summer

August 22nd continued

…I go up in just under six weeks…

I wrote masses of letters, including one to KP that wasn't as witty as it should have been, one to Daniel that wasn't as convincing as it should have been, one to Charlotte that wasn't as long as it should have been, one to Steve that wasn't at all as it should have been and one to Chris that was more sentimental than it should have been.

So, not a very spectacular day… Was it?

August 25th

Had a beautiful letter from Stevie, a card from Barney, and replied to the former, hoping to see him soon. He's going to University College London. Chris, though, still doesn't know what's going to happen to him.

Trundled the wheelbarrow down the lane to Miss Bennett's. Loaded Pippa the squirrel, in her big cage, onto the wheelbarrow and trundled it all the way back up the hill. Pippa the squirrel is coming to stay with us for her holidays.

Then Mrs C came with a load of guinea-pigs for us to look after. So I looked after them, and collected for Lifeboat Week, and made apple champagne, <u>and</u> mowed all the lawns, <u>and</u> got my own tea (mother was out, playing quartets) <u>and</u> got cross-questioned by prospective buyers of the house opposite <u>and</u> baby-sat for the couple who are staying in Miss Bennett's cottage while she is away, reading RW Chambers' Thomas More, and made ten shillings… Worth it?

August 26th

The History department at Durham have given us a preliminary reading list, to be tackled before the start of term. Included is St Matthew's Gospel in Latin, to get us used to reading medieval Latin fluently, and Bede's Ecclesiastical History of the English People.

Drove to Rye and asked at the public library. Had to fill in reservation cards… Author: Matthew, Mark, … And then Bede. What were his initials. TV? The Venerable?

In the evening I heard that hop-picking is to start a week earlier than expected. And I'm supposed to be seeing Steve… Damn! Have to sort this out…

Clare Fosbree, by the way, has 'already heard' I'm going to Durham. (So, as it happens, is she.) And the Ashleys, who I'm going to be hop-picking for, 'were told yesterday'. Why don't I get to hear these things? Damn it all, as a winemaker I ought to be in touch with the grapevine, oughtn't I?

August 27th

A surprisingly good day with the Catterall family at Bognor, including a swim and a good drive, though marred by phoning Stevie and finding him sounding like a different person – one who probably can't come down in the near future. I shall probably have to go to London.

I'm now inexplicably depressed. I don't want to go to Durham, I don't want to go hop-picking, I don't want to stay here, I want to be with the old school gang – or at least, with three of them. Guess which…

G'night.

August 28th

A letter from Charlotte. Enclosing, astonishingly, a fourth-hand, dog-eared copy of Alpha. But it's quite a treasure, as it must be the only copy ever printed. Can't imagine how she came to have it...

No phone call from Steve.

With some difficulty cleaned out the squirrel's cage and bought a 'respectable' suit and a pair of cords in Hastings.

Baby-sat for Doctor Rogers in the evening. A dull day.

August 29th

Received very nice letters from Paul (Jagger) and KP. Paul has got into Newcastle, to read Architecture. He will be just up the road from me, so we can see each other during term time. He, like me, is now very occupied with sorting out his long-distance move. Wondering whether he needs to take sheets etc...

Spent the evening at the Fosbree's with their three daughters and became briefly infatuated with Clare. She has the most astonishing flame-red hair.

August 31st

Melanie, the six-year-old from next door, dropped in, and wouldn't drop out, despite the entire Walker family and Jonathan's fiancée Sue coming for coffee. Melanie had twenty biscuits and turned cartwheels on the lawn and teased the squirrel and punched Jonathon in the balls.

The squirrel looked constipated this morning so I gave it a laxative and made elderberry wine all afternoon.

Sept 1st

Got stung by a wasp and had a good supper at the Walkers' and have just now squashed a bluebottle between these pages. (You can see the remains in the top LH corner.)

Sept 2nd

My first day hop-picking. Started at 7.30, my job being the clearing away of the spent bines and the waste leaves. The picking machine broke down for an hour in the morning so we had a long break.

Sept 3rd

Unsurprisingly, today was much like yesterday, except the machine broke down for only half an hour, I drove around on one of the tractors quite a lot and there were five full pockets of dried compressed hops at the end of it.

Sept 4th

Went to the Fosbrees in the evening. A whole crowd of people from my first school were there. Wendy is off to Newcastle, her fiancé is going to Durham. RB has got into Oxford... They were having supper. I kept them company with a glass of cider. Since we all have to be up and hopping tomorrow I left at ten.

No post. Nothing from Chris, Steve... Nothing.

Saturday Sept 5th

Lost the seat of the tractor and had to ride bareback on the metal – until David produced it from somewhere. Being a Saturday, work finished at 11.30 and we collected our pay £8 for three and a half days. Not bad.

Lunch was steak and kidney. A letter had come from Barry M. He has got into Kent. And a short note from Chris. *Big Brother, Chris*, as he signed himself this time. He's coming to England next week and will be coming to see me before I go to Durham. I'm glad.

Sept 7th

Rotten day: too hot, rotten hops, got the bines tangled in the tractor's lifting gear, and then the hub-cap flew off.

Sept 9th

Squalls. Soaked. Kept up spirits as I drove the tractor by singing – Beatles, Mother Courage, Gilbert and Sullivan…

Mother had two punctures, and I continued to read St Matthew's Gospel in Latin.

Sept 11th

Poured. Hops wouldn't dry. Rotten day.

Saturday Sept 12th

Rained cats and dogs. Poodles everywhere. Found my trusty steed replaced by a modern monster tractor the size of a mammoth with two gear levers, independent brakes, a speedo that didn't work and a cockpit that gives you a fantastic view of the back of your headlights but little else.... So I had to have a demonstration. Once you've climbed aboard you're wherever you want to be before you've hardly started.

Soaked to the skin. Got home. A busy afternoon. A letter from Jaggy.

Sept 18th

After a foggy start, a sunny day. In the evening I got things ready for packing, did wine, washed my hair, cooked supper and drove over to the Fosbrees after. Nearly broke my neck on the way back, swerving to avoid a rabbit at 60mph.

Sept 21st

Life is full of surprises... Got a new job ... in the hop garden. Less lonely than my last post outside the machine shed and on the tractor. Got an electric shock on the spark-plug of the grain elevator, filled the kiln, did a stint up on the crow's nest, and John M and I gave Alice a mouse for lunch.

Back at home, read Bede. Lots of it. That's all.

Sept 22nd

Found a frog in the hop garden. Mediocre day. Steve phoned once, but not twice, and I finished Bede.

Sept 23rd

I phoned Steve.

And John M, showing me how to stop the elevator without getting a shock, got one himself.

Sept 25th

Last day of hopping. We all wore flowers in our buttonholes and swapped jobs around. Funny how other people's jobs look easy till you go and do them. John M brought a tape recorder and embarrassed everybody by playing back what they'd said behind each other's backs in front of them. Beer, sherry, cider, Dubonnet and homemade wines (and some vinegar!) were provided and various mixtures were drunk in the barn. One mixed, drank and felt various. Round of sad goodbyes. We'll all be back next year. And I believe that.

Picked sloes. Steve didn't turn up but phoned up. Coming tomorrow – I hope.

Saturday Sept 26th

Made sloe wine.

Met Steve off the three o'clock. He wasn't on it.

Met Steve off the four o'clock. He was on it. Lovely to see him again. I took him into the bedroom we are sharing… and things simply carried on from where they left off on June 21st. He is without pubic hair at the moment, having been shaved by a girl at a drunken party in London for a dare. He is also wearing a brown leather jockstrap instead of underpants, which is quite sexy.

Chris is expected to arrive tomorrow. I'm told he has grown a moustache and looks like Che Guavara.

Watched television. Steve is now reading last term's diary…

Sunday Sept 27th

Up early – I think, and went to Mass, followed by a drink at the R and C. Chris didn't arrive.

We had afternoon tea, with damson jam and scones, with old Miss Manders and her niece Jane at Watcombe Farm. Something new for Steve…

Sept 28th

Beautiful weather. Steve and I cycled to see the Fosbree girls. Nobody was in. So, on the way back Steve smacked my bike into a bridge, spinning down the hill too fast and coming off on the bend. His knee was too badly cut and grazed to cycle back, so I had to leave him lying in the wood, and bike the three miles back to fetch mother with the car to bring him back home. The doctor was called, and made him take his jeans off, which was embarrassing because of the jockstrap and shave underneath, but doctor made no comment, and was very entertaining. Then Chris phoned, a letter arrived from Daniel, we had lunch, picked wild fruit and Chris arrived, complete with Che Guevara moustache, having hitched from Tenterden.

Both he and Steve are amused and fascinated by the visiting guinea-pigs, the squirrel, and of course, the bumble-bees.

After tea, prepared by me, Steve went to bed. Chris and I went to the R and C. Two pints. Percy the landlord bought us a third. We got into conversation with an old chap. Then all the people I'd been hop-picking with walked in. Quite a jolly time.

Walking back with Chris, I said, 'Life isn't the same without you.'

'There's always the element of missing you,' replied Chris. Our friendship is nothing if not sentimental.

Cooked supper, feeling particularly jolly and had a bottle of homemade champagne … we'd had one for lunch too. Dear old Big Brother. Where would I be without him?

Sept 29th

Chris cut my hair. We went to Rye and I was late for my first appointment with 'my' bank manager. Later we met a rather famous actor in the R and C and we all talked rubbish till lunchtime. Then we picked fruit, had tea, went back to the R and C, and I cooked mackerel for supper. After that Steve went to bed, he is still suffering the effects of his accident, and Chris and I – despite our day's intake – got through two bottles of homemade wine. We watched a TV play in the Menace series and then talked and talked, me sitting on Chris's lap in one of the big armchairs, though we seemed to stay as sober as we've ever been. It is obvious at times like that why Chris is my best friend and big brother.

We said goodnight. Rather sadly.

***

Wonder, though, if Steve is really feeling rough after his crash, or is he going to bed early because his nose is out of joint as a result of Chris's arrival and the attention I'm paying to him?

Sept 30th

Had to take Steve to the doctor's to be checked over. I've lent him some underpants. While he was inside I took Chris round the corner and showed him over the old Tudor house that is falling down. I'd peered through the windows once and it was ghastly. Old 'Nurse' who lived there in wellingtons has obviously died, but the state of the place…

With Chris I was bolder and we went inside. It has been a beautiful cottage once, but now the plaster is hanging from the ceiling, the roof is naked of thatch, the sink and the washing copper are full of dirty water, the Range all rusted up... I wonder what price they are asking.

Later we had a last visit to the R and C, and a bottle of wine with lunch. We got relatively sloshed. Finally we had to say goodbye.

I was left feeling very conscious of the imminence of my lonely journey north, and my nerves convinced me I had appendicitis. They haven't done that for ages.

I told Chris how his visit would make me all the lonelier at Durham. But then, I can jog along OK with most people... So...

Anyway, no point wasting ink on such corny stuff.

Went over to the Fosbrees in the evening. Clare very busy packing for Durham. Told her about Steve's accident. She very apologetic. So was the cat, Ginger. He came and sat on my lap....

Oct 1st

Less sad today. Round of Goodbyes. Neighbours came round for a drink, we drove to Elham for tea, had supper at the Oxney Ferry on the way back, and coffee with the Walkers. I'm rather tired. Can't sit on Chris's lap today.

Earlier, like in a scene from Great Expectations, I went across to the farm to see Harry the pig-man and told him where I was off to the next day. He shook my hand and said very warmly, 'I wish you all the luck.'

Oct 2nd

Up early. Waited ages for the train at Robertsbridge, but caught it eventually, thinking hard. I thought, among other things, how wonderful it would be if Chris happened to be on the platform at Tonbridge...

But I didn't have to wait till Tonbridge. Chris and Steve were together on the platform at Tunbridge Wells, incredibly, peering in through the windows looking for me. They caught sight of me and sprinted along beside the train...

Somehow we got three seats together. Then we sang Simon and Garfunkel songs at the tops of our voices all the way to Charing Cross. It was a very happy journey (for the three of us at any rate...) all of us very high on one another's company. We drank in the station bar at Charing Cross, then went down to the underground where I had to say Goodbye to Chris. Steve came with me as far as King's Cross, and we parted there, bound for our new lives. God bring our next meeting soon.

TWENTY-THREE

Love and Friendship

Oct 13th

Two lectures – not too bad, then, after lunch and a shopping expedition, took a train to Noocastle. It took just fourteen minutes. Then one was in Northumberland, pigeon-stained Noocastle.

I looked for Jaggy's hall of residence... (When I found myself among open fields I turned back and had another look!) Found it, a smart new place in the middle of Leazes Park, and the porter phoned his room but on-one in. I sat on a wall and scanned faces for half an hour, then walked into town, but, not finding him in the vivid red-brick section, returned to hall and not finding him in the dinner queue, was beginning to wonder what to try next – I'd been in Newcastle for 2 hours by now – when there he was. He didn't recognize me 'because I'd grown' ... and he was NOT wearing a sports jacket (as Steve had guessed he would be). He is cultivating a new image and went to great lengths to demonstrate his popularity. Fortunately this included persuading a 'friend' to lend me his meal card, so, by dint of keeping my thumb over the identity photo, obtained a free meal – and a load of shit it was, too.

Jaggy – though I should call him Paul – then took me to the Union for some drinks, and we talked and talked and talked, till we split up. He showed me the way to the station, we said goodbye and he patted me on the back – that must be the first time after nearly two years, so perhaps he's not so keen on his new friends as he makes out.

I missed the train by 15 seconds and had to wait an hour and a half. I had a depressing, solitary whisky in a ghastly Victorian Baroque waiting room bar, and mused. After seeing Newcastle, I think Durham is a paltry little place; I have no group there – I have no group anywhere, except the Eternal Triangle – only a lot of disjointed acquaintances and one friend here at Newcastle, where I'd prefer to be anyway. I believe it is not absence that makes the heart grow fonder but parting, and the memory of parting, and I never knew how fond I was of Paul, and how false my assured and cheerful airs at Durham are.

There were crates of minks or ferrets on the platform, which I fed with crisps through the wickerwork, boxes of pigeons, and a parcel from 'Harbour Road, Rye'. How funny.

PS. Paul is growing a beard. As he's on a seven year course, I suppose he stands a chance.

Oct 30th

No letter from Paul, no letter from Chris, no letter from Steve. One begins to wonder whether London and the back garden of England are any more than figments of the imagination. Still, one can't complain; the soup we had for lunch was, 'excellent,' as Jagger would say; 'repulsive', as Steve would; or as one of my new mates here would say, 'classic.' I called it mushroom.

Saturday Oct 31st

Did my final audition for Pinter's The Caretaker... I got a part! No cigars, no pipe – but a roll-your-own ciggy. Very pleased. So was my room-mate Bill, so was mother – who's up here, staying for the weekend – and so was Paul, from whom I received a letter. He wanted to come over today. Quite impossible. I wrote a note, and we drove to N'castle with it… You can imagine driving in N'castle in a hurry, in pouring rain and mist, on a Saturday morning, during Rag Week … and being quite lost? Well, that was me. Well, I delivered the note, but in the afternoon after I'd shown my mother the Bailey and the cathedral (including the orgasmically worthwhile Monks' Dormitory, full of Saxon illuminated manuscripts, medieval vestments, and the only Saxon embroidery in existence) I saw a wet-haired figure sitting on the inside window-sill of my own room as we approached the front door beneath it through the rain. It was Paul! Funny, it was the first time I'd forgotten to lock my door all term. Anyway, he hadn't got my note, and had come down on the off-chance. We had coffee and took him to the station after an hour or so. It was worth seeing him again, even for such a short time. He tells me he's just bought The Caretaker and 'a lot of Chekov'.

Nov 3rd

Wrote, unaccountably, to Cyprian, and … wished Chris were here. Despite appearances it would make all the difference.

Nov 10th

Surprised to get an entertaining letter from Cyprian. I actually did some work, and learnt a few lines of The Caretaker, becoming aware gradually that my room-mate Bill hadn't spoken to me all evening. On being questioned he produced the explanation that 'I should know' why he was gloomy, that it was 'something I'd said'. And since I hadn't spoken to him all evening it is hard to imagine – unless he's been nosing through my diary????

We may never know.

Nov 11th

But we do now. It appears I called him a bumpkin. But that's all settled now.

I finished writing to Chris and started writing to Steve.

Nov 17th

A letter from Chris. It didn't cheer me up too much though. But it's nice to know that Big Brother's still alive and well, and working in an art dealer's show-room in Bond Street. Possibly a little more inspiring than this morning's lecture on the depression in the 1930s. 'A professor is one who talks in someone else's sleep'. (W.H. Auden.) Too bloody true.

Dec 9th

Got up late. A letter from Chris, a very nice one, arrived. So I'm going there on Friday. Good.

Wrote a lousy essay in the dark under the impression that it was yet another power-cut – in fact the bulb had gone.

Dec 11th

It took a while to get to Clapham on the tube from Kings Cross, lugging my luggage, with that stupid feeling in the pit of the stomach that is inevitable when you find yourself doing the thing you've been looking forward to for seventy-one days.

I walked up the unlit street to Larkhall Rise. Found the flat and was shown into a room. A little bloke came in. So I'm nearly as big as my big brother. 'It's good to be home,' I said.

Saturday Dec 19th

Left really early and after paying respects to cousin at Elham and doing shopping got to school at 11. Weird sensation. Thank God everyone pleased to see me. I thought Barnabas looked fatter. He thought I did. Had a long talk with Malachy. He was most impressed I'd been asked to do a part in Pinter's latest, next term.

Of course Smith had to appear. He's had a fantastic interview at Christ Church, Oxford. Of course there's no accounting for taste, but sometimes I think there's no taste left either.

Found the school at the Foy Boat. Dick (formerly known as Dick-the-Dick) has turned into my bosom friend, it seems. Found Frankie, ten minutes before lunch. Could I run his whole family over to Margate to pick up a few things?... Arrived half an hour late for lunch. Talked to Fr Sebastian. He was reading a letter from a former class-mate in which I was mentioned. Sebastian scoffed at my acting ambitions, yet praised my keyboard performance of the summer. (All The King's Men.) !!!!!

Just as I left lunch, up rolled Chris...

Back to the Foy Boat...

Phallus-head was pleased to see me back.

The school play – Oh What A Lovely War – Was excellent. People like Chris's younger brother have improved vastly as actors.

We congratulated Mr Johnson (Johnnie) on his engagement. I congratulated Barnabas on the nice length of everyone's hair. He gave me one of his twinkles and said, 'Nasty child.'

Did the fifty miles back in ninety minutes, which is bloody good.

Sunday Dec 20th

Good lunch, so a sleep after. Woken by a phone call from Steve. That's fantastic. I was wondering how to compose a questioning, reproachful, beseeching. McKeanian letter to him. Instead I'm going to his place on the outskirts of London tomorrow. I will be eighteen and a half. Yipee. (Is that how you spell it?)

Dec 21st – 23rd

Three rather difficult days to write up... After a lot of letter-writing I set off for London in bright sunshine, black cloak and black trilby hat.

It was nice to see Steve again. He read the school magazine, read this diary. Said I was getting sentimental – What the hell d'you expect in a diary? ...Tabulated tables of emotions, giving their square roots and anti-logarithms, with explanatory notes after the index?

Steve's sister is nice. His father may be nice too, but he clearly doesn't think I am.

Went to London, among other more or less normal things, and saw bits of UCL, and had a bottle of wine and a good bit of cider – also a dance. Which was rather funny, seeing that neither of us can dance...

And I shared a bath with Steve and had sex in it. 'Experiments in living,' Steve called it.

I was sorry to have to leave. Found my train was earlier than advertised. Also found it raining...

...Forgot to say, we phoned up Jagger, rather drunkenly. I don't know what he will make of that. And now ... it beginneth to snow.

Dec 24th

To Rye on slithery snow for midnight Mass. Singing was appalling. But this is the first white Christmas I have known.

Dec 28th

It thawed. There was nothing really to go out for. Steve phoned and promised to come. I did a hell of a lot of piano practice, and watched a very good documentary about the Tay Bridge disaster. They seem to know just about the whole story now. Pity they didn't show the programme ninety-one years ago. Now it beginneth to snow again...

Dec 29th

Deep snow. Did some Latin. Met Stephen at Robertsbridge. On time!

Fantastic to see him again. (What rot!)

We spent a typical, untypical, evening and now – nearly one o'clock – we are contemplating bed. Respective beds, I should say. As I have so often done...

...Er... We might have contemplated separate beds, but only briefly. Because that was certainly not the way it turned out...

Christ!!! ???

Dec 30th

We went to Rye. Had a drink in the Railway Hotel. People were playing Euker. Uker? Uchre?

Lots of snow. We went to the village shop. Had haddock for tea. Watched TV. And, um, after...?

Dec 31st

Long day. Steve was introduced to Tom, mother's old gardener. He asks, 'Is Steve Italian?'

Drinks in the R and C. Saw the New Year in. Steve and I made a resolution...

Watched the film Anastasia. One of the most fantastically unsentimental sentimental films I've ever seen. We got to bed about four or five.

Jan 1st 1971

Steve discovered his true metier as a kindling chopper...

Made our way to the Fosbrees for coffee and tea. Amusing afternoon. Very.

Coming back we met a lorry stuck on the ice in the lane and had to reverse all the way down to Pooh-sticks bridge (where Steve had crashed my bike back in the summer).The two-mile journey took half an hour.

Saturday Jan 2nd

Chris came down and joined us in the evening. Driven down by one of his flat-mates, Kevin, who stayed. We went to the R and C after supper, then had some more drinks when we got back. Fantastic evening.

(Chris and Kevin had the twin beds in my bedroom, I had the ancient military camp bed at the other end of the

room. Steve occupied the double bed in the spare room on his own. I could have insisted on sharing it with him, but did not. Chris doesn't know that Steve and I have sex together. If he did it would only complicate things.)

Sunday Jan 3rd

All went to Mass in Rye. Great fun. Chris and I sang the customary duet.

A drink at the R and C. Good and merry lunch. Afternoon at the Fosbrees, tea back at home, after which Chris and Kevin had unfortunately to leave.

Last ever episode of Doctor Finlay's Casebook on TV. Steve and I got sad and melancholy after. Perhaps because Big Brother has gone... I also felt rather ill.

Jan 4th

Steve got some money from the bank, paid his rent, we had a drink and had tea with Miss Bennett, with a Maltese lemon and an atmosphere like a percussion band – and at night we threw matches into the fire.

(The diary doesn't record much more about those winter nights. Steve and I naked together on the hearthrug, lit by the flames, exploring each other endlessly and playing with each other's cocks. After my mother had gone to bed, of course. Diaries are for recording the things we would otherwise forget, perhaps. And we wouldn't be forgetting that...)

Jan 5th

We went for a walk. It was very cold. We also drank quite a bit, here and there. Saw a very funny film, and a TV play with our local star actor in it, playing opposite Gwen Watford. On his recommendation. Enjoyable.

Jan 6th

To the Fosbrees in the afternoon. Found that my friend and Clare's friend Terry from Durham was there, so we spent quite a long time there.

In the evening even my mother came to the pub, and we discussed last night's TV play with its leading man. He was most disappointed with it – too much editing.

Long and searching conversation with Steve.

This was the night we talked about the nature of our relationship. I maintained that people never changed, they only developed. Steve maintained the contrary. We went on splitting hairs over this, both refusing to give way, until three in the morning, by which time we were both crying tears of frustration. We went to sleep, leaving the question still unresolved.

Jan 7th

Drove to Epsom. Steve played cowboys with my little cousins – so for that matter did I – and Steve was most amused by my older family's reminiscences of Barney as a golden-haired little boy.

Drove home in the dark: appalling traffic, torrential rain, floodwater, frost-battered roads, fog patches and gusty winds, but still did it in two hours.

Very amusing TV play about a public school.

Jan 8th

Steve and I walked to Northiam across the fields and woods, boots thick with clay. It was a warm vibrant afternoon when we set off – and twilight when we got back, rather hot and smelly.

But we enjoyed it.

Watched the Marx Brothers in a film later. Brilliant in parts.

No more damp-eyed quarrels though, thank God.

Forgot to mention my mother's surprise, on waking us this morning (we are now back in the twin beds of my own bedroom) to find the wrong head in the wrong bed. Somehow in the course of the night we had swapped beds. But what else can you expect?

Saturday Jan 9th

Spent a busy morning packing, drinking sherry etc, and an afternoon with the Fosbrees, then watched The Chalk Garden on TV. Dreadfully sentimental, but somehow it appeals to me.

Steve can't be bothered to read this till tomorrow. I think I shall sulk … only there's not much time. After tomorrow evening I shall be back in the company of … dear old Durham room-mate Bill. Ha bloody ha!

Sunday Jan 10th

To Mass, then to the R and C. Rather quiet, though less sober. Then lunch with booze, and Steve got talkative – there may have been no connection – then we listened to the Mozart record. The D minor piano concerto, whose slow movement is, for me, a portrait of Steve.

Drove to Robertsbridge and said goodbye to mother. The journey to London soon passed, teasing a couple of little girls … poor kids.

Made our way to Clapham. Found Chris in depression and white socks. A Chinese and five pints later we all – Kevin included – made for the nurses' house where, after chatter, we all kipped down on sofas and floors and things. Chris had shown me my last letter to him, told me he always carried it round with him, and had laughed for twenty minutes over the post-script... I think we were both a little influenced by the booze.

Jan 11th

Had a series of nightmares and awoke depressed. Hung around with the nurses all morning, shopped, and had Scotch eggs and ham roll with Tankard in a pub for lunch. Rather a sombre meal.

A silent journey to Kings Cross and protracted farewells all round. Chris and Steve horsing around on the platform, giving each other piggy-back rides and waving to me through the carriage window till the train finally pulled out.

Now, after waiting an hour for a taxi at Durham station, a Wimpy, some unpacking and a half-pint, I'm off to bed.

No Steve, no Chris, no Big Brother to hold my hand. Very sad.

Jan 27th

Went to Newcastle to see Paul. (Jagger.)

When I go to see him, Durham crumbles away like a nightmare and I return to reality, to genuine friendship and some (if small) degree of honesty.

Of course it took a while to peel off layers of degeneracy, but underneath, Paul is the same old fellow – and when I come to think of it, one of the few people I really like within a 245-mile radius of Durham.

We had a look around his department, and met somebody who knew people I know in Durham. We had beer and turkey sandwiches in a pub. Then I came back. The train took only eleven minutes to do the 15 miles from the bridge over the Tyne to Durham, which is bloody good, and the journey was enlivened anyway by some drunken Pakistanis discussing religion.

Not too despondant on returning … but there's plenty of time for depression still. 43 days, in fact, before I get back to humanity. (What little of it there is.)

TWENTY-FOUR

Happy Easter?

March 13th

After listening to an Irishwoman railing against immigrants in the buffet at Charing Cross, caught the train home. It went slowly till we reached Wadhurst. Then the driver looked at his watch and we picked up speed so fast that all the passengers were rolling about and much luggage tumbled from the rack. Well, it's nice to be home. The lambs are in the fields. But I wish 'the boys' as mother calls Stephen and Chris, were here too.

March 15th

Wrote to Stephen. Read, played the piano, shivered; it snowed.

March 18th

Very very cold. The phone rang in the morning, and a very quiet voice said, 'This is the Sundance Kid.' Of course, I only know one Sundance Kid, and that's Chris. Well, it seems I'm going up to London next weekend. Good. 'Er, just you keep on thinking, Butch,' said Chris.

I did.

Then Steve phoned up. It being of course, bloody good to hear from him after all this time. (Not his fault of course: the postal strike, y'know.)

Well, it seems I'm going up to London next weekend.

(The postal strike explains why I didn't meet Steve or Chris on my way down from Durham. We were all out of touch for weeks, and the single pay-phone in college was impractical and expensive to use.)

March 19th

A letter came from Chris at lunchtime. Actually it was two letters, one written pre-strike but too late for posting. Well, it seems I'm going up to London next weekend. And I'm still appreciated. Chris should take up letter-writing professionally; he's damn good at it. At least *I* think so.

March 22nd

Sunny but windy. Dreamed that Chris had broken his leg.

March 26th

After lunch, off to Robertsbridge. Long wait for a train so I walked halfway to Etchingham and back. Then I thought I'd be clever and catch an earlier train – not for some time did I realize it was going to Cannon Street. And then it broke down half in and half out of the Sevenoaks Tunnel. The driver came running back along the track as the first spots of rain put an end to a beautiful afternoon. We crawled all the way to London and at Cannon Street it was announced, 'We apologize for the lateness of the Hastings train due to a defective unit wot's got to be serviced.'

Then, for the hell of it I walked to Charing Cross, taking a look at the Temple en route, and Steve met me. Chris soon found us both in the bar. Good to see them. Steve's sister's birthday. So we drank, talked to a queer

– who looked like Zebedee! – had an Indian meal, put Steve's sister on her train at Kings Cross – where to my amazement I got upset by being on that station, and felt depressed on the way back to Stockwell, where Steve and Chris now share a flat, on the bus. Walked the last bit arm in arm with Chris, who had to be put to bed, then spent part of the night in his bed with him and part in bed with Steve. It is now four o'clock in the afternoon. Steve has gone out, Chris's younger brother has come, and Chris and I are not, properly speaking, up yet. Well, it was a grand reunion anyway.

Saturday March 27th

When finally we got up we had a meal in the Chinky, then got a bus to Marble Arch – this was me, Chris and his brother – where we saw Cromwell, sitting so near the front of the curved screen that we had to keep turning to look over our shoulders to see what was going on at the edges of the curve. Well, it was a superb film, especially Alec Guinness as Charles I.

Then, with difficulty, we caught a bus back, and went to a party under the roof of the nurses' house in Clapham. We went in with no booze and came out with a little. Suppose we should be thankful, so OK.

Sunday March 28th

Didn't get up none too early again either. Spent the afternoon at the nurses' house and got given omelettes – Chris and I insisted that they contained onions, so of course they did.

Well, in the evening we went to an Up-the-Junction cinema and saw 10 Rillington Place, gloriously gruesome, and kept up to standard by Richard Attenborough. Then one went back to Stockwell and to bed but, it being rather hot, nobody slept very well, whoever's bed they were sleeping in.

March 29th

Woke up and said Goodbye to Chris, who has to go to the Foreign Office, because he works now, being quite a big boy.

Well, Steve cooked some breakfast and we got the train from Clapham Junction, changing onto the Hastings train at Waterloo. The train was full of such interesting people that I need hardly describe them to you.

Well, it was a bloody good weekend, even though two men in the Cornet of Horse on Lavender Hill did say that Chris was better looking than me, although they had to admit that we were both very handsome blokes.

There are not many people whose company I'm not lonely in. But Chris is one. I'm so lonely without him.

Well, two films and an onion omelette later, yes I enjoyed my stay in London!

March 30th

Drove to Rye in the morning. In the afternoon Steve and I sat on the grass verge by the churchyard in Beckley. The sun was warm and Church House looked particularly nice. But there's a wind about today.

Sawed up some wood, and we all watched Civilization on TV and listened to 'Steve's' Mozart concerto.

March 31st

We sawed up more wood this morning. We had a very good rabbit for lunch, a drink at the R and C and a drive to Appledore.

Nothing much else happened, only we had a very long chat this evening, in fact, it is now getting earlier and earlier tomorrow morning and we're still talking.

April 1st

The bank rate was lowered and our local famous actor explained to us what this meant in the R and C. Later we watched him on TV at the Fosbrees where, as usual, they were choc-a-bloc with cousins. We all went to the White Hart and Steve gave a sex lecture.

Later he became depressed, and we came back home and spent the rest of the evening together.

(And you know by now what that last bit of code means.)

April 2nd

Letter from Fr Peter. Monastery for Easter seems no go. So I wrote to Chris. Asked him if he could come here instead.

(We had written to the abbey, asking if we could repeat our last year's visit. But apparently the more serious retreatants had found our boisterous presence a bit disruptive. Fr Peter, the guest master suggested we could go along for a night or two the following weekend.)

This afternoon we went to Hastings and Steve nearly bought a parakeet. We walked on Castle Hill – then back at Beckley we took a walk through the newly cleared woods near the City Stores and said hallo to a girl who was picking primroses. She was not overly friendly. A bitch in a ditch, I called her.

Saturday April 3rd

Had a bonfire and watched the Grand National and then Chris phoned, said he was on his way, so we met him at Robertsbridge. So the family is complete again. 'The place feels like home again, now you're here,' I said. Chris laughed.

Sunday April 4th

Breakfast all together, Mass, then Rose and Crown, where Mrs Percy got stroppy with us for eating all the free cheese and biscuits. Cold chicken for lunch, with pickled onions (of course).

In the afternoon, after playing word games, we drove Chris to a point on the A21 where he could hitch-hike back to London. A sort of grey, going-back-to-school, sort of afternoon. On the way back there was a bang under the bonnet and the oil light came on. Convinced the sump had blown open I stopped and after playing around with an old phone in a garage we produced two men from Hurst Green who discovered what I should have seen at once – a simple case of a broken fan-belt...

...So we arrived at the Manders', where we'd been invited for supper, a little late. Their living-room looks lovely at night, and Miss Manders' reminiscences were, as always, interesting.

We drove home and watched a film on TV. (Last night we'd seen James Cagney as Lon Chaney. Till then I'd thought he was just a pretty face.)

Chris will be back on Thursday.

April 5th

After mother had gone to bed... Well, you've had the description before – only this time we discussed it afterwards – and are still doing so, which is a bit of a bore. However...

Don't ever let me get into a rut. Any rut.

April 6th

Still minus a fan-belt – so I had to cycle to Northiam to the butcher's for the meat. In the afternoon Steve and I walked to Stent Farm and beyond and back. Steve said I destroyed the beauty of those fields for him by telling him how marvellous I thought they were. But they are.

We came back through the woods, with a rustic interlude among the bluebell roots.

(It was Steve that started it this time. He caught me by the hand and said, 'Lie down,' and we pulled each other down eagerly, using his unbuttoned greatcoat as a groundsheet, pulling our jeans down to our ankles and our shirts and jumpers up under our armpits. I was on top. It felt very wonderful. Just as food tastes better out of doors, so it can be with sex.)

Then we got a little lost among the woodland paths but finally got home and in the evening watched TV. Stravinsky has died, James Mossman the broadcaster has taken an overdose, there has been a Welsh mine disaster... But Kenneth Clarke's Civilisation showed Peter de Hooch and Vermeer of Delft as placid and magical as ever.

April 7th

I am making a summer dress for my mother. This morning I cut it out, from the pattern.

This afternoon Steve and I went to Stent Farm to pick primroses for primrose wine. We found a badger caught in a fox-wire. After trying to rescue the poor thing which snarled and snapped, I returned to the farmyard and got one of the men (rheumatic, with Wednesday stubble on his chin, and a wife who cleans his gun for him). His boss persuaded him to take freeing equipment, in the form of two hammers, as well as his gun. When we got back to the spot the badger was really wild, couldn't be got near enough to release, so the little old fellow pulled the trigger. The badger had stopped moving some seconds before. Now a red and white gap appeared at the back of its head, the shot sounded faintly, and then the blood ran out, rich and warm.

We picked nearly three gallons of flower-heads, and explored the funny lonely house in the woods on the way back, discovering it to contain leather armchairs and a toilet roll, a map of Paris and some Windowlene, poetry books, the Bible, and a dead jackdaw.

A vast oil slick is approaching the holiday beaches from Thanet to Dungeness. But there is a hint that the end of the Vietnam War may be in sight. At least, that's what they said on TV.

I'd never seen a live badger before.

But I'd played on farms before. Before Chris, before Steve, before Canadian David, before Phil...

And the memory is clear, though many years passed before I wrote it down.

...I am stretched out in the bath's warm shallows, alongside Roger. We've been sharing baths at intervals for the best part of a year, and still manage to fit in side by side – though with a little adjustment of the hips these days: we've been growing quickly since we both turned eight.

'Lighthouses,' Roger says, for that is what our two upstanding dicks remind us of, poking up out of the water among the reefs and headlands of our bellies, thighs and knees. No light beams from them however, so Roger does the next best thing, projecting his own water in a brief upward spring that then tumbles down again like rain upon his groin. A second later and I bring my own lighthouse sparkling into commission in just the same way.

Roger's elder sister looks up from the washbasin just alongside the bath. 'Stop that,' she says. She has come in here to brush her bedtime teeth – and perhaps also to cast her eye over the spectacle of her little brother naked in the water with his best friend. 'Stop it. It's dirty.'

'Can't stop till it finishes,' Roger answers, sweetly, reasonably, un-chastened. And for a further half minute he and I continue to pretend we are lighthouses as if to prove the point. I think of other things we do together, and have been doing during the course of this last wonderful year and which Roger's sister has never seen us at. She might think us even dirtier if she knew. But to me, and to Roger, they don't seem dirty. Just good.

It's almost an effort now for me to remember how it all began. The wonderful improbability of it. The serendipity of it. Not that that word had entered my vocabulary back then. Roger joining my school last September. Three months older than me and bigger, burlier and more boisterous. Better at football too. But it was football that became his undoing – and the happier sparking off of what has followed…

There am I, standing at the edge of the playground where the ground rises just a few inches as asphalt gives way to turf – on a rough grassy patch where a lichen-clad, still leafy apple tree stands. Raised voices a little distance away, and I turn to see that Roger has tried to join a football game played by the nine-year-olds. I could have told him it wouldn't do. Roger is roundly told to get lost and then the ball is kicked gratuitously against his backside as he turns rebuffed away.

By chance he is now walking towards me. I call to him, 'Hey Roger!' And Roger comes on towards me, relieved, unconsciously, that my greeting has given him a destination, somewhere to make for when a moment ago he had only somewhere to retreat from, and this masks to some extent the ignominy of his dismissal. It's a matter of a few yards only. So now here is Roger standing facing me and, because of the tiny rise in the ground under the apple tree, Roger's eye-line is an inch or two below mine instead of the usual half inch above, and for the first time Roger finds himself looking up at me. The high afternoon sun is more or less behind Roger but not so completely as to reduce him, in my eyes, to a silhouette. 'They wouldn't let me play with them,' he says, his deep blue eyes meeting mine in a candid gaze. It's the first time he's taken much notice of me, let alone confided to me such an ego-bruising summary of events. And I see that Roger's admission has cost him something. Tears have welled up in those blue eyes, have overflowed their lower lids and are now balancing among his long black eyelashes like dew on spiders' webs.

This in turn makes something well up inside me, though it isn't tears. I don't know what it is. If I've ever had intimations of this feeling before, they've never been as strong as this. All I know is that it's the most important feeling that I've ever had. Wonderful, shocking, surprising, like sudden light and heat. And also – puzzlingly – it hurts. I feel as if my heart will burst. And the sensation is doubly powerful, doubly strong, because somehow, mysteriously, the knowledge is given to me that Roger is experiencing the same thing.

Some gesture seems to be needed. But none comes easily. If we were standing side by side I might risk placing an arm across Roger's shoulder. (Risky because normally only the older boy is supposed to do that, and it might in any case be roughly shaken off.) A hug is out of the question – we're both too old for that. Words then, perhaps. But what words? Older people have phrases in their heads like, 'I love you,' and, 'Be mine for ever', or simply, 'Darling.' None of these is available to me, aged not quite eight. Which is probably just as well. Instead I say, quite softly, 'Show me your willy,' and I'm moved rather than surprised when Roger unquestioningly obliges, hitching up a leg of his shorts to reveal his ivory-skinned little soldier to his new friend. And I, with only the briefest look around to check that no teacher is at close range, follow suit.

It hasn't been a very public sort of friendship. We don't spend all our break times together at school, nor always sit next to each other at lunch, nor have we asked to have adjacent desks. So not everyone is aware how close we have become. Most of the time we share together is out of school. We are forever visiting each other's houses. For Roger home is a working farm, and for me there's one conveniently just across the road, with all that these entail in the way of open spaces to play in, and private outbuildings where we can enjoy our secret pleasures in the dim light. Our long-suffering parents spend much time at weekends driving us to and fro. We sleep over at each other's places often, and always, always demand to sleep together in a double bed. Like the shared bath and the lighthouse game this has become a tradition – honoured now with some eleven months' observance.

Twenty minutes after bathing and we two boys are tucked up together in the spare room double bed. The routine is pretty fixed. Roger calls, 'Pyjamas down below knees.' His pyjamas are blue like his eyes; mine, though my eyes are also blue, are green. Both pairs slide down. I switch on the torch which lies – placed there with some forethought as always – between our two torsos, pointing down. The top sheet, tented over raised knees, becomes a bright-lit cyclorama in front of which our two cocks take centre stage. They're stiff of course – which we are hardly aware of, since that's how they always are when we get them out or take notice of them for any purpose whatever. Now they're to be played with and explored. They are slightly different, because I, unlike Roger, have been circumcised. We don't take much account of this either. People are born differently after all. It's probably just like the fact that older generations were born with wildly different shapes and sizes of nose. Like the fact that my hair is fair and curly while Roger's is straight and nearly black. Just one of those things.

W.T. is what we call our nocturnal game. Willy tickling. Which is exactly what it is. Even today, I can never hear the initials, referred to in news bulletins, of the World Trade Organisation, without experiencing a tug of memory that takes me in imagination back into bed with Roger. 'Lovely W.T.,' says Roger as he runs a finger for the umpteenth time along the underside ridge of my small erection, and traces its continuation in the seam that rides up over the dome of my ball-sac until it disappears mysteriously into the tight vortex of my bum: a place that Roger has occasionally explored with a tentative finger, amid my feigned protests, and to my secret delight. Lovely WT. Funny, the use of the word lovely by an eight-year-old. Roger doesn't consciously make the connection between that word and the shorter one that it derives from. One might almost say, a pre-pubescent Freudian slip. Half an hour later the two of us are fast asleep and in a position we would never consider adopting while awake: enfolded in each other's arms...

***

April 8th

Spent most of the day awaiting a phone call from Chris. In the end it was the Etchingham station master, who phoned in the middle of tea... Anyway, I went to meet him. He has a new suit and has written some bloody good poems. The Fosbrees came for coffee in the evening. Good to have Chris back again.

April 9th

In the afternoon we went to Dungeness, climbed the lighthouse, saw the little train, and ran along the Ness Beach as if in a film. Chris and I always do things as if in a film.

In the evening Steve got depressed and Chris and I had one of those conversations that only Chris & Me could ever have... We have the most fantastic friendship in the whole world, but it wouldn't be possible without Stephen. Goodnight.

PS. Today was Good Friday. While Christ died, magpies copulated in the grass and rabbits gambolled in the meadows.

Holy Saturday, April 10th

A beautiful day, but difficult to write up, so I'll do it tomorrow.

We went to Rye in the morning, looked at the Ypres Tower museum and rode piggyback down the street. After lunch we chopped up mother's old wardrobe in the garden, then the sun came out and Chris and I sat on the

roof in the warm. It seemed very much a day of nostalgia
– we then decided to go for a drink.

We got to the R and C at closing time and had a pint,
then we slumped over a wall on the farm and watched
the pigs, walked through a field among a cloud of seagulls, and talked of nothing more profound than sex and
onions.

So then, of course, we walked to the City Stores and
bought some – onions, not sex – and walked home
munching them. That is life. It may be an illusion. There
will be a day when C. D. Kirkman is just a name, and
memories are cheap and false, but for today… Today we
walked two years into the past – I may forget the feeling,
but for today, I can not conceive of forgetting. This is
Chris'n'me, life as it should be.

Stephen had been for a walk. After tea we watched
TV and drank at the R and C. Then back here. And one
by one, we went to bed.

Sunday April 11th. Easter Day

It's great to get up and find the first person who says
Good Morning is your old friend Chris. It's Easter
Sunday – or Sundance – and we all had mushrooms with
breakfast – and went to Mass. A drink at the R and C, a
good lunch, and port afterwards. We three walked over
the fields towards Stent Farm, as far as the stream, and
sat there and climbed trees, then Chris and I stripped
naked and galloped and leapt in the fields as we've
always wanted to do. It sounds corny, and it might have
looked ludicrous … but maybe you've never done it.
Steve didn't. We tried to cajole him, but on this occasion
he wouldn't take his clothes off and we did our nude
tree-climbing while he watched derisively.

The handwriting ain't too good. Sorry, but Chris'n'me
have been drinking. Well, all three of us started, and

eventually Steve got pissed off and stormed, damp-eyed, out of the room. Chris'n'me were bloody depressed by this… We had spent much of the evening trying to cheer each other up (both were a little depressed) and now we had to begin all over again. But we succeeded. 'If you didn't have confidence in me, I'd have none in myself,' I told Chris, which was true. In fact, everything I tell Chris is true … even if *Carissimus lector,* (Steve) thinks it is all fiction.

We said Goodnight. 'But it's not really Goodnight,' said Chris. 'I'll be seeing you at breakfast in a few hours.' …Which is true. Chris'n'me is nothing if not a philosopher.

April 12th

Went to the Fosbrees in the morning. Listeed to Leonard Cohen. Chris and I felt a bit grotty. Too much booze and not enough sleep. Steve was very quiet.

After lunch at friends of mother's I drove Chris to Etchingham station. I felt really grotty. It was hot; crowds of traffic around Bodiam. We had to get out and have a shit in Hurst Green, queuing up outside the only bog.

We agreed it had been quite a traumatic weekend, and said Goodbye-till-Friday, which isn't so bad as Goodbye.

Funny, how despite precedents, human nature (and Rich's: 'You know what's likely to happen, Chris,') a schoolboy friendship that should have burnt out long ago carries on… or has done, so far. The sky is brilliant blue before the storm clouds gather … or they may never come.

And even if honesty doesn't play the lead role in our friendship, we've admitted to each other that it doesn't.

So perhaps there is a bit of honesty of a different sort after all.

I suddenly realized why Durham is unreal. It's because I am unreal in Durham. Going back will be a step into a void. And one of my own making. But could I have created a new world up there, drawn down the portcullis on the past and left my two friends behind me? Knowing myself even as little as I do, the answer is No. No, no, and I'm glad of it.

April 13th

A very long bedtime talk with Steve last night. As foreseen.

April 14th

In the afternoon Steve and I dug over Miss Manders' vegetable plot for her, and had tea there, with damson jam and scones, and Steve making twelve-year-old type double-entendre jokes and embarrassing me.

Steve didn't know that the spit of soil you dig up on the end of a spade is also called a sod. So when Miss Manders instructed him to 'turn the sod right over' he thought she was swearing.

Sardines for supper.

April 15th

The doctor, who is a good pianist, came for music and tea with my mother while Steve and I mowed the grass. A phone-call from Chris to confirm about tomorrow.

Watched a good TV play about officers in training and a good film about a brother and sister having a fuck.

(That must have been after my mother had gone to bed.)

April 16th

A last drink at the R and C, lunch, then Steve and I off to Rye, to get the train to Thanet. Arriving at the monastery, everything seemed so real: the monks, the guests, the kitchen, and the cockroaches. After quite a good supper, Fr Cyprian, Fr Sebastian, Steve and I went to Compline and then tried to contact my father and other dead people by means of a tape recorder. Nothing came of it – except Chris, who materialised from London… Though he is anything but dead.

After a little more food then, we retired for the night. The clock in the cloister is striking twelve.

April 17th

Had breakfast with Chris and Fr Sebastian. Then we talked for a while and wandered over to the school, looked at our old room, looked in our old mirror like we used to, and complained about the décor. We went to see old Mr Lavin at his shop, we met Matron, strolled in the sunshine, and then went down to Stella Maris to see Teddy. Mrs Teddy is pregnant. Both seemed pleased to see us.

Then we walked up to see Mrs Pring, but she was out – so we left a box of chocolates and an invitation to join us in the Regency in the evening. Barry M is already going to join us there.

Chris and I had a quick drink in the Tart n Bitter pub on the way back to lunch.

Over coffee we talked to Father Barnabas about the move to Westgate which all seems to be turning out very well. In fact, talking and chatting, and watching the monastery cat climb trees occupied us till teatime, after which Chris and I walked over to see if the Roland-

Butters were in. They were not, so we went down and looked at the sea. It was fine; the sun shone on the water, the gulls dropped like petals onto the waves, or circled methodically above them.

Finally Mr Roland saw us on our way back to the abbey and we went over to their flat for tea. Mrs Roland enveloped us both with one large kiss and after tea and protracted hovering on the doorstep, we were late for our kipper supper.

After that, over to the Regency. Barry M is reassuringly unchanged. Soon we went over to the Foy Boat; many old familiar faces. Including, surprisingly, Phil, who bought us all a drink. Chris and I dared each other to get our cocks out under the table, and we did, though Phil and the others didn't. I think everyone had a look at Chris's and mine, though.

On the way down to the pub Chris and I had acted out the final scene from Butch Cassidy and the Sundance Kid – where they get shot – just like we used to act out old jokes in the refectory. Though Barry M did ask, deadpan, which was the Sundance Kid. As I say, he hasn't changed.

(Chris, like Robert Redford in the film, is the one with the moustache. I only started shaving just after Christmas.)

Back at the abbey I said to Chris, 'Funny to think that Phil was my best friend seven years ago.'

'Don't say that,' said Chris.

So I went on to say that in seven years time Chris would still be my best friend and also in fourteen.

'But what about in twenty-one years?' he asked earnestly.

'You'll be my best friend still,' I said. I told him I sometimes felt (as I did then) that he was the only friend I'd got... Then, having said Goodnight on his corridor, I spent half an hour in bed with Steve in his room, which is around the corner and next to mine. So I'm a bloody hypocrite. Or maybe it was just the influence of alcohol. I hope I'm not a hypocrite anyway.

April 18th

Breakfast with Chris again. Then Fr Sebastian reproached us for forgetting the Prings. For we had! They had gone to the Regency at our invitation and we'd already left. They had then had the whole monastery scurrying round looking for us.

Then we went to High Mass in the Abbey church and sat in our old, old place at the back, and Chris and I read the Epistles. Fr Sebastian's aunt complimented us on our reading. Even Steve did. And that's praise worth having.

Down at the Foy Boat, met Jerry and others, and Daniel. Chris was right about Daniel: he's altered beyond recognition. The bright brown eyes are turned dull and strange. The old bond of sympathy has gone for good. I could see that at once. It's a shattering experience.

(How wrong that is! Daniel must have been off-colour that day, or on something of very dubious quality. His letters to me of around this time are full of affection, and some of the sweetest I've ever received from anybody. Signed off always With Love.)

Lunch was quite good. Followed by coffee, and talking with Fr Malachy. Eventually Chris, Steve and I went over to Mrs Pring's for tea and double entendres. She now has one of those lamps with wax in it that, when heated, makes beautiful shapes in water.

Back for supper, then a long round of Goodbyes – only till Sunday in the case of Steve and Chris. Got a lift to the station…

How often now do I seem to be waiting on stations at dusk, red lights shimmering in a mist that eats into the bones, silver rails standing out in the dusk, and finally the train comes in, and the wandering in the wilderness is over.

It was a slow ride to Ashford and Rye. I wish the others had been on the train too.

TWENTY-FIVE

Changes – Or Developments

April 20th

A summer's day. The cuckoo called, the swallows came to stay. I racked my wines, mowed the grass, sat in the sun, wrote to Chris, and the Manders came for coffee.

April 21st

The Queen's birthday. My 10/12 birthday. I saw a cuckoo, was attacked by the cockerel on the farm and caught the boar having a fuck. And I worked on the summer dress for mother who was in Faversham playing quartets.

April 22nd

Continued work on mother's dress, and being disturbed by a great noise from my bedroom, discovered a dog under the floorboards. A terrier. It had burrowed under the house in search of rabbits! Angrily, I chased it out into the road where it was nearly run over by a bus.

Sunday April25th

Good lunch, and wine with it. Drove to Robertsbridge, but found the next train due in an hour and a half – so I went for a long walk round Salehurst and the Abbey Farm.

…And, my train fare had gone up by a whole pound, and the train was an additional quarter of an hour late. I made the acquaintance of a 60-year-old woman whose fiancé had just died. Poor old thing. I let her talk all the way to Tonbridge where she mercifully got off. I felt quite sad for her. And I think I've got troubles?

Got to Waterloo and got a train quickly. Carried my baggage up from the junction to Lavender Gardens (They've moved back to Clapham from Stockwell.) Chris was cutting out nudes, Steve was present. We sat quietly, and later went to see Up Pompeii, really unsubtle and crude, but quite a laugh.

Talked again with Chris and Steve. Said Goodnight and got a bit depressed.

April 26th

Chris woke me up to say Goodbye as he was leaving for work. We said just that. 'Goodbye,' … and, 'See you soon,' etc. Then he left.

It was some time before Steve got up, and then it was raining. So we got a goldfish bowl for his goldfish, and then went to Kings Cross.

Where we had two Scotches. Then we said Goodbye. Happily it is not for long this time.

Sunday May 2nd

Two years ago today I went to sleep with Chris on the railway carriage seat. That was the first moment of consciousness I knew about that friendship that after another fortnight was to seem as if it had been going on for ever. I suppose you could say it had been going on for four years, but that wouldn't be quite right. Chris and I knew each other slightly, but weren't friends. He was older than me and friends with an older set even than that. *(Though there was a moment on the Rugby field all those years ago when Chris was injured and sat on the ground hugging his knees and couldn't stop himself from crying a bit, when I found I wanted to hold him.)*

May 7th

Thought about how one always thought of relationships in terms of past ones. How some new friendships here at Durham were replacing older ones from the past. Though Chris and Steve remain in place as always.

But has Paul (Jagger) been replaced by someone else? Paul H, for instance? My relationship with Paul (Jagger), never queer in practice, but always homosexual in concept – he used to call me Macky-Darling and I used to call him Micky-Darling, which was a play on his Jagger nickname, and he used to come up behind me and stroke my hair and make me guess who was doing it … it was always him, nobody else did that … well, that was over years ago – is gone. My affection for him has been shared out perhaps between Chris and Steve… though not, I think, Paul H.

I sat on the wall outside my front door to sober up and thought of a time when I need not have sat on cold damp stone but upon Chris's lap, with my arms round his neck. And I remembered how, when on June 22nd 1969 I was frightened by being blanket-bumped, Chris stroked my hair and smiled at me as if to say, 'You'll live.' And I did.

And I wished Chris were with me now. But then, I always write stupid things when I'm drunk.

Sunday May 9th

When I said Goodbye to Steve at Kings Cross two weeks ago he was going on to collect some law books which he'd left in a luggage locker at Cannon Street, in a parcel I'd helped him pack and wrap. I've written this.

If I do
Ever get back
Will you
Still be there
Motionless
In mid-stride
At the top
Of the subway?
Or will you
Be gone for ever
To Cannon Street
And your cardboard box
Tied up with string
Full of paper books?

May 14th

Sat on my wall in the sun till lunch, watching the world pass by, and forgetting the unreality of this place. Why bother, I wondered, to maintain a life based on old school friends as well? They're no better than anybody else.

But when, a few minutes later, I found an envelope addressed in unmistakeable writing and containing a letter from Chris, I changed my mind rapidly. Who else would put as a PS: 'I'm sorry I couldn't find an envelope that doesn't match this paper.' ? Good old Chris.

May 29th

Two years ago Chris bought me a drink – lager and lime in a quiet pub – and there was a high wind that nearly blew your charcoal-grey school suit jacket off on the street corners.

June 9th

Terrific day. After early breakfast found a telegram in my pigeon-hole – someone must have died. I ripped it open. 'Avenge your clan,' it read. What?! But it continued, 'Good luck in exams.' It was from Steve. Much appreciated.

The exam was hilarious. Dr M invigilated. The Latin proved easy and the French ghastly, contrary to expectations. When it was over, all forty of us marched into the adjacent Dun Cow and drank to the end of exams for two whole years.

June 25th – now aged 19 and 4 days

(After getting a lift down to London…) Caught a train to Clapham Junction, feeling like Joe Buck in New York, not knowing quite what to expect.

To my surprise Steve opened the door at Number 43, so I didn't have to trek over to his father's place at Woodford. But I obviously wasn't expected, though it was nice to see Steve again. Sally cooked me an omelette with onions in it.

Much later Steve and I went to a party near Southwark, by taxi, whose driver got us lost… and grotty it was too. But while talking to someone on the staircase I became aware of two brown eyes and a moustache looking at me through the banisters. Chris, who should have been in Tonbridge and, according to

Steve, not expecting me at all, had come up to London. It was tremendous to be with him. But then it always is.

Well the party dragged on, I was satisfactorily rude to a few people, then found myself being woken up to go home. It was four o'clock, and I found myself paying a quid for the taxi. So much for saving money on train fare.

June 26th

Had to get up, not surprisingly, when the nurses came back off night duty, since I was sleeping in one of their beds. Had some breakfast, said Goodbye to Steve, and went shopping with Chris and Sally. Left them and went on the bus to Charing Cross, where I bought a ticket, queuing behind a man who wanted a ticket for a chair he was transporting, saying the inspector had to let it go for half price. But the clerk seemed to think the chair was old enough to need a full-price ticket…

Anyway, as I had travelled with Chris from Tonbridge to London at the beginning of the year, so we returned as far together – Kent looked beautiful in the sunshine. Chris got out at Tonbridge, I went on to Etchingham, phoned mother in the middle of her lunch and got her to bring me home.

Steve should be coming down on Monday. Hope he'll be back to normal by then. Perhaps it's me that's out of joint, but then Chris seemed unchanged as usual, so I don't think it can be that. Steve says Chris has changed. Chris thinks Steve has. But what the fuck would it matter anyway? They're my friends, aren't they?

Sunday June 27th

Spent the day tidying up, trying to get a farm job for the summer, and receiving a phone-call from Chris about Thursday.

Tomorrow I've got to be up very early and dash up to London – to Hill's, since mother's dropped and cracked her £3,000 violin and it's got to be seen to.

June 28th

Up very early and dashed to London. Crowds of pin-stripes on the quarter to eight train.

Phoned up Steve from Charing Cross, asked him to join me for the return journey. London looked beautiful, with the sunshine, a real Mrs Dalloway morning – 'Life, London, this moment of June.'

Walked through the Burlington Arcade to Hill's where my mother's old friend was on holiday, so service was a little colder than usual.

Anyway, relieved of my burden, I retraced my steps, looked round parts of the National Gallery, admiring Seurat, Gainsborough and Bosch who had till then meant only glossy colour plates in arty books, but were now seen to be captured moments, congealed movements, in coloured oil and very impressive.

Also walked round St Martin in the Fields. Then, to my surprise, met Steve on the platform at Charing Cross, and we rode down in the sunshine to Etchingham. And of course he hasn't changed, but he read my diary, and liked the poem about him, also liked my new trousers; and in fact, though he talks more and more about academic matters at UCL (though he doesn't appear to be much involved in them) nothing has really changed – indeed, scarcely developed.

Another bit of code. There had been no indication from Steve's behaviour towards me in London that he wanted our sexual contacts to resume. Back at my mother's house, though, I put this to the test. Steve was already in his bed when I undressed, slowly at the other end of the room. I had a full erection by the time my pants came down, and walked slowly back, naked and cock-wagging, towards the space between his bed and mine, though deliberately a little nearer to his bed than mine. Within arm's-reach... He watched me approach, reached out from under the covers with his left hand and took the bait. I got into bed with him.

June 29th

Church, it being SS Peter and Paul. (Good for them.) Nothing much happened, except we went into Hastings. Steve and I got the bus back, mother gave her violin lessons at her school and lost her car keys, so there was a bit of a chemozzle all evening, especially when, after being given a lift home, mother found the key in her pocket.

Steve looked at me during the final stage of this and raised his eyes to heaven. 'Actually,' he said, 'what she needs more than anything is a jolly good screw.'

He's probably right. I'd never thought of that.

Then Steve and I went off and had a quiet drink in the R and C.

June 30th

Up early. A lift had been arranged to take me into Hastings with the car keys to bring back the car. After that Steve and I went for a walk in the fields by Watermill Farm where they were haymaking while the sun shone. Then my trunk came, back from Durham. So I unpacked it – which was quite a logical thing to do.

In the afternoon mother went teaching and Steve and I stayed in together, very much together, in the old juvenile way. He lay back on my bed and said, 'Give me a cuddle, Ralph,' and I did that, after we'd both taken our clothes off, and we ended up doing a bit more than that.

In the evening we drove over to Elham where Steve was very taken with Dorky, a very elegant old lady, wearing an old-fashioned choker neck band with a cameo broach on it, who is now lodging with mother's cousin there.

And back home, Steve and I talked from eleven to half past three. About all manner of things, including Steve's character, and, as usual, my relationship with Chris. I was quite astonished to discover that Steve actually rather admired it.

No mention of this in the diary, but at some point during these wonderful few days together Steve and I tried to fuck each other. It was something we hadn't tried before. I mean, us two together. Steve was pretty experienced when it came to fucking women by now, which I was not, but it turned out that penetrating a boy was of a different order of difficulty, and needed skills we hadn't yet learned. We took it in turns to use our cocks as battering-rams, but made no impression at all. The end result was the same for both of us. We couldn't hold back our ejaculations and came unheralded between each other's thighs. (Every time. We each had several goes.)

July 1st

And once again up early. Steve left for the station with mother.

Chris phoned to say he wouldn't be coming over today.

So not a great deal happened. Steve has gone, with a paper bag tied up with string, full of paper books, a copy of my poem and a photo of me on my first day at University.

He said last night I didn't have to be his friend if I didn't approve of many things about him. The thing is, though, that I do have to be his friend, because that's the way things are. And besides, I like him.

Funny how different that is from my friendship with Chris, in which we only offer the best parts of our characters to each other (which isn't what I mean to say at all, so hang it and stop the analysis.)

Remember though the end of Easter weekend, when Chris and I drove to the station, ever so slowly, and stopping here and there in the sunshine, feeling like the end of the world, though we would see each other again in five days anyway, and I almost said too much when we said Goodbye (and I don't think I understand what I mean by that either. It's just that that's how it felt.)

Saturday July 3rd

Up early again, and drove to Thanet in the fog, or rather haze. Got there. Talked for a while to Uncle Ron, Mrs O and others in the office (my piece about Durham <u>was</u> put in the magazine) then walked over to the sports field and met Barnabas, Mr (Johnnie) Johnson (with his fiancée) and Teddy, whom I later met with baby Eleanor, achieved after five years of trying. She is four weeks old.

Then along came Chris with parents, who are over from Hungary and staying in Tonbridge. Mr Kirkman is very quiet for a diplomat, shortish, and looks like one of my ancestral photos. Mrs Kirkman is more or less how I imagined her. So, after talking and reminiscing with

Chris for some time, I drove all the family to Westgate to look at the school's new buildings (from next year), and then to Minster Abbey. I had by then earned myself a share of the Kirkmans' sandwiches, which we ate perched around the base of St Augustine's Cross near Sevenscore, and then went back to school.

A Mass was going on on the lawn. Fr Cosmos was preaching, so Chris and I sloped off as inconspicuously as possible, meeting up with a whole crowd of old mates including Barry M and a great many others. Tea on the lawn followed, the usual scrimmage, we met Mrs Pring, her inevitable self, and listened to the speeches and prizegiving, which seemed more informal and friendly than in the past – as the last one beneath that grim Victorian front wall could afford to be. Barney's speech was indeed quite charming.

Anyway, I drove the senior Kirkmans to the station, and Chris and me down to the Foy Boat. 'Not you again!' said Phallus-head, her hair still done up in a great peak above her forehead.

So, as we've often done, and as I've often said we've done, we sat and drank, and talked about Steve – and a few other people got a mention. I had met Daniel earlier, and so had Chris. I think we formed slightly different impressions, but anyway, that doesn't matter.

Finally we left. It was a nice drive, getting out to piss together in the road in front of the passing cars, singing Simon and G in falsetto voices and Leonard Cohen in rather deeper ones, until we arrived at Elham at dusk. Cousin Ethel and Dorky were pleased to see us. We talked about the theatre for twenty minutes and then departed; we found Ashford station without difficulty, said goodbye for a few weeks, and I drove back to Beckly in half an hour.

Saturday July 17th

In the afternoon went to the antiques fair at Brickwall in Northiam, where there were many beautiful objects on show, including Wendy P whom I haven't seen for thirteen years. She's changed – or at least developed.

Sunday July 18th

Phone call from Steve in the evening. He's got a year off university. Lucky sod. I really don't know why I bother to stay on. It's most disheartening. First, Chris doesn't go to university, now Steve's got a year away, and I'm still destined for two more years of being treated as a dependent inhabitant of cloud-cuckoo-land.

July 22nd

Following last night's excess I got up seeing double. Felt dreadful when I started work on the farm at 8.30, loading what seemed to be two lorries. But, as Chris says, 'All bad things come to an end,' and so I now feel a little better.

July 26th

No missive from Stephen. Spent most of the day at Watcombe Farm cutting the hedges for old Miss Manders. The place is too lovely to be left to rack and ruin. Needs looking after ... so yours truly has offered to cut the hedges.

July 27th

Had a badly written letter from Stephen. Still, he hasn't had much practice in the last year, and it was nice to get it anyway.

To Hastings in the morning. Bought a book. 'Teach Yourself Italian.' For the Italian Renaissance course next term.

In the afternoon I taught myself Italian. It poured with rain.

July 28th

Watched Ian McKellen as TE Lawrence in 'Ross' in the evening. He's quite good, but can he only play homosexuals and neurotics?

July 29th

Went to London in the afternoon to see Stephen, to get a wine press, and go to Hill's about mother's violin. But actually I went in the morning, went to Hills (where to my surprise I ran into someone I know from Durham) looked round Savile Row, went to Charlotte Street for the wine press I've been meaning to buy for years, and then walked to Clapham, taking three hours – taking in a visit to the National Portrait Gallery, a walk up Downing Street, St James' Park, Westminster Abbey and cloisters, Victoria station, a piss at Sloane Square, and the King's Road. Quite hot when I got there, but Steve was this time agreeably surprised to see me. In the evening we went to the pictures – to see The Wind In The Willows, and The Love Bug – which was quite good fun.

Later it became Steve's birthday.

July 30th

Steve's birthday. Spent listening to Leonard Cohen's new LP, drinking sherry, having a Chinese lunch, having philosophical discussions of a most beautiful and ethereal nature and going to the pictures again... Carry On Up The Jungle. Breathtakingly predictable.

July 31st

Got up gradually, and went home – came home, to Beckley, with Steve. Another hot day. And well, here we are.

(Here we are where? In bed together, probably.)

Sunday August 1st

Nice day. Went to Church. Tidied out the garage. Sherry, champagne, lunch in the garden, drove to Bodiam in the afternoon, walked round the castle, played silly games, watched a film about Freud in the evening, and talked for hours – and still are.

August 2nd

To Rye in the morning. Bit of a nightmare, but had a drink in the Royal Oak on the way back – that will be our localest as from the 18th. For we heard at lunch that the point of no return has been reached. Tye Cottage (which she has been trying to buy for six months, just a mile's drive from where we now are) is now my mother's. So be it.

Ralph: Diary of a Gay Teen

August 3rd

In the afternoon we all drove to Sissinghurst Castle and found not only wonderful gardens and herbs but an unexpected Bloomsbury shrine – the original Bloomsbury Press, with type, which fascinated Steve.

Then to the new house. Steve likes it.

In the evening talked and drank till three o'clock. Memorable and enjoyable conversation. Produced this gem (among many others) from Steve, *au sujet de* my relationship with Chris. 'A pinta a day keeps us merry and gay.' Like Gratiano's grains of wheat among the chaff … only this time they <u>were</u> worth the search.

August 4th

Up early, feeling grotty. Shopped in Rye. Drove to Ashford, stopping for a drink at the Duke's Head, Ham Street.

Steve's new girlfriend's house is beautiful, her mother less of a dragon, more refined, than I'd imagined, and his girlfriend herself, Steve's Alter Ego, is perfectly sweet and, I think, rather beautiful.

After a good lunch we drove to Court-at-Street, and walked through the Manor Farm. One encounters a hidden precipice, a view of the coast from Dymchurch to Eastbourne, and below are the crumbling remains of the chapel where Elizabeth Barton, the 'Maid of Kent' had her ergot-fungus inspired visions in the sixteenth century.

A cup of tea, then I drove back alone to Beckley in time for the Big Game… Inter-farm stool-ball, a Sussex speciality, played despite rain. I made about ten runs, we lost, and Billy's Bashers won the trophy (an old potty).

Drinks – horribly fizzy beer in the open air – followed by chasing around the field after one another, to make everybody sit on the potty. Rather ridiculous, though I found myself almost the fittest person there – second only to young Richard – and of course the racing around, the cartwheels, the wrestling with Richard, the revolting sandwiches, and the beer, made me somewhat sick.

Cycling back home in the dusk, shushing noises followed me up the hedgerow, and led me to the churchyard where, rather apprehensive by now, I found only the magnificent silhouette of a barn owl, on tip-toe on a shed rooftop, brandishing his wings above his head, calling his mate. I approached, he gave a shriek and slid off into the air, sailing round above me, eerily reminiscent of Tolkien's Nâzgul.

I retreated. Back home I found I'd lost my door-key and practised the virtue of patience on the doorstep until mother returned from Wittersham.

August 6th

No word from Chris.
'And would I know if he's alive or dead
I'll bid my footman put it in my head.'
To misquote Pope.

August 9th

This evening I wrote a letter to Chris, while eleven people died in the fighting in Northern Ireland.

Friday August 13th

Busy packing for the move. Chris phoned. Bloody nice to hear from him. He'd like to come down next weekend but might not be able to. But he'll think of something. (Just keep on thinkin', Chris.)

Sunday August 15th

The bare boards of the house now echo to our footsteps and the night peers crudely in through uncurtained windows.

Big Brother phoned. He can't come at the weekend – plus, his grandmother has had a heart attack. So I'm going to Tonbridge on Friday night. Not very convenient, my mother says. But what has convenience to do with it? Bloody hell. I hardly ever see Chris, and he's hardly the least among my friends…

(We finally moved house on the 18th.)

August 20th

It poured. In the evening I drove to Tonbridge to see Chris. Horrible drive, slow and wet, imaginary punctures etc. Had a Guinness at The Primrose on the way into the town, then waited for Chris at the station. He still doesn't look like a commuter.

We went to The Angel and, to put it in a nutshell, got pissed. We discussed my purchasing a brown velvet evening suit, as an alternative to the ubiquitous black dinner jacket at Durham dances. Chris thinks it would suit me. He also offered to lend me as much money as I needed for it. I was most touched.

Drove around Tonbridge looking for fish'n'chips – a miracle we didn't hit something.

Chris and I ate our fish and chips in the garden of his grandmother's house and listened to the trains rumbling towards Hastings. Then we took a trip down memory lane and listened to some Bob Dylan. The record-player wouldn't turn, so Chris had to turn it with his finger – but it sounded alright.

We phoned Steve up, but I can't remember what we talked about. And then we crawled into bed. Without the usual qualifying parenthesis.

(Yes, I climbed in with Chris again. He didn't want me there, but was too drunk to do or say much about it. Nothing occurred, of course.)

Saturday and Sunday August 21st – 22nd

Having told mother I'd be back at ten I had to hurry along, since I didn't get up till 9.30, but I was only half an hour late despite shopping for coffee, bread etc. and the bloody slow traffic – and one hell of a hangover. I drove most of the way fast asleep I think.

Pretty shattered later, but livened up when Chris came down in the evening. We had our 'pinta a day' (or several) at the R and C, more at the Royal Oak. Back home for a bottle or two of homemade wine. Spilt some on the clean tablecloth. We watched TV draped over a couple of chairs, and at one point I put my hands down Chris's trousers, though met with no encouragement and withdrew them. Neither of us mentioned it this morning.

Morning was ghastly. Both of us had been very sick, mother had not failed to notice the wine-soaked table-cloth, and breakfast was one of the great ordeals of all time, eaten in double-visioned silence. But at least there were two of us.

After breakfast we fixed up a run for the guinea-pigs, and explored the new garden. Then we took a door off its hinges and planed it down, and Chris cut my hair, as I hoped he would, in the garden. So instead of flowing around my shoulders it just covers my ears and looks extremely moderate. A change of image. I'm pleased with it, Chris is pleased with it. Good.

After Mass, and feeling a little better, we tried to take a wheel-back armchair up the ladder into the attic, but got it wedged in the hatch and I was stuck up there. Eventually, drenched with sweat, we had to saw it into pieces before we could get it down.

After lunch, over to the Fosbrees. New hair cut got a mixed reception.

Chris does like the new house. It feels lived in now he's been here.

Paul H phoned about arrangements for Wednesday's journey to Edinburgh, and I took Chris to Etchingham, after a call at the Junction Inn. Waiting for trains alone is horrible at night, so I waited with Chris till the train came. Said Goodbye till Tuesday; I'm staying with him on my way to Edinburgh... Same old Chris – same old Ralph.

August 23rd

Felt grotty and played the piano most of the day. Sad not to have Chris here any more.

Also sad to have to kill off a wasps' nest – with fly-spray, now DDT's illegal. I admire wasps, their noble and selfless devotion to duty and to their organisation. True socialism, and I have to go and squirt it into ignominious collapse. But the fruit crop has to come first.

August 24th

I needn't have worried about wasps and their nobility. All were fine this morning. So I resorted to burning paraffin. A flaming rag wrapped round a long pole...

Eventually Chris phoned to say he wouldn't be at Tonbridge but at Clapham. So up I went, looking forward as much to an evening with Chris as to the three-week ego-trip on the Edinburgh Festival Fringe ahead...

Steve was amazed to see the haircut. He was pleased to see me, and I was very taken by this. We went for a drink. Chris arrived and it became several. Great to see him. Had chicken and chips and finally went to bed. Chris and I implored Sally to tell us a bedtime story. She told us about Cinderella and the marijuana plants and we went gently to sleep.

August 25th

Up early. Mild hangover. Said Goodbye to Steve; went on the bus with Chris. There was silence for a few minutes before we got to his stop, and when he got up it became apparent that both of us had been preparing a short farewell speech, for we recited them simultaneously and very fast. So neither of us heard very much, except that I said I only wished Chris were coming to Edinburgh too, and he said that he wanted me to write to him from there.

I will, Chris, I will!

TWENTY-SIX

The End of Teen

Sunday Sept 12th

(The three weeks at the Edinburgh Festival Fringe are up. A couple of new feathers in my acting cap.)

Up at eight, and to our surprise, got away from Edinburgh before nine. Beautiful empty roads among the hills of Peebleshire and Dumfries, a motorway drive to Birmingham, and then Paul H and I waited two hours by the roadside, thumbs outstretched, waiting for a lift.

But it was worth it. Beautiful journey down to London – and, incredibly, our driver was a Durham graduate, and from our college.

Got a train from Twickenham to Clapham and No. 43, where Paul thought he might come along and scrounge floor space for the night, but in the end changed his mind and went on to Reigate. It turned out that he, like Chris a few weeks earlier, had prepared a little farewell speech, but this time I had forgotten to, and had to improvise.

No Steve at No. 43, so I had to get a bus to his sister's flat in Gloucester Road. Here I am, and so is Steve, and I for one am bloody tired...

...Only a friend of Steve's turned up and we talked till four in the morning.

Sept 13th

Steve seems to have shrunk to a pathetic and inarticulate shadow of his old self – and is obviously very unhappy. Poor old Steve. What the hell can I do?

At six o'clock we met Chris outside Charing X, me sitting on a bollard, when along comes the same old figure with white socks and broadly grinning moustache. We drank a considerable quantity of Guinness; I read my Edinburgh press reviews to Chris, and he, as usual, showed me the last letter I wrote to him, which he kept, as usual, in his wallet. Reading it, it seemed a very nice letter, ending, 'And next time I come to Edinburgh, you better bloody come too. Love, Ralph.'

After some chips, we returned to Gloucester Road, Chris carrying my suitcase for me, as a matter of course, as a big brother should (-)) Then I went to sleep on the floor.

Sept 14th

Got up at eight, without a hangover, and set off to the accompaniment of a blind accordionist. Said Goodbye to Chris across a sea of cobble-stone faces in the tube (where my suitcase was none too popular) and got the train home... Had I phoned home earlier, I'd have known mother's violin was ready, so I've got to go to London again tomorrow!

Listened to the Enigma variatios. First time in ages. My tastes are changing. Six months ago I dismissed Elgar and Tchaikovsky as beneath my notice. Now I like them better. I wonder why.

Sept 15th

I begin to wonder whether there will ever again be a *Carissimus Lector* to read this diary. A serious thought: I told Steve it would take two years to get to know anyone else well enough to let them; only one year has gone by since then. Paul H has read random samples. I suppose Chris might read some of it. And maybe Steve will read some again one day. But I don't know – and I care very much...

...But today, got a train to London from Robertsbridge. Phoned up the Sundance Kid at the Foreign Office, and arranged to meet for lunch.

Then walked to Bond Street to collect the violin – they brought it up from the safe, placed it firmly in my hand and said, 'Don't drop it.' I didn't.

Walked back through St James's Park, and Queen Anne's Gate (most beautiful houses) to the Westminster Arms. There Chris turned up as arranged, with a few Foreign Office colleagues. Some are quite nice guys, others are bloody creeps, but at least Chris and I are agreed on who were which. After Guinness and shepherd's pie and conversation that was not as esoteric as usual, we split and more or less arranged for Chris to come down in ten days.

Sept 25th

Rafe, how could you be so foolish as to doubt your old friend, to doubt yourself, and allow those haunting words to repeat themselves continuously? Steve's words: 'You're being taken for a ride, Ralph, and one day it will end.' Rich's words: 'I know what you're likely to do, Chris.'

Forget them. Big Brother is still looking after you – I met him at Etchingham station, and we drove home – stopping for the proverbial 'pinta a day' at The Junction, for onion omelette.

Then we went to see the West Kent Youth Theatre at Brickwall in Northiam – doing Mother Courage! My mother came too. They did it very well for the most part, a production strikingly similar to ours, and a fascinating experience to live it all over again – especially with Chris...

…You see, we are living on nostalgia, but at least we don't fight about it, and our memories make us happy, not sad.

After it was over, we went home, discussing it endlessly, had some soup, and watched an old film, drank some wine – enough but not too much, unlike last time…

Then we just talked till 2 o'clock, like we used to every day at school, only now it's just a few times each vac. – and less this one than before. Still, a very pleasant evening.

In front of a mirror we look the same height, which is amusing, since he used to be eight inches taller than me once. But actually, he's quite a bit bigger than me – and lately, rather fatter…

Goodnight.

Sunday Sept 26th

Breakfast. Ate all of it, and talked about ships, shoes, sealing wax, old times at school… All the best old times, of course. Never mentioning that for about three years we didn't get on well together (at least, not all the time) but just picking and choosing the good bits: Johnnie Johnson's English classes, our breakfasts of beer, rides in the Moke, acting…

We discussed the apparent change in Stephen, and the letter I have written to his girlfriend – then Paul (Jagger) and others came under the wheels of our conversation.

We went to church, very entertaining, and walked round the garden in the long wet grass, looking over the fence into the fields. For this has become a tradition, a nonsensical whim of the sort that makes other people laugh. So let them. What can not be shared may be laughed at, perhaps?

Back to the station, the train came, and went. And I went back home.

...So there we are. Ralph the old codger, Ralph the conventional, Ralph the simpleton, the dull, the predictable, Ralph the fool... Or so Steve would maintain. And am I? Whoever in hell you may be, reading this: am I really? Or do you, like my Big Brother, believe more in me than that? Please do, then I may believe myself ... but perhaps Chris has convinced me already.

But enough of this emotionalism. Ralph, you're supposed to ne reserved and hard, and slightly masculine, aren't you? Then so be it. For a little while, a little while...

Oct 1st

Wrote to Steve in reply to the letter he wrote me. His girlfriend rang me up to say, among other things, that it was she who had prompted him to write his letter to me – still, that was two replies to one letter, a good investment, I think, for I usually only get half as many letters as I write ... and I don't write all that many.

Nov 16th

A letter from Steve – out of which dropped a pound note and a St Christopher medallion. Reading this un-Steve-like letter I could hardly prevent myself crying, sitting in the college bar before lunch, and it was only with great effort that I kept up conversations over lunch. The letter was apologetic, kind, and so full of feeling, I didn't know what to think.

...Started to write a letter to Steve... Whom have I ever misjudged more seriously or more often than Stephen?

Dec 22nd

Got a very grand Foreign Office Xmas card from Big Brother. Drove Jane Manders into Hastings and back – old Miss Manders had had another heart attack.

Then Stephen phoned. He's coming down tomorrow. Though only for a fleeting visit. Really, really nice, man.

Dec 23rd

Finally Steve came. Drank at the R and C with mother, and Michael Miller and his twin sister.

But nothing is quite the same as it used to be… Very sad.

Dec 24th

Nice breakfast. Over to the Fosbrees where we listened to Nashville Skyline with all its associations … Chris and so on.

Saw Steve off on a train at Rye. He's going to see his girlfriend. So he doesn't need my company any longer. Perhaps it's just as well.

Dec 25th

A very good traditional dinner with that bottle of 1966 Volnay I had the foresight to purchase in Dieppe nearly three years ago.

I tried to phone Chris but got no reply. I haven't seen him since October and very much want to.

By the way, when Steve was here the other day I let him read this diary. He read some of it. SOME of it, with the discriminating taste of a connoisseur, I suppose. Well, that really is the last time. We've never had much in common. Now even less. I find his conversation boring, he finds my company uninspiring. Let him. And he hasn't phoned to say whether he's coming down again, and I can't ask Chris down until I know. …Which Steve knows perfectly well. Always so bloody thoughtful.

Sunday Dec 26th

Phoned Chris in the afternoon. He'd just gone out with his new flat-mate, James, who we were all at school with. I tried to read Arostotle's Politics and fell asleep as I usually do when I read Aristotle's Politics. A little later a knock came at the door. And there was really no doubt at the back of my mind about who it was. Funny, every time I see Steve now it is a disappointment, but when I see Chris it never is. He and James just came for tea, toast, and home-made champagne around the fire, and talked of nothing serious, but we were delighted to see each other again. We talked about Steve and his girlfriend, and old times at school. The best days and best friends of all our lives. Quite true… For the last year or so, that is. And with the exception of one – or maybe two – people at Durham. But as I said at Easter, in twenty-one years I'd still be Chris's best friend… Which is very banal, but we were pissed at the time, so allowed to be banal. Or maybe we're both just very dull people. But I don't really think so, somehow! Goodnight.

Jan 4th 1972

I drove to Tonbridge in the dark and the pouring rain which I find so lonely and depressing. It was very nice to arrive in one piece and see Chris pacing up and down outside The Angel which wasn't open yet … but it soon did, and we ensconced ourselves and talked, about the past, as usual, and about Steve, and about ourselves. We had a curry in the Chinese place across the road later, then adjourned to the Railway Bell for more beer and whisky. Back at Chris's place we stood round the glowing embers of the late fire drinking whisky. We must be growing up a bit because we had enough (for a change) instead of the usual 'too much'.

Then went respectively and respectably to bed.

Jan 5th

…And slowly fell asleep. Somehow I only hate going to bed so much in a room by myself. I suppose that's what boarding school does…

Up at eight with not too awful a headache. Chris's grandmother cooked breakfast, I drove Chris to the station and, on a clear road, got home in under forty minutes.

Sunday Jan 9th

I've decided it's time I wrote something about my father, for I did have one.

He was 5' 6", a commander of a destroyer in World War I, of minesweepers in World War II, having acquired a limp through numerous hip operations following an (I'm told) necessary leap from bridge to deck. My mother was his second wife. To me he was perfect. Strong, brave, never frightened, or worried or unable to cope. A ruddy-faced, white-haired man of the world, a god to me. I loved him passionately. I used to pray that if one of my parents had to die first, it would be my mother, as I didn't want to have to deal with her on my own, without his calming, buffering presence. But that prayer was not answered. When I was eleven I left

Stella Maris and moved up to the senior school. He warned me about the advances older boys might make, saying it was just the same in the navy. A week later he suffered a stroke. When I saw him at Xmas his face was thin, unshaven, yellow and long-haired, the whites of his eyes dull. He couldn't quite remember my name, but held my hand between the bones and withered skin that was all that was left of him. At Easter he died. I wasn't quite twelve. But I had rehearsed the emotions I ought to feel for months.

So Father is still god-like to me. And if there's any man I desire to emulate, it's him, or at least my eleven-year-old's idealised picture of him, Harry McKean the perfect father.

Since he died, have I been looking, in my search for love and friendship, for someone to replace him? As well as for a big brother and a twin?

Jan 25th

Got up late. Very depressed. Dull day. Read William Golding's The Brass Butterfly – preparation for play readings I'm supposed to organise. Pissed off with people, especially Paul H. Oh my god, he made me want to shout abuse and scream and holler at him; and I couldn't. I can't. I can't bring myself to it. Because he would look at me and shrug his shoulders and walk away. So would everyone else. No-one likes me that much; not even Chris. I pretend that he does. I have to pretend that I really mean something special to someone. But it's a lie. I try to deceive myself. There is no-one. Really. No-one.

Read Arthur Miller's Death of a Salesman to myself. Didn't put me in any better a mood. Morbid, Ralph, morbid. And manic-depressive.

March 7th

Up late, wrote an essay, wrote a really nasty letter to Stephen.

March 9th

Had a reply to my letter to Stephen. He's most cut-up and tear-stained. What can I reply? What am I supposed to do? I don't even know where I stand. Underneath everything I suppose I still like him...

March 10th

After an early lunch Paul H and I zoomed off down the M1 in his car. Heavy showers, a few anxious moments, and a little map-reading at Hendon, then Paul and I said Goodbye – a little less warmly than in the summer, I fear, and I got a tube from the Edgware Road to the Oval. Then walked a mile with heavy luggage to Chris's new place, a very smart basement flat which he shares with James and James's sister. Very good to see Chris again, as always. He had some food keeping hot for me. Having eaten it, listened to (of course) Leonard Cohen – One More Night – and compared notes on playing Moon in The Real Inspector Hound – which we've both recently done, and then proceeded to the pub. Later we were joined by James, and another old face from school I hadn't seen for years. We drank a lot and, after driving home, played at being Arabs, with knives, tea-towels tied to heads, and war-whoops – it was these last that brought the landlord down with the cry – 'Cut the bleeding noise out!' I was lying on the floor by then, pretending to be in my death throes. I winked at him. He surveyed the scene with some astonishment, and then retreated.

Saturday March 11th

After falling asleep on the floor, got up at about 10, and read the whole of John Wyndham's The Chrysalids before Chris got up.

We had some boiled eggs and toast, and by the time we'd got the place tidied up after last night, it was time for me to go, rather regretfully. Anyway, James drove us to Charing X. I said G'bye to him and Chris, and took the train to Etchingham, talking to a young and charming mother and kids all the way down.

Nice to be home again, home cooking, log fires, the piano to play. My mother had a very bad skid with the car the other day – she was very lucky not to go over the edge of a steep bank, a hundred foot drop to the Tillingham valley below. Anyway, all safe and sound, so no complaints.

(On June 21st 1972, at approximately seven thirty in the morning, my teenage years came to an end.)

July 16th – 20th

Three exchanges of letters with Steve. He asks me to go and see him. I say, why not come down here? He says, Sorry, can't. His girlfriend's just suggested they go to France together. Next, he's surprised my reply to this seems unfriendly.

No letters from Chris. Surprising how soon one learns to do without people who have seemed indispensible to one's whole life. One returns to that cocoon of emotional detachment one promised oneself never to break out of again … frequently.

August 2nd

Still no news of Chris. I begin to see how the last three years have only been about trying to recapture the mood of a just a few odd hours over a few weeks, three years ago in May. So sad.

Sept 12th

I wrote a postcard to Chris, and got no reply. That old all-pervading friendship disappears further into the murk astern, and I stand, as always, leaning over the rail, looking sadly backwards, not knowing or caring where I am going.

Sept 22nd

A letter arrived from Chris – with apologies for his long silence; he's been laid up in hospital following a car smash.

I phoned him and arranged to see him in London next Wednesday on my way to Durham. Great to hear his voice again.

Sept 27th

Lovely sunny colourful morning. Caught the train to London. Took a little walk, then met Chris in a pub in Queen Anne's Gate. Fantastic to see him again How just like himself he always is. A marvellous person. We had three or four pints and talked, of course, non-stop. We said Goodbye cheerfully, almost nonchalantly; I remember when a parting for so many weeks would have been heralded by sentimental speeches and silences and back-slappings... Now we so seldom meet that Goodbye means that much less. I suppose it means we've both grown up a bit. Sad, really.

Oct 1st

My thoughts are clear but often contradictory, my dreams vivid and psychedelic – but nightmarish. I dreamed I noticed an old friend from school in the street, called his name, and he, on turning round and seeing me, bent down and picked up a sharp stone, and flung it in my face. I saw also spaceships exploding in the sky, a tree full of coloured birds and rabbits in the dining room at home – and felt my teeth kicked out with much pain and blood.

I walk the streets of Durham in the small hours in the rain. I sit alone moping on my wall in the dark and the wet. Like Terry Carleton at the end of Lord Dismiss Us. *How did he come to be standing alone and friendless here, on a hill, in the rain?*

I am found at last by the college nurse. So banal.

TWENTY-SEVEN

To The End Of Time

It was just a month later, on November 4th, that I first successfully fucked another boy – or man. And I was fucked by him on the same night. In my own bed in Durham. But I was four and a half months out of my teens by then and he – a French lad called Christophe, coincidentally – had had his twentieth birthday just six weeks before.

So that particular adventure does not belong to this story, the story of my teens so recently ended, but is the beginning of a new and different one, and I'll leave it there.

Except to say that I fell in love with Christophe. That was bound to happen. He didn't fall in love with me. But forty years later… well, we're still close friends.

Lovers? Friends? Still not sure what the difference is. The matter of sex might play a part. (Come on, we all know it does.)

But love and friendship? I had sex with Steve, on and off for years after I left my teens behind, despite his girlfriend, and a few years later I shared a flat with him for a time. I never had sex with Chris – for all my efforts in that direction. And yet… the wonderful thing I had with Steve felt – still feels – more like friendship. The wonderful thing I shared with Chris… and Christophe… Well, it was more like love.

Whatever love means.

Is it just biological? A hormonal thing? Something that wakes up inside us at puberty, and flexes its muscles in our late teens? Is love no more than that? The thing that bursts our hearts asunder and shows us the infinity of the night sky beneath the pavement of our pedestrian world; the thing that breaks the wall between two separate rooms and makes them one; the thing that puts an end to *me* and makes me into *us;* the thing that makes me able and ready to fight to the death for my man when the time will come: is all this no more than a chemical reaction in the brain?

And is friendship what lives on when love has fulfilled its function, produced the sprogs, and, like the stork, migrated away south again? Is the whole process no more than that? That's what I thought I'd learned about love and friendship from the experience of my teen years. Only much later did I find that sometimes – in some special cases – the stork forgets to fly away…

*

Michael Campbell wrote in Lord Dismiss Us about First Love. The love that was supposed to make the difference to all the others that followed. Yet which experience, and involving whom, was First Love for me? Chris, of course. Of course? There were precursors even to him.

Canadian David. Remember him? This book began – *So what did you do today?* – with David's daily words to me.

And Phil…

Before Phil came Roger, of course. A picture of him, aged eight, at the wheel of his father's tractor, is in my wallet still…

Before Roger came Tim. Curly-haired, golden-haired, blue-eyed, snub-nosed, rose-petalled lips, and thin and small like me. He had piano lessons, like I did. Like me he was crazy about birds and insects and animals. We met aged five, but not till we were seven did he seem important. He was the first person with whom I articulated the concept of wanting to find my twin. The first boy with whom I shared those phrases of wonder: *so do I; so am I.*

I regret to say that our relationship didn't long survive the advent of Roger and his fall of tears under the apple tree.

*

Memories of love fit one inside another like Russian dolls. They bounce off one another, like multiple reflections of a candle flame. They pare down, like a peeled onion, to a thread-like, almost invisible thing…

Micky was his name…

My first time-identifying memory was of me, aged just two, on holiday at Hayling Island, in a caravan and atrocious weather. There is just me, and my parents, in this memory – no other children.

I am an only child. My cousins were big teenagers when I was born. And though I did meet other children and play with them, they were always the children of my parents' friends. I didn't choose them, nor did they choose me. My memories of them are ghostly blurs.

Then came Micky. I was about to be – or had just turned – four.

I'd had an imaginary friend of course. I think his name was Arthur but am no longer sure. He didn't exactly have a shape or face – he was just a presence, comforting and competitive by turns and very vaguely he had a colour: he was a fuzzy scribbly mixture of grey and brown and pink. But with the arrival of Micky he disappeared. He has never returned.

A small strip of field ran between our house and the next. I could see the house next door through the hedge where it was thin. And one day, when I went near the hedge there was a movement on the other side and when, curious and excited, I stooped and peered through the gappy part low down, a boy of my own age, also curious and excited, was peering back.

I had never before experienced the sensation that I felt then, unless it was when I first viewed with understanding my own reflection in a mirror. I felt warm and wonderful inside. It was as if Arthur had come magically to life. 'Hallo,' I said. 'What's your name?' The greeting came easily. It was, after all, what every adult said to me.

'Micky.'

'Mmm – Rafe.'

'Hallo.' Pause. 'Rife.' A minute later, with a little help from our respective mothers, he was with me in my garden.

We played together every day from that day forward and were as happy as we knew how to be. Micky was three months younger than me; the little differences between us were a source of infinite wonder to us both. I had blue eyes, his were brown. My hair was wavy and golden-biscuit colour, his was straight and chocolate brown. I dropped my shorts around my ankles when I wanted to pee, he hitched up one leg of his, his willy poking out from underneath and firing like a miniature water-pistol. I thought this was rather swashbuckling and debonair. Though the technique didn't always work. It occasionally resulted in a waterfall that cascaded down his inside leg and into his shoe. Unlike me, he did not wear socks.

The other thing he didn't wear was underpants. I thought that an attractive feature too. In his own house he would walk around without shorts either, his apple-cheeked bottom and tiny pointing penis on show underneath. I thought the effect was lovely. Even at that age we used always to take our cocks out and play with each other's when unsupervised for any length of time. Sometimes if I went to his house in the morning I'd find him clad in nothing but a vest, beneath which he dangled most prettily. Sometimes he wouldn't notice, in the excitement of my company, that his bladder was full, and the inevitable fall-out was a turn-on for me. I think I can date my fondness for my own sex, and my enjoyment of the sight of men naked from the waist down from my friendship with Micky...

We played with toys indoors and in the gardens of our parents' cottages. His sister, Pat, had a tricycle which we borrowed, and I had a pedal-car. At his house there were chickens, in a run outside the back door, and a cat, which obligingly had kittens, prompting an earnest debate between us about where she had produced them from.

How long did our idyll last? Three months, or six, or twelve? We had nothing to measure time against in those pre-school days. There was no term-time, no holidays; we hadn't lived long enough to register the seasons as a recurring pattern. There was just an eye-widening, wonderful, ongoing now.

But then Micky and his family moved, to a town some sixty miles away. I don't remember our parting; I don't remember if I felt lonely after he had gone; if I missed him. We never met again. The cottage he'd lived in was pulled down and rebuilt almost at once. I watched the building work from close at hand, learned about 'footings' and how cement was made, how bricks were laid. When the new house was finished a new family moved in. They too had a little boy of my age. We liked each other and played together. But it wasn't at all the same.

There was nothing like the joy I had experienced in Micky's company, the excitement, the sensuality, the bubbling up of feelings whenever we met. He stirred up something in me that I hadn't known existed until then. Micky was my first and only friend, and I was his. Micky was my other self, a wonder more mysterious even than the image in the mirror. With Micky I tasted for the first time the most wonderful thing that life can offer us; the sameness-difference, the difference-sameness, of another human being…

***

Chris Kirkman grew up and got married, and was posted far abroad. Just once or twice, in later years, his letters to Ralph were signed, With Love.

Steve also grew up. And got married too, though in a slightly different way. His letters were fewer in number than Chris's, but Love was the word at the end of them all.

As for Ralph, he grew luckier in love after he escaped his teens. In search of a replacement for his dead father, and looking for his ideal twin, he came close to finding both in one and the same man, in a partnership that survived for thirty years; until death called time. By then he was no longer looking for a father figure. Nor a big brother even. But that other thing, the twin thing… He seems to have got that sorted, once again.

After all, he was a writer. In Lord Dismiss Us this is Terence Carleton's final comment on himself. And Ralph became a writer too. He didn't find it easy to make sense of his teenage self. But like Carleton he owed it to his calling to try.

Oct 17th 2014

So what did you do today…?

THE END

****

Anthony McDonald is the author of more than twenty novels. He studied modern history at Durham University, then worked briefly as a musical instrument maker and as a farmhand before moving into the theatre, where he has worked in every capacity except director and electrician. He has also spent several years teaching English in Paris and London. He now lives in rural East Sussex, England.

Novels by Anthony McDonald

IVOR'S GHOSTS

ADAM

BLUE SKY ADAM

GETTING ORLANDO

ORANGE BITTER, ORANGE SWEET

ALONG THE STARS

WOODCOCK FLIGHT

THE RAVEN AND THE JACKDAW

RALPH: DIARY OF A GAY TEEN

SILVER CITY

THE DOG IN THE CHAPEL

TOM AND CHRISTOPHER AND THEIR KIND

DOG ROSES

Gay Romance Series:

Gay Romance: A Novel

Gay Romance on Garda

Gay Romance in Majorca

The Paris Novel

Gay Romance at Oxford

Gay Romance at Cambridge

The Van Gogh Window

Gay Romance in Tartan

Tibidabo

Spring Sonata

Touching Fifty

Romance on the Orient Express

Also:

MATCHES IN THE DARK: 13 Tales of Gay Men

All titles are available as Kindle ebooks and also as paperbacks from Amazon.

www.anthonymcdonald.co.uk

Printed in Great Britain
by Amazon